MICHAEL O. GREGORY

Copyright © 2023 by Michael O. Gregory

ISBN: 978-1-77883-008-2 (Paperback)

All rights reserved. No part of this publication may be reproduced, distributed, or transmitted in any form or by any means, including photocopying, recording, or other electronic or mechanical methods, without the prior written permission of the publisher, except in the case brief quotations embodied in critical reviews and other noncommercial uses permitted by copyright law.

The views expressed in this book are solely those of the author and do not necessarily reflect the views of the publisher, and the publisher hereby disclaims any responsibility for them. Some names and identifying details in this book have been changed to protect the privacy of individuals.

BookSide Press
877-741-8091
www.booksidepress.com
orders@booksidepress.com

CONTENTS

Dedication v
Prologue vi
Chapter I: The Harem 1
Chapter II: The Dig 13
Chapter III: The Cave 22
Chapter IV: Random Violence 29
Chapter V: Cassandra Moves Out 36
Chapter VI: Two Mothers No Father 46
Chapter VII: Assault 53
Chapter VIII: In Hiding 62
Chapter IX: Men Isolated 70
Chapter X: Plans Made 77
Chapter XI: Internment Camps 84
Chapter XII: Hijack 89
Chapter XIII: Cryogenic Sleep 97
Chapter XIV: Rescue 104
Chapter XV: A Second Beginning 117
Chapter XVI: Secret Kept 133
Chapter XVII: Slide to Extinction 149
Chapter XVIII: A Secret Revealed 161
Chapter XIX: Allies Sought 176
Chapter XX: Plans Made 190
Chapter XXI: Going Public 201
Chapter XXII: Bishop Langley 214
Chapter XXIII: Conspirators 224
Chapter XXIV: The Plan 232
Chapter XXV: Martyr 241

CHAPTER XXVI: WEDDING 246
CHAPTER XXVII: PLANS COUNTER PLANS 254
CHAPTER XXVIII: ATTACK 262
CHAPTER XXIX: TASCOSA 276
CHAPTER XXX: INVESTIGATION 285
CHAPTER XXXI: TASCOSA REBORN 291
CHAPTER XXXII: BISHOP LANGLEY'S END 299
CHAPTER XXXIII: RECOVERY 305

Dedication

In writing a book you usually work alone. However, there are most often people in the background that give support, their expertise and encouragement. The first was my late wife, Jeanne who tolerated me spending so much time alone writing. The others were the Augusta Georgia writer's group, led by Elizabeth Estes. They have been very helpful to me in developing my writing skills.

PROLOGUE

For most of man's history, since he gave up his hunter-gather lifestyle, it had been a struggle to make the land produce. The premium locations for early agriculture were the fertile river valleys where the land could be renewed annually by floods. As man's population increased more land was brought under the plow. At first man could rotate the use so that the land could rest and become fertile again. Over time man's population increased to the point where all land suitable for agriculture had to be constantly under the plow. Man learned that crop rotation would help, but the land needed nutrients. They learned to reuse plant matter, by plowing under what was left after the crops were harvested; and also, animal and human waist. This worked well for thousands of years.

With the beginning of the industrial revolution and the dawning of the twentieth century, man learned to make chemicals for use on the land. There were fertilizers to enrich the land, as well as pesticides and herbicides to kill insects and weeds attacking their crops. Now, with enough water, any land could be made productive. These chemicals were used first-in the rich industrialized countries, and eventually, all over the world.

Just after World War II the first flaw in the new technology showed its head with the failure and recall of Dichloro-Diphenyl-Trichloro-Ethane (DDT). However, most people were not very concerned; the attitude of the time being that technology could overcome anything. It was the genie in the bottle. If there was a mistake from time to time, no problem, it could be corrected. Technology had the ability to overcome its faults. We had just won the war; we could do anything.

Thanks to technology the world underwent a population explosion. At the same time standards of living were being raised. Science and technology made man's future unlimited. In 1950 the United States was in the middle of a baby boom. For every one-thousand girls born, there were one-thousand-six boys born. Not a significant difference; less than one percent. Life was wonderful. The American dream that all men were created equal; that a man's station in life was limited only by his own ability somehow became the right to a three bedroom, two bath house in the suburbs, with three-quarters acre of green lawn; a spouse and two or three children, two cars in the garage, a dog and a cat. It was a time of fast cars, fast food and instant gratification.

Farming had also changed. It was now called agribusiness. Everything was mechanized. Now a score of men or less, worked land that used to be worked by hundreds of people. The hoe had become obsolete; weeds were controlled by agrichemicals. With chemicals man had finally tamed the land. With agrichemicals they also controlled pests and enriched the soil. Agrichemicals were used by agribusiness, and also by everyone with a three-quarters acre green lawn. Millions of tons of chemicals were dumped into the environment. They were used by the train load, by the truck load and by the ton. A lot of these chemicals mimicked natural hormones. Antibiotics and hormones were being used with poultry and livestock to control disease and to increase production. All this was being passed up the food chain to the human population.

By the late sixties medical science noticed that the sperm count in males had started to drop. Of course, most people didn't pay much attention to it. After all it wasn't much of a drop, and males had plenty of sperm anyway.

There was a further drop in the sperm count through the seventies and eighties, and more couples were experiencing infertility. In 1998 there were fifty-thousand less males and fifty-thousand more females born in the United States. A six percent difference between males and females. In the mother's body we are all destined to become females, that is until conception, then about half are altered by the 'Y' chromosome to become male. Something had upset the balance. At the dawn of the twenty-first century, this trend started to reverse its self, mostly in under-developed, or as some called them, Third World countries. With ultrasound a female fetus could be identified while still in the womb. This led to the abortion of a large number of human females. This trend, however, could not last.

The environment, both land and sea, continued to be saturated by agrichemicals and other toxins. It impacted not just the human race, but all species on earth. By 2038, the birth ratio was five females to four males; that was for all animal species on earth. By 2044, the birth ratio was sixty-two percent female to thirty-eight percent male. This disparity in the birth ratio had commenced to have a profound social impact worldwide. No world political or industrial leader could ignore the problem any longer. There was already a ban on most suspect chemicals for domestic use. However, with world population levels so high, they had to continue the use of them in agriculture in order to feed everyone. They needed to find alternatives before they could stop using these suspect chemicals.

In 2049, the birth ratio was seventy-one percent female to twenty-nine percent male. Males were starting to lose control of their political, industrial, religious and military institutions. Even the most male dominated societies had no choice. They had to let women have power; they no longer had enough men to maintain it. Were men used to wield power, they were becoming second class citizens.

Under social pressure, the traditional idea of marriage, as a monogamist paring of one man and one woman, was first discouraged and finally banned. Men were now expected to have long-term relationships with more than one woman; or at least make themselves available to many women. There could be no other way. Women had to share their men.

If you think that men were getting the best of everything, think again. Men were now too valuable to be risked. Their options were diminished. They were banned from all hazardous occupations. Men could still serve in the military, but they were banned from serving in combat arms, or combat support. In the police force, they were restricted to administrative duties.

Science and engineering were making great strides. Technology in engines and cryogenics had reached a point that deep space travel was possible. NASA planned a deep space mission that would last for years, but men would not go. Only women were allowed to go into space.

By 2061, the birth ratio had stabilized with males occupying fourteen to fifteen percent of the population. By 2064, all males were banned from any sport that could cause injury. This spelled the end to American football, rugby, boxing and many other full contact sports. They still had baseball and basketball, but most of the players were by now women. In numbers and influence, men had become insignificant. It was now a woman's world.

When by law marriage had been abolished, one of the new family units was, for lack of a better word, a harem. It was a group of women associated with one man. They jointly owned property, and all had an equal voice in the group. When a person wanted to leave the group, they just sold their interest to another party.

This arrangement wasn't universally popular with all women or men. A large percentage of women preferred to live alone, in pairs, or in small groups. They found the idea of a group of women living with and being serviced by one man annoying and demeaning.

A lot of men also preferred the single life style. They also saw the harem as annoying and demeaning, but for different reasons than the women. They felt that being the only man in a group of women, their vote wouldn't count. They felt that the women would have the power over and dictate to the man. For them the single life style allowed them to be independent, and women were available whenever they were wanted.

Most single women from time to time would have an affair and move in with a man. However, with so much competition between women for the limited number of men, the woman in the relationship would be under constant pressure to keep her man interested. After a while the woman burned out from the stress and the affair would end.

After a while many women realized that they were playing a game that they were destined to lose and dropped out. Once they came to terms with reality, they found a celibate life less stressful. They now needed a man solely for reproduction; and they didn't need the whole man, just the sperm. All men were expected to make regular deposits at the sperm bank, even men that were celibate for religious or other reasons.

The custom of children's surnames was that all girls adopted their mother's surname. All boys had their father's surnames, if the father was known. Otherwise they had their mother's surname.

Women now had sole custody and responsibility of their children. The ratio of men to women being what it was made it impractical for women to expect any meaningful support from fathers, even if their fathers were known. It was unfortunate that it had to be that way, but they had no alternative. Some women accepted it as the reality of the times. Most, however, felt that they were unfairly exploited and wanted someone to blame. They saw all men as having a position of privilege in the social order and resented them for it. Slowly the resentment turned to hatred.

In 2073, Nedra Granger, a Catholic Priest, broke away from the Catholic Church and founded her own church. She called it the New Christian Truth Reform Church. At first, she attracted converts by preaching the bible from a woman's point of view. By 2079 she had a small following. It was then that she started to change her message. At first, she preached that the Bible wasn't complete; that the men who had written the Bible hadn't given women credit for their contribution. From there she went on to attack parts of the Bible as not being divinely inspired; and demeaned it as simply a historical document, with little or no religious value. She was slowly writing men out of her version of the Bible. When she was unable to write men out, she just excluded those parts from her version of the Bible.

In 2078, Nedra Granger elevated herself to grand Bishop of the New Christian Truth Reform Church and established a priesthood. To make her priest distinctive, she rejected the cassocks and robes of the Catholic Church with the colors of black, brown, red and white. She chose for her priest an emerald-green caftan with navy-blue trim, embroidery and waistband. The sisters of the church wore an emerald-green caftan without embroidery or trim and an emerald-green waistband. As a bishop, her caftan had golden-yellow trim, embroidery and waistband. There was a navy-blue cloak with hood for wear when needed.

Nedra Granger sent her new order of priests and sisters out to get converts for the church. They concentrated on schools and college campuses. The church was for women only; no men were encouraged or wanted. They found that there was no shortage of converts. By now most women wanted to have nothing to do with men. They even felt that the human race would be better off without them.

THE HAREM

April 17, 2085, the rain had started early that afternoon. A heavy-driving rain with strong wind and lightening. The heavy overcast blocked out most of the light, making it almost like driving at night. As usual, there were slick roads, causing the hydroplane condition sensors on all vehicles to force them to drive slower. The rain was drumming so heavily on the roof of his vehicle, that he couldn't even hear the almost silent electric motor. Stewart Vaughn, in preparation for a right turn, had moved into the outside lane. He would be home soon. He longed to be warm, dry and comfortable in his private quarters.

Stewart Vaughn, an agent of the Texas Department of Agriculture, had spent the day checking soil conditions with farmers northwest of Amarillo. The trip only had purpose until the rains came, then the soil quickly became saturated. His clothes were soaked, despite the raincoat with hood he wore. He was cold and miserable, but he had at least kept the mud off his boots by wearing overshoes. It had been a terrible day to be out in the weather, but worth it. The winter had been dryer than normal. If the rains continued, there would be a good harvest this year. Even with all the advancements to science, man still couldn't control the weather.

Tomorrow he had to go to the L S Ranch north of Vega. He needed to check on a new hybrid maize growing as a test for the agriculture department of the Texas A&M Amarillo campus. He liked going out to the L S Ranch. They were hospitable people; and if he timed his visit just right, he could expect to be invited to an excellent meal. Perhaps, he could even get invited to hunt pronghorn this fall. It was really good hunting there along the Canadian River.

He cut his speed and pulled off the main road, into the entrance to his home. Everyone living in the building had finally agreed on the parking grid for the parking lot; and the addition of a portico to the entrance of the building. He should manually park his vehicle, and plug in the charger. However, just as he pulled in, the skies opened up with lightning and thunder. Sheets of rain was being driven across the parking lot by strong winds. He looked again at the torrents of rain sweeping across the parking lot and debated it he really had to put the vehicle on charge now. He decided to let his vehicle park its self. He had to go into the office early in the morning anyway. He could put it on one of the quick chargers at the office.

Coming to a stop under the portico, Stewart got out of his vehicle and gave it a verbal order to park. The vehicle pulled out from the portico and following a preprogramed order, drove remotely to the proper parking space.

Stewart turned and spoke his name into the speaker at the door then entered the main lobby of the building. Once inside the main lobby, he removed his raincoat and overshoes, then shook off as much rain water as he could.

When he was ready, Stewart turned to the elevator doors and said, "Elevator going up."

After a few seconds the elevator doors opened. He stepped into the elevator and said, "Third floor."

The elevator doors silently closed. The elevator operating system had recognized his voice. "Good afternoon, Mr. Vaughn. How was your day?"

Stewart didn't like machines that inquired as to his well-being; as if they really cared. He said, "Who cares."

The elevator stopped moving and the doors opened. "Have a nice day, Mr. Vaughn." The electronic voice of the elevator said.

"Go to hell!" Stewart said as he stepped out of the elevator. He wondered why he even bothered to say anything to the elevator. Afterall, it was just a machine. It didn't care if you said anything or not. He didn't even know if it had been programmed to listen.

Standing in the third-floor lobby, he turned to the entry to the apartments and said, "Open door."

The entry door to the apartments recognized his voice and opened to admit him. After sensing that he had passed through the door, the door closed automatically. In the entry hall he put his raincoat and overshoes in the cloakroom next to the front door.

Stewart Vaughn was a large man, six foot five inches tall, two-hundred fifteen pounds, light-brown hair and azure-blue eyes. He had a high forehead, with prominent straight-bridged nose and a strong jaw line. His lips were not so full and he had a dimpled chin. He had the look of someone who spent a lot of time outdoors. He was twenty-eight years old.

The building where he lived had been an old three-story warehouse, that had been converted to domestic use. A family group, or harem occupied each floor. The living quarters were laid out with a cloakroom, two parlors, a family room and game room, kitchen, dining room and laundry room in one wing. The individual living quarters took up the rest of the floor. Stewart had a sitting room, one bedroom and a bathroom. The women each had a sitting room, two bedrooms and a bathroom.

The harem was not the image that the word called up; that being a group of women dominated by one man. The harem could more accurately be called a commune, with each member contributing to the upkeep and sharing the work.

The female members of the harem were, Charity Engle, Serena

Bassett, Betty Tredway, Theresa Fuentes, Alberta Singletary and Patricia Key.

Charity Engle was a forty-eight-year-old department store buyer. Her hair may be graying, but no one could tell; she kept it dyed a brassy-red and short styled. She had had an excellent figure in her youth, but she was now thick in the waist that she tried to hide with loose fitted clothing. She had two daughters, Cassandra, age nineteen a college student and Crystal, sixteen, a high school student.

Serena Bassett was thirty-five and a travel agent. She had brunette hair, cut above the shoulder and styled. Being before the public, she always took good care of herself and dressed well. She had one daughter, Virginia, age thirteen, a student.

Betty Treadway was a thirty-three-year-old police detective. She had chestnut-brown hair that she wore long, below the shoulder and straight. She had an athletic body kept in excellent shape by working out at the gym and lifting weights. She dressed conservatively, in keeping with the requirements of her job. She had been able to keep the stress and pressure of her job from impacting her open and caring personality. Her fourteen-year-old son, Thomas Owens was a student.

Theresa Fuentes was twenty-nine and an air traffic controller. Her long-raven hair hung in loose curls half way to her waist. She had a petite-compact body with accentuated curves. She had a high-stress career. To cope with the stress, she liked to run when the weather allowed. She also liked to paint with watercolors and was quite good at it. Stewart had one of her paintings displayed in his private quarters. She had two daughters, Juanita, age nine and Carmen, age seven.

Alberta Singletary was a twenty-three-year-old auto technician. She had short-light-brown hair and was of average height and build. She had a youthful, but otherwise unremarkable appearance. Her only interest outside of work were her girlfriends and her daughter. She really enjoyed being a mother to Daisy, age two.

The last member of the harem was, Patricia Key, sixteen, with long-ash-blonde hair and attractive-youthful appearance. She was a high school student. She had inherited her position in the harem from her mother three years ago when her mother died of breast cancer. Since the death of her mother, she had been the ward of the harem. Along with her share in the harem, she had inherited enough in savings and insurance to meet her needs and provide for her college education. Even with all her advantages, the loss of her mother meant that she had to learn to grow up fast. She was already tall at five-foot seven-inches and would most likely add a little more to her height in the next couple of years. Her slender figure would fill out as she matured.

Stewart had started to walk toward his private quarters, to get out of his wet clothing and into something more comfortable, when he smelled the aroma of food coming from the kitchen, and made a detour to see what was for supper. He entered the kitchen and found Patricia, Crystal and Virginia cooking the evening meal. He looked into the dining room; Thomas and Juanita were setting the tables for dinner. Stewart looked to see what they were having.

Patricia stood in front of one of the stove tops, stirring the contents of a pot with a large wooden spoon. Crystal and Virginia were busy with other tasks to get dinner ready. Patricia was dressed in a gray sweatshirt, faded denims, an old pair of running shoes and a red and white apron with pink ruffled lace trim. She looked really cute standing at the range. On impulse he gave Patricia a pat on the behind, wrapped his arms around her and gave her a kiss on the back of her neck. Releasing the spoon, Patricia, with a warm smile, turned in the circle of his arms, wrapped her arms about his neck and kissed him on the lips. Stewart felt her lips part and the tip of her tongue search the inside of his mouth, as she slowly rubbed her pelvis against his. He felt the soft-warmth of her body as she pressed up against him. She really knew how to excite him. He could feel his manhood starting to become erect from the rubbing.

Conscious of the children around them, he broke the embrace. "Good God, woman! What will the children think?"

Patricia's eyes flashed as laugh lines appeared at the corners of her eyes, her nose crinkled and a smile lit up her face. "Oh, don't worry about the children; they're just getting a lesson from their older sister on how to take care of their man."

Stewart gave Patricia another pat on the behind. "You're incorrigible, what will I ever do with you?"

Patricia just laughed and kissed him on the cheek. The other girls looked on. Virginia with a smile of approval, Crystal with a look of indifference. As Patricia went back to her cooking, he said hello to the other girls. He then lifted the lid from the pot. "What are we having for dinner?"

Patricia looked up from the pot that she was stirring. "We're having salad, spaghetti with meatballs, green beans, garlic bread and apple pie with vanilla ice cream; and put that lid back on."

Replacing the lid on the pot, Stewart gave Patricia a quick smile. "Yes, Madame."

Patricia gave him an amorous look. He knew that she had strong feelings about him. Being young, she still believed in love between a man and a woman. He knew that she loved him; and if it were possible, she would want him all to herself. He tried to return her affections as much as he could. He didn't want to ruin her youthful fantasies if he could help it. Reality would eventually catch up with her, but why rush it. He embraced and kissed her again, then gave her a parting pat on the behind that made her giggle.

He left the kitchen and headed back to his private quarters to take a hot shower and get into dry clothing. As he went through the living quarters of the harem, it didn't take long to see that this was a habitat for women. Everything, the furniture, furnishings, drapes, curtains, paintings, other art works, even the color of the paint and wall coverings exhibited the feminine idea of beauty and scale. His private quarters were the only male bastion within this female enclave. He had it decorated in a style and in colors that suited his taste.

The time that he arrived home from work, until dinner was his own time to be alone. Back in his private quarters he relaxed for a minute, then got out of his wet clothing and stepped into the shower. The hot water banished the cold and relaxed his tense muscles. He spent a few more minutes in the shower just luxuriating in the hot water running over his body. When he had determined that he'd had enough, he turned off the shower and toweled himself dry.

After the shower and change of clothing, he fixed himself a bourbon and water and turned his attention to one of his hobbies, collecting kachina dolls from the Hopi Indians. He also had several pieces of American Indian pottery, some artistic pieces of silver and turquoise jewelry, dream catchers in the sitting room and bedroom and other Indian artifacts. His hobbies were important to him. He made the most of the little private time he had.

Dinner was the time when everyone in the harem got together. After dinner, they had a social hour in the family room; then they were free to stay in the family and game room, or go to their private quarters. Stewart sometimes had one of the women visit him in his quarters, or would visit them in their quarters, depending on what arrangements were made. Sometimes the visits were intimate and other times they were simply social calls.

The relationship that he had with each woman was different. With Charity Engle, the oldest, there was no intimacy, just a cordial relationship. She planned to sell her financial interest in the harem, and move to a private residence as soon as her youngest daughter, Crystal, started in college.

He and Serena Bassett were good friends, there was occasional intimacy, but they had little in common. The infrequent times that they were intimate it was urgent and frenzied. There was never love or romance involved, just an overwhelming need for sexual gratification; like she had an itch that only he could scratch.

With Betty Treadway, he had a very close relationship. In some ways they were like a married couple, that had been together long enough to be very comfortable with each other. Their love making was slow paced and romantic; taking time and effort to satisfy each other's needs. They were close in age and they both liked the outdoors. Betty also shared Stewart's interest in pre-Columbian history and artifacts. Stewart had also taken an interest in her son, Thomas Owens, and she appreciated that. Stewart and Betty were intimate on a regular basis.

With Theresa Fuentes, there were intimate relations on a regular basis. Their love making was very lively. She always wanted the top position to be in control, as she put it, of her own orgasm. They both liked to play cards and spent a lot of time doing so with each other. Theresa's daughter, Carmen, was Stewart's first child.

With Alberta Singletary, there was no interest in common. She preferred the company of her girl-friends. Her only interest in him was his sexual services, which she required on a regular basis. Her interest in sex tended to be very creative. She liked to play fantasy rolls, sometimes dressing in costumes and experimenting with various positions. Her daughter, Daisy, was also his child.

Patricia Key, after turning sixteen and reaching the age of consent, took full advantage of her rights of membership and became sexually active with Stewart. When Patricia's mother died, he had taken on the role of big brother to her. He had wondered at first if it was wise to also be her lover. His concern turned out to be unfounded. The change seemed to have no adverse effect on their relationship. She was in love with him and looked to their intimacy as being very special. She was inexperienced in love making and let him take the lead. He always took care to make it a tender and fulfilling experience.

At 7:00 PM, everyone was seated in the dining room except Daisy, who had been fed earlier and now slept in the family room in her playpen. The dining room was large enough to accommodate two dining tables that seated up to twelve people each. Everyone agreed that the two-table arrangement was better than one long table. They had no formal seating arrangement at the tables. Everyone just sat where they pleased. Cassandra said the blessing that evening. After everyone served him or her selves, the dinner conversation began.

Cassandra was sitting at the same table with Stewart, Charity, Crystal, Theresa, Juanita and Carmen. Casandra, being fervent in her religious beliefs, kept telling everyone at the table about the new reform movement that she was into at the college. "I tell you; the Reverend really knows what she's talking about. We were talking about the New Testament today and do you know that it's incomplete."

She gave Stewart a spiteful look, just waiting to see how he would react. She had no interest in what he had to say, as such. She was just interested in making a scene.

Stewart had just taken a sip of wine and put his glass back down on the table. It was obvious that she wanted him to respond. She was trying to bate him again. He took his time to answer. He knew that it would be useless to try and debate her. She only wanted to rub her hatred of men in his face. He had tried before to ignore her, but to no avail. She would just become disruptive to the point that no one could enjoy their meal in peace. By now all conversations at both tables had stopped. Everyone looked at Stewart and Cassandra to see what was coming. Stewart decided to meet it head on. "So, she said that the New Testament is incomplete. How is it incomplete?"

A cunning smile came upon Cassandra's face. Her ploy had worked, Stewart had risen to the bate. "It's about the twelve disciples. They are the only ones mentioned in the Bible."

Stewart looked at Cassandra with a forced smile to hide his true feelings of rage at her disruption of the evening meal. She was getting ready to make her point, whatever it was. Stewart was getting tired of the constant negative rhetoric against men in general and him in particular. With a condescending tone in his voice, he said, "As far as I know, there were only twelve disciples."

That had been the response that she had been waiting for. She jumped right on it. 'That's according to the male version."

Stewart raised his eyebrows in mock surprise and responded with levity. "Oh, I didn't know there were more than one version."

The effect on Cassandra was immediate. She slammed her fists down on the table and words exploded from her. "Don't give me that patronizing look! You know damn well there's only one version, and that's the problem! Christ had women followers; and they worked just as hard to spread the gospel as the men, maybe more! Are they mentioned? No, because men don't value women!"

Cassandra's mother, Charity, reached out to take her daughter's hand and gave her an imploring look. Cassandra angrily threw her mother's hand off. Charity was embarrassed by her inability to control her daughter. Everyone else at the tables felt uneasy at having to witness another confrontation between Stewart and Cassandra.

Stewart looked at the ceiling. *Here we go again. I have to hear this male domination of women crap again. If anyone is being dominated its men, being that we're out numbered six to one by women. Now Cassandra has this new religious crap to back up her argument. Where does it come from?* He thought.

Patricia became incensed by Cassandra's behavior and was about to respond on Stewart's behalf. Stewart noticed her and gave her a quick signal to stay out of it, so she just bit her lip and remained silent. Cassandra and Patricia were half-sisters, but there was no sibling love between them. Most of the time they could tolerate each other's company, except for when Cassandra started to attack Stewart. Then Patricia had to be restrained from attacking her sister.

Betty had also become fed-up by Cassandra's repeated disruptions of the tranquility of the harem, but knew better than to try to intervene. It was between Cassandra and Stewart, and nothing that she could add would make any difference.

Theresa had also been listening and decided to speak out. "Cassandra, you shouldn't be listening to those radicals. They are spreading false information. It's blasphemy!"

Cassandra now turned-on Theresa with venom in her voice. "I expect as much from you, being that you're a papist! The Pope tells you that black is white and you believe it!"

Now Theresa was angry and speaking with deliberate forcefulness. "Cassandra, I believe what the church tells me, because it's the truth that has stood the test of time and the scrutiny of biblical scholars!"

Cassandra, having temporarily forgotten about Stewart, shot back at Theresa. "Ha! The Catholic Church was forced to take women into the priesthood because of the shortage of men. There are now more women in the priesthood than men. The College of Cardinals has just elected a new Pope and she's a woman. The Catholic Church will now have to join the twenty-first century."

Stewart had had about enough of this. He had to try to put a stop to it. "Cassandra, please, that's enough now! Let's find something else to talk about."

Cassandra directed her anger back at Stewart. She wasn't finished yet. "Okay, you don't want to talk about religion, then let's talk about men. Let's talk about how men have always been dominant and how men have always run everything. Well, look at the mess you have made of everything. Now we women will have to clean up the mess you men left us. We don't need you; well, the one thing we need from you we can get at the clinic. Some day we may even find a way not to need that anymore." Cassandra threw her napkin on the table and stood up. "I'm not hungry anymore, I'm going out." She stepped away from the table and left the room.

Everyone remained silent for a minute, then normal conversation resumed. Charity spoke, "Stewart, I'm sorry about Cassandra's outburst."

Charity felt embarrassed by Cassandra's behavior and felt the need to explain. Stewart had heard it all before, but decided not to interrupt, knowing that it made her feel better. "Yes, but I feel that I must explain. You see, Cassandra is a sensitive child. When her father, Leonard Owens left, she was twelve years old and entering puberty. It was a time that she most felt the need for a father and he left her. She only understands that she can only rely on men for reproduction, but not for love. As you know, relationships are just for convenience, not for love."

Stewart nodded. "Yes, I know the reality of the times."

Charity reached out and put her hand on Stewart's forearm. "I know how you care about your children; more so than some men, but in the end you will go too. Individuals come and go, only the harem survives. We just stay together for economic advantage."

Stewart looked at Charity and knew that she shared his insight "You're right. I guess the only love left is that between mother and child."

The rest of the meal was taken in silence. After dinner, Stewart skipped the social hour and returned to his quarters. After the confrontation with Cassandra, he needed some time to be alone.

After the social hour, Theresa came to his quarters. They played gin rummy for over two hours; then had intimate relations.

THE DIG

By the next morning there had been a marked improvement in the weather. The sky was still overcast with occasional light rain, but the wind had died down. Stewart checked the weather forecast and found that the rain would end by noon, with gradual clearing to follow in the afternoon. After breakfast, he went to the office to catch up on his reports and other paperwork. He disliked paperwork, seeing it as a necessary evil of his job. He had rather be out in the field, and usually put off the paperwork until it had to be done.

At 10:00 AM, Stewart left the office for the L S Ranch. After entering the destination into his navigation system, Stewart headed to the nearest ramp for Interstate 40 West. He got onto Interstate 40 West, moved to the inside lane and engaged the automatic guidance system. The guidance system locked onto the line of buried magnets running down the center of the lane; and his vehicle sped along at ninety miles-per-hour, keeping proper distance with the vehicles to the front and rear. Not having to control the vehicle, he sat back and watched the scenery go by. The first alarm sounded two minutes before the Vega exit. The vehicle automatically moved into the outside lane and started to decelerate. When the second alarm sounded one minute later, he took manual control and turned off onto U S Highway

North. He continued north until he came to the entry road to the main headquarters of the L S Ranch. He arrived at the main headquarters for the L S Ranch at 11:10 AM.

The ranch foreman, Peggy Bagley, had been expecting him. Peggy just could not pass up the opportunity to make the observation that Stewart always managed to show up at lunch time. Stewart laughed, then pleaded guilty to availing himself of their excellent cuisine. Peggy laughed with him. She enjoyed having him visit.

Following lunch, Peggy took Stewart to show him the fields where they had planted the maize. It was a new hybrid that could produce the same amount of food, while using fewer agrichemicals. After looking at the fields and conferring with Peggy on the program for treating the crop, he left for Amarillo. He arrived back at his office a little before 5:00 PM.

This was the evening that Stewart usually went to his club after dinner. It was an all-male club where he could get together with friends and have a pleasant evening. Since all-male clubs were no longer the seats of power, women were no longer interested in them; they had their own clubs where men were excluded.

When Thomas Owens turned thirteen, his mother, Betty, started to let Stewart take him along with him to the club. Thomas was becoming a man and Betty knew that he needed to associate with other men. Stewart had become a role model for Thomas.

After dinner, Stewart took Thomas and they left for the club. On arrival, Thomas met up with some other young men he knew and went to the billiards room to play eight ball. Stewart went to the bar, ordered a drink, then had a seat at the table with two of his friends. They were Arthur (Art) Smith, a high school teacher, and Dr. Ernst Nichols, an orthopedic surgeon at Northwest Texas Hospital. Stewart sat down at the table and was greeted by Art and Ernst. "Hi, Stewart," Art said, "how has things been going?"

Stewart took a drink from his glass, then said, "Oh, just fine. I was out to the L S Ranch today; I saw Peggy about the new maize crop."

With a knowing smirk on his face, Dr. Nichols gave Stewart a playful pat on the shoulder. "Yea, I bet that you got there just before lunch."

Stewart laughed. "You win that bet, Ernst." Dr. Nichols and Art joined in and they all laughed together, Stewart continued, "They have a great cook out there, but enough about my culinary adventures. What have you two been doing?"

With his hands out in front of him palms up, Ernst shrugged. "Oh, just the usual broken bones and other problems. I had a fourteen-year-old girl in surgery to correct a back problem. Everything went just fine."

Stewart took another drink from his glass, then said, "That sounds good, but that's routine for you." Stewart looked down at his drink for a couple of seconds, then continued, "To change the subject. The weather is good now and the forecast for the coming weekend is sunny days. I'm planning a trip this weekend to the pueblo Indian ruins on the Canadian River that I learned about from the Bivens Ranch foreman. How would you like to come with me?"

Ernst was very interested and wanted to go, but he had other commitments for the weekend. "I'd like to go, but you'll have to count me out; I'm on call this weekend."

Stewart looked at Art. "What about you?"

Art thought for a few seconds before he answered. "Who else is going with you?"

Stewart counted on his fingers. "So far there's Betty, her son Thomas and Patricia."

Art was interested, but he wanted to know more about the pueblo, "Just where on the Canadian is this pueblo?"

Stewart responded, "It's several miles west of where U S Highway 385 crosses the Canadian. It's close to where the Rita Blanca and Punta de Agua creeks run into the river. You go about one-half mile north of the bridge over the river. There's a dirt track that will take you to within three and one-half miles from the pueblo."

Art thought that it would make a fine weekend adventure. "Okay, count me in. There's a teacher I work with, Ruth Griffin, she's interested in this sort of thing. Can I bring her along?"

Stewart didn't have any objections to anyone else coming along. "Yes, bring her along. We'll be out overnight, so bring your sleeping bag and tent; and don't forget rations."

Art said, "I won't."

Stewart saw that everyone's glasses were empty. He offered to buy the next round. After Stewart got the drinks and sat back down, he continued the conversation, "I had another confrontation with Cassandra at dinner yesterday evening."

Ernst took a drink, then spoke, "This is happening more often now, isn't it?" It wasn't a question, but a statement.

Stewart thought of his relationship with Cassandra. It was stormy now, but it hadn't always been so. "Yes, it is. She never liked me. She resented me for taking her father's place in the harem. Until recently, we mostly just ignored each other, but now she has been trying to provoke me every chance she gets. Yesterday evening she started running off at the mouth about how the Bible is wrong and how men have messed up everything."

Art knew just what Stewart was talking about. He had been experiencing the same problem with some of the students at the school where he worked. "So, she's one of them now."

Stewart's eyebrows came up in surprise. "One of who?"

"Guess that you haven't heard of then yet." Art said, "They're a new religious movement. It's called the New Christian Truth Reform Church. They are anti male. Even more, they fantasize about a human society without men. They believe that the Bible was written to glorify men and demean women, so that men could dominate them. They say that the Bible is slanted to the male point of view and incomplete. Their Bishop, Nedra Granger is rewriting it."

Stewart set back with a scowl on his face and shook his head. "No, I haven't heard of them."

Ernst sat his drink down and sat back in his chair. "well, I have. A lot of the women at the hospital are starting to believe this crap; and that's not all, they are saying that god is a woman. The way they see it, God is a creator of life; woman is a creator of life and man isn't. So, therefor, God must be a woman."

Stewart had been paying close attention to all of this. He had his own ideas about religion and the identity of the Supreme Being. He could not see how anyone could claim to know God that well. "It's my belief that God's identity has nothing to do with gender. I see God as a divine force in the universe. I can't see God as a man or woman that lives up in the sky, but a divine force for creation without gender."

Art nodded. "Yes, I believe as you do, but women are getting turned on to this new religion. It's starting to get into the high schools now. Women are frustrated and want someone to blame. They look to us men and say that it's our fault."

Ernst put his glass down and shook his head in disgust. "They think that they have a raw deal! Well, it's no picnic for us either! I for one, would like to have what used to be called a normal life, but that's not possible. When you really look at it, women are just using us. We don't have any say; we are out voted on everything. Just look at how we're banned from all contact sports, or any duty in the military or police that is considered hazardous. Look at all the career fields that are closed to men. We are now thought more as a resource than as real people. We have become second-class citizens."

Stewart found himself in complete agreement with Ernst, he said. 'Yes, women think that as men we have it made. Well, let them spend some time with us. That will help to get their heads screwed on straight." That brought a burst of laughter from everyone, Stewart continued, "They say that men are too valuable to risk. Well, I would still like to have the freedom to do anything I want."

'Hold it," Art said, "enough of this talk! I came here to have a good time. All of this is depressing me." He looked at the table, and continued, "It's time for another round; I've got this one."

Art got up, ordered the next round; then brought it back to the table. He then spoke to Stewart, "When do we leave on Saturday?"

Stewart said, "Be at my place at 6:00 AM ready to go. I want to be at the pueblo and have our camp set up before noon."

Art nodded. "Okay, we'll be there at 6:00 AM."

They continued to talk. Ernst got the next round and a deck of cards and a box of poker chips from the bartender. They played a few hands of five card stud. By then it was getting late. Stewart got Thomas from the billiards room and they left for home.

Because of the drinks that he had consumed, Stewart didn't want to take a chance of being in violation of the law; so, he set the vehicle on self-drive, entered home as the destination and let the vehicle take them home.

At 6:00 AM Saturday they left from the parking lot of Stewart's home. They drove west on Interstate 40 to Vega, then north on US Highway 385 toward Channing. They crossed the bridge over the Canadian River. One-half mile north of the river, they turned left and crossed a cattle guard onto a dirt track. It didn't look like much of a road, but it was hard packed, with good ground clearance and no washouts. There were no sharp turns or steep grades. The track followed close to the river. About three miles further on they passed what the local residents referred to as the bluffs. A limestone cliff formation on the north bank of the river, rising from forty to sixty feet high and close to one-half mile long, with narrow ledges and small cave openings. Four miles past the bluffs, the dirt track ended at the railroad line running from north to south and crossed the Canadian River. From there, they took their packs and walked the three and one-half miles to the pueblo; arriving at about 10:00 AM.

Upon arriving at the pueblo, Stewart picked a campsite where they would be sheltered from the cold north wind, that still blew this early in the season. After setting up camp, they unpacked the sandwiches and had lunch, while they planned their afternoon activities.

Following lunch, they set to work readying the site. The pueblo had been a small settlement for just a few family groups. All the structures fit within a square, one-hundred-fifty feet to a side. The first thing they did was to establish a square, one-hundred yards to a side around the site, with a stake driven into the ground at each corner.

After they had the area staked out, and the reflectors attached to the stakes; They split into two groups. The first group, Stewart, Thomas and Betty were going to take some photographs and make some sketches of the ruins. The second group, Arthur, Ruth and Patricia were going to look for artifacts laying exposed within the staked-out area, other than the ruins. They would be looking for arrow or lance heads, scrapers, pottery shards, or anything else that had been uncovered by wind or water. When they found an artifact, they located it by taking a triangulation to at least three corner stakes. They then gave it a catalog number, tagged it and removed it.

At the end of the day, they built a fire to heat water for their dehydrated meals and instant coffee. After dinner, they sat around the fire talking. Everyone was having a wonderful time, especially Patricia. She loved being able to spend the whole weekend with Stewart, even if they were not alone.

The pueblo had never been investigated. No one knew who the inhabitants had been. They talked about it for a long time. They recalled the Indian nations that were in the area at the time Europeans first started to settle the Americas. There were the Jicarilla Apache to the northwest, the Paducah Apache to the north and the Lipan Apache to the south. They could have been from any of these groups, but no one thought that Apaches ever built pueblos like this. There were the Keres and Tanoan. They built pueblos, but they were to the west in New Mexico. It couldn't be the Wichita or the Tawakoni; they were too far to the east and southeast. Before they turned in for the night, they had decided to do a dig as a summer project.

The next morning, they all surveyed the ruins. They decided to start the did in what appeared to be one of the larger living quarters.

They cleaned the place up, clearing away all the brush and debris. They were careful to leave anything that may be of archeological importance where it lay. They made plans to come back the following weekend with tools and equipment to do a proper job. They wanted to set up a grid and do it right, documenting everything. After lunch, they broke camp and started walking out. They got back to the vehicles and started for home.

They had some time to spare, so when they came to the bluffs, they decided to stop and explore. The bluffs had a reputation for being a haven for rattlesnakes, so the local residents avoided the place. Stewart cautioned everyone to watch their step.

When they got to the edge of the bluff, they walked along the edge and looked down at the riverbed. At this point the riverbed was over one-hundred yards wide. The riverbed was mostly dry sand, with white streaks of alkali on the surface. The only water in the river was a small trickle about one foot deep, that could almost be jumped at some places, that meandered down the riverbed. The only time the riverbed was full, was at flood stage.

Walking ahead, Thomas spotted a ledge approximately eighteen inches wide, about three feet below the edge. He wanted to check it out, but at first his mother didn't want him to take such a risk. Thomas wouldn't relent, in the end Betty got curious and went with him. The ledge led along the face of the bluff at a slight down angle for about eighty feet, more or less, to where the bluff made a turn away from the bluff for a few feet. There they found an opening at least six feet wide by over seven feet tall. Stewart, standing above them, asked, "What do you see?"

Betty and Thomas looked inside. They could only see darkness beyond the entrance. Betty said, "It's an opening in the bluff. It looks like a cave, but I can't tell how big it is."

They didn't have a flashlight with them, but Betty had a pocket mirror. She took it out and focused the sunlight into the opening of the cave and moved it around. "Stewart."

"Yes, Betty."

"It looks like a very large cave. I can see the walls, but I can't see the back. It makes a turn to the left a few feet back."

Stewart thought for a moment if they should try to explore the cave. He decided that it wasn't a good idea right now. "We don't have the time to check it out now. We can come back later. You and Thomas need to come up now."

Betty and Thomas back tracked to where they had jumped down on the ledge. Stewart and Author helped them back up to the top of the bluff. They took a few more minutes to look around then returned to their vehicles and drove back home.

THE CAVE

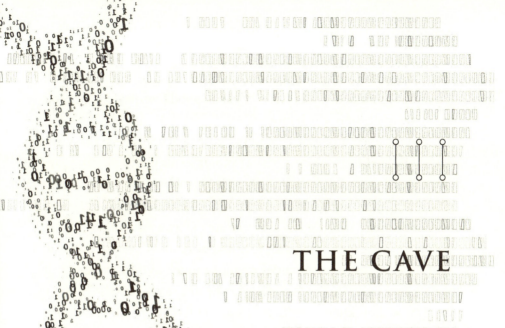

They went back to the pueblo ruins the next weekend. Everyone had been able to make it this time, including Dr. Nichols. Two friends of Dr. Nichols had also come along. They were Anthony Cooper, a business machine repairman and Lesley Hawkins, a shoe salesman. They also had an interest in pre-Columbian archeology and wanted to be included in the dig. Stewart was glad to have them along. There had been a lot of equipment to be brought to the site; and extra hands made it a lot easier to pack in the tools.

After arriving at the pueblo, they quickly set up their camp and unpacked their tools. They then set up a one-meter grid at the dig site, then broke for lunch.

After lunch, they commenced the dig. They started by removing the top layer of dirt; and putting it in a pile to be sifted. They didn't expect to find much in the top layers of dirt, but they sifted it anyway, to make sure that they didn't miss anything. The site had been unoccupied for over three-hundred years, or more. Anything they found would most likely be deep.

After a long afternoon of work, they called a halt about thirty minutes before sundown. They built a fire and boiled water for the evening meal. Later, everyone was sitting around talking. Stewart and

Dr. Nichols had their dinner and coffee, and were sitting a little apart from the others talking together. "We had a good first day," Dr. Nichols said, "we got a lot of earth moved."

Stewart took a bite of rehydrated beef stew and washed it down with coffee before he spoke. "Yes, we did. It seems like hard work now, but this is the easy part. Once we get down to a layer where we start to find artifacts, we will have to switch to smaller tools and work slower, with more care. You will feel that you are like you are working just as hard, but doing less. Some people would be tempted to rush it, but in doing so they might end up destroying as much as they recovered. If we're going to do this, we should take the time to do it right."

Dr. Nichols knew that Stewart was right, that they should do the dig in a careful way, instead of digging everything quickly with a pick and shovel, grabbing anything that they could. "Yes, I agree that you're right. As much as we may be tempted to rush it, we need to do it right. Besides, we have all the time we need."

Stewart kept looking at the fire, as he ate from the pouch of beef stew. "That's true," he said, "I'm sure that we'll find flint tools and most likely a maize grinder or two. What I'd really like to find is some pottery shards. That may tell us more than anything else who these people were."

Stewart and Dr. Nichols finished their dinner and kept on talking about the dig as they drank their coffee. Dr. Nichols said, "I tell you, Stewart, it's been a busy week. I was really glad to get away this weekend and relax."

Stewart took a sip of coffee and zipped his coat up a little to shield himself from the coming cold of night. "So, you say it was a hard week; how's that?"

Dr. Nichols was looking at the fire. He first looked down, then at Stewart before he answered. "Well, really not any more than other weeks. It's just that I keep thinking about one patient. They brought him in Tuesday night. He had three broken ribs and a fracture of the left wrist. That was easy enough to fix. The difficult part was the hip and femur. We worked on him for over five hours to put him back together. He will set off airport alarms from now on and walk with a limp, but otherwise he will be okay."

Stewart took another sip of coffee; it didn't sound like anything unusual to him. "So, what's so special about this one? You've put a lot like him back together again."

Dr. Nichols took some time just looking into his coffee cup before he answered. "I spoke with him the next day. It was no accident that he had. It was about eight-thirty in the evening and he had been walking back home from the restaurant as usual, when a car came at him. He almost got out of the way, but not quite."

Stewart shook his head. "I don't see what you're getting at. It sounds like an accident to me."

Dr. Nichols gave Stewart an astute look. "He said that the car was accelerating when it hit him, and that the driver aimed the car at him. It was a hit and run; it was deliberate, not accidental."

Stewart took another sip of coffee. "So, he has an enemy."

Dr. Nichols shook his head. "No, I questioned him about his life style; I don't think he has any enemies."

Stewart gave Dr. Nichols a questioning look. "What are you trying to tell me, Ernst?"

Dr. Nichols took a sip of coffee. "I'm not sure, it just has me thinking."

Stewart and Dr. Nichols just looked at the fire, thinking. Random violent crime wasn't very common nowadays. When it did happen, it got people's attention. At that time Patricia came over to sit beside Stewart. She had been sitting with Betty and the others, but had wanted to be close to Stewart. It was her intention to sleep in Stewart's tent with him that night. Her arrival ended their conversation on the hit and run.

The next morning, they were back at the dig. By mid-morning they struck something hard in the corner and switched to trowels and brushes. It wasn't long before they could see that it was a maize grinder. Betty became the recorder. She drew in the maize grinder on the grid where they had found it and at what depth.

At 1:00 PM, they put away the tools, broke camp and started back to the vehicles.

When they reached the bluffs, they stopped. Stewart wanted to check out the opening in the bluff, that they had found the week before. Stewart took a powerful flashlight from his vehicle, that he had brought for the purpose. He noticed that everyone else had also brought a flashlight. Stewart asked Betty to go down with him. Thomas and Patricia wanted to come along and Stewart allowed them. When they started down the ledge, Patricia was nervous about the narrowness of the ledge and the distance to the riverbed; she insisted on holding Stewart's hand all the way down. Art brought up the rear of the party.

When they arrived at the entrance, Stewart cautioned them to be careful of rattlesnakes. At the mention of rattlesnakes, Stewart felt Patricia squeeze his hand tighter and move closer to him. Stepping through the entrance, they found a chamber about forty feet long, that widened from six feet at the entrance, to about fourteen feet. The ceiling ran from over seven feet at the entrance to about nine feet. There it turned left about thirty degrees and widened out into a chamber over two-hundred feet long, forty to forty-five feet wide and over thirteen feet high at the highest point. The flashlights of the party were playing around to illuminate ever corner and crevice in the cave. If there had been any rattlesnakes in there, they had already left for the summer. The floor of the cave was fairly level and hard packed. There were two small passages, so narrow as to discourage investigation in the back that led deeper underground.

"Wow!" Stewart said, "What do you think of this?"

Art played the beam of his flashlight around to try to see everything. "I didn't think there was a cave this big around here."

Stewart kept looking around. "You're right. You're not likely to find one this large around here, but as you see, it can happen. Most are formed by wind erosion; like the ones you can see on the saddleback, just the other side of the river. This one must have been formed by water seeping through the stone through the ages to erode it away."

Betty and Thomas kept together as they checked around the walls, all the way to the rear of the cave.

Patricia had continued to hold Stewart's hand, to give her a more secure feeling in the cave. She looked at Stewart. "Is the saddleback that red sandstone hill west of the highway about a mile or more south of the bridge?"

Stewart knew that she had made reference to the right hill. It was a distinctive landmark in the area. "Yes, that's it. In it are several small wind-eroded caves; some large enough to stand up in and a few feet deep." Stewart took one last look around. "I think that we've seen all we need to see today. Is everyone ready to go?" Everyone indicated that they were.

Stewart let Betty lead the group out of the cave and up the ledge. He was the last one out with Patricia. She wouldn't let go of his hand until they were safely on top of the bluff.

After they were back up, the second group, led by Dr. Nichols, went down for a look.

When the second group got back to the top of the bluff, they talked about their discovery of the cave; and how they should handle it. Everyone agreed that, except for size, there was nothing remarkable about the cave. They all decided not to say anything about the cave. They didn't want any curiosity seekers roaming around and perhaps messing up their dig. The decision made, they returned to their vehicles and started home.

Through the spring and summer, they continued the dig. They were finding mostly stone tools for cutting and scraping, also some lance and arrow heads. The first maize grinder that they had found was broken. The jackpot was pottery shards. By the end of the summer, they had enough to compare with known shapes and decorative patterns. They now believed that they had an early pueblo culture, from four-hundred fifty to five-hundred years old, related to the Keres pueblos. Everyone was excited about the dig. There were at least five persons each weekend working at the Pueblo, usually more. Only three weekends were rained out.

Stewart's work and home life continued on as usual. There was an occasional confrontation with Cassandra. Stewart managed to avoid her for most of the day, so that their confrontations were limited to dinner. She seemed to take pleasure in disrupting the tranquility of the harem as much as she could. She would attack men in general; and seemed to get a sadistic pleasure in attacking Stewart personally. There was no way that Stewart was going to win a debate with Cassandra. She didn't want to debate; she just wanted a shouting match. She was really hung up on this New Christian Truth Reform Church thing. Her sister, Crystal, had started to take her side in any arguments with Stewart. Charity was embarrassed by Cassandra and Crystal's behavior, but rarely intervened.

Stewart would like to know more about this New Christian Truth Reform Church, but he couldn't learn much from Cassandra. When he inquired of her, he got no answers. When they argued at dinner, she just made quick reference to the church, then attacked his manhood. This New Christian Truth Reform Church was also a topic at the club with his friends. No one knew much about it. With the women in the church, the men became the enemy.

It wasn't as if men would want to join it anyway. The message was apparently meant only for women. Stewart found out from the other men at the club, that when women turned toward this church, they turned away from men. They weren't lesbians, or such; they just didn't want to compete for men anymore. In fact, they didn't want to have anything to do with men. They lived a celibate life. When they wanted to have children, they used the sperm bank.

Stewart's friends at the club that lived alone, said that although there were still plenty of women to choose from, there was a noticeable decline in the overall numbers. Most women were finding the competition for men too stressful. They were just looking for someone to them that it was okay to get out. The men were starting to see a lot of women in the emerald-green caftans, some with navy-blue trim and waistband, but mostly with emerald-green waistband. The church membership seemed to be growing at an alarming speed.

In late October the weather started to change. It would be turning cold soon and hunting season was near at hand. They decided to postpone the dig until next spring.

As expected, Peggy Bagley invited Stewart to hunt on the L S Ranch. He was able to bag a good-sized pronghorn. The week before Thanksgiving, Stewart went hunting for turkey with Peggy Bagley. Betty was also invited along on the hunt. Both Stewart and Betty were able to bag a turkey.

The harem made a big deal of putting up the Christmas tree after Thanksgiving. Presents from one to the other accumulated under the tree. After dinner on Christmas eve, everyone gathered in the family room, in front of the tree. Serena Bassett told the Christmas story to the children that year. The next morning, there were toys under the tree from Santa for the children. Everyone then opened their presents. At 1:00 PM they all sat down to Christmas dinner.

On New Year's Eve, all the women celebrated by themselves. Stewart went to his club with Thomas to celebrate with his friends. At midnight, Stewart made a toast. "May this New Year, two-thousand eighty-six, be better than the last." Everyone put their glasses together, then drank.

IV

RANDOM VIOLENCE

The New Year of 2086 came in with a blast. On the ninth of January a blizzard swept across the southern plains and hit Amarillo, Texas. The blizzard blew for three days, with temperatures down to minus twenty degrees Fahrenheit. It was very brutal, if not a deadly time for man and beast. Everyone remained indoors, braving the elements only when it became necessary to do their work. Or for an emergency.

At a time like this when everyone, more or less was confined indoors, care had to be taken not to upset the tranquility of the harem. It was also the time when it seemed to Stewart that the women of the harem made the most demands of him for intimacy. The first evening, Alberta came to his private quarters for a very lively and imaginative evening. The second evening, Serena had one of her infrequent urges. Stewart always found their episodes of intimacy very exhausting; and was glad that they were not more frequent.

On the third day of the blizzard, Cassandra again started to disrupt the evening meal. Patricia became angry, and before anyone could react to intervene, she assaulted Cassandra and they came to blows. Embarrassed by her loss of control, Patricia fled from the dining room in tears to her private quarters

Stewart gave her a few minutes to get most of her crying done, then went to her private quarters. At first, she didn't want to let him, or anyone else in, but after a while, she relented and opened the door to him. Stewart spent a couple of hours with her. First to comfort her and give her a shoulder to cry on; then at her insistence, to make love to her. When he left her, she was again in good spirits.

When Stewart got to his private quarters, Betty was waiting for him. The first thing that she wanted to know, was how Patricia felt. Stewart assured her that Patricia had gotten over her altercation with Cassandra; and was once again in good spirits. Concerned that he might be tired and want some time to himself, Betty was starting to leave. Stewart urged her to stay, expressing the desire to have her company for the night. After comforting Patricia, he could use a little comforting for himself.

Stewart couldn't get out to the field, so he spent his time catching up on paperwork. Which ironically, was mostly on the computer now, but the name stuck. This was the part of his work that he put off as long as he could. He only worked hard on it when bad weather kept him from the field. He could have made into his office despite the blizzard, but he didn't see the need to go to all that trouble If he didn't have to. He linked his home computer and everything from his private quarters at home. After three days, he had nothing more to do in the office. He was now anxious to get back in the field.

On the twelfth of January, the weather broke and the sky finally cleared. The temperature was still frigid, but the farmers and ranchers could now get into their fields, to check on their property and livestock. A farmer just west of Panhandle, Texas, in Carson County, was checking her fields, when she found the body of Dudley Morgan draped over the barbwire fence. Dudley was twenty-three years old, an employee of the Texas State Technical Institute in Amarillo. His throat had been cut. The murder became a sensation, with all the news stations on it right away. The police vowed to find whoever was responsible and bring them to justice. They sounded really sincere, but by now, most people were skeptical of their willingness to look for the killers.

Two days later, when Stewart went to the club with Thomas, everyone was talking about the Dudley Morgan murder. He had happened to be a member of the club; and his friends were very upset. They couldn't think of anyone who would want to kill Dudley.

Stewart sat at the table in the bar, with Dr. Nichols, Anthony Cooper and Leslie Hawkins. They were talking about the Dudley Morgan murder. Leslie was speaking, "I tell you; I've been talking with some of his friends. No one knows why he was killed, or who may have done it. They say that he was a really nice man; that he treated all his friends, both men and women well."

"You know," Stewart said, "they always say that about the deceased. No one speaks ill of the dead. However, you know as well as I, that most people have secrets; and that with some of these people, the secret can be really egregious. How do you know that this good guy didn't have a dark side and someone decided to get even?"

Lesley knew that Stewart had a point, but he knew some of Dudley's friends; and believed them to be a good judge of good character. "Yes, I've heard that one too, but I believe them when they talk about him as being someone without enemies. I don't understand this one. What reason anyone have to do something like that?"

Anthony took a drink of his beer, then said, "What I gather from talking to some of his friends, is that he wasn't a person to take risks; he wouldn't have been out looking for trouble. If you're right, this is just a random killing. Now, the question I have, is why the killer or killers displayed the body the way they did, there's something going on here. Something like this doesn't happen for no reason."

Dr, Nichols nodded. "You're right, Anthony; as much as I wish you weren't. It started about a year ago, maybe more. There had been assaults, hit and runs and murder, mostly against men; and they are on the rise. No one knows who is doing it, or why."

Random murders and random violence against men. Stewart thought. He thought of the hit and run that Ernst had told him about last year. Is it possible that these two events are linked? What's going on?

Anthony looked down at his drink for a minute, trying to put things together in his mind, before he asked, "I'm wondering, are they just random-unrelated events, or is some organization behind all this?"

Anthony looked around the table. Everyone was deep in thought, but no one had any answer to his question. He continued, "Stewart, Betty Treadway is with the police. Has she said anything about this happening in other cities?"

Stewart thought back to any conversations that he had with Betty before answering. "Yes, I didn't pay much attention at the time, but she did say something about random events happening around Albuquerque and Santa Fe, New Mexico. This was just something that she said in passing. She didn't mention any place else. I'm willing to bet though, that it's happening in other places."

Lesley then asked the question that was on everyone's minds. "Why is all this happening? What does anyone hope to gain by it?"

Everyone was silent for a while in thought. Nothing ever happened in a vacuum, there was always a cause and effect, but where was the connection? Finally, Stewart said, "I don't know, it's a mystery to me. Do you think this New Christian Truth Reform Church has anything to do with it?"

"I don't know," Anthony said, "you have to come up with suspects and motive first, before you can start connecting one to the other." Anthony held up his right hand with the index finger pointing up for emphasis. "I, for one, would like to know more about this New Christian Truth Reform Church."

Dr. Nichols looked around the table, as someone who had a secret he longed to impart. He had taken an interest in the New Christian Truth Reform Church; and had been trying to information about it. He had soon realized, that it was hard to discover anything about the church. For a man to try to get information, was like trying to get

Masonic secrets from a Mason. "I have some information on them. It seems that they couldn't do much about the Old Testament, so they just declared it to be a sexist and almost worthless document, then threw it out completely. They say that had only historical, but no religious value. They have rewritten the New Testament as a radically feminist document. They now call it the Testament of Christ. They haven't gone as far as to claim that Christ was a woman yet, but it wouldn't surprise me if they did."

Lesley saw that everyone's glasses were empty. He got up to get the next round. When Lesley returned with the drinks, Dr. Nichols continued, "About the possibility of a connection between the random violence and the new church. The church couldn't do this alone; they would have to be conspiring with other groups; even people in the government and police would have to be in on it."

Everyone was silent again. It was hard to believe that anything like Ernst had implied could ever happen.

Finally, Anthony broke the silence. "Well, I'm telling you, I watch where I go now; and I don't spend any time alone in parking lots."

Stewart had been thinking about what he should do to look after his own security. "You know the revolver I have?"

Dr. Nichols said, "You mean that old forty-four magnum?"

Stewart nodded. "Yes, that's the one. I carry it with me in the field during the warm months. I keep it loaded with a special birdshot load, to take care of rattlesnakes. I'm going to start carrying it with me all the time; and not loaded with birdshot."

Dr. Nichols had been giving the problem some thought as well. He also planned to get a gun and start carrying it. However, they also needed to start thinking of more than just personal protection. He said, "To start carrying a gun for personal protection is one thing, but we need to do more than just look to our own personal security. If there is a conspiracy, the question is, why/ It can't be for women to gain power over men; the women already have the power in every aspect of society, because of their overwhelming numerical dominance.

There's something here that we're not seeing. It seems we have a lot of questions and no answers. We just can't sit and wait for things to happen. If we do that, by the time we have the answers, it may be too late. I suggest that we start networking with our friends around the country. We need to have answers," Everyone nodded in agreement, Dr Nichols continued, "I suggest that we meet here the same time each week to share information.' Everyone agreed.

They continued to talk for a while longer. When it was time to go, Stewart got Thomas from the billiards room: and they left for home.

When they got back home, Stewart got his revolver from the closet. It was a large frame Smith & Wesson .44 cal. Magnum model 2036 with six-inch barrel. He cleaned it, then took a fifty-round box of cartridges from the closet. He first loaded the revolver. He then loaded three hard rubber quick loaders. He then took his coat and put the quick loaders in the lower left front pocket. He put the remaining rounds from the box in the lower right front pocket. He would carry the revolver in his under-arm holster, under the left arm.

Through the internet, they started to get in touch with old friends all over the country; and what they discovered was alarming. There seemed to be the same pattern of random violence directed at men throughout the country; and it was not just in the United States. There were reports on the internet of the same thing happening in other countries as well. It seemed like a plot to intimidate men, in order to curtal the freedom of their movement. The whole thing was making Stewart and his friends uneasy.

In February, he thought of the cave that they had found at the bluff last summer. He decided to start laying in supplies and equipment. He had no plan. He simply thought of it as insurance against some as yet unknown emergency. He started to take something with him to drop off at the cave, every time he went out to the L S or Biven's

Ranch, or anywhere around Channing or Dalhart. He then put in some camping Gear.

In March, Alberta Singletary let Stewart know that she was pregnant. Stewart would have a third child, most likely a girl.

CASSANDRA MOVES OUT

In mid-April, when the weather started to warm up, they decided to resume the dig at the pueblo. Everyone who had been involved in the dig last season, opted to continue on the team. Patricia had participated in the dig last year, more for the purpose of being close to Stewart as much as possible. She still wanted to be close to Stewart, but she had also developed an intense interest in pre-Columbian archaeology.

On the first weekend, they carried in all their tools, set up the grid as before, then continued the dig where they had left off the previous fall. During the second weekend, they started to uncover the remains of a basket. Everyone became excited and eager to see their find. However, it was so fragile, they had to proceed with caution. They were using dental picks and fine camel hair brushes. Basket weaving could reveal a lot about the people who had once lived there; especially the time it was made, being that it could be carbon dated. Everyone wanted to recover it without any further damage.

At dinner, Stewart sat at the table with Betty and Patricia. The three of them were talking about the dig. Charity, Cassandra and

Crystal were sitting at the next table. Cassandra had been listening to the conversation between Stewart, Betty and Patricia. Betty was talking to Stewart about where in the pueblo they should dig next, after they finished with the family unit, when Cassandra interrupted. She threw her head back and rolled her eyes in mock disgust. "Oh, God, can't you talk about something else besides that damn dig?"

Everyone was startled, but not surprised by Cassandra's outburst. It was, however, very disruptive to everyone at the tables.

Betty became angered, but determined to maintain her composure. She stopped eating, put down her knife and fork, then gave Cassandra a cold look. "Please, Cassandra, this isn't your conversation. Kindly stay out of it."

Cassandra wasn't about to stay out of it. She had been spoiling for an argument. She glared at Betty and Stewart with hatred in her heart and voice. "Oh, it's not your conversation that I'm interested in, Betty. It's how you and all the rest of the women in the harem keep sucking up to him all the time."

Betty was about to answer her, when Stewart waved her off. This was something that he had to handle. Stewart faced Cassandra, with an exacerbated look on his face. No matter how often it occurred, it never became a routine matter. He was getting sick of it. "Cassandra, I know that you don't like me, but do you always have to interrupt everyone's peace?"

By now, everyone had stopped eating. Instead they were watching the give and take of the argument between Cassandra and Stewart. They argued so often now, that it had become a spectator sport. Cassandra glared back at Stewart, with menace in her eyes. When she spoke, it was with venom in her voice. "I speak to you when I can! I don't care where when or where it is! However, it's not you I want to speak to; I don't give a damn about you!" Cassandra waved her arm about to encompass everyone in the room. "It's these women, I don't see why they don't throw you out."

Betty could no longer contain herself; she jumped to her feet and

CASSANDRA MOVES OUT

faced Cassandra. With a furious look, she shook her finger at Cassandra. "Cassandra, we've had enough of you! Why don't you just leave?"

Cassandra, by now, had also gotten to her feet. "I plan to do just that, but first I'm going to say what I want to say and no one is going to stop me!" She looked around to make eye contact with the harem members at both tables. When she spoke, it was with a condescending voice. "You women are pathetic! You pamper and kiss up to this man, so that ever once in a while he'll stick his penis in you! For me, I don't want that!"

Charity was shocked. She had gotten used to Cassandra's behavior, but this time she had gone too far. She sprang to her feet, barely able to control her rage, as she tried to face down her daughter. "Cassandra, that's enough! Your behavior this evening is reprehensible! I believe that you owe an apology to Stewart and everyone else here!"

Cassandra gave her mother a despotic look, clearly showing disrespect and a feeling of superiority over her mother. "No, Mother, I don't owe him, you, or anyone else anything! I don't need to apologize for the truth! You don't need him! I don't see why you demean yourselves by keeping him! The very idea of a man between my legs, forcing himself into me is revolting. Cassandra now directed her words at Stewart, ignoring her mother. "You men are superfluous! We don't need you anymore! We don't need anything you have! You are obsolete!"

Cassandra's mother was really angry now. It was all she could do to keep from slapping her daughter in the face. "Cassandra, you apologize to Stewart and the rest of the harem, right now!"

Cassandra snapped back at her mother. "No, I won't apologize! I just wanted to have my say, before I moved out!"

"What!" Charity screamed.

Cassandra said, "I'm moving out, Mother. I'm moving to Chicago. I'm entering the sisterhood; and will be training to enter the priesthood. I'll call you, when I get there." Cassandra then turned and left the dining room to pack.

Charity just stood there mute, as Cassandra walked out of the dining room. She wanted to rush after her daughter, to speak about all of this, but first, she felt that she had to say something to Stewart. "Stewart, I want to apologize to you for Cassandra's behavior. I should've seen it coming, but I didn't know how deep she was into this new religion."

Stewart gave Charity a wave of the hand and a reassuring smile. "Thank you, but you have nothing to apologize for. It was not your fault."

Charity then turned and left the dining room.

Everyone else put the incident behind them and went back to dinner. Betty and Patricia continued to Talk about the dig. Charity came back to the table. Her daughter, Cassandra, had refused to talk to her. Stewart kept thinking about the incident. He kept thinking about what she had said. What did she mean by, 'you are obsolete'?

Cassandra came back into the dining room a few minutes later. She was dressed in the emerald-green caftan and waist sash of a sister of the New Christian Truth Reform Church. She said good-bye to her sister. She didn't say good-bye to her mother. Charity, being scandalized by Cassandra's behavior, turned her head away from Cassandra, refusing to acknowledge her. Cassandra just turned and left the room.

That evening, after the social hour, Patricia came to Stewart's private quarters. She was too young to drink, but Stewart would indulge her anyway. He would make her a rum and coke, putting just enough rum in, that it could be tasted, but not enough to make her drunk. He would then make himself a bourbon and water. Patricia was in an exceptionally good mood that evening. She had never had any love for her sister, Cassandra, and had been glad to see her go. She thought of how much more pleasant it would be without her.

After the drinks, Patricia wanted to look at Stewart's collection of Indian pottery and other artifacts. As he stood behind her, explaining what each item on the shelves were, he placed his hand on her shoulder. She reveled in his touch and leaned back against him. She loved to feel the strength of him and to smell his masculine aroma.

After Stewart had showed her his collection, they again got

comfortable in his large easy chairs and talked. Patricia, now being very interested in pre-Columbian history, wanted to learn as much about it from Stewart as she could. Stewart had an excellent collection of books on the subject. He took a book on the Zunis Indians to show her and they talked about it.

After a while, Patricia asked Stewart for another rum and coke. They got up and went to the bar, where Stewart mixed the drinks. When they went back to the chairs, instead of taking her seat in her chair, she sat in Stewart's lap. She lay up against him, with her arm around his neck. He put his arm around her waist. She snuggled up against him, feeling the warmth of his body. Her sitting on his lap was just her way of saying that she wanted to spend the night with him.

Stewart had a special relationship with Patricia. He found himself in the role of being everything male to her, like father, big brother and lover all rolled into one. It was a difficult role; and one that had been awkward when she had reached the age of consent and had exercised her rights as a member of the harem. Stewart's worries that the start of a sexual relationship would lead to difficulty in their other relationship proved to be unfounded; and a very good relationship had developed between them. Patricia loved him.

Patricia sat in Stewart's lap and swirled her drink around in her glass, listening to the ice tinkle against the glass. She put her glass down on the side table, next to Stewart's drink and fished out an ice cube. She reached up and started to rub his neck with the ice cube.

Stewart gasped, "You!" He put his other arm around her waist and pulled her close. She giggled, then kissed him on the lips. He tickled her on the ribs and she squirmed in his lap laughing. "Oh, you!" She gasped, "Quit it!" Stewart stopped his tickling and they kissed again. She got comfortable against his shoulder and chest again and looked into his eyes smiling "I'm so happy, this had been a memorable day."

"Oh, why is that?" Stewart asked, while raising his eyebrows in mock surprise.

With a crafty smile, she said. "The bitch is gone."

Stewart knew, that despite their being half-sisters, there was no love lost between Patricia and Cassandra. "Yes," Stewart said, "she was a disruption to the harem. She had always been cold to me; blaming me for taking her father's place. However, for the last two years, she had been especially hostile towards me. Now, at last we should have some peace around here. I know that she didn't care much for you either."

Patricia had Stewart's shirt unbuttoned and was running her fingers through his chest hair. "That's right, she is my half-sister, but we didn't get along together at all. She is so uppity, she always had her nose so high in the air, it's a wonder that she knew where she was going."

Stewart laughed at her remark. "Yes, I'm aware of the falling outs you had with her, one in particular, the one in the kitchen."

Patricia kept running her fingers through Stewart's chest hair, as a wicked little smile crossed her face. "Yes, how could I ever forget it? It was right after I came of age and started to take advantage of my conjugal rights. Cassandra and I were here in the kitchen, having some words about it. She said that I couldn't wait to spread my legs for you, that I was your little whore. I called her a stuck-up, love starved little bitch. She struck me and grabbed my hair. I hit her back and grabbed her hair and we started rolling on the floor, kicking, scratching and pulling hair. Alberta and Betty heard the fight and broke it up.

Stewart nodded with an amused look on his face. "Yes, I remember Betty telling me all about it."

Patricia said, "I had a bloodied nose, a cut inside my mouth and my scalp hurt, but it wasn't so bad. I'm sure that Cassandra's scalp hurt even more than mine; and she had a lovely shiner. It got all black and swollen, with a blood-shot eye. There wasn't any amount of make-up that could cover it. She had to wear sun glasses all the time for a few days. She wouldn't say why she was wearing them, so that she wouldn't have to tell her friends that her younger sister had beat her ass."

Stewart laughed and gave her a pat on the hip. "Yes, I remember that shiner; and what a beauty it was. You must have gloated every time you saw it."

Patricia grinned. "Yes, I did."

Stewart drew her close and they kissed. "Are you ready to go to bed?" He asked. Patricia nodded. Stewart got to his feet, still holding Patricia in his arms and carried her to the bedroom.

The next week, Stewart was at the dig. With him were Patricia, Dr. Nichols, Author, Ruth, Anthony and Thomas. Betty couldn't come; she was on duty that weekend. The campsite was set up before noon. They had lunch, then spent the rest of the afternoon at the dig.

After dinner, they were all setting around the fire. Ruth and Thomas were talking with each other. Stewart, Dr. Nichols, Author and Anthony moved away from the fire to talk in private. Author said, "I've been networking with some of my friends in Denver, Lubbock and Tulsa. They say that they are having the same pattern of Random violence as we are."

Everyone nodded. This surprised no one. Anthony said, "I've many friends on the internet and I can tell you it's happening on the east coast, west coast, mid-west; it's happening everywhere. It's even happening in other countries around the world."

Everyone was very thoughtful for a few moments before Stewart spoke. "Well, I'm sure we all have the same story. What we need to know is why? Does anyone have any ideas?" Stewart looked around. No one had any answers. Stewart continued, "Okay, we don't know why, but this is what I believe. We are just seeing the tip of the iceberg so-to-speak. We can see what is happening; and I'm sure that they know we would see it, but that's not the real problem. What we have to discover is the purpose behind all this. We can't just sit around waiting for the hammer to drop. By then it'll be too late."

Dr. Nichols nodded to Stewart. "That's a good speech Stewart and I'm sure we all agree with you, but do you have any ideas on how to find out what's behind all this?"

Stewart shook his head in resignation. "No, I don't. I've been racking my brain, but so far, I haven't come up with anything. We may not know until it's too late. I may not know what's coming, but I don't plan to be caught without options. You remember the cave at the bluffs?" everyone nodded. "Well, I decided that it's a good idea to have someplace to disappear for a while if we need to. I have been laying up stores, like dehydrated meal packs, canned goods, camping gear and sleeping bag. You might think of doing the same. If you can't bring it out yourself, just give it to me, I'll bring it out for you."

Everyone agreed with Stewart. They might not know what they were guarding against, but now at least they had a plan that they could act on. Everyone would start laying up supplies.

Author said, "We now have a place to hide if we need to, but we still don't know how to get at the real problem. Damn, this is all so frustrating! If it's a conspiracy, it's a conspiracy of women. Women are such a majority, that they hold all the key positions. They have the Presidency, Vice Presidency and the Cabinet. They have ninety percent of the Congress. They control the armed forces, police and industry. It's the same in all the Governors Mansions and State Houses. If you have to trust women to get information, how do you know which ones to trust?"

Everyone thought for a while, before Stewart spoke, "Art, you've gone right to the core of the matter. How do we break into a system and get information, when we don't know whom to trust? I suggest that we give this some thought, then discuss it next week at the club. Now, if there is nothing more for now, we can go back to the fire. Everyone looked around; no one had anything more to say.

Dr. Nichols said, "Well, I guess that's it for now."

Everyone started to get up and move back to the fire. Dr. Nichols grabbed Stewart by the arm to keep him from rising. "Stewart, Thomas has been telling me that things are a lot quieter at your home now?"

Stewart nodded. "That's right; Cassandra moved out after her last outburst during dinner. She just had to take a last parting shot at me, before she left and it was really ugly. She's now a novice with this new religion. I'm sure that even her mother was glad to see her go. There was, however, something strange about her parting words. They were, as best as I can remember. 'You men are superfluous. We don't need you anymore. We don't need anything from you. You are obsolete.' That's as close as I can remember."

Dr. Nichols nodded. "Yes, that's a strange statement. Are you sure that she used the words obsolete?"

Stewart nodded. "Yes, she did use those words."

Dr. Nichols sat for a minute, looking at the ground, playing Cassandra's words in his mind, before looking back up at Stewart. 'Well, that's really strange. Why would she choose that word? I need to think about this."

Dr. Nichols and Stewart then got up and moved back to the fire.

Monday evening after dinner and the social hour; Stewart returned to his private quarters. A few minutes later, there was a knock at the door. He put the book that he was reading down and answered the door: it was Betty. He invited her in and served her a glass of white wine. She had come to talk about the dig.

For twenty minutes they talked about the did, then Betty changed the subject. "Stewart, you've really been good to Thomas. You're sometimes like a big brother and sometimes like a father to him."

With a wave of his hand, Stewart said, you don't have to thank me. I'm glad to do it; I like Thomas."

Betty looked down at her wine glass, it was empty. "Oh, Stewart, may I have another glass of wine?"

Stewart's glass was also empty. "Of course, Betty, let me get it for you." He got up and refilled both glasses, then sat back down. He could tell that something was on her mind, but that she was reluctant to bring it up.

"Betty," he said, "you have something to say to me, but are reluctant to do so. I like to believe that whatever it is, we can trust each other."

The time had come to be frank with Stewart. Betty took a sip of wine and put her glass back down. "I have been talking with Thomas. I know that you and some of your friends are concerned about something: and I think I know what it is. It's this pattern of random violence against men. Am I right?"

Stewart nodded. "Yes, Betty, you're right."

Betty continued, "It's a concern of mine too. I have a son and what affects him affects me. I also know that you have been provisioning that cave against some as yet unknown emergency."

Stewart knew that he needed to be honest with Betty. Of all the women that he knew, Betty was the one that he felt he could trust the most. "And what about the rattlesnakes; don't you think they will use that cave for a den?"

Stewart shook his head. "No, that cave is too big and open. It would get too cold for them in the winter."

Betty was thoughtful for a minute before she spoke. "I want to help you. I can help you provision the cave; and I can help you gather information. I do have some sources that aren't available to you. In return, I want you to include Thomas in your plans and take care of him."

Stewart had no problem about taking care of Thomas. He readily agreed and held out his hand. "It's a deal, Betty." They shook on it.

Now that the business was taken care of, the atmosphere turned pleasant. Betty said, "Thank you for agreeing to take care of Thomas. I have one other request; can I stay with you tonight?"

Stewart smiled at Betty. "Why, yes, I'd love your company.

TWO MOTHERS NO FATHER

It was mid-summer now and Stewart's busiest time of the year. As a State Agriculture Agent, he had a large area to cover and a lot of farmers and ranchers to service. Some days were really long and he didn't get home until late in the evening. He did, however, make sure that he could be present for all the weekly meetings with the group at the club. They had a meeting each Wednesday at 8:00 PM. Everyone who could make it was present.

Betty was now a member of the group, but for obvious reasons she would not be able to attend the meeting at the men's club. At the request of Betty, Thomas was now a member of the group. At fifteen, he was old enough to take the responsibility for keeping everything discussed at the meetings in confidence. He had the maturity to be an active and contributing member of the group. Thomas was therefore able to keep Betty up to date, without her having to spend so much time at home with Stewart, so as not to arouse the interest of the rest of the women in the harem.

The first week of July, the weekly meeting at the club was in progress.

Lesley was speaking, "Most of my friends are here in Amarillo. We talk a lot about what is going on. So far, no one has a clue as to the reason for the violence. I do have some friends on the internet in Miami, Boston, South Bend and Santa Cruz, but none of them know anything either."

Dr. Nichols, with a smug smile on his face, looked around as if he was about to reveal something profound. "Stewart, do you remember what you told me that evening at the pueblo ruins about what Cassandra said?"

Stewart thought for a moment, before he spoke, "Yes, I remember, she said, "You men are superfluous. We don't need you. We don't need anything from you. You are obsolete." Is that how you remember it?"

Dr. Nichols replied, "Yes, that's it. I just wanted everyone to hear it, before I told you what I've found out." Dr. Nichols paused for a moment, to make sure that all eyes were on him. "Well, I've been looking into human reproduction research. They have perfected a technique where they take an ovum, or ova, that's what you call the human female egg. They take two ovum each from two women. They then extract the genetic information from the two ova of one of the women and inject it into the two ova of the other woman. What you now have is two fertilized ova. You now implant one ovum in each of the two women. Each ovum will become a female child, with two mothers and no father. It doesn't matter which fertilized ova goes into which woman, because both embryos will be sisters, with the same two mothers." Dr. Nichols paused. to look at the impact his words were having on his audience. He could see it in their faces. "So, there you have its gentlemen, conception without the benefit of a male."

No one spoke; they just sat there in silence. Finally, Stewart let out an audible sigh that broke the silence. "Damn!" He said, "Now I know what Cassandra was saying. Maybe we are obsolete."

Suddenly everyone wanted to talk all at once. There was a rapid back and forth exchange; as Dr. Nichols tried to answer everyone's questions at once.

After a few minutes, order was restored to the meeting. Dr. Nichols said, "My explanation of the procedure may have been a bit simplistic, but you get the idea. What you may not grasp are the implications. A woman would no longer have to reproduce two times, once for herself, then once for her male partner. She just has to reproduce one time to replace herself. You will end up with a population of only females, with every member a reproducing member. Now the myth of an Amazon society can be a reality. A world without men."

Most of the men were still finding it hard to grasp the idea. Finally, Arthur exclaimed, "Oh, my God! It's much more serious than we imagined!" His face became a mask of concern; he banged the table with his fist for emphasis. "You know what we are talking about! We're talking about the extinction of the male half of the human race.

Everyone around the table became very somber. The implications of what they had been hearing were unthinkable. Could women go as far as to breed men out of the human population? After a few seconds, Anthony sat back in his chair and let out an audible sigh. "I can't believe what I've been hearing. Even if there is a conspiracy, I can't believe that every woman would be in on it, or in favor of it."

Stewart had been thinking of something that had come into his mind. At first, he couldn't believe it was possible, but perhaps it could be. He looked around the table with a grave look on his face. "They all don't have to be in on the conspiracy. You just need enough and in the right key positions."

Anthony shot back. "Good God, man! Do you hear what you are saying? You're talking about a conspiracy that would be worldwide. Can that be possible?"

Stewart said, "Possible or not, I don't know. However, women now control the world, we must assume that anything is possible. Now, I know that there a lot of women who wouldn't be for it, like Betty. She has a son to think about."

The mention of Betty's name made Authur think of Ruth. "Ruth has a son; his name is David Cushing. He's nineteen and attends Texas A&M at Amarillo Campus. Ruth may want to help us. I can talk to her and see if she would help us."

Dr. Nichols looked at Authur. "I have a better idea. Let's allow Betty to do it at the pueblo dig this weekend. Betty will know best how to bring up the subject with her."

Stewart nodded agreement with Dr. Nichols. "Okay, Thomas and I will speak with betty. She can sound out Ruth this weekend. Now, if there are no objections; I believe that we have enough to think about until next Wednesday. I suggest that we adjourn." Stewart looked around the table. No one else had anything more to bring up, so everyone agreed and the meeting ended.

That evening, when they got back home, Thomas briefed his mother. The next morning, Betty let Stewart know that she would talk to Ruth that coming weekend.

Saturday they were at the pueblo ruins. They continued to work on the remains of the woven basket; and were successful at removing it without any further damage. They congratulated each other on their success. This was by far, the most valuable artifact recovered. Stewart and Arthur packed it up for transfer to the Museum in Canyon, Texas.

They were almost finished with the dig in the family unit. There next dig would be the ruin of a circular structure of approximately twenty feet in diameter. Stewart figured it most likely a place for religious ceremonies. Everyone looked forward to it.

That evening at dinner, everyone let Betty and Ruth have the space to talk alone. Stewart made sure that Patricia stayed close to him, and out of earshot of Betty and Ruth's conversation. He invited her to go for a walk with him, taking a blanket along. They stayed out in the dark for over an hour, Making love under the stars. When they finally returned to the fire, Patricia had not been aware that Betty and Ruth had conversed.

Betty had first engaged Ruth in conversation about the dig. After a while, Betty steered the conversation around their jobs. Ruth spoke about some of the problems that they were having in the schools. Betty then started to talk about the random violence against men. "I tell you, Ruth, I'm worried for Thomas. I don't want him to become a victim of these attacks. I don't know what I would do if he were hurt."

With a knowing thoughtful look on her face, Ruth nodded. "Yes, I know what you mean, although Thomas is still younger than David, we both have to think of their safety after they leave home and are on their own. Maybe by then something will have been done about it."

Betty nodded with a concerned look. "Yes, perhaps they will have done something about it by then, but I wouldn't count on it. This I can tell you. I have been checking and this is not just a local problem, it's everywhere and it's getting worse. Now each incident is investigated, but so far nothing has become of the investigations and I don't think anything will."

Ruth gave Betty a questioning look. "Aren't the police giving this a high priority and organizing a task force to look into it?"

Betty shook her head. "No, nothing is being done, they are just going through the motions." Betty reached out, touching Ruth's forearm and looking into her eyes. "Ruth, there's something I have to tell you."

Ruth was surprised by Betty's sudden serious demeanor. She wondered what betty was trying to say.

Betty continued, "There's nothing random about these random attacks. We don't know what it's all about, but there's some kind of conspiracy behind it."

Ruth was stunned. It took her a full minute to recover. She still didn't know if she should take everything Betty said on faith. She looked at Betty. You say that there's a conspiracy. What proof do you have?"

Betty looked down for a few seconds, then looked back up at Ruth. "Listen, Ruth, as of yet we have no proof, but that's what things are starting to point to. By the time we have proof of a conspiracy, it may be too late. Those who are behind this and their intentions we're not sure, but I doubt it's good."

Ruth still wasn't sure of what to believe. She wondered why Betty was telling her about this. "You say that there's something behind all this? What can we do about it?"

Betty said, "Well, since we don't know what exactly it is, we don't have a definite plan. Instead we have, let's call it an option, a refuge for our men, in case there comes a time that they have to disappear for a while. I thought that you would like to have David included in the group."

Ruth didn't have to think about it for an instant, her answer was immediate. "Yes, I would. What do I have to do?"

Betty smiled; she had been sure that Ruth would want to be included. "You remember that cave at the bluffs?"

Ruth nodded that she understood what cave Betty was talking about. Betty continued, "We are stocking it with food supplies and camping gear. If you can't take it yourself, give it to Stewart or myself and we will see that it gets there."

Ruth nodded. "Yes, I'll do it."

Betty had one last point to cover. "One other thing, all the men have a meeting at their club each week. You could have David start attending the meetings."

Ruth nodded again. "Yes, I'll do that; and I will also have David join the group here at the dig."

Betty was pleased that Ruth had now become a member of the group. Ruth had a lot of friends from college and others that she had met on the internet. She would be a valuable asset to the group. Ruth's son, David Cushing, had a lot in common with Stewart. He would be a natural addition to the group.

July passed into August and the days were beginning to get shorter. The pattern of random violence had taken a new turn. Armed gangs were starting to invade and attack single men in their homes. Most simply received severe beatings and were robbed. However, three men in Amarillo had been murdered in their homes.

Since men were now regarded as a national resource, steps were being taken by state and local governments to safeguard them. Luxury apartments with limited access and twenty-four-hour security were offered to all men who were living alone. The government made them even more attractive by offering them at subsidized rates to entice men to relocate from their old residences into the new apartments. Nine out of every ten men living alone agreed to move to the new apartments. Dr. Nichols and Leslie Hawkins were two such examples.

VII

ASSAULT

By mid-September they had finished with the living unit; and had moved on to the ceremonial site. It was late in the season, but they were sure that they could get a good start before they had to suspend the dig for the winter. Everyone was excited, they wondered what treasures they would find in the ceremonial site.

The group dig went well, but not their investigation into the random violence against men. They were sure that something was going to happen, but what it would be, they had no idea. Betty used her position in the police department to try and gather information without attracting attention. All they had were police reports on the crimes, but no clues or suspects. Betty tried her best to ferret out information, only to find silence or dead ends. She had even drawn the attention of her supervisors and other police agencies; and was told to stay out of investigations that had not been assigned to her. She knew for certain that something was up, but had no way to get to it.

Ruth was a graduate of Texas Tech University at Lubbock, Texas. Many women were networking in an attempt to find out what was going on; and trying to find others that they could trust. She had many friends in education and industry, including the aerospace industry and NASA. She tried to determine by their reaction to events if they could be trusted. She had also made some tentative contacts.

At first Patricia had not noticed it, but after a while it was hard for her not to start seeing some changes in the group. Some of the members of the group would from time to time go off by themselves to talk. It was not always the same members that made up the group. The one thing that she could not fail to notice, was that no matter how the group was made up, she was never one of them. She also noticed that when, on occasion, two or more of the members of the dig were in conversation and she came near, they stopped talking. She knew that they were keeping something from her; but what?

By now Patricia had started to drive her own car to the dig each weekend. She noticed that she was most often the second car, behind either Betty or Ruth. The men always seemed to come in last, often delayed by several minutes. She began to wonder what the cause for the delay was.

Sunday afternoon, after they had packed up and started out, Patricia announced that she had forgotten her flashlight and had to go back for it. She assured everyone that she would soon catch up; and for them not to wait for her. By the time she arrived where they parked the vehicles, everyone had already started back. She made sure that she would be the last car out.

When she got to the bluffs, she stopped, took her flashlight and got out of the car. She was curious and wanted to check out the cave again for herself. After dropping down onto the ledge, she made her way to the cave. She then turned on her flashlight and entered the cave.

Once inside the cave, she soon found all the supplies and equipment that had been stored there. It didn't take long for her to figure out why the cave was being stocked. She knew as well as the others, what was going on and how uncertain the times had become.

She spent some time looking about the cave, interested in what had been brought in so far. At first, she was angry at having been left out of the group. By the time she got back to her car, she had started to feel ashamed of her anger. She understood that security dictated that she be kept out of it., but it still hurt that they didn't trust her. She was now determined to confront Stewart about this.

Thursday evening, after dinner and the social hour, there was a knock at Stewart's door. It was Patricia, he invited her in. He had some Bailey's Irish Cream. He offered her a glass and she accepted. Rather than wanting to sit on his lap, she sat in a chair on the other side of the end table from his chair, sipping her Bailey's

Stewart could see by the expression on her face and her body language, that something was on her mind. He would just wait and let her bring it out in her own way. After a couple of minutes, she said, "I've really enjoyed this summer. We really learned a lot from the dig."

Stewart nodded; he could tell that this was but an opening ploy. The dig was not what she had come to talk about. "Yes, we have done well. The Museum in Canyon is going to carbon date those basket fragments. We should get a good idea as to when the Pueblo was abandoned."

Patricia finished her Bailey's and sat the glass down on the end table. "Why didn't anyone ever dig there before?"

Stewart decided to push her to come to the point. He took a sip of his Bailey's, then looked at her. "Well, it's a small site and I guess that no one ever got around to it before, but you know that already. What do you really want to know?"

Patricia's pout intensified, tiny wrinkle lines appeared on her chin and between her eyebrows and she started to cry. "Oh, Stewart, why don't you trust me? I thought that we meant a lot to each other."

Patricia sobbed. "You know what it is."

Now, Stewart was really confused. He had no idea what she was talking about. "Okay, Patricia, you have me beat; what's the problem?"

Patricia took a handkerchief from a pocket in her skirt, dabbed her eyes, wiped her nose and looked into Stewart's eyes. Stewart took her hand and gave it a little squeeze to reassure her. She took her time in answering. "It's the group you might say. I've a feeling about something.

It seems that there's some big secret and I'm the only one not in on it."

So, that's what it's all about. Stewart thought. When they were putting the group together, Patricia had been overlooked. First off, they had just been taking in those that had a reason to be in the group; and he had just not thought of her. Later, he had considered her, but had decided to keep her out of it. He should have known that she would notice that something was different. Now, he had to do something about it. He felt that he could trust her, but he had to be careful now, to try to find out how much she knew without tipping his hand. "I don't know what you mean. I can't think of any secret. You must be imagining it."

Patricia shook her head. "No, I don't think I am. I'm sure that something is going on. I can feel it."

Stewart kept trying to make light of it. "Okay, what makes you think there's some big secret?"

Patricia started to pout again and he could see a hurt look coming to her eyes. "There are a lot of private conversations and I'm never a part of them. There's also a lot of looking over shoulders."

Stewart shook his head. "I really don't know what you mean. I don't see anything."

By now, Patricia could see that Stewart was trying to keep everything from her. His skipping around the truth hurt her. Didn't he know that she loved him and would do anything for him? Why didn't he trust her? "One last thing, David Cushing. He joins our group and from the first he seems more of an insider than I am."

Stewart didn't like the way the conversation was going. He had to try to end it. He gave Patricia a reassuring smile. 'You're imagining all this. People talk with each other, it's just talk. No one is trying to shut you out."

Patricia looked straight into Stewart's eyes. "Stewart, what is all the stuff in the cave for?" Stewart was taken completely by surprise. Before he could think of what to say, Patricia continued, "And don't try to tell me it's nothing. I can see it on your face."

56

Stewart knew that no lie would satisfy her. He had to trust her and tell her the truth. He picked her up from her chair, carried her over to his chair and sat down with her in his lap. "Okay, Patricia, I'm sorry that I hurt you, but it wasn't intentional. We had been trying to keep the group small and just overlooked the fact that you might want to help us. You want to know everything, now here it is," He told her everything, leaving nothing out. He outlined how they had become concerned about random violence against men and the suspicions about a conspiracy.

When he had finished, Patricia smiled boldly at him. "Thank you for telling me everything. You have always been good to me. You really helped me through my grieving when mother died. I knew that I could depend on you then. Do you know that I love you? Why didn't you trust me? I would be glad to do whatever I can for you. Besides, I would also be doing it for Thomas. After all, he is my brother and I love him too."

Stewart could see the love in her eyes. He was convinced of her loyalty, and that she could be trusted. "okay, I know that I can trust you. From now on you're one of the group. What we're stocking the cave for is some unforeseen emergency that may cause us to have to disappear for a while. The cave is just a refuge of last resort. We hope that we never have to use it. Now speak about this only to members of our group and no one else."

Patricia looked at her empty glass sitting on the table. "Oh, Stewart, can I have more of that Bailey's?" Stewart said, "Why, yes, you can."

Stewart got up, refilled the glasses and sat back down with Patricia in his lap. They finished their Bailey's with some kissing and foreplay between sips. Afterwards, Stewart carried her into the bedroom.

By late October the days were a lot shorter. On the eleventh, Stewart had to go up to see a rancher in Dallon County between Dalhart and Texline. He went by way of Vega and dropped off some dehydrated meal packs and a bag of winter clothing at the cave. He took the time to look over what had already been deposited in the cave. Everyone now had clothing, sleeping bag and other camping gear. There were enough food stores for several weeks, along with cooking stoves and fuel to cook meals and heat water.

He then drove up to see the rancher that he had the appointment with. He spent the afternoon with the rancher; it was late when he started back home.

The last light of day was fading in the western sky when he left. When he reached Dalhart, it was completely dark. When he got to Hartley, he kept going south on U S Highway 385 to Channing and Vega.

As he left Hartley, he noticed headlights in his rearview mirror. The vehicle seemed to be staying back about one-hundred to one-hundred fifty yards. He had no reason to suspect the vehicle, so he didn't pay much attention to it.

About two minutes later, the vehicle following him started to accelerate to pass. The headlights in his rearview mirror grew large. When the vehicle should have pulled into the oncoming lane to pass, it kept on coming and rammed his vehicle with force. The seatback slammed Stewart in the back and his head snapped back against the headrest. The force of the blow knocked the air from his lungs. The impact caused Stewart to almost lose control of his vehicle.

While he tried to regain control, he was rammed again. He was again slammed into the seatback, knocking the air from his lungs. He stomped on the accelerator and sped up. That gave him time to regain control of his vehicle and look at the other vehicle in the rearview mirror. He could see that it sped up to keep pace with him. He was now traveling at over eighty miles-per-hour and still accelerating, but he didn't have the speed to get away from his pursuer.

The pursuing vehicle pulled into the oncoming lane and pulled up alongside of him. He glanced to the left and could see several people in the car, but in the dark, he could not see their faces. He could only tell that they all appeared to be women. The pursuing vehicle swerved to the right, slamming into the side of his vehicle. His vehicle was pushed to the edge of the pavement, his right-side wheels running on the edge of the shoulder. Stewart jerked the wheel to the left and his vehicle swerved back into the lane, fishtailing. The pursuing vehicle started to slam into his side again. He swung to the left and made contact with the pursuing vehicle. The pursuing vehicle went on the opposite shoulder and came back on the highway fishtailing. He took the opportunity to pull ahead. The vehicle came on and he was rammed again three more times. He had to struggle to maintain control and keep his speed up.

The pursuer now tried to pull alongside of his vehicle again. He moved over to try to block his pursuer. The pursuing vehicle struck his vehicle on the left rear corner Stewart lost control and started to skid. His right front wheel was on the shoulder, then he left the road. He ran across a shallow ditch with gently sloping sides. He was headed right for a barbed wire fence. He was able to turn the vehicle enough to miss the fence. He kept his foot off the accelerator and rolled to a stop in a cloud of dust paralleling the barb wire fence.

The pursuing vehicle came to a stop on the road about fifty yards ahead of his vehicle. He had unfastened the seat belt, and was getting out of his vehicle. Four people got out of the pursuing vehicle with pick handles. In the light of his headlights, he could clearly see that they were all women, but they were not close enough to be able to identify any of them.

Stewart moved to the far side of his vehicle, drew his 44-magnum, took up a two-handed grip and rested his arms on the hood of the vehicle. His first shot smashed the rear and left-rear windows of pursuing vehicle. The second shot went over the head of one of the attackers. The third shot put a crease in the hood of the pursuing vehicle. The assailants retreated back to their vehicle and sped away. He continued to fire at the retreating vehicle until his revolver was empty.

He didn't even take time to check the damage to his vehicle. He reloaded his revolver, then got back inside and started the engine. His vehicle had full-time all-wheel drive, so he drove it back over the ditch, onto the highway. By now he shook so much, that he had to take a couple of minutes to settle down.

He continued on south to Channing. Instead of continuing south to Vega, he turned east on Texas State Highway 354 and drove to Four Corners, then south on US Highway 287 to Amarillo.

When he arrived back home, instead of getting out at the portico, he pulled into his parking space and got out. There was severe damage to the left side of the vehicle. The rear hatch, bumper and rear lights were also damaged. He may find more damage in the morning, but there didn't seem to be anything mechanical wrong. The Vehicle belonged to the Texas State Department of Agriculture. He would have to report the incident to his supervisor in the morning. Right now, he just wanted to have dinner and relax in his private quarters.

Everyone else had already eaten dinner when he got home. He took the dinner that had been set aside in the kitchen for him, and went directly to his private quarters. He was in the living room with his dinner in front of him on the coffee table, when Betty knocked at the door.

He invited her in, then went back to his dinner. Betty took a chair across the coffee table from him. "You look like hell. What happened?"

Stewart put his knife and fork down and looked at her. "Someone forced me off the road. It happened on the highway just south of Hartley."

It showed on her face that she was concerned. "Was it deliberate?"

Stewart had gone back to eating. Between forkfuls, he said, "Yes, they rammed me several times until I went off the road. When I stopped, so did they. Four of them got out of the vehicle. They were all women, and they had pick candles. I fired at them with my 44-magnum and they took off. There's nothing like the sound of a large caliber bullet breaking the sound barrier next to your ear to make you rethink your priorities. I guess that they decided that their venture was getting too costly."

Betty chuckled at Stewart's humor. "Did you hit any of them?"

Stewart stopped eating and looked at her. "I don't think so, but you can look for a vehicle with the rear and left-rear windows shot out and one or two bullet holes."

Betty wondered if Stewart would report it. If he did, his office would find out about it and restrict his movements. "Are you going to report it?"

Stewart let out a sigh; he didn't want to, but he had no choice. "My vehicle has damage, and it belongs to the state. I have to report it."

"Did you get a license plate number, or anything?" Betty asked.

Stewart shook his head. "no, I wasn't close enough to see the license number. They stayed on the hard-top, so there aren't even any tire prints. I'll make a report, but nothing will come of it."

"You're right about that. Well, the important thing is that you're safe."

Stewart was waiting to get back to his dinner. "Betty, I'm sorry I'm not such a good host right now. I do want to have someone with me tonight. If you will give me time for dinner and a shower, then come back, say in about one hour. I promise to be at my best."

Betty got a big smile on her face. "Yes, that's fine." She got up, kissed him on the lips and let herself out. Stewart went back to dinner.

The next morning Stewart made reports of the incident for the police, and his department supervisor. He turned his vehicle in for repair, then drew another one from the motor pool. His supervisor had cautioned him to plan his trips to the field, so as to be back in Amarillo before dark. This random violence had started to affect him personally. He didn't like restrictions being placed on his work, but that was what his supervisor wanted, and she always got what she wanted.

VIII

IN HIDING

By mid-November no man in the group was living alone in an unsecured location. Stewart and Authur both lived in harems. Thomas and David lived with their mothers. Dr. Nichols, Anthony and Leslie now lived in the same security apartment complex. David had been thinking of moving into a secure apartment, and had spoken to his mother about it. Ruth wasn't keen about letting him go with all the trouble going on. She knew that eventually she would have to let him go, but she wanted to hold on to him as long as possible.

The men who lived alone and went out at night to the clubs and nightspots to be picked up by women were becoming more cautious. The night life was no longer as safe as it used to be. Some men had left a club or nightspot with a woman, expecting a night of pleasure, only to be assaulted and severely beaten, or even killed. Few men were now willing to consider going anywhere with a woman that they didn't know, no matter how willing or eager she appeared to be. It was just not safe to do so. From what Stewart had heard from his single friends, most of the younger women had abandoned the club scene. Things were changing and everyone wondered what was going to happen next.

On the fifth of December, Stewart's third child, a girl, was born. Her name was Iris Singletary. He was pleased that he had a new daughter. He would like to take pride in his daughter and take an active part in her life, but he knew that it wasn't practical. The way things were now, children were solely the mother's responsibility. Men were not expected or encouraged to take a role in their children's lives, as it would be likely to cause problems later on. In the end, he did what he was expected to do; congratulate the mother, then let her raise the child as she pleased.

Patricia was now a sophomore at Amarillo State University, having finished her freshman year at the university, while still a senior at Palo Duro High School. She had an excellent academic standing in high school; and had been able to keep up with her high school classes and college work at the same time. She had decided on a career in bioengineering. Stewart and Betty took a special interest in her; and helped her with her studies as much as they could.

Everyone had been networking, but so far, they had a lot more questions than answers. Every time they tried to get information from official sources, they were either sent in circles, or hit a blank wall. No one had been kept from making official inquiries, but it seemed that any information they got was worthless. Anyone who had any information of any value wasn't sharing it on the internet. Even as they tried to find out what was going on, they knew that what they were looking for was a closely guarded secret.

The new reproduction procedure that Dr. Nichols found out about was now in use in special reproduction clinics. As it turned out, it wasn't any big secret that Dr. Nichols had uncovered, but a new procedure that hadn't yet been made public. The government claimed that despite all efforts to reverse the trend, there was still a slow but perceptible decline in the birth ratio of males to females. The government felt that because of the coming decline of the male population, an alternate means of human reproduction would be needed as an option. It did seem odd, however, that there being so few males, more and more women were opting for the new procedure that guaranteed only a female child.

The government had declared males a national resource. As of January 2087, all males were banned from service in the armed forces, police and the space program. Men would no longer have even an indirect role in any occupation of risk. Men were being isolated even more from the agencies that controlled the government. Men began to feel that they were outsiders from society.

Stewart spent Christmas with the harem. They had the tree in the family room, with the usual Christmas party and the exchange of gifts. Patricia was given the honor of reading the Christmas story to the young children. Everyone tried to pretend that things were normal, but they knew that times were changing.

Stewart spent New Year's at the club as usual. At the club, Stewart made his annual toast that everyone has a happy new Year; and that the coming year be better than the last. However, he and the others had an uneasy premonition that it wouldn't be. They just couldn't set aside the foreboding feeling about the coming year.

The first week of the New Year, they were having their meeting at the club. Absent was Leslie, who had gone to Clovis, New Mexico for his mother's birthday. Authur was speaking. "The government had an explanation for the new procedure. To the unsuspecting it sounds right, however, I don't think they're telling us the whole truth. I believe that they're hiding something." Everyone around the table nodded, Authur continued, "More and more women are opting for the new procedure. It makes no sense. Why, when the ratio of women to men is so high, would a woman opt for a procedure that will guarantee only a female child? I don't like it. It's like they are learning to do without us. It gives me the creeps."

Everyone was silent foe awhile. Then David pounded his fist on the table. "This damn New Christian Truth Reform Church! Does anyone believe that it's just coincidence this happened at the same time that this new religion has taken control?"

Stewart nodded, his sentiments about the New Christian Truth Reform Church was the same as David's. He saw it as much of an anti-male movement as a religion. The very mention of it made him feel uneasy and sent chills up his spine. "Yes, I know what you mean. This new religion, or whatever you want to call it, preys on the vulnerabilities and frustrations of women. They think that they have it harder than men do. They see men as like kids in a candy store, with women getting the short end. They don't realize that this imbalance is just as hard on us as it is on them. I don't know anyone that sees this as a utopian existence for men or women."

Everyone around the table nodded and voiced agreement. "I agree with you," Authur said, "but I doubt that you would be able to convince many women of that. Most women see men spending much of their time enjoying the pleasures of the flesh. Not having to accept the responsibility for it. Some women are starting to believe that they no longer need men for anything. Why make any more of them?"

David said, "I see it with the girls at college. When they get involved with this New Christian Truth Reform Church, they stop competing for men and look to other women for friendship and support. They have no more use for men."

Everyone was pensive for a while. Authur got up to get the next round. When he returned with the drinks, Stewart said, "About what David is saying, it's happening in my house with Crystal Engle and Virginia Bassett. It's the same as with Cassandra all over again, well, almost. They are not as in your face as Cassandra was, but they have made it clear what their feelings for men are. There's one thing for sure, we're becoming more isolated all the time." Stewart paused and looked around the table. "We may have to go into hiding on short notice. I suggest that we keep a bag of essentials in our cars." Everyone nodded, Stewart continued, "Okay, that's all I have for now. Does anyone have any more business?"

David banged the table again. "Damn, this doesn't make sense! Can you imagine a world with only Women? A single gender species.

It's unbelievable, it's unnatural. How can they get along without us?"

Dr. Nichols muttered under his breath. "They may not be able to, but I know a few women who would like to try."

Everyone at the table laughed, but it was a nervous-halfhearted laugh. They all felt uneasy at how close to true the remark was.

After the laughter subsided, Stewart said again, "Any more questions?" There were no more questions. "Okay, then I believe that's all for now. Thomas and I have to get home." The meeting broke up and Stewart and Thomas left for home. The other men stayed on at the club for a while longer.

The second of February was Patricia's eighteenth birthday. The harem had reserved a private room at the Sundowner restaurant to celebrate her birthday. They had an excellent dinner, followed by cake and ice cream. For this night, all diets were off. After the cake and ice cream, Patricia opened her presents, then there was a round of speeches. There was a general consensus around the table that everyone was having a good time, especially Patricia. Everyone considered the party a success. Later, Stewart and the other women started to plan a celebration for the completion of Patricia's second year of college in May.

The first day of March, and spring was not far off, but winter had not yet lost its grip. After dinner and social hour, Stewart retired to his private quarters. A few minutes later, there came a knock at the door. Theresa Fuentes had a new deck of cards. They spent the next one and a half hours playing gin rummy. Afterwards, they retired to the bedroom for the night.,

Twenty minutes later, they heard a powerful explosion that rattled the windows and awakened everyone in the house. From the windows of their home on the third floor, they had a good view. It wasn't long before they saw the glow of a fire about three miles to the northwest.

Stewart went back to his quarters and turned on his television to a local news station. A few minutes later he learned that the explosion had been at his club. Upon hearing of the bombing of the club, he became very concerned for the safety of his friends.

He spent most of the night watching the news. There were other bombings in Shreveport, Louisiana, Bridgeport, Connecticut, Minot, North Dakota, Lansing, Michigan, Cedar Rapids, Iowa, Tampa, Florida and other cities around the country. The targets were Men's clubs and other places where men gathered.

Stewart had been on the phone with the other men in their group. He had been able to contact everyone, except Arthur and Lesley; they were not at their homes. Stewart couldn't locate them anywhere. After breakfast, he had Betty come to his private quarters. As soon as they were inside and the door closed, Stewart said, 'Betty, it's time that we go into hiding. I'll take Thomas and Patricia with me and pick up Dr. Nichols. I need for you to pick up Anthony and David. We'll all meet at the bluffs."

After what had happened the night before, Betty knew that Stewart was right. She also felt that if they didn't move now, they might not be able to later on. Betty nodded. "Okay, I'll have Thomas get ready to go with you; then I'll leave to go get Anthony and David. I'll also tell Patricia to meet you at your vehicle. How long will you be?"

Stewart said, "As soon as I can change clothes; make it fifteen minutes. I already have everything in my vehicle. Anthony will be at Ruth and David's house. You'll pick them both up there. That way, you don't have to sign in with the apartment security. Dr. Nichols is already waiting for me outside of his apartments. I'm taking Patricia with me so that she can dive my vehicle back home."

Betty asked, "What about Arthur and Leslie?"

Stewart shook his head with a concerned look on his face. "I don't know. I've been trying to get hold of them all night. They aren't answering their phones. I hope that they are safe, but I have a feeling that something has happened to them."

Betty looked at Stewart, her eyes betrayed her feelings of anxiety for the safety of their friends. "I'll try to locate them and bring them out later on."

Stewart placed a hand on Betty's upper arms. "Well, thank you, Betty. I know that you will do your best,"

They embraced and kissed. Betty then left to tell Thomas and Patricia to dress and meet Stewart at his vehicle in the parking lot. She then dressed and left to pick up Anthony and David. Stewart met with Thomas and Patricia at his vehicle; then left to pick up Dr. Nichols.

Stewart, Dr. Nichols, Thomas and Patricia arrived at the bluffs at 11:20 AM. Betty, Anthony and David arrived fifteen minutes later. When they arrived, Stewart and Patricia were waiting for them at the top of the bluffs. Dr. Nichols and Thomas had already gone down into the cave,

Betty got out of her vehicle and handed Stewart a couple of large sacks. "I stopped off to get something for you. Those meal packs are going to get monotonous. I wanted you to have at least one good meal. I got you all some fried chicken and biscuits."

Thomas had heard his mother's vehicle drive up, and had come up from the cave to see his mother.

Stewart said, "Thank you, Betty, we appreciate it. When you find Arthur and Leslie, if you can, bring them on out here. From now on there must be as little direct contact as possible. After the first of April, it should be warm enough to start the dig again. You can then start using the prearranged drops to leave messages if it looks too hazardous to make direct contact."

Betty nodded. "Okay, we'll start as soon after the first of April as we can Stewart gave her a smile and pat on the shoulder. "Okay, now say good-bye to Thomas. The rest of us will get our things into the cave. We need to start turning it into a home."

Betty gave Stewart a pleading look. "Look out for Thomas for me."

Stewart gave her a pat on the shoulder. "I will, don't worry."

Betty kissed Stewart good-bye; then went to say good-bye to her son.

Patricia came to get the electronic device from Stewart, that would allow her to operate his vehicle. After he handed it over to her, he kissed her good-bye. As she turned to leave, there was a tear in her eye. She got into Stewart's vehicle and started back to Amarillo. Betty was only a few minutes behind her.

Stewart and Thomas watched them until they vanished over the crest of the hill. They then went down into the cave and had chicken and biscuits for lunch. They then started to turn the cave into a home.

That evening, Stewart listened to the report of the club bombing on their battery powered radio. Twenty-seven were dead and forty-two injured. Among the dead were Leslie Hawkins and Arthur Smith. The attacks and bombings continued through the weekend. From the news they learned that the that the attacks were not confined to the United States, but were worldwide. Sunday, the President of the United States declared a state of national emergency. Monday, the Congress gave the President emergency powers to protect a national resource, the male population.

MEN ISOLATED

The same day that congress granted the President emergency powers, she started to take action to protect men from further assault. All men's clubs and other places where men congregated were ordered to close indefinitely. A curfew for all men was established in the interest of safeguarding them. The curfew had been set so early in the evening, that it killed what was left of nightlife; as if it really mattered anymore. There had been very little nightlife left anyway. By now there were few men on the streets. About the only time that men were seen, was when they were going to or from work, or on quick shopping excursions before curfew.

One week after receiving emergency powers, the President ordered that all men, without exception, were to live in the secure apartment complexes. No man would be exempt, not even those living in harems. Only males under the age of twelve could live with their mothers. Some of the man, fearing this to be too much of an infringement to their liberty, were hiding out; mostly in the apartments or homes of women who wanted to help them. When they were found, they were ordered to move to a secure apartment. No punitive action was taken against either the man or woman. All men could come and go as they pleased and keep their employment. They just had to live in secure apartments and observe the curfew.

The first of April, Betty, Ruth and Patricia were at the pueblo ruins. They got there before noon Saturday; set up camp and had lunch.

After lunch, they laid out the grid and started the dig again. They didn't have much enthusiasm for the dig anymore without the men, but they had to go through the motions in case they were being observed by anyone. They worked through the afternoon.

They quit for the day in time to build a fire before dark to heat water for their meals and coffee. They kept by the fire and talked until after 9:00 PM, then turned in for the night.

The next morning, they had breakfast, then went back to the dig. They had been working for almost an hour when they saw a woman approaching the pueblo ruins from the direction of where the vehicles were parked. Betty went out to greet her. When they came face to face, Betty put out her hand with a smile. "Hello, I'm Betty Tredway. Can I help you?"

The woman took Betty's hand and shook it. Betty noticed that she had a firm grip. "Hi, I'm Ramona Parker, the foreman for the Bivens Ranch. I'd like to speak with you."

Betty pointed back from where she had come. "Okay, let's just go over here and have a seat." Betty took the time to get a good look at Ramona Parker. She wasn't a big woman, only about five-foot five-inches tall, with black hair and hazel eyes. You could tell by looking at her that she was accustomed to hard work; and had an air of self-assurance about her. Betty wondered why the foreman of the Bivens Ranch was out here to see them. Betty knew that the dig was on Bivins land; and that they were there at the good grace of this woman.

They went over to the remains of a wall. When they were seated, betty turned to Ramona. "All right now, what do you need to talk about?'

Ramona looked over to where the other two women were still digging, then back at Betty. "For starters, I'd like to know how the dig is going."

"It's going all right." Betty said.

Ramona nodded, then spoke in a casual manner. "That's good to hear. I was wondering how you're going to get along with your project without the help of the men?"

Betty became suspicious of Ramona. She wasn't here just to inquire about the dig. She had something else in mind. Betty would just have to play along until Ramona was ready to reveal what she had on her mind. "It'll take us longer, but we'll be able to finish without them."

Ramona nodded as she watched the other two women go through the motions of working on the dig. "That's good to hear. It's good to talk to someone who's interested in the history of the area, which brings me to my point. I have a place close by that I'm sure that you would be interested in. I'd like for you to come with me, so that I can show it to you."

This woman's behavior was perplexing to Betty, but the woman was the Bivens Ranch foreman and they were using Bivens Ranch land. She would just have to play along until Ramona was ready to reveal what was on her mind. "It sounds interesting, but I don't have the time right now."

Ramona replied, "Then you will have to make the time, it's important."

Betty didn't feel like going with her, but she knew that she had to please this woman and go with her. Betty slapped her hands on her thighs and started to get to her feet. "Okay, then I can make the time. I'll just tell the others we're going; and please, call me betty."

Ramona also started to get to her feet. "Okay, you can call me Ramona."

Betty told Ruth and Patricia that she had to go with the Bivens Ranch foreman. She told them to pack up in about an hour, and head back to the vehicles. She would meet them there when she was finished with the Bivens Ranch foreman. She then left with Ramona.

They walked back to the vehicles and got into Ramona's pickup truck. They drove back to the highway, turned north, drove two-hundred yards, then turned right. The road that they were now on had been paved at one time, but it hadn't been maintained for a long time. They drove for about half a mile before coming to a place where the road had long been washed away by a creek. The creek was shallow and easy to ford with Ramona's pickup truck. The ford ran off the road to the left, crossed the creek, than ran back up on the road.

Once they were back up on the road, Ramona turned to Betty. "Okay, we begin our history lesson here. This place used to be the town of Tascosa. It was named after the creek that we just crossed. It was the county seat for ten counties here in the Texas panhandle, during the last half of the nineteenth century. It was also the southern end of the Dodge City trail. The Texas cattle herds were marshaled here before being driven north to the railroad head at Dodge City, Kansas, to be shipped to the stockyards in Kansas City, Kansas" Ramona pointed to the creek that ran from north to south. "The main street of Tascosa ran parallel to the creek on the west side. Behind us, on the west side of the creek, once stood a three-room adobe house. It was much like most of the houses in Tascosa. It had been the home of a lady that went by the name of Frenchie McCormick. She was the last living resident of the town. She was married to Mickey McCormick, the owner of the Tascosa Saloon in the late nineteenth century. It is said that she once hid the notorious outlaw Billy the Kid in her bed from the Sheriff's posse, after he was wounded in a shootout in town. She nursed him back to health, then helped him sneak out of town. Tascosa became a ghost town after the railroad and stockyards came to Fort Worth, Texas and the cattle herds stopped coming. The house was demolished sometime after she died in 1950.

Ramona drove on; they crossed a cattle guard and under an old-rusted iron-gate. Betty could see several buildings that were abandoned and in disrepair. Ramona stopped the truck and pointed to a large two-story limestone building, with a covered porch across the front supported by four large-square limestone columns. "That is the old Tascosa Court House. It was built in 1884 and is the only building from the old town still surviving. The rest of the buildings here are from the last century. This wasn't a new town. There was another town on the other side of the river. Everyone moved away after the sand and gravel pits were closed. There were two huge-old cottonwood trees flanking the front of the court house, with others around the sides and back." Ramona pointed again at the court house. "You see those trees in the front? They say that they had a hanging judge here, and that he hung thirteen men on those trees, but that's only legend around here."

Betty was just listening while Ramona gave her the guided tour. Ramona continued, "About one-half mile behind the court house we have a large barn. It became ours when we got the land back."

Ramona started up the truck again; and they continued to drive down the road. They passed a large building to the left that at one time had been a school building. About a quarter of a mile beyond the school, the road turned left around the base of a hill. On the other side of the hill were still more abandoned buildings. At the end of the road was a very large hay barn. The barn was a steel frame covered by corrugated steel. It had a large double door at each end; so that a tractor-trailer loaded with bales of alfalfa hay could be driven into the barn, unloaded, then driven out the other end. The barn was big enough to have two tractor-trailers, one behind the other, in the barn unloading at the same time.

Ramona parked at the far end of the barn where the road ended. "We have to get out here and walk the rest of the way."

They got out of the pickup truck, and started walking down a footpath. Ramona continued to speak, "Betty, there's a reason why I've brought you here and given you this tour. I'm the foreman of the Bivens Ranch. I know the land; I know the history and I know everything that is happening on it."

They came to a creek between three to four feet wide. They jumped the creek and continued on to a spring in the side of a hill that had been improved to make a pool about ten feet in diameter and about five to six feet deep. There were trees and brush here that made it hard to see the spring until you were almost on it. They stopped and had a seat next to the spring. Ramona looked at Betty. "I know that Stewart and his friends have gone into hiding, and that it's somewhere around the pueblo ruins. I also know that you know where they are."

Betty was taken aback by Ramona's bold statement. She wondered what she knew about the men and what problems she could cause. She started to perspire and nervously wiped her sweaty palms on the thighs of her jeans and measured her words before she answered. "What makes you think that I know anything about where they are?"

Ramona was the foreman of a ranch that covered over three-hundred fifty square miles in Hartley, Moore, Oldham and potter counties. She supervised a large work force and made executive decisions all the time. She was a woman of action, and didn't want to get caught up in a verbal sparring with Betty. She came right to the point. "Listen, I don't want to beat about the bush about this. Seven people go up the track in two vehicles. Later, the same two vehicles come back, each with a single occupant, you and that young woman over at the pueblo."

Betty knew that to try to bluff would just anger Ramona, and perhaps make the situation worse. She wondered what Ramona's interest in the men was all about. If she wanted to turn them in to the authorities, then why would she have to play this game? She just had to contact them and tell them what she had seen. Betty realized that she needed to be honest with Ramona. "Okay, say that I know where they are. Why do you need to know?"

Ramona smiled, she could tell by observing Betty, that she knew where the men were hiding and that she and the other women were aiding them. She decided it was time to show her hand. She stood up and called out, "Ben…Ben, come on down here!"

It was less than a minute before a boy came down the trail to the spring. He was the age where he was transitioning from the boy to the man. He had Ramona's coloring, hair, eyes and some of her features. He had the promise of being a handsome man. Ramona took him in her arms and they embraced. "You doing all right, Ben?"

Ben nodded. "Yes, Mother, I am."

With her arm still around her son's shoulder, she turned to Betty. "Betty, this is my son Benjamin Weaver. He's fifteen years old; Ben, this is Betty Treadway.' Betty and Ben shook hands. Ramona continued, "I have had Ben camped out here for over two weeks now. Eventually people will see this madness for what it is and put a stop to it; then Ben can come back home. In the meantime, I need a safe place for him. I don't want him shipped off to one of those male prison camps. They don't call them that yet, but you watch; that's what they're going to end up being. I don't trust people in power."

Ramona and her son took a seat at the edge of the spring next to Betty. Betty looked at Ramona. "Yes, I know what you mean. I don't trust them enough to turn my son over to them either. As for your son, he can't stay here by himself. If you keep coming here all the time, they will figure out where he is. Let's get his things, and I'll take him to where the others are."

Ramona was relieved by the outcome of events and expressed her gratitude. "Thank you, Betty. You can count on me for any support you need. As for security, this is Bivens land, I run things here. No one comes on Bivens land without my say so." Ramona turned to her son. "Okay, Ben, get your things and put them in the truck."

It took less than a half-hour to pack Ben's camping equipment into the truck. Ben rode in the cab with his mother and Betty. There was no traffic on the highway to speak of; so, there was hardly any risk of him being seen by anyone. They drove back to the bluffs. Betty showed Ramona where the cave was; and they made contact with Stewart and the rest of the men. Ramona was surprised to find that there was a cave at the bluffs. She, like most local residents, seldom came around the bluffs because of the threat of rattlesnakes.

Stewart was glad to see Ramona, and to have her pledge of support for taking care of Ben. No one knew yet how long this madness would last.

PLANS MADE

Even with the steps the government had taken to safeguard them, men were still being attacked. The men were now allowed out of their enclaves only to go to work; that was only if they had a job where they could be transported to and from work, and their security being ensured while on the job. The men were upset by these extreme measures, but the government was firm, no man would be allowed out in public without an escort.

To make up for this, commissaries and shopping outlets were set up in the enclaves. What they couldn't get there, they could get through mail order on the internet.

By the end of June, the male presence, except for the men who were being escorted to and from their jobs, had been removed from the general population. If a man tried to venture out into public unescorted, he was instantly placed in protective custody and returned to his enclave. By now all men that had been hiding in the homes of their mothers or girlfriends had been found and ordered to the men's enclaves. The only men at large now were the ones that had prepared ahead of time and were hiding out in places not obvious to the authorities. The men would like to have the freedom to come a go as they pleased, but it was no use to even try to slip out. Within minutes they were back in protective custody. The men complained to anyone that they could think of to no avail. No one in a position of authority in the government cared what the men had to say.

Some of the women protested the treatment of the men, but most of the women just didn't care. Women were already their own breadwinners, with sole responsibility for their children. Economically they no longer needed the men. Most women were burned out from the stress of competing for the men. Once they adjusted to an all-female society, they found it much less stressful. They did have to give up the idea of romantic fulfillment, but that was a very remote, if not impossible dream anyway. They were able to reproduce without men. Life would be a lot simpler without them. By now most women were ignoring the fact that the men no longer had any civil rights.

Starting the fourth of July, Ruth Griffin went on vacation for two weeks to Denver, Colorado. She had arranged to be joined by a friend of hers, Ms. Sherry tiller; who had flown up to Santa Fe, New Mexico from Houston, Texas. She had then rented a car, and driven up to the Denver Airport to meet Ruth. Sherry was a friend of Ruth's from college. Sherry now worked for NASA; her field of work was biophysics. She worked in the cryogenics lab at the Manned Space Flight Center in Houston, Texas.

After picking up Ruth at the Denver Airport, they started on an auto tour of the Rocky Mountains in Colorado and the desert southwest. They drove west over the Rocky Mountains into Utah. Then they turned south and drove through Monument Valley, Grand Canyon, Flagstaff, Phoenix and Tucson. From Arizona, they drove on to New Mexico and visited Carlsbad Caverns, Roswell, Albuquerque, and Santa Fe. From New Mexico, they drove through the Texas Panhandle and back to Denver. Once in Denver, Ruth took a flight back home. From Denver, Sherry droves back to Santa Fe to return the rental car and fly back to Houston.

On their drive through the southwest they had used false identities and paid cash for everything to make sure that there was no record of credit card receipts. They never discussed their route with anyone, or called ahead for motel reservations. They just got a motel room where they were at the time they wanted to stop. They never discussed anything personal or of a business nature in the car, motel rooms, restaurants, or other public places. They only spoke privately in natural settings. They had a lot to discuss and plan for. They wanted to be sure that no one could overhear or record them in any way.

The weekend after Ruth returned from her vacation, she went with Betty and Patricia to the pueblo ruins. She waited until that evening when they were around the fire eating dinner to tell the others about the trip. "I've learned a lot from Sherry. What has happened here in the United States is worldwide. The script may be different from country to country, but the outcome is the same. We are becoming a world of women. Of course, we network worldwide and know that. Now, there's something that isn't so well known, at least not yet, and not by the men at all. They're still collecting sperm from the men for the sperm banks, but it isn't being used. All women are now being impregnated using the ovum fusion method. The men's sperm is being thrown out." Betty and Patricia were shocked by what they were hearing. Ruth continued before Betty or Patricia could say anything. "That's not all; Sherry has found out that all women pregnant with a male child in her first or second trimester are being told that their fetus is severely deformed, and should be aborted. No more males will be born."

Betty and Patricia couldn't believe it. "This is madness." Betty said, "Are you sure of this?"

Ruth nodded. "Yes, as sure as I can be."

Patricia was very troubled by this. She thought of Stewart and Thomas, and had to fight to keep the tears from coming. "What's to happen to all the men?" She said.

Ruth just shook her head. "I can't tell you what is to happen to the men. I just hope that all this madness ends. I can't imagine a world without men." Ruth paused for a few seconds before she continued, "Sherry has told me that she has a son in hiding along with three other men in the Odessa area. She said that they are safe from discovery for now, like our men. However, it can't go on indefinitely. With luck, they can stay in hiding for a year, perhaps a little longer, but eventually something will happen to compromise them and they will be picked up." Ruth paused again for effect, and looked at her companions before she continued. "Betty, Patricia, Sherry had an idea; it's a very radical one, but we may have to consider it. She works in the cryogenics lab at NASA Manned Space Flight Center in Houston. She told me about NASA having developed a cryogenic unit, or capsule. They call it a 'cryogenic couch'. This cryogenic couch has been exhaustively tested in the lab and has worked flawlessly. It is going to be field tested in space starting next year. It's designed for interstellar flights. It's completely self-contained with its own power source. It is guaranteed to keep its occupant viable for at least one-hundred years or more. Now the units have a safety margin of another one-hundred years or more; so, they can keep a person viable for two hundred years, or much longer.

"You know about the interstellar ramjet that NASA is building in orbit. It'll be completed soon. Then they are going to send it on a test flight way out past the orbit of Pluto and back. It'll take about nine years. Now this is a short test for the unit, but if they work flawlessly for that long, they can work well past the designed endurance.

"Sherry plan is to hijack a truckload of cryogenic units when they're being shipped from Houston to the Kennedy Space Flight Center. A truckload is sixteen units. The units go by commercial carrier without an escort. They don't think there's much chance of them being hijacked. The idea being that even if you hijacked them, what would you do with them anyway; there's no market for them but NASA. They're to be shipped starting in December and continuing until March. Now. They can get the truck, but they need a place to put the units where they can't be found; and our cave fits the bill. We also have to be able to dispose of the truck so that it can never be found. So, what do you think of it?"

Everyone just sat and looked at the fire. This was a lot to take in all at once. It was over five minutes before Betty spoke, "You know that the men would have to go along with it." Ruth and Patricia nodded, Betty continued, "As I see it, we don't have to use them if we don't need to. We do have to get them when they are available. We can use them later on only when we feel that it's necessary. Okay, Ruth, if the men are in favor of it, then it's all right with me."

Ruth turned to look at Patricia. "What about you?"

Patricia nodded. "Okay, let's do it."

Betty turned to look at Ruth. "We're all in favor of taking the units. I assume that you and Sherry have a plan?"

"Yes," Ruth said smiling, "we have a plan. If we agree I'll place an ad on the internet to sell a two-karat diamond ring with yellow-gold setting. This will also be the signal to gather all the men that will be making the trip to join our men here. Three days before the hijacking, Sherry will post an add on the internet to sell an antique Seth Thomas mantel clock. Now these are the only signals that will be passed between us. We have a prearranged point just north of Littlefield on US Highway 385. The hijackers will park the truck at the transfer point and leave. There will be no direct contact between the hijackers, the people transferring the men and us. None of them will know where the units and men are going. What do you think about it?"

After a few seconds, Betty said," It sounds great, if they can hijack the truck and get it to us."

Ruth smiled. "Then we present it to the men?"

Patricia and Betty nodded. Betty said, "Okay, then we'll lay it out for the men when we stop by tomorrow. They can tell us if they're for it or not."

They finished their dinner, as Ruth filled them in on the details of the plan. They talked for a while longer, then went to bed.

PLANS MADE

Sunday morning after breakfast, they broke camp and walked back to the vehicles. On the way back to the highway they stopped at the bluffs. They had some supplies to drop off; and they had to tell the men about the cryogenic units. They took some of the supplies from their Vehicles, then started down the ledge to the cave. The men were at the entrance to greet them. The men went back up with them to bring down the rest of the supplies.

After the supplies were in the cave, they all gathered near the entrance of the cave where the light was good to have their meeting. Ruth went over the plan to hijack the cryogenic units.

When she had finished, Stewart had some questions for her. "First off, how big are these things. I mean overall dimensions?"

Ruth said, "They're ten foot eight inches long, three foot nine inches wide and four foot seven inches tall. They have a polished titanium alloy outer shell. They're rectangular in shape, with a seven-foot-long hinged lid that raises up to expose the couch. Inside the outer lid is an inner lid of clear acrylic. All the controls are recessed into the rear of the unit behind a door. There are operating instructions engraved on the back of the door. The units are easy to operate; Sherry has given me a copy of the manual on them."

Stewart stood at the entrance to the cave. He turned to look out upon the river in deep thought. The other men carried on conversations between themselves. After a minute Stewart turned back to face the others, everyone fell quite. "Okay," Stewart said, "they're big, but they will fit through the entrance to the cave. Now, how much do they weigh?"

Ruth said, "They weigh five-hundred sixty-four kilos, or about one-thousand two-hundred eighty-four pounds."

Stewart and the other men thought for a while and conferred with each other before Stewart answered. "Alright, now as we see it, we have a good plan to get the units to the top of the bluffs. However, we don't yet have a plan to get them the last few feet to the entrance of the cave. As you know, we can't just back the truck up to the entrance and unload."

Ruth smiled at Stewart's humor. "Yes, we know. I can't give the okay to Sherry until we know that we can get them into the cave."

Stewart spoke again for the men. "We can't make the decision now. We need to talk it over and decide if this is what we want to do. I also need to speak with Ramona. We'll need her help. She said that she would be looking in on us this week. Why don't you check back with us next Sunday? We may have some answers for you by then."

Dr Nichols made the motion that the meeting be adjourned and everyone agreed. The business over with, the women stayed to visit for about two hours. They then left for the drive back home.

Tuesday, Ramona was down on the southern boundary of the Bivens Ranch checking fence lines, cattle guards and the alfalfa hay crop growing in the fields next to the river.

By 10:00 AM, Ramona was in the cave visiting her son, and talking with the rest of the men. She spent over three hours talking about the cryogenic units with the men. When she left, they had a workable plan for getting the cryogenic units into the cave.

XI

INTERNMENT CAMPS

The next Saturday, **Betty, Ruth** and Patricia were back at the pueblo ruins. After breakfast Sunday morning, they packed up and started back. When they got to the cave at the bluffs, Ramona was already there.

Everyone gathered at the entrance for the meeting. Stewart started off the meeting. "Okay, first off we have talked it over and have decided that we would like to have the cryogenic units. So, Ruth, you can let your friend Sherry in Houston know that we're in on it." Betty and Patricia were relieved to hear it. Ruth, however, wanted to hear of the plan before she could feel confident that she could notify Sherry to proceed. Stewart continued, "Now, as for how we will move the units from the truck into the cave." Stewart nodded in Ramona's direction. "Ramona, you have the floor."

Ramona looked around at everyone, then started her presentation. "Now the problem we have is to get four feet by four and a half feet by ten and a half feet object down from the top of the bluff, about twelve feet above the top of the entrance, and into the cave. There's one more problem; once the units are in the entrance of the cave, you must move them back into the cave. Now, let us take one at a time. We'll be able to bring the truck up close to the edge of the bluff. I'll have a back hoe with a chain hoist attached to the bucket, that we can use to lift the units off the truck, and lower them to the entrance to the cave. From there the men can pull them inside the cave.

Now the second problem. You have sixteen units that weigh between one half to three quarter ton each that you have to move from the entrance to the back of the cave. For that you will have to have something on which to transport them. I have a special trailer. It's small, light and very low to the ground with small wheels. The bed is covered with rollers, and it has a two-ton winch on the front. It is used to pick up and haul away a steer carcass for disposal. It's just large enough to hold one unit, and small enough to move around inside the cave."

Ramona looked around; everyone was nodding; she could see that everyone was pleased with her plan so far. "Now, we will have to hide the truck until we are ready to transfer the units to the cave." She looked in Betty's direction. "Betty, do you remember that hay barn where we parked?"

Betty nodded. "Yes, I remember."

Ramona said, "We'll keep the trucks there. After we've transferred the units to the cave, I'll dispose of both the tractor trailer and the truck that the other men are transported in. About one-half mile north from the barn that's behind the old Tascosa Courthouse, there's an old ground silo that had been used to store corn silage for winter feed that's no longer in use. It's a large cut through a hill, over four-hundred feet long, sixteen feet wide and over twenty feet deep at its deepest point. I'll take the Caterpillar tractor, dig it deeper, and then drive both trucks into the silo. I'll then crush the trucks down with the Caterpillar tractor and bury them. Any questions on my plan?"

Ramona looked around to see if anyone had any questions. Ruth had a question. She had to be sure that it could be done. "Are you sure that we can lower the units without any problems?"

"There's no problem." Ramona said, "The backhoe can handle the weight. The chain hoist can handle two tons, and can be operated by one person."

Ruth was satisfied that they had a workable plan. She now felt confident that she could give Sherry the signal. However, instead of feeling pleased, she experienced sadness for the desperate measures that had been forced on them. She was sure that once they had the units, they would have to use them. She was going to lose her son forever to an uncertain future. At least it had the promise of being a better future than that of the internment camps. She hated society for having driven her to this desperate choice.

Stewart said, "Ramona, we'd like to have some tools, so that we can prepare places to put the units."

Ramona replied, "No problem, I can get you all the tools you need; just give me a list."

Stewart continued, "The trailer that we're going to use to move the units around in the cave; can we have it a day or two ahead of time, so that we can get used to moving it around in the cave?"

Ramona again nodded to Stewart. "No problem, I can do that."

The men had already taken a vote and decided to take the cryogenic units; provided that they could get them in the cave. Stewart looked around; all the men nodded approval. Stewart said, "Okay, we're all in favor of taking the units."

They were committed now. The next step was up to Ruth. The meeting over, they stayed and visited for more than two hours, then left for home.

Monday morning, Ruth posted an ad on the internet to sell a two-karat diamond ring with yellow-gold setting. Sherry Tiller saw the ad and called her fellow conspirators to let them know that the operation was on. She also started making plans to have the rest of the men in the Houston group moved to their sanctuary in Odessa, Texas. Sherry had been planning this ever since she realized what was happening to the men. She knew what she needed to carry out her plan. She went about it carefully, recruiting the people she needed to accomplish it. She could call it off at any time up until they actually took the units.

After that, they would be irrevocably committed. There would be no going back. She prayed that the madness would end. However, she was a realist and knew that it was unlikely. She couldn't dwell on that now; she had a lot to do, and not much time to do it.

By August, men were no longer allowed out of their enclaves to work. The men who still had jobs were those who could work out of their homes. All visits by women to men in the enclaves had been stopped. The men were now completely isolated from the general population.

On the fifth of August, the government decreed that there would no longer be coeducational schools. All males from kindergarten up would be educated at boarding schools set up by the government. All boys five years of age and older, would have to leave for boarding school in two weeks. There would be no exceptions; no wavers would be given.

At the same time that the five to eleven-year-old boys were being taken from their mothers and sent to boarding schools; twelve to seventeen-year-old boys were being shipped from the male enclaves to boarding schools.

In September, all the men fifty-five years of age and over were being removed from the enclaves and relocated to senior citizen communities. As with the boys, there would be no exceptions; no waivers would be given.

When the men were transferred from their apartments in the enclaves by bus, they were allowed one carry-on bag and one suitcase. The rest of their things were packed for shipment to their new homes. Before shipment, everything was searched for firearms and contraband. These items were removed and the owner's compensated for them.

When they arrived by bus at the transit centers, their bags were turned over during processing to be placed on the train for them. All bags were search for firearms and other contraband. A receipt was given to them for these items when they boarded the train. No private

INTERNMENT CAMPS

property would be taken without compensation. All profits from the sale of private property were placed in special accounts to be used for their living expenses. The senior citizen communities and boarding schools were really internment camps.

In September, a service was set up for the unemployed men in the enclaves. The service matched up men with jobs that were available in other cities and states. Since most of the men by now were unemployed, they jumped at the chance for a good job in another city. Men sent in resumes and were quickly accepted for the new job.

There was a slow, but steady exodus of men from the enclaves to their new jobs. The same procedure was followed with the men going to their new jobs as for the senior citizens. That way all firearms and other contraband were removed from them. The men were going to new jobs, but not in another city. What they didn't know and were not told, was that there were no jobs for men in any city. They were going to internment camps being built in remote areas of the country. Companies were to be located next to the camps to give the men work.

By December, the occupancy of the apartments in the enclaves was down to twenty percent, or less. Residents were told that their enclave would be closed; and that they were being moved to a new apartment in another enclave. They went through the same procedure in moving as the rest of the men.

By Christmas, all men were in internment camps and the enclaves closed. In the internment camps they would be given work, and paid a fair wage. They would be allowed to have any luxury or hobby that they could afford, within reason. They could do anything they wanted with their free time, again within reason. However, they could never leave the camps.

If by chance a man were able to get away from a camp; he would be picked up and returned to the camp as soon as he reached a populated area. There was no way for a man to stay at large in an all-female population.

XII

HIJACK

By late October, the dig at the Pueblo ruins had been closed for the winter. The only contact the men had been with Ramona. She would stop by at least once a week to drop off supplies; and take care of any needs of the men.

The other women couldn't risk coming out to the pueblo ruins during the winter. Their friends knew that they had quit the dig for the winter. To go there would arouse attention. Ramona kept the other women informed about the men when she came into Amarillo, and relayed any messages that they had for the men.

Before they closed the dig for the winter, the women made plans for what they would do when they got the word that the operation was on. Betty and Ruth would be the ones to pick up the men at the transfer point, and deliver them to the cave. Ramona had a license for a tractor trailer; so, she would drive the truck with the cryogenic units. Patricia would meet Ramona at the hay barn the day of the hijacking, then drive Ramona to the transfer point. Patricia and Betty had already driven there with Ruth to make sure that they knew where it was. As soon as the ad for the clock was posted on the internet, Ramona would come to Amarillo to confirm with one of the other women.

Sherry was also ready. She knew the shipping dates, and by what carrier. Sherry had a dispatcher of United Van Lines Houston terminal in her group of conspirators. United Van Lines would be shipping a load of sixteen cryogenic units on the ninth of January. The dispatcher already knew whom she was going to assign to drive the truck. They already had false driver's license and other identification made out for their own driver.

The regular driver had been deliberately chosen for this run by the dispatcher because she lived alone, and kept her tractor parked next to her house overnight. It would be easy to kidnap the driver and take the tractor at her house.

It was scheduled that a flatbed trailer would be delivered to the cryogenic lab at the NASA Manned Space Flight Center on the eighth of January; and left to be loaded, covered and lashed down.

The next morning at 5:00 AM the driver would return with her tractor, connect up to the trailer and leave for Florida.

They would kidnap the driver the next morning of the ninth, when she started to get into her tractor. Their own driver would then take the tractor and pick-up the loaded trailer. She would also have another bill of lading for a shipment of refrigeration units to Phoenix, Arizona.

After leaving the NASA Manned Space Flight Center, the second bill of lading would be shown if they were stopped. Also, the existence of the second bill of lading would eventually be uncovered by the police, and lead them in the wrong direction.

Everything was ready. On the sixth of January, Sherry put an ad on the internet to sell an antique Seth Thomas mantle clock. Betty, Patricia, Ruth and Ramona all saw the ad for the clock.

That afternoon Ramona drove into Amarillo on business. When she got to Amarillo, she contacted Betty to confirm that Patricia would be at the barn at the proper time. Betty assured her that Patricia would be there on time. The forecast for the next seven days was for good weather. Picking up the tractor trailer at the transfer point, and driving it back to the hay barn would be the easy part. The hard part would be the transfer of the units to the cave.

At 2:00 P.M. the 8th of January, a United Van Line tractor pulling a flatbed trailer pulled into the Houston, Texas NASA Manned Space Flight Center. The driver delivered the trailer to the cryogenic lab, disconnected the trailer and left.

As soon as the trailer was delivered, the loading started. Sixteen titanium alloy cryogenic units were loaded onto the trailer, stacked two abreast, four deep and two high. The loading was supervised and double checked. The load was then covered with a gray waterproof covering and carefully tied down. The loading operation took five and a half hours. After loading operations were completed, the load was checked one last time and signed off by the load supervisor.

That evening after loading the special package into her van, Sherry had a quite dinner at home. The special package would be transferred to the chase vehicle in the morning. After dinner, she got out her photo album and looked at it. She then played videodisks of her son on her entertainment center. Sherry loved and missed having her son around. She wished that the madness would soon end, but she knew that it wouldn't. There was an agenda at work that wouldn't be denied. It wasn't just the United States, but worldwide.

Sherry had never thought of herself before as a crusader, however, there were some things that you had to take a stand against. If her son went into a camp, he would grow old and die without a future, if he were even allowed to grow old. Rumors had it that illegal drugs and alcohol were widely available in the camps; and the authorities were turning a blind eye to it. The drugs gave the men an outlet; And every overdose would be one less man to worry about. It was clear that the only place her son may have a chance would be in the future.

January ninth 4:00 AM, Finescia Emerson, a United Van Line driver emerged from her house and walked to her tractor that was parked on the side of the road in front of her house. The morning was cold and dark. She had her coat collar turned up against the cold wind. She didn't see the two women with guns coming up behind her as she approached the cab of her tractor. Before she realized what had happened, she had been shoved face first into the side of the cab of her tractor. A gun was put to the back of her head, and she was ordered in a strong-forthright manner to do as she was told or die. She wondered who it was that had assaulted her like this; and if they planned to kill her. Her nose was bleeding and a bump had started to rise on her forehead. She was ordered to Put her hands over her head, she complied. Her hands were handcuffed behind her back and a gag put in her mouth.

A van pulled up alongside the tractor. One of the women took the keys to the tractor from Finescia. They opened the side door of the van and pushed her inside. One of the women got in the van with her and closed the door. As the van drove off, her feet were bound and she was blindfolded. By now she was terrified that these people would kill her.

The other woman got into the cab of the tractor, started the engine and headed for the NASA Manned Space Flight Center. The whole thing took less than two minutes; and there was no one close by to witness it.

At 5:00AM, the United Van Line tractor pulled into the cryogenic lab loading area and connected to the trailer. The driver was given the shipping documents and instructions. By 5:40 AM, the tractor trailer rolled out of the Houston, Texas NASA Manned Space Flight Center. The destination was Cape Canaveral, Florida, where it was scheduled to arrive in two days.

When the tractor trailer got to Interstate 10, it turned west instead of east. The tractor trailer continued on through San Antonio, Texas on Interstate 10. At Boerne, Texas the tractor trailer picked up a second driver and a chase vehicle. At Comfort, Texas they left the Interstate highway and headed north on US Highway 87. They drove north through San Angelo, Texas and Big Spring, Texas to Lamesa, Texas, where they took State Highway 137 to Brownfield, Texas. At Brownfield, they picked up US Highway 385 north to Littlefield, Texas. The driver then parked the tractor trailer at the prearranged transfer point. Sherry's special package was then transferred to the tractor.

After the successful hijacking of the cryogenic units, a message was sent to get the men at the Odessa, Texas sanctuary moving to the transfer point. The men would be moved by truck, followed by a chase vehicle. Betty and Ruth would pick up the truck with the men of the Houston group at the transfer point, deliver them to the cave at the bluff, then park the truck inside the barn behind the Tascosa courthouse. Being that the distance the Houston group had to travel was far less than the hijacked cryogenic units, they would arrive at the cave early.

At 10:00AM, Betty and Ruth left Amarillo in Ruth's car. They headed for the transfer point just north of Littlefield, Texas. They arrived just after 1:00 PM to find the truck and the men waiting for them at the transfer point. They headed north, with Betty driving the truck and Ruth following in her car. They arrived at the cave just before 4:00 PM. They had the men and their supplies unloaded, the truck parked in the barn behind the courthouse and were back home by 6:30 PM.

At 3:00 PM, Patricia departed from her home in Amarillo for her rendezvous with Ramona at the hay barn. When she arrived, Ramona was already there. She got into Patricia's vehicle and they started south on US Highway 385. To Littlefield, Texas. They took their time and arrived at 7:15 PM. The tractor trailer wasn't there yet. They continued to drive south until they found a restaurant where they stopped for dinner.

After dinner, they drove back north. When they arrived back at the transfer point the tractor trailer was there. Ramona climbed into the cab. The key was in the ignition. She started the engine and drove north on US Highway 385. Patricia followed behind the tractor trailer in her vehicle. It was an easy trip without any problems. They arrived back at the barn at 10:25 PM.

Ramona and Patricia then left for home. Patricia arrived back home at 11:40 PM. Betty was still up and saw Patricia as she arrived back home; they could tell by the looks on each other's face that they had been successful.

When Finescia Emerson had been kidnaped in front of her home that morning, Sherry had driven the van. They took Finescia to a vacant warehouse where they had set up a room to keep her confined for twenty-four hours. Sherry had the help of Dorothy Hyde to keep Finescia confined.

Sherry had been able to find a few trusted women in key positions to make this conspiracy work. They all had one thing in common, a son or brother for whom they were concerned. Sherry was in a unique position. She was the only one who knew everyone in the conspiracy. She was the only link with Ruth Griffin. Ruth had been a lucky find, an old alumnus with no professional or social ties to herself. To keep the cryogenic units from being found, they had to be turned over to a group with a secure hiding place and no ties to the Houston group. They wouldn't get anything from her computer. Her computer was part of the special package that she had her friends put on the tractor trailer with the cryogenic units. The tracking device on the tractor trailer had been disabled soon after the hijacking. She had been the loading supervisor and knew that there were no tracking devices on any of the units. The police would never find them by electronic means.

All that day, Sherry followed the progress of the tractor trailer mentally in her head. Every few minutes she looked at the clock and recalled the schedule. She would visualize what highway the tractor trailer was now on, and what city or town it was close to. By midnight she started to relax. When the tractor trailer failed to show up at Cape Canaveral, Florida tomorrow, all hell would break lose. By then it would be too late for the authorities to find the tractor trailer. It would be safely hidden away in a place where they wouldn't be looking for it.

At 4:00 AM the next morning, Sherry and Dorothy got Finescia blindfolded and handcuffed, then put her into Cherry's van. Sherry released Dorothy to go to her own vehicle and leave.

Sherry drove Finescia out into the country, to a place from where it would take her about three hours or more to walk to some place where she could get help. When Sherry reached the place, she stopped the van and took Finescia from the back. Sherry walked Finescia two-hundred yards back in the direction from which they had come. Sherry then removed the handcuffs, but not the blindfold. She instructed Finescia not to remove the blindfold for five minutes. Sherry then returned to the van and drove away.

As soon as Finescia heard the van drive off, she removed the blindfold and looked about. It was still too dark for her to get a good look at the retreating vehicle, or to get a license number. She threw the blindfold in the ditch and started walking down the road.

When Sherry got home, she parked the van in the garage and went into the kitchen. For the last twenty-four hours she had felt the pressure as the leader of the group that everything goes right. Now it was out of her hands; she now felt relieved and at ease. She made a cup of coffee, and sat at the kitchen table with her coffee. They had pulled it off. The cryogenic units and their men were safe. Now they would start to feel the wrath of the authorities. Everyone connected with the cryogenic lab and the trucking company would be suspect. There would be the questions. Everyone would be asked to account for their time. There would then be the interrogations and the polygraph tests.

Sherry got up from the table and went to the bedroom. She changed into her best nightgown and brushed her hair. She looked at the photo of her son on the dresser. She hoped that his future would be fulfilling.

After she finished brushing her hair, she got a glass of water from the bathroom and lay down on the bed. She was the only link between the Houston group and the Amarillo group. To insure her son's future, she must remove the link. She had thought of sleeping pills, but she wanted something more certain. She had a capsule of potassium cyanide. Her last thought was of her son.

XIII

CRYOGENIC SLEEP

On the fourteenth of January warm-moist air moved up from the Gulf of Mexico and collided with a cold mass over the central plains. The result was a solid overcast and snow. Ramona and Betty were ready. Betty met Ramona at the hay barn. Ramona drove the tractor trailer up to the bluffs. Betty followed with the backhoe. The weather was just what they needed to protect them from air reconnaissance.

When they got to the bluffs, Ramona took the backhoe and positioned it at the top of the bluff, directly over the opening to the cave. She then pulled the tractor trailer up in position to life off the first four cryogenic units. They hooked up the chain hoist to the backhoe and started unloading the cryogenic units.

Dr. Nichols, Steven Picket and Douglas Hamilton were at the top of the bluff to help the ladies unload. Even with the backhoe and chain hoist to do all the lifting, it was still a very tricky operation, that required some muscle at times to keep the units from being damaged. Stewart and the rest of the men working with the trailer in the cave to move the units from the entrance to their final position. It was very hard work. One by one they were lifted off the trailer, swung out over the edge of the bluff and lowered by the chain hoist to the level of the cave; where they were pulled into the cave, onto the trailer, then maneuvered into position at the back of the cave. As each four units were lifted off, the tractor trailer was moved up for the next four. The whole operation took a little under five hours.

After all the cryogenic units, and Sherry's special package were in their final position, the small trailer was lifted out of the cave and placed on the bed of the tractor trailer. All the other tools were brought up and put on the bed of the tractor trailer. Ramona and Betty then drove the tractor trailer and backhoe back to the hay barn; then returned to the cave.

When they entered the cave, they saw how the men had arranged it. In the back of the cave they had the units lined up eight to a side about seven to eight feet apart. Sherry's special package, that seemed to be some sort of time capsule was in the center behind the last two units. Betty and Ramona stayed to visit for about an hour, then left for home.

The next morning Ramona returned to the barn. She drove the truck that towed a lowboy trailer with a Caterpillar bulldozer. She got the pit in the trench silo ready for the tractor trailer and the truck that had delivered the men. She then drove the tractor trailer and truck up from the barns and into the pit. After slashing the tires to let the air out; she ran the Caterpillar over them several times to crush them down. She then pushed the dirt back into the pit to cover the tractor trailer and truck. After she finished the job, she loaded the Caterpillar back onto the lowboy and left for the ranch headquarters. It continued to snow on the fresh earth in the silo.

After the death of Sherry Tiller, and the hijacking of the cryogenic units, the police were in a frenzy to recover them. Roadblocks were set up on likely routes that the tractor trailer could have taken from Houston, Texas. The police were also stopping all tractor trailers that matched the description of the hijacked tractor trailer. They had tried to locate it using the tracking system without success. It was like it just vanished from the face of the earth. The authorities could see only one use for the cryogenic units, and were determined to get them back.

In the resulting investigation, the police turned over every stone that they could think of, but the only other conspirator that they could find was Rose Daladier; she was the dispatcher for the United Van Line terminal in Houston, Texas. The police and FBI tried everything to get information out of Rose on the rest of the conspirators. The only problem was that she knew of only one other conspirator, Sherry Tiller; and she truly had no idea where the cryogenic units were.

The police and FBI knew from Rose Daladier of the phony documents that sent the refrigeration units to Phoenix, Arizona. They were aware that Sherry had gone on vacation to Santa Fe, New Mexico. Then from there, she had rented a car and gone to parts unknown. They were putting a lot of investigative work into Santa Fe, New Mexico and Phoenix, Arizona. They were also looking in Colorado, Utah, Nevada and California. They were determined to find the cryogenic units. At the same time the police were cracking down everywhere, trying to round up fugitive men. The pressure was on. If they couldn't recover the cryogenic units; they might be able to round up the men before they could be used. Everyone they suspected of harboring a man was being watched.

The first week of February, Betty, Ruth and Ramona were at the cave. They were having a meeting with the men. The group was so large now that they could no longer have the meeting in the entrance to the cave. They had the meeting in the main chamber by lantern light. It was informal with everyone sitting on the open floor with their backs against a cryogenic unit, or standing to lean against them.

The meeting would be to decide if they should make use of the cryogenic units now, or wait until later. Theodore Conway, one of the recent arrivals was speaking. "I don't know about the rest of you, but I need to be really sure before I take the step of going into the deep freeze."

There was a lot of nodding and murmured comments from the

men. The debate, as to whether or not to use the units, had been going on ever since they had received them. The idea of using them was at first seen as a last resort. No one was eager to use them, but they could all see the desperation of their situation. Most had by now come to realize that it might be their only hope. However, a hardcore minority still held out, not yet ready to take the step.

"Well," Anthony Cooper said, "I don't like the idea of going into the deep freeze very much either. However, we've been hiding for a year now, and things have gone from bad to worst. Betty you're on top of things with your job in the police department. What do you think?"

All eyes were on Betty. She cleared her throat, then said, "To be truthful with you, the heat is really on now. It wasn't hard to take these cryogenic units. NASA didn't think that anyone would want them. Where would a thief sell such a thing anyway? Well, you can bet that they'll guard them well from now on. To get back to what I was going to say. Before when a woman was caught harboring a man nothing was done to her. Now the woman gets jail time. The authorities are desperate to get the units back, or at least keep them from being used."

Everyone was silent for a while before Pablo Quintana spoke. "I don't know what the rest of you think, but I believe that we'll have to use them soon."

Most of the men nodded and murmured agreement. Thomas Owens spoke, "I don't know about the rest of you, but I don't know how much longer I can hold out here. It's really hard spending all your time in this cave, and it's a lot more crowded now."

Betty looked at her son. "Do you want to use the units?"

Thomas nodded. "Yes, Mom, I do."

Clifford Johnson then sprang to his feet to give voice his opinion. "I for one am not ready to use the units. What if the right people gain control of the government in the next couple of years and put an end to all this nonsense; we would have then taken a risk for nothing."

Pablo Quintana got to his feet and looked at Clifford Johnson. "You think it might get better? I doubt it! You hear the rumors about the camps just the same as I do; it's not getting better. They are allowing drugs and alcohol to get into the camps to keep the men disorganized. No man will ever get out of the camps, at least not as a man. The only ones allowed out of the camps are those that undergo gender reassignment surgery to make them a girl. Are you willing to let them chop off your dick and balls to have your freedom?"

Pablo's last remarks drew uproarious laughter from everyone, but the subject was no laughing matter.

"I have a question," Horatio Sikes said, getting to his feet, "we don't have a lot of supplies with us; and it will be difficult to get any more for us. How long can we hold out?"

Dr. Nichols said, "With what the new group brought with them, we have supplies for two and a half to three months. As far as the long-term prospects for holding out here; that depends on how our women can keep us supplied."

Stewart spoke out. "To stay confined here we'll eventually reach a breaking point where we'll have to either separate, or start fighting each other."

Ramona now addressed everyone. She didn't want to lose her son, but she knew that she was going to lose him one way or the other. "With care you can stretch your supplies a little. The other women and I can supplement your supplies, but we can't start looking like an army on campaign every time we come up here. Eventually someone will get suspicious. One of us will be followed and you'll be found out. It's crunch time! We must decide now!"

Everyone nodded in agreement. It had become clear to everyone that they were out of options. The only way to stay out of the camps would be to use the cryogenic units. The time for talking was over, they had to act now. Ramona looked at Stewart to take the lead.

Stewart paced before the men as he spoke. "This Madness has gone on for a year now without abatement. It can go on for another five, or ten or more years; and what will become of the men under their control in the meantime. There are still people of conscience, but they are not in charge, and not likely to be. The vast majority of women are now in support of the present leaders, and condone their actions. Cryogenic sleep is our only way to endure. I say that we take a vote now. All in favor of using them now?"

Stewart raised his hand. Five other hands came up, then three more. One by one the rest of the men raised their hand until it was unanimous. Even the ones that had been reluctant to enter the cryogenic units could see that it had become their only hope of survival.

Each cryogenic unit had a storage container that had to be removed before the occupant went in. The containers were designed to safeguard clothing and equipment for extended periods of time. The men spent the next week cleaning their clothing and equipment for storage.

Friday, they had what might be called a going away party. They raided their stores for the best of everything and had a good time. Everyone tried to be festive, but the uncertainty of what they were about to do hung heavy over them all.

Saturday morning at 8:00 AM, Ruth, Betty, Ramona and Patricia were at the cave. They were already familiar with the procedures for putting people into cryogenic sleep. Dr. Nichols would be with the women to help them put the other men into cryogenic sleep. He would then be the last. The whole process would take thirty hours. The men had already been assigned cryogenic units by the drawing of numbers. On the right were odd numbers one through fifteen and on the left were even numbers two through sixteen.

Without delay or fanfare, the process began. Stewart was the first to enter his unit. He removed his clothing and put them away in the equipment container. Patricia was almost able to hold back the tears, but not quite. She was certain that this would be the last time that she would see Stewart. Seeing her discomfort, Stewart gave her some encouraging words and a parting kiss. He also had a warm good-bye for Betty and the other women. He then took his place in the unit and

Dr. Nichols gave him an injection to put him to sleep. Then with the help of the Women, he hooked Stewart up to the unit and started the automatic process of putting him in cryogenic sleep. He then showed the women how to wrap the men in their protective wrap.

After finishing with Stewart, they took the rest of the men one by one and put them in cryogenic sleep. When it was time, Betty, Ruth then Ramona had tearful good-byes with their sons. Dr. Nichols was the last to enter cryogenic sleep. He got undressed and took his place in the unit. Ramona gave him the injection, hooked him up to the unit to start the automatic sleep process and wrapped him in his protective wrapping.

All the women had to do now was to monitor the process. By 6:00 PM Sunday the process was complete. All the men were in cryogenic suspension. The women took one last look, then left the cave for the last time.

XIV

RESCUE

It was a beautiful fall morning in the first week in October. A cool wind blew from the northwest at from ten to fifteen miles per hour. Small fluffy clouds drifted by in a mostly clear azure-blue sky. The only sound was the wind blowing through the grass and mesquite branches. An occasional tumbleweed could be seen bounding by.

Over the hill from the south came five four-wheel ATV's, each pulling a small trailer. Driving the ATV's were drovers from the Farrow Ranch. They all had carbines in boots mounted on the side of their ATX and pistols in holsters at their hips. They were dressed in work clothes, boots and broad-brimmed hats as drovers had dressed through the ages. Their bodies were lean and hard, and they all had dusky complexions. Theirs was the dry wind-burned skin of people spending long hours working outdoors in the harsh semi-arid climate.

The ATV's had to get really close before you could hear the almost silent hum of the electric induction motors running off hydrogen fuel cells. The wide low-pressure tires were almost silent as they rolled over the soft ground. The ATV's were very efficient vehicles. They were constructed mostly of ultra-light weight, but extremely strong composite materials and exotic ceramic compounds. To provide for extended range, the tops of the trailers were covered with photoelectric cells that converted sunlight to electricity and stored for use in the vehicle's storage batteries.

The drovers had been out checking the stock to the north of the ranch headquarters when they found the partly eaten carcass of a calf. The evidence was clear that a large predator had attacked and killed the calf. This had happened before and the lead drover, Lawrence Sherman, had decided that they had to track the predator down. They had been tracking it since late yesterday afternoon and were very close now.

The ATV's continued on until they came to another hill. Just short of the crest of the hill, Lawrence signaled a halt, dismounted, took the carbine from the boot on the ATV, moved with stealth to the crest of the hill and took up a prone shooting position. Lawrence spotted the predator through the scope of the carbine. It was a large male cougar about four-hundred yards away, moving north through the scrub and mesquite trees in an easy bounding gait capable of being sustained for a long time. Lawrence felt certain that the cat sensed that they were tracking it, and was heading for the wilderness zone. It was a long shot for a carbine and getting longer with each stride of the big cat, but Lawrence had to take the shot. The cougar had developed a taste for bovines and had to be stopped. The shot was quick and should have been fatal, but the bullet was deflected by a mesquite branch and just wounded the cougar in the right fore leg. With a sudden bound the cougar took off at a run in the direction of the river.

Sean had been lying next to Lawrence, watching the cat through binoculars when the shot had been fired. "You missed."

Lawrence looked at Sean. "No, I didn't miss. Did you see him when he took off? He was favoring his front leg. I hit him all right. Besides, at that range you wouldn't have even taken the shot."

Sean chuckled. "Okay, you're the better shot, but you still missed."

Lawrence gave Sean a sour look, got up, and with Sean following, started back to the ATV's "It's only wounded." Lawrence said, "We have to finish the job."

When they got back to the ATV's Lawrence put the carbine back in the boot and remounted. Lawrence gave the signal and they started forward again.

When they got to the spot where the cougar had been hit, they found blood on the ground. They continued tracking the cougar north. They were in open terrain with clumps of buffalo grass and other grasses, prickly pear, barrel cactus and mesquite trees. The soil was mostly sandy loam. It wasn't hard to follow the cougar's tracks, especially with the blood trail of occasional drops on the ground, or on the grass.

About one-hundred yards from the riverbank, they encountered a thicket of tamarack. Lawrence called a halt. "We're not far from the river. He's heading for the wilderness zone on the other side of the river. Now, when we cross the river, we'll go single file. I know the riverbed looks mostly flat and dry, but it can be deceptive and treacherous. I don't want to risk getting more than one machine bogged down. Okay, now let's go."

Lawrence started into the tamarack thicket, with the rest of the drovers close behind. It took Lawrence and others over fifteen minutes to bash through the thicket to reach the riverbank. The river was less than two-hundred yards wide at this point. The riverbed was mostly dry sand, with white streaks of alkali. There was a small stream of water that a person could almost jump across only a foot or less deep, that meandered down the riverbed. Lawrence found a way down onto the riverbed and they struck out for the other side. They had no trouble picking up the cougar's tracks in the soft sand of the riverbed. They could tell by the unsteady stride that the cougar had been weakened by the loss of blood.

They found a place to drive out of the riverbed and picked up the track again. The tracks were leading west, up river. The cat was heading to a bluff at the edge of the river, about one-half mile ahead.

When they reached the top of the bluff, they dismounted, took their carbines, and followed the track on foot. The track led to the edge of the bluff, then down onto a ledge about eighteen inches wide. They followed the ledge from the top of the bluff and saw that it led to an opening in the bluff. That was where the cougar had to be hiding. Lawrence knew that someone had to go down after the cougar, and the leader always led the way.

There wasn't the room to use a carbine, so Lawrence with back to the bluff, pistol in the right hand and flashlight in the left hand, slowly advanced down the ledge towards the entrance to the cave. As Lawrence started around the turn in front of the cave entrance, the cougar let out from deep in its throat a menacing growl. Lawrence shown the flashlight into the cave and caught the cougar in the beam of the flashlight, just as it started to spring. Lawrence fired three times and the cougar fell dead at the entrance to the cave. Lawrence moved forward into the entrance to the cave and checked to make sure the cougar was dead; then decided to check out the rest of the cave. When the light was shown into the back of the cave, it reflected off something metallic.

Lawrence went back to the entrance of the cave and called the rest of the drovers down. When they were all in the cave, Lawrence led them all back into the rear chamber. Everyone was amazed at the immense size of the cave. As they played the beams of their lights around, they noticed that there were several large rectangular shiny metal objects lined up on each side of the cave. Beside each of the larger objects were smaller rectangular metal cases. At the rear of the cave was another square object of a different size and shape of the others. They counted the larger units, there where sixteen, eight to a side. The smaller units appeared to be part of the larger units.

Sean said, "What are these?"

Lawrence kept playing the beam of the flashlight around the cave. "I don't know."

They turned to the first unit on the right. Whatever these things were, it was apparent from the thick coat of dust that they had been here for a long time. They started to inspect the first unit. They could see that there was a hinged lid on the top. Lawrence noticed a plaque on the side and started to read.

NASA MANNED SPACE FLIGHT CENTER

CRYOGENIC SUSPENSION UNIT MARK 1-D

Lawrence pointed and the others looked. "Well," Lawrence said, "we know what they are; now, what in the hell are they doing here?"

Everyone just shook their heads. They looked the units over and found a panel door at the rear of the unit. They opened it and found the unit controls. Inside the door were etched instructions on how to operate the controls. They read the instructions and ran a test of the unit. The unit was in operation, and there was a viable human being inside it. They checked the rest of the units. Three had lost power, their occupants were dead. The rest of the units were still in operation; and their occupants were viable.

They checked out the stainless-steel box at the rear of the cave. Inside they found what looked like a very old computer, with stacks of disks.

They held a conference to decide what to do. "Okay," Lawrence said, "what we have here is human beings in cryogenic suspension. Three are dead; the rest may still be alive. Now, the question is, what do we do about it?"

After a few moments Brigitte said, "Whoever they are, they have been here for a long time. I doubt that anyone who knew them is still alive. My question is, who are they, and why are they in this cave where they may have never been found?"

Nancy Cleveland indicated the cryogenic units with a wave of the hand. "We can't just leave them here. We must do something. We have the instructions; why don't we just reanimate them."

Lawrence had the last word. "That's what I have in mind. We have the instructions; and I can't see why we shouldn't do it. Besides, we'll have to do it anyway to get them out of here. Does anyone have any objections?" Lawrence looked around, no one objected. "Okay, we'll reanimate them. According to the instructions, the reanimation process takes ninety-six hours. Nancy, you take Sean and Brigitte with you and return to the ranch headquarters. Get the carryalls, load them with additional supplies, blankets and anything else we may need and return here. Now when you get back, don't cross the river with the carryalls until I'm there to guide you across. Henry will stay here with me. Once we start the process it's automatic. All we have to do is monitor he units. You will be back long before the process is completed. Any Questions?" There were no questions, Lawrence continued, "Okay, we have work to do, let's get going."

The meeting broke up. Nancy, Sean and Brigitte returned to their ATV's and started out for the ranch headquarters. Lawrence and Henry started the reanimation process on the units that still had power. After they had started the reanimation process on the units, they went up to their ATV's and got their bedrolls and other supplies.

Nancy, Sean and Brigitte were back with the carryalls by late afternoon of the next day. Lawrence guided them safely across the river, and had the carryalls park at the top of the bluff. They then set up hydrogen fuel powered heaters in the cave, then brought everything they needed into the cave.

The morning of the fourth day the outer lids of the units automatically opened. There was a clear acrylic lid under that. Inside they saw something wrapped in a silver-coated shroud. The object was human in shape, like a mummy. Four hours later, the clear acrylic lid opened. The time had come to start removing the wrapping from the occupants.

Everyone gathered around and started at the first unit on the right. First, they unfastened the straps and folded back the outer quilted cover to expose a body wrapped in what looked like aluminum foil. The occupant was definitely human, but there was something odd about the body proportions.

They started to peel away the inner aluminum foil wrapping, beginning with the head. They were surprised to find that the person had such strong facial features and a large amount of facial hair. They got down past the neck and shoulders. The muscular development of the upper torso was amazing. They were down to the waistline. There was a lot more hair, and the mammary glands were under developed. They got down to the groin and stopped. They just stood there looking at the groin area of the person in the cryogenic unit with amazement. Finally, Nancy said, "Male!" It was as much a question as an exclamation. What they were looking at was a protruding organ from the groin, a male penis and testicles. After a while they regained their composure and finished removing the wrapping.

The next person was also a male. By now the shock had started to wear off. By the time that they unwrapped the last person, they were no longer surprised at what they found.

Stewart slowly returned to consciousness. He became aware of the light and opened his eyes. He saw a group of women standing around him. One he noticed right off because she was much taller than the rest of the women. She was at least six-feet tall; and Stewart estimated that she weighed about one-hundred sixty pounds. She had straight-black hair that wasn't styled, but just cut short. She had dark-brown eyes, like mahogany, a fine nose and full lips. All the women had dark eyes and black hair, either straight or curly. The color of her skin, as was all the women here in the cave was a yellow-brown, like the butternut dye. It was hard to tell what race they were. To Stewart they looked most like Polynesians. He spoke to the tall one. "Who are you?"

She smiled at him. He was taken by how her whole face lit up when she smiled. She had a certain rugged-honest beauty that appealed to him. He gave her a smile in return. She said, "I'm Lawrence Sherman." She pointed to the oldest woman. "This is Nancy Cleveland." She then pointed in turn and introduced the rest of the women as Sean Anderson, Brigitte Fowler and Henry Perkins. She then asked Stewart. "And you are?"

Stewart said, "I'm Mr. Stewart Vaughn." The first thing that Stewart wanted to know was how long they had been in cryogenic sleep. "What's the date?"

Lawrence answered, "It's the tenth of October, twenty-three sixty-eight. The other males have asked the same question. You've been in cryogenic suspension for two-hundred eighty-six years."

All that Stewart could say was, "Wow!"

Lawrence was really intrigued by these males. They weren't just different physically, but their speech was really antiqued and difficult to understand. There was one honorific that all the males so far had used. She was curious about what it meant; she could also use it as a way to start a dialogue with Stewart. "Every one of you so far has used the honorific of mister. What does it mean?"

Stewart felt his strength coming back and felt like talking. "Oh, that's easy. It's used as a title prefixed to the name of a man. It also used to mean husband."

Lawrence looked perplexed. "What's a husband?"

Stewart thought about Lawrence's question. It seemed an odd question to ask. He started to suspect that these women had no knowledge of men. He wondered what kind of human society now existed. He said, "A husband is the male member of a married couple. The female member of a married couple has the title of missus. To write them, mister is abbreviated Mr. and missus is Mrs. You also have a title for a maiden, it is Miss, it also means an unmarried woman or virgin."

Lawrence was even more confused than she had been before she started asking questions. These males were so alien that nothing about them made sense to her, they were not even supposed to be. She would have to question him more to get a better explanation when she had more time.

She noticed that another male had started to move and sent the other women to help him. She remained with Stewart to talk with him; and to help him to sit up and get out of the unit when he was ready. She said, "I don't know what to think. Everyone knows that God made humans in her own image, and that we are all female, the same as God. Then we find you; you are different in many ways the most profound being a male organ like animals, and you refer to yourself as a man and refer to true humans as women. There are just humans and they are all female."

Now it was Stewart's turn to be confused. How can that be? Am I hearing her right, that the whole human race is female? He couldn't hold back, he had to ask the next question. "Are you telling me that all humans are the same gender?"

Lawrence gave Stewart a look like he was a child that didn't know any better. 'Why, yes, everyone knows that all humans are made female in God's image; and that only animals have males to reproduce by copulation."

Stewart just had to laugh. Her statement seemed so absurd to him, he had to respond with a comeback. "I hate to upset your idea of a perfect world, but there are two human genders, the male called man and the female called woman; and they do reproduce by copulation."

Stewart's response shocked Lawrence, and she started to get frustrated by this verbal exchange. The idea of humans copulating was so disturbing. Everyone knew that human reproduction was a medical procedure, she couldn't even imagine humans copulating. She responded in a defensive manner. "That's not right! All humans are female!"

Stewart showed a devilish smile. He could see that she had started to lose her composure. He knew that he should not goad her, but he couldn't help it. "Than what are you looking at?"

By now Lawrence had become flustered by this exchange with Stewart and tried hard to keep from showing any anger. She could see that this male was having fun with her. She would like to have a rejoinder for him, but this was all so out of her realm of knowledge that she had no answer for Stewart. She needed to get off the subject. "Okay, Mr. Stewart Vaughn, are you ready to sit up now?"

Stewart, seeing that Lawrence was a little unsettled and not in the mood for jest, curbed his quip manner, and gave her his cooperation. "Yes, I think so."

Lawrence grabbed Stewart under the arm. "okay, but take it easy. You may be dizzy at first; I'll help you."

With Lawrence's help, Stewart sat up and swung his legs over the edge of the cryogenic unit. No one had to speak about it. They all knew that whatever life had for them, they would now be leaving the cave. Stewart spent a couple of minutes just sitting on the edge of the cryogenic unit, before he felt ready to stand. With Lawrence's help, Stewart got out of the unit and stood on the floor of the cave. Stewart felt like moving around now. He opened his storage container to get his clothing. He reached for underwear and it came apart in his hands.

Lawrence chuckled at Stewart's plight at not having any clothing to wear. It also made her feel better than this male that was now at a disadvantage. "I'm sorry to say this, Mr. Stewart Vaughn, I don't think that storage container was meant to be used for such a long time in these conditions."

Stewart sighed in disgust at not having anything to wear. He stood up, pulling the blanket close about himself. "I see what you mean. Now, one other thing, I don't like to be so formal all the time, so if you just call me Stewart, I'll call you Lawrence."

Lawrence had also felt a little odd with all this formality and was glad to get on a first name basis. "Okay, Stewart, for now you will have to make use of the blanket until we can get you clothing. Right now, if you go out to the front chamber of the cave, we have some hot soup for you."

Lawrence went to help the other women. Stewart went out to the front of the cave. Thomas, Benjamin and Allen Worley were already there. There was a field stove with a large pot of steaming hot soup with beef, vegetables and barley. Stewart took a bowl full of soup and spoon and had a seat next to the wall, where he could see out of the cave. Stewart felt good about that. He also thought about Betty, Patricia, Ramona and Ruth. He knew that they were all long dead. He wondered what kind of a life they had after they had said their good-byes. He wished that there was some way that they could know that they had made it through.

Of concern to Stewart was the fact, made apparent by his conversation with Lawrence, that they would be facing a society that was totally unprepared for them. What kind of a reception would they receive? Would they be welcomed in this society? They couldn't go back. For better or for worst they had to make the best of their situation.

A few minutes later, Dr. Nichols came out to the front chamber of the cave, got a bowl of soup and sat down beside Stewart. In between spoonsful of soup, they congratulated each other on making it, and exchanged ideas about what they needed to do. They agreed that for now they were dependent on the women who had found them.

After a while, Lawrence came out to talk with Stewart again. He learned that when they were found, three of the men were already dead, and that two more died when the power failed in their units during the reanimation process. The dead were, Anthony Cooper, David Cushing, John Boatright, Horatio Sikes and Pablo Quintana.

The women had brought robes in the carryall and handed them out to the men. They were ill fitting and so small, that some of the men had trouble getting them on, but they were grateful to have them.

By the time that everyone was ready to travel, it was too late in the afternoon to make the trip. They decided to spend the night at the bluff, then head back to the ranch headquarters in the morning. The women camped out on top of the bluff. The men would have also liked to sleep in the open, but they didn't have the equipment to do so, as their sleeping bags had deteriorated like their clothing. They stayed in the cave where they could be more comfortable sleeping rolled up in their blankets next to the heater.

Stewart and the rest of the men couldn't help but to notice how the language had changed. It was still English, but it had evolved and sounded different. To be better understood, they would have to refrain from using slang and speak proper English. Everything else must really be different, they had a lot to learn. They had a quick meeting in the cave that evening. They all agreed that until they got their feet on the ground, so to speak, they must rely on the hospitality of the women.

That evening, when they were alone at the top of the bluff, the women also had a discussion about the men. It had been an eventful day for them all, to say the least. No woman alive today could even imagine a male human being. They were members of a single gender race, and had not been prepared to come in contact with male human beings. Now they had among them eleven male humans that they had rescued from cryogenic sleep. They were not really sure how they should deal with them.

According to religious teaching, in the distant past there were subhuman males. The true humans shared the world with them until the true humans reached spiritual maturity; then God banished all subhuman males from the earth. If anyone asked Lawrence if she believed in God, she would say yes. Otherwise she didn't give it much thought. If religious teachings seemed illogical, she would be more likely to follow her own beliefs. If the church was right, then these males shouldn't exist, but here they were. They were real, that was for sure. They were really exotic beings, and not just for their gender. They were from a time when there had been a lot more diversity in the human race. They were from mostly a light-skinned race. However, two had really dark skin and one had tawny skin. Their hair color ran from black like hers to brown, reddish-brown, red and the color of new straw. Their eyes were from dark like hers to brown, gray and blue. They were broad through the shoulders and narrow through the hips. They were on average taller and more muscular than true humans were and had deeper voices. All that Lawrence and the other true humans had ever known told them that these males were subhuman, but after being with and talking to them, they had a hard time seeing them that way.

After talking it over, they agreed that regardless of the differences, the males were to be regarded as human. They were also in agreement that until they could assess the impact the males would have on the local population; they would keep them a secret.

One thing that Lawrence didn't bring up was what the male, Stewart Vaughn had said to her about human copulation. If any of the others had heard anything about human copulation, they didn't want to talk about it. Working with animals, she knew what copulation was, they all did. She tried to imagine what human copulation would be like, but she only had the example of other animals to go by. From her observations of other animals, she doubted that it would be a very pleasurable experience for the female. Having a male organ inside her was a repugnant idea that she'd rather not dwell on.

As Lawrence lay in her sleeping bag trying to get to sleep, she kept thinking of the male, Stewart Vaughn. She didn't know why, but she couldn't stop thinking about him. He had a disquieting effect on her psyche. She thought back to what he said. It had just been something he had said in passing, but it really piqued her curiosity. What was marriage? It had something to do with relationships between males and females. Miss, an unmarried female wasn't hard to figure out, but what was a maiden? And what was a virgin?

Life had been so simple until they had found these males. Now everything she knew was being challenged. Her life would never be the same again. Her world had changed forever. After what seemed to be several exhausting hours, Lawrence finally got to sleep.

XV

A SECOND BEGINNING

The next morning everyone was up at daybreak. The women soon had breakfast ready. They served it atop the bluff, next to the carryalls. Stewart and the rest of the men reveled in being able to leave the cave in the day and enjoy their meal in the sunlight. During breakfast the men and women both had further opportunity to get to know each other better. Some of the awkwardness of the day before was gone, and they were starting to feel more comfortable with each other. Stewart conversed with the other men.

After breakfast, they loaded up the carryalls. The carryalls were eight-wheel all-wheel drive, all terrain utility vehicles, with wide low-pressure all terrain tires. They were twenty-four feet overall, designed to carry cargo or personnel. They had a rear and top hatch for the cargo compartment and side doors for the crew cab. Lawrence and Henry would drive out on their ATV's. Brigitte and Nancy would drive the carryalls. The men and Sean were divided between the two carryalls.

Before they left, the men went through their storage containers to see if they could selvage anything. All the clothing and footwear were unusable. Anything made of metal or any other durable material, provided it had been well packed, was still good. Stewart's .44 magnum revolver was still good, having been greased and wrapped in grease impregnated cloth. As for the ammunition, the powder was probably too old and unstable. He had two belt buckles, one made of nickel-silver with an enamel inlay thunderbird on it. The other was made of brass, with a star within a wreath on it. There was also a coffee cup with the Texas A&M logo on it and other small items.

Before they left the cave, they said a prayer for their departed comrades. Lawrence had assured them that they would return with tools to lift the bodies up from the cave and properly bury them.

At 8:00 AM, they started out on the trip to the ranch headquarters. Lawrence called the ranch headquarters on her portable hand-held visidatacom unit to let them know that they were coming in. She took care to make the message sound routine. It could not do to have eavesdroppers get too curious. The ranch owners knew that they had found cryogenic units, but they had no idea that human males were in them. Lawrence decided not to say anything over the visidatacom about them.

Stewart and the other men had the top hatches of the carryalls open and were standing up in the hatches so that they could see where they were going. Everyone was so thrilled to leave the claustrophobic confines of the cave for the open country. Everything looked much the same as it did before. However, having been liberated from the cave, it seemed as if they were looking at it for the first time.

They went down river about one-half mile to where they could drive onto the riverbed and cross. To Stewart the river looked the same as before. He looked down river to see the highway bridge. He then looked up river to see the railroad trestle. Neither the highway bridge nor the railroad trestle was there. He had expected to see them, but wasn't really surprised when he didn't. After all it had been a long time. Just the same, he had to know what had happened to them. Brigitte was driving the carryall. Stewart ducked down inside to ask her about the bridges. "Brigitte, what happened to the bridges?"

Brigitte glanced quickly back at Stewart. "What bridges?"

Stewart said, "There was a railroad trestle up river and the bridge for US Highway 385 down river."

Brigitte took another quick glance at Stewart. "There has never been a bridge here that I know of. There is no US Highway 385. There's nothing north of the river except wilderness zone."

Stewart just shook his head in wonder, he had no idea what this wilderness zone was. There used to be productive farms and ranches north of here. There were also the oil and gas wells around Borger, Texas. What happened to it? He had to know. "Brigitte, what is this wilderness zone? Isn't there any towns or cities north of here?"

Brigitte nodded. "Yes, up in Colorado there's Pueblo, Colorado Springs and Denver."

Stewart was surprised by Brigitte's answer. "A wilderness zone that large. How can that be? What else is there between those cities and us?"

Brigitte took another quick look at Stewart. "Nothing, just wilderness."

Stewart just stood back up in the hatch, and rested his elbows on the edge of the roof hatch and looked around. With the world population in the billions; how could they afford to abandon such vast tracks of land, to let it go back to wilderness? They must have made marvelous advances in agriculture, animal husbandry, engineering and manufacturing to be able to have such wilderness zones. Stewart knew that he was going to have to look into this wilderness zone more, but not now. He relaxed to enjoy the ride.

They drove out of the riverbed onto the south bank. They retraced their track back through the tamarack thicket, then turned southwest. They crossed the flood plain and climbed the first hill. Stewart could see that they were heading in the direction of Adrian, Texas. Stewart and the rest of the men kept looking about. It was true that you could never go home again, home no longer existed. At least the countryside hadn't changed.

Ben and Sean were next to each other leaning on the lip of the hatch, looking about and talking with each other. They were about the same age, and it appeared that a friendship had started to develop between them. Sean, as the youngest of the drovers, seemed to have the least problem in finding common ground to begin a friendship with the men. Stewart turned his attention elsewhere and watched Lawrence as she rode her ATV ahead of everyone else. She was a fascinating woman, so independent and self-assured, a natural leader. She, like all the other drovers dressed in work clothing that, although comfortable and functional, didn't give much regard to style; despite this in appearance she was very feminine. Stewart could even imagine that with make-up and in a dress, she would be a really beautiful woman. As for acting feminine, he doubted that any of the women even knew what it meant. They were indeed different than the women in his last lifetime.

Up front on her ATV, Lawrence was not so at ease. Since finding the males her whole world had changed. Everything that she had been taught to believe as the truth was now suspect. She wondered what other surprises lay in store for her. She had questions, but no one to give her the answers.

She could not get that male, Stewart Vaughn, out of her mind. Of all the males, he was the one to have the most profound effect on her. She couldn't stop thinking about him. He was inside of her head and she couldn't get rid of him. She couldn't understand it, no matter how much his questions or comments infuriated her, she couldn't turn her back on him. She felt compelled to engage him. She had started to think that the males were not just different physically, but they also thought different from true humans. All she wanted to do now was to get back home so that she could have some time alone to relax. She yearned to be in her shower, to have the hot water to wash over her and carry her doubts and uncertainties away.

Just before noon they drove over a hill and the men got their first look at the Farrow Ranch headquarters. The headquarters complex was located in a broad-flat valley surrounded by low hills. An asphalt road came into the complex from the south. At the end of the road and nearest to them stood a very large barn, surrounded by a series of corrals. Stewart could see horses in some of the corrals. Stewart looked, but couldn't see anyone moving about. He could, however, see some dogs lying about. Two hundred yards south of the barn was the main complex. He could see a water tank, tractor and equipment sheds, an enclosed swimming pool, recreation center and other buildings. Stewart noticed several one-story buildings built of red sandstone, with clay-tiled roofs. Attached to these buildings were large barn like structures. Stewart ducked down inside the carryall to ask Brigitte about the buildings with the strange barn-like structures. "Oh, Brigitte, what are those buildings with the barn-like structures attached?"

Brigitte took a quick glance at what Stewart was pointing to. "Those are the bungalows for those of us that work at the Farrow Ranch. The large barn-like structure is the holograph room." Pointing to one of the bungalows, she said, "That's my bungalow there."

Stewart continued his survey; on the west side of the road from the buildings were four large silos for feed grain and several rectangular haystacks covered with blue plastic weatherproof tarps. South of the silos and haystacks on the west side of the road, was a twenty-acre fenced in square, that had been further subdivided into five-acre squares. These were livestock feed lots. Each one was equipped with feed and water troughs. Stewart had a good look at it. It looked like an efficient operation.

They drove on past the barn to the ranch office; the smallest building, and closest to the road. In front of the office were three vehicles. One, a small, light-orange color, three-wheeled utility vehicle with oversized tires, intended to carry small loads for a short distance. The other two vehicles were really strange two-wheeled vehicles. One, a red color, was just a little larger that a large motorcycle with a fully enclosed body. Stewart could see that it was capable of carrying two riders. The third vehicle, a dark-green color, was larger than the other, with room for four to five occupants; and although having only two wheels, appeared to be a sedan. It was apparent that the vehicle required gyros to maintain stability. Each of the two-wheeled vehicles had two wheels on the sides that were down when the vehicle was not in motion, otherwise they were retracted. They both had very sleek body styles, most likely made of the same strong and light-weight composites and ceramics as the ATV's.

They stopped in front of the office and Lawrence dismounted from her ATV. A large golden retriever ran up to her barking and wagging its tail. Lawrence stroked its coat and scratched it behind the ears. At this time a stout woman, about five and a half feet tall, came out the front door of the office. She was in her mid-forties, with streaks of gray in her hair, that was cut short. She had the same dusky skin and features as the other women. She wore a green-plaid shirt, blue denim skirt, wide brimmed hat and boots. Lawrence spoke briefly to her; then they came up to the carryall. The woman was Jerry Lawton, co-owner of the farrow Ranch. After Lawrence had told her that the humans from the cave were males, she had to get a close look at them. She stared into the lead carryall in wide eyed amazement, as if she couldn't believe what her eyes were seeing.

After a few moments she remembered her manners as a host and sent them on to the dining hall for lunch. They drove to the dining hall and went in. On the way, Stewart had a good look around. He saw more of those strange two-wheel vehicles, and two other vehicles that were four-wheeled vans. He had noticed that all these vehicles had wheels that didn't have pneumatic tires. The wheels were of an ingenious design that allowed them to maintain its shape and have a flexible tread without being inflated.

When they entered the dining hall, the ranch cook, Dee Andros, had been waiting for them. She was a heavy-set woman in her early fifties that looked as though she really enjoyed her own cooking. She had gray-streaked short hair, and the same dusky skin and features as the rest of the women. She was a hands-on woman with a joyful personality. She had been told to expect additional people for lunch, but she wasn't prepared for the arrival of the males. At first, she didn't believe that there was such a thing as a male human being. She had to touch them and stroke their beards. Only then did she accept them as real. After that, she couldn't take her eyes off them.

The men were joined right away by Jerry Lawson. Her curiosity being so great that she couldn't stay away. She wanted to meet them, and learn all that she could about them. Lawrence introduced Jerry to each of the men. All during the meal, she spoke to first one, then to the other. By the time the men had finished eating, Jerry had spoken to most of the men, at least briefly.

After lunch, they were taken to the quarters where they would be staying for now. It was a dormitory to house temporary workers. It was a long rectangular single-story building with a communal living and recreation room at one end of the building. A hall ran from the living room down the center of the building to the back door. The first door to the left was as you went down the hall was a communal bathroom. The rest of the doors opened into private bedrooms. The bedrooms were small, but well furnished. Each had a single bed, two comfortable chairs, a small table and a video wall, with entertainment console. All the men were pleased with the accommodations.

Shortly after Stewart had settled in his room, there came a knock at the door. "Come in."

The door opened and Lawrence entered the room with Jerry. Jerry had with her a bottle of wine and three glasses. Stewart welcomed them, and had them take the chairs, while he sat on the bed. Jerry opened the bottle and poured everyone a glass of wine. Stewart took a sip; it was a very good sherry wine. He got as comfortable as he could on the edge of the bed and rolled the stem of the glass between thumb and fingers. He could see that Lawrence was watching him closely.

Jerry opened the conversation. "As I see it, the first thing we need to do is get clothing made for all of you."

Stewart glanced down at his state of undress. "Yes, we do need clothing. We thank you for the robes, but they're not really adequate to cover our nakedness for modesties sake."

As casual as Stewart's statement seemed, it really brought a fact to Jerry's attention. Human nudity had never been an issue before. In a world with only a single gender, it just didn't matter. She would have to talk to the other humans about this. They were going to have to modify their behavior around the males, so as not to offend them. Jerry Continued, "We have a tailoring machine that can reproduce any standard pattern, or copy any item of clothing once it's disassembled and the parts are scanned into the Visidatacom. With pattern adjustments to allow for your body measurements, we can make any item of clothing in just a few minutes. We can make you shorts, shirts, trousers, skirts…"

Stewart interrupted her. "Wait just a minute! I think that I need to explain something to you about clothing. Although men and women both wear shorts and trousers, they are cut and styled differently. For starters, women's shirts, blouses and coats close right over left. Men's shirts and coats close left over right. Also, I have noticed that your trousers have no front opening. Men's trousers require a front opening, or as we call it, a fly. Now skirts and dresses are strictly women's clothing. Men don't wear them."

Lawrence shook her head. Here we go again. Males and true humans, or as he calls us, women, have different titles; and now he's saying that men wear different clothing. This is all just silly. Lawrence wanted to speak out and tell this male how silly this all was, but she didn't want to embarrass Jerry.

Jerry then recommended an alternative, "We could go back and get some of your clothing and reproduce them, but you need something right now. I thinking that sweat suits would be good for now."

Stewart took another sip of wine, then put his glass down on the table. "Yes, sweat suits sounds just fine; they're one item of clothing that will fit men and women equally well. It will do until we can retrieve some of our clothing. We can get them when we go back to bury our dead."

Jerry was glad that they had settled the clothing issue for now. She now thought of foot wear for the males. "As for boots, I don't think that we would be able to find any large enough to fit you. However, we do have some fine leathers here on the ranch that you could use to make sandals and moccasins. That's about the best that we can do for now."

"That'll be just fine." Stewart said, "I would like to thank you for all the help that you have been so far."

Jerry smiled. "Okay, we can have the sweat suits ready for you by dinner. I'll have the leather sent over to you, along with everything that you will need to make footwear for yourself."

Now that they had the business out of the way, Jerry wanted to hear of the things that Stewart had told Lawrence. "Stewart, Lawrence has told me that there are certain titles that you and the other males go by."

Stewart wondered how many times he would have to go over this. "Yes, that's true. During our time men were addressed as Mister. We are all addressed as that, except for Ernst Nichols. He's a doctor, so he's addressed as Doctor Nichols."

"Yes," Jerry said, "we do have persons that have titles that are professional, political, religious, police or military. Most of us, however, just have our names, we need no titles."

Stewart went over the different titles again for Jerry's benefit. After the titles, he went on to other differences. "Now, different titles and different dress wasn't the only thing. There was what was called a feminine mystique; what I mean is that women went out of their way to display their differences from men. One was clothing. A lot of their clothing was utilitarian, but they also had clothing that flattered and emphasized the female figure, some of it was even provocative. It was meant to attract a man. Hair was another way to that women displayed their femininity. The hair was thought to be the woman's glory. They wore their hair very long, much longer than the men wore there's. Some of women's hair was down their back as far as their waist. Some women would even wear their hair in elaborate styles. Women also wore cosmetics to enhance their beauty. To be feminine was to be demure and a little mysterious; at least that was men's idea of femininity."

Lawrence had been listening closely to Stewart and thought that it was ridiculous that humans should behave that way. No way would she ever behave like that, or display herself to males in a manner as Stewart suggested. She regarded Stewart with a confrontational look. "That's the most ridiculous thing that I have ever heard. Why would a human ever want to act like that and display herself to a male? Now I imagine that you are going to tell us that there was also a masculine mystique."

Stewart looked at both Lawrence and Jerry, but his remarks were mostly for the benefit of Lawrence. "Yes, there was, but

I would not call it a mystique. It was an accepted belief that women were more complex than men. Men were seen as being more open and straight forward as women; in other words, with men, what you saw was what you got."

"What do you mean by that?" Jerry said.

Stewart took a sip of wine, then put the glass down on the table, before he answered, "What I mean is that was just the perception, not necessarily the truth. Like the perception that in a relationship that it was the man who always pursued the woman. In reality women were just as aggressive going after a man, but their tactics were subtler. Men and women had different roles in the relationship called marriage. The woman's role was to nurture and to be the primary care giver for the children. The man's role was to go out and work to provide for the well-being and a safe and secure environment for the family."

Lawrence had been listening and heard the custom of marriage mentioned again. This intrigued her. She wanted to know more. "This custom of marriage, can you explain that?"

Stewart smiled at Lawrence, wondering just how far he could go in explaining marriage before irritating her. "Okay, marriage was a religious and legal union of one man and one woman for life, for the purpose of procreation and to form the family unit for the children to be raised in. Marriage was the most important of all human institutions. That was the reason why it was given legal sanctions that no other institutions had.

"Let me explain it to you this way. Now, everyone knows of the bond of love that exist between parent and child, and that it lasts a lifetime. Well, when a man and woman leave home, fall in love and marry, they create a bond of love between themselves that is stronger than that between parent and child. They become as one."

Jerry found all this talk about marriage interesting. "Stewart, were you ever married?"

Stewart shook his head. "No, I was never married. By my time the institution of marriage had been abolished."

"Why was that?" Jerry said.

"Well," Stewart said, "in my time there were so few men that we had to share ourselves with many women. We couldn't be exclusive to only one woman."

Lawrence found all this talk about how humans behaved rather bewildering. It seemed to her this idea of displaying one's self for the benefit of a male to be a distraction for no good reason. Even if she thought it all nonsense it still intrigued her. "You said about how humans in your time used clothing and cosmetics to enhance the difference in their gender, and make themselves more attractive to the other gender. Did the males also do that?"

Stewart had to stifle a laugh at the thought of men dressing provocatively and using make-up. "As for cosmetics, men didn't use them. With men's clothing, what was most emphasized was the shoulders, which were sometimes padded. Some men would spend long hours in the gym building their muscles."

Jerry paid close attention to everything that Stewart said. With all this talk about family unit and children, she was curious about procreation; Lawrence not having time to tell her everything that she had learned from Stewart. "You talk about the family unit and children. How did you procreate?"

Stewart got a big grin on his face. He was glad to have the question asked. He realized that this would be one subject that would need a lot of explaining. "Well, we procreated by sexual intercourse."

Jerry was shocked by the answer. Lawrence already knew the answer and only felt uneasy about it. Jerry said, "You mean that you copulated like animals?"

Stewart could see that the women were having a hard time dealing with this, but he felt that it had to come out, and the sooner the better. "That's exactly what I mean; and we did it not just for procreation, but also for pleasure. Now I know what you're thinking, but it wasn't like that at all. If a man took a woman and had intercourse with her, thinking only of his own pleasure and getting his genes into the next generation without thought of the woman's needs or pleasures, then it was no more than animal copulation. However, when a man and woman have love and respect for each other and they care as much for the other's needs and pleasures as they do for their own, it can be a beautiful and pleasurable experience for both. That is why we call it making love. It's part of the bonding process between husband and wife."

"What is a husband and wife?' Jerry said.

Stewart said, "In marriage the man is referred to as the husband, the woman as the wife."

Lawrence felt uneasy every time that Stewart spoke of human copulation, and wanted to get off the topic. "Stewart, there were two words that you used yesterday. They were maiden and virgin. What do they mean?"

Stewart looked at Lawrence. "Well, maiden is a girl, or a young woman, and a virgin is a woman who has never has sexual intercourse with a man." Stewart grinned, "Right now that's the whole human race."

Jerry and Lawrence felt the flush of heat from a blush in their cheeks. All this talk about male/female sexuality was still uncomfortable for them. The very thought of humans having sex was stressful. Jerry said, "Even with your explanation of the subject, this is hard for us to understand. True humans don't reproduce sexually, like animals. It's a medical procedure. You and your friends are something that shouldn't be. All true humans are female; they are made in the image of God. Now the question is, how did you come to be, and where did you come from?"

Stewart took a sip of wine and regarded the two women in front of him. To Stewart it seemed an odd question to ask. How could they be ignorant of men? Perhaps the fact of the male demise had been covered up by their history. "Okay, if you have some time to listen, I have a story to tell."

Jerry nodded. "Yes, we have the time. We would like to hear your story."

Stewart started out by giving them a description of how it had been in his time, and the reason for them being in the cave. He ended up by telling them why they made the decision to enter cryogenic sleep in February 2082.

When Stewart had finished, Jerry said, "The conditions that you speak of no longer exist. There are no longer any males in detention camps. There are no male humans in the world, except for you and your friends. Now, you can do what you want and we feel obligated to help you. However, bear this in mind. You and your friends are an abnormality, outside of everyone's experience. If you just show up on the street in Amarillo, you'll at least cause a riot."

Stewart nodded. "Yes, I understand what you're saying; and we're not ready to go out in the world yet. As you can see, we don't even have the clothes on our backs."

Jerry now had a proposal. "Stewart, this brings us to my proposal. I propose that all of you stay with us here at the ranch for now. We won't tell anyone of your existence. You and the other males have a lot of catching up to do. I don't think that you should try to integrate yourselves into our culture until you understand it."

Stewart nodded, pleased that they for now had a safe haven. "I understand and agree with you. I'm sure that I speak for all of us when I say that we would like to stay here; and that we'll do anything to earn our keep."

Jerry smiled, relieved that they had reached an agreement. "That's good, we want to do everything we can for you."

Stewart said, 'Good, now there are some things that will make things more harmonious. Everyone should start thinking in gender specific terms. The first thing you can do is instead of saying the words male and human, you can start using the terms man or men and woman or women."

Lawrence had gotten tired of all this, and it had started to wear on her patience. This gender specific talk annoyed her. "Okay, now we have titles and clothes that are gender specific. What else?"

Stewart could see that Lawrence was a little irritated by the whole thing. He decided to take it a little further to see how she would react. "Well, for one thing people's names are gender specific."

The mention of names grabbed Jerry and Lawrence's attention. Lawrence said, "This is absurd! A name is just a name, there's nothing gender specific about it!"

Stewart looked at Lawrence and smiled. "You're wrong about that. Most names are either masculine or feminine. There are some names that can be either masculine of feminine. Also, a lot of masculine names have feminine variants. To give you an example, your friend has a feminine name. Your friend Henry has a masculine name,"

Lawrence cut in, "It's masculine? I don't believe any of this!"

Stewart continued, "Yes, it is. There's a feminine variant to Henry, it's Henrietta." Stewart pointed to Jerry. "Now your name can be either masculine or feminine." He pointed to Lawrence. "You have a masculine name."

Lawrence almost jumped to her feet. "What, my name isn't masculine! There's no masculine or feminine difference in names!"

Stewart said. The feminine variant of your name is Laurel. Laura is also used quite often as a variant for Lawrence."

Jerry could see that Lawrence was almost out of control. She decided that the time had come to go. They could talk about other things later. She assured Stewart that they would have the men clothing by dinner time. They then took their leave and departed.

As Lawrence approached her bungalow, she said, "Door open." The bungalow visidatacom recognized her voice and the door slid silently to the side. Her golden retriever, Mansfield, followed her inside and took her accustomed place on the carpet in the center of the living room. Lawrence was glad to be back in her private quarters. She ordered the visidatacom unit to display in the background a tropical shoreline, with waves lapping on a sandy beach on the video wall, the sound of surf, the smell of a tropical island and soft music in the background.

Lawrence's bungalow was typical of the domicile of the average person. The rooms were large and lavishly appointed with fine woods, fabrics, carpets and furnishings. There were systems to take care of all cleaning, to include laundry. The visidatacom unit handled all domestic chores.

Lawrence got undressed, threw her dirty clothing into the receptacle to have them cleaned and sanitized for their next use and stepped into the shower. The spray of hot water felt good on her skin. It was great to wash away the dirt and fatigue after such a long time. She had been out in the bush for over a week, and a shower was way overdue.

As she stood in the shower with the water running over her body, she thought of Stewart. She had always been such a self-assured person. However, every time she was with him, she became confused. He had a way to get inside her psyche with his disarming smile and quick wit. She knew that for her own piece-of-mind she should avoid him, but she couldn't bring herself to do that.

She had really been disturbed by what he had told about what had happened to the males, or men as she would have to start thinking of them as, in the past. She still found it hard to believe that women could have deceived men to get control of them, and put them in camps. If that were true, then women were guilty of a grievous wrong done to men. She knew that she had nothing to do with it, but she still felt guilty that it had been done in her name. She wondered if this wrong could ever be addressed.

After her shower, she stood in front of the mirror wall in her bathroom toweling dry. She did a critical appraisal of her body. She hadn't done that since she had been in puberty and becoming an adult. She didn't know why she needed to do it. She ran her fingers through her hair and wondered how she would look if she let her hair grow long.

After the shower, she put on a red silk caftan with buff trim, embroidery, sash and red velvet slippers. She made herself a drink, then sat in her favorite chair. Mansfield came up and put her head in Lawrence's lap. Lawrence stroked her head and scratched her behind the ears. "Mansfield, are males as much a bother to you as they are to us?" The dog looked to her as if trying to understand her words. "No, I guess not."

Lawrence thought about the men. Ever since they found the men, her life had been turned upside down. They were exotic creatures with their pale skin, facial and body hair and other oddities. She would like to ignore them, but she couldn't, especially the tall one, Stewart. When the sun shone through his head and facial hair, it shown a reddish-brown, or chestnut color; and those eyes, they were the color of a clear-blue winter sky. All that she had ever seen was dark eyes like her own. She couldn't keep from looking at them. She had always been so self-assured, but now every time she got around him, she had to struggle to keep her composure. She had started to have feelings that she had never had before, and she didn't know what they meant. That youthful anxiety that she had learned to control so well had come back stronger than ever, and she didn't know what to do about it.

XVI

SECRET KEPT

After breakfast the next morning, they loaded into one of the carryalls and started out for the bluffs. Stewart took with him Dr. Nichols, Clifford Johnson, Carlos Valenzuela and Theodore Conway. Nancy drove the carryall. Lawrence and Henry were leading the way on their ATV's. They followed the same route back and arrived at the bluffs before 11:00 AM.

They got to work right away hauling the bodies up to the top of the bluff by rope. It took about two hours to dig the graves and bury the bodies. They then had a graveside service.

After the service, they went back to the cave and brought up Sherry's time capsule. Stewart and the other men went through the storage containers and brought them out of the cave. When the time capsule and storage containers were loaded into the carryall, there was too little room for the men. Two of the men would have to ride double with Henry and Lawrence on their ATV's. Henry rode with Henry while Stewart rode with Lawrence.

When they started back, Stewart rode tandem behind Lawrence on her ATV. Lawrence felt the closeness of him, the strength of his arms around her waist, and his breath on her hair and the back of her neck. It was almost more than she could stand. Every nerve in her body went into overload. Her skin tingled when his thighs, or any other part of his body touched hers. She tried to resist, but couldn't help the feelings that she experienced when Stewart was so close to her. She had a feeling of excitement from his arms about her waist. She had never had these feelings before from another's closeness. She was emotionally confused. Each breath of his on her hair, or the back of her neck sent a charge racing down her spine. She wondered why Stewart had such an effect on her. She had never heard of any person having an effect on another person like this. There must be something wrong with her? Perhaps it had been a mistake to let Stewart ride with her. Maybe she should have taken one of the other men, but she didn't know if they would have the same effect on her.

Riding on the back of the ATV behind Lawrence was also having an effect on Stewart. The warmth of her body, the scent of her hair and the feel of his arms around her waist were also stirring up feelings of passion in him. Her exotic beauty and independent spirit were a mixture that intrigued and piqued his interest. Having the experience of other relationships, he could tell that he was having a profound effect on her, and that she found the effect confusing.

After a while Lawrence had been able to bring her emotions under control. She had begun to find the closeness of Stewart to be a pleasurable experience. She had become more at ease with him now, and they had started to converse with each other. They spoke about themselves and found that they had some things in common, like music, hunting, guns, horses and other things. Stewart told her about his .44 cal. Magnum revolver. Lawrence was very interested in it. She had heard of some revolvers in museums, but she had never seen one. He agreed to bring it over to her bungalow so that she could see it. By the time they got back to the ranch headquarters, they were starting to become good friends. She had started to get used to the closeness of him and enjoyed it.

When they arrived at the ranch headquarters, they first unloaded the time capsule at the ranch office. They then unloaded everything else at the men's quarters. Then everyone went to dinner.

After dinner, Lawrence and Stewart went back to the office. Lawrence was very interested in Sherry's time capsule. The package had been placed in one of the back rooms. They unpacked it and found the computer discs had been packed and preserved well. All seemed to be in good working order. After assuring that the power supply was compatible. Stewart showed Lawrence how to set up and operate the computer. At first, she found it most difficult to operate; being used to the visidatacon unit that you only had to give voice commands to. All the discs were arranged by subjects, like art, music, classic cinema, history, the Bible and other subjects. They found a catalog of the discs. Lawrence liked music, so they started out with music.

When Lawrence returned to her bungalow, her golden retriever Mansfield followed her inside. Mansfield took her accustomed place on the carpet. Lawrence ordered the visidatacom unit to make coffee for one. After the coffee; she went to take a shower.

After the shower, she dressed in a silk cobalt-blue caftan with lime-green trim, embroidery, sash and matching cobalt-blue slippers. She then sat in her favorite chair and ordered the visidatacom unit to mix her favorite drink. She then ordered it to display a mountain meadow with wild flowers on the video wall; and also, with the fragrance of wild flowers and mood uplifting music in the background.

Mansfield came up and put her head in Lawrence's lap. Lawrence stroked her head and scratched her behind the ears. Mansfield was a loyal pet and Lawrence loved her. In a society where most members led a solitary life style, pets were important as companions to relieve the loneliness. Nancy had a large male gray Prussian cat named Smoky; and a large aquarium full of fish. Jerry loved birds and had several pair of parakeets and a parrot. Henry had a beagle named homer and a calico cat named Snooker. All the women had a dog or cat or both.

Lawrence sat there stroking Mansfield, while she listened to the music, but her mind was on Stewart. She seemed to be thinking about him all the time. Even when she tried, she couldn't stop thinking about him. She had no idea where it would end. The idea of human males and females copulating was no longer upsetting to her, just strange. She now toyed with the idea of copulating with Stewart, or as he said, making love. How would a man and woman do it? Do they do it like the horses, dogs, or other animals do it? She tried to imagine herself on all fours with Stewart mounting her from behind. She didn't know rather she should laugh or grimace. Perhaps if she got the right time, and could manage to have the nerve to, she might ask him how a man and woman do it. The subject was embarrassing to her, but she had to know.

After Lawrence finished her drink, she decided to go into the holograph room and watch a recording of a concert. Perhaps that would take her mind off Stewart for a while.

The next morning, they started making patterns for new clothing. They took the old clothing apart and laid them out on the grid table, then scanned the parts into the visidatacom unit. They instructed the visidatacom unit as to how the parts were to be assembled. They then selected the fabric and loaded the bolts into the machine; the machine did the rest. In two days the men had at least three changes of clothing, to include underwear.

With the various grades of leather, they were able to make new belts, sandals and moccasins. The women had some hats that were the right size for some of the men. Jerry offered to get hats for the others the next time she went into Amarillo.

Now that everyone had proper clothing, the men could take part in the work at the ranch. Stewart would be especially useful with his training in agriculture. The ranch had a small dispensary in the office building. It had been stocked with medical remedies for minor aches and pains, colds, coughs, sore throats and other common ailments. There were all kinds of bandages, splints, tourniquets and the material to make casts. There was also a diagnostic machine for use by non-medical personnel in remount areas where medical care wasn't readily available. It could be used to run urinalysis and blood tests. Dr. Nichols took the job of ranch physician. The rest of the men helped out according to their own talents.

Four days after the men returned from the burial, the other co-owner, Robert Edison, and the rest of the drovers, Crystal Laster, Carl Seabolt, Jeff Tarver and Sandra Emory returned. They had brought a herd in from the west range to be fattened up in the feed lots before being shipped to market. After herding the cattle into the feed lots, they headed for the ranch office.

The first of the men that they encountered was Benjamin Weaver. He was in front of the ranch office as they rode in on their ATV's. At first sight what they saw was a somewhat odd-looking stranger with pale skin and a strange style of clothing. They had no idea that they were looking at a male human being. Then Douglas Hamilton came out of the office. He was a large muscular man of just over six-feet tall, with blonde hair and beard and gray eyes. His effect on the drovers was profound. As surprised as they were, it still hadn't dawned on them just who or what these people were. Sean then came out of the office. When she told Robert Edison and the drovers that the two strangers were human males, their first reaction was disbelief, to be replaced by amazement and intense curiosity.

They had been aware before they left on the roundup that cryogenic units had been found, but they had no idea what was in them. Robert could tell that her drovers were so interested in the men, that it would be hard to get much more work out of them today. Some of the men went with them to put out feed for the cattle, so that the drovers would take care of it.

That evening at dinner, introductions were made all around and the newly arrived drovers were cautioned not to talk about the men to anyone outside the ranch for now. That was just fine with everyone.

They wanted to get to know the men first; and would just as soon not have people nosing around the ranch getting in the way.

Aside from the fact that there were now men at the ranch, Lawrence had noticed other changes. Some of her co-workers, who used to not pay too much attention to their appearance, were dressing better now and paying more attention to their grooming. Some of the women had even decided that they needed to add to their wardrobes. The tailoring machine was kept busy. Jerry would have to replenish her stocks of cloth earlier than expected.

Lawrence had become aware that she had started to spend more time in front of the mirror each morning. She would even spend time some mornings before getting dressed in front of the mirror wall in the bathroom looking at her body and thinking what Stewart would think about it. Would he find her as desirable as the women of his century? After some consideration she decided not to cut her hair anymore. She had found herself thinking before she put anything on if Stewart would like it. She knew it was silly, but it seemed to be an unconscious act on her part. She thought to herself that she had to end this nonsense and get herself under control. But she couldn't bring herself to do it.

She started to notice other things; like wherever Benjamin was, Sean would usually be close at hand. Where you found Thomas, you were likely to find Henry. Even Nancy was acting strange. She always seemed to be close by to give Dr. Nichols a hand when he needed it. Everywhere Lawrence could see the tension between the women and the men. It wasn't a hostile tension, more the opposite. She could also sense it between Stewart and herself. There was some sort of attraction that kept drawing them together. It was a new experience for her, and she wasn't sure what to do about it.

One other thing that had changed was the swimming pool. The women had invited the men to use the swimming pool. However, they had to have bathing suits. Whoever heard of wearing clothing while swimming? It was enough that you now had to be dressed to answer the door, and be clothed whenever you may be seen by someone else, but this was going too far.

As it turned out, the bathing suits were like underwear, but made of different fabrics and in bright colors. Since the men were so sensitive about the issue of nudity, the women decided to make bathing suits for themselves. The men mentioned something called a bikini for women. It had a halter to cover the mammary glands, but if the men didn't cover theirs, then why should they.

By the second week of November the weather had started to get cold. All the men now had warm footwear and gloves. They used a standard work coat pattern in the visidatacom unit, made adjustments for their size, and made themselves coats.

Jerry and Robert were pleased that the men had integrated so well with the women. They were grateful for the help that the men readily gave with the ranch work. The only thing that they had to be careful of was that the men were out of sight when anyone came to the ranch, which wasn't very often. There was a truck from the dairy that came at the same time every day to pick up the milk from their dairy herd for delivery to the dairy in Amarillo. There had also been trucks to pick up the cattle for delivery to the processing plant in Amarillo.

Lawrence and Stewart were spending a lot of time at the computer from the cave. She had become very interested in Stewart's time; and Stewart was very interested in how things were now. What he found out from Lawrence didn't sound good. All the small towns around Amarillo had been abandoned. Everything north of the Canadian River into Oklahoma and Kansas and west into parts of New Mexico and Colorado was a wilderness zone. This wasn't the only wilderness zone. There were wilderness zones all over North and South America, Europe, Asia and Africa. Stewart wanted to know more.

One afternoon, while they were watching a history program on Colonial American history on the computer, Stewart asked, "Lawrence,

I'd like to know how are they able to set up all these wilderness zones?"

Lawrence kept looking at the computer as she said, "It's just that we don't need all the area now, so the government lets it go back to wilderness."

There was something about this wilderness zones that didn't make since to Stewart. How could they afford to just abandon vast tracts of land? "Tell me, what's the population of Amarillo now?"

Lawrence put her index finger to her chin and thought for a few moments. "Let's see, it must be around twenty-eight thousand right now."

Stewart was astounded by this revelation. "What! Twenty-eight thousand you say! When I was living there the population was two-hundred-thirty thousand! What happened?"

Lawrence didn't feel much like talking about it now, but she knew that he was concerned about it. She turned from the computer to face him. "I don't know what happened. It has been about the same size for as long as I have known. Maybe it's a little smaller now."

Stewart didn't want to ask the next question, but he had to. "Do you know what the population of the United States is?"

Lawrence had turned back to the computer, she nodded. "Yes, according to the twenty-three thousand sixty censuses, it was about thirty-seven point four million."

Stewart couldn't believe it. What had happened? In his former life the population of the United States had been close to half a billion. What had happened to cause the crash in the population? He had to know. "Okay, can you tell me what the world population is now?"

Lawrence thought for a while before she answered. "as best I can remember, it's about seven-hundred sixty-million more or less."

This was astounding news for Stewart. Something was very wrong; he needed an answer. "What's wrong? The world population used to be over eight-billion. Aren't women having babies anymore?"

Lawrence had started to feel uncomfortable with this conversation. When she turned to answer him, Stewart could see that she had a remorseful look, and her eyes were starting to tear. "As a matter of fact, no; most women don't have babies anymore. Some of us are blessed by God to be the mothers, but most of us are infertile. I wanted desperately to be a mother, but it wasn't to be. All of us here on the ranch are infertile. The mothers have soft jobs and are supported by the state,"

This was worse than any of his suspicions. What was going on with the human race? Didn't they have a sure method of reproduction? "Okay, can you tell me how many women can have babies?"

Lawrence took a few seconds before she answered, Stewart could see tears starting to run down her cheeks. It must be stressful for her to talk about it. Finally, she said, "It's about eight out of one-hundred. We're all tested when we're sixteen-years-old to see if we can reproduce. Most of us are not blessed. We desperately want to have children; we need them badly. It hurts when you're told that you are infertile."

This was something really big. Stewart would have to talk to Dr. Nichols about this. He could see that the subject made Lawrence very distraught and decided to change the subject. "What are you looking at now?"

Lawrence turned back to the computer, relieved to be talking about something else. She looked at the screen. 'We're still on Colonial history, but I feel like some music." Lawrence hit a few key strokes and the picture on the computer changed.

Stewart looked over her shoulder at it. On the screen was a list of military music. Stewart spotted something on the list and pointed to it. "Say, this is really good."

Lawrence looked at what he was pointing to on the screen. "Edinburgh Tattoo. What's that?"

"A tattoo is a military band parading at sunset. These are Scottish pipers. They are really good."

With the cursor, Lawrence pointed to Edinburgh Tattoo and clicked. A picture came up on the screen of a parade ground in front of the Edinburgh Castle. There were bleachers full of people on both sides of the parade ground. A voice announced, "Ladies and Gentlemen, the Edinburgh Tattoo." There came the shrill of pipes and the tap of drums. The camera showed a band of pipers marching out of the castle gate onto the parade ground.

They watched the parade for a couple of minutes. Then Lawrence pointed to the screen. "Look!"

Stewart looked at the screen, but had no idea what she was pointing at. "What do you want me to see?"

Lawrence kept pointing. "Just look, you said that men didn't wear skirts."

Stewart kept looking at the screen. "Yes, that's right, men don't wear skirts."

Lawrence said in an accusing voice. "Then what are those men wearing?"

So, this is what it's all about. Stewart thought. "Oh, those are kilts, not skirts."

Lawrence turned to face him. The sad face and tears were gone; she was her usual self again. She wasn't going to let him get away with this one. "Well, they look like skirts to me."

"Believe me," Stewart said, "they aren't skirts, they are kilts, there's a difference."

Lawrence said in a condescending voice. "Oh, please, tell me. I want to hear you explain this one."

Stewart let out a sigh. "Okay, for one thing, a kilt is made from a tartan."

Lawrence knew what a tartan was, but didn't know what it had to do with it. "Yes, I know what a tartan is. Now what does it have to do with it?"

Stewart said, "Well, each Scottish and Irish clan have their own tartan. Also, Each Scottish or Irish military unit have their own tartan. The kilt is also made to a traditional pattern. The kilt closes different than a lady's skirt. The lady's skirt closes from right to left. The kilt closes from left to right."

Lawrence gave Stewart a quizzical look. "What does that mean?"

Stewart chuckled and got a mirthful look. "Well, if a Scotsman or

Irishman wears it it's a kilt. If any other man wears it it's a skirt. Now do you understand?"

She shook her head. It was still confusing to her. "No, I don't but I'll try to figure it out."

They were now facing each other just a few inches apart, looking into each other's eyes. Stewart saw her confident look, her dark-flashing eyes and full-soft lips. He could smell the fragrance of her hair and see her breast rise and fall as she breathed. He was suddenly overcome with an urge to have her. He swept her into his arms, held her close and kissed her on the lips long and passionately. At first, she didn't resist, nor did she encourage him; then her lips parted and she gave herself to him. When the kiss was over, they remained in a loose embrace for a few seconds looking into each other's eyes.

Suddenly Lawrence broke from Stewart's embrace and ran from the room. Stewart just watched her go. He wondered if he had acted too quickly. She was an enigma, a feminine being that had not yet become aware of her own sexuality. He would just have to give her more time.

Lawrence went directly to her bungalow. She needed the security of her own space. Her mind and emotions were in turmoil. Stewart's attention to her had been unexpected. Lawrence knew what a kiss was. A mother kissed her daughter, friends kissed each other, but a kiss like this was a kiss like she had never experienced before. It had lit a fire in her and melted her resistance to him. She liked it, but were women supposed to behave like this with a man? What was she supposed to do? For the first time in her life Lawrence didn't know what to do, and had no one to ask.

Lawrence became very agitated and started to pace her living room. Mansfield moved to the corner of the living room to stay out of her way. Lawrence was having a hard time coming to grips with Stewart's recent attentions towards her. She struggled with this new development in her life. She was forced to face everything to try and see the truth in it.

After a while, Lawrence came to the conclusion that the pacing didn't help. She decided to take a long shower, which usually had the effect of calming her down. Once in the shower, she turned on the water and just stood under the shower head letting the hot water wash over her body. After a while the effect of the hot water melted the tenseness in her muscles to give her that relaxed feeling of warmth, but did nothing for the turmoil in her mind.

After the shower, Lawrence dressed in a turquoise caftan with silver-gray trim, embroidery and sash and turquoise velvet slippers. She sat in her favorite chair in the living room and tried to ease the turmoil in her mind with a glass of burgundy wine. After a few minutes the wine wasn't working either. Lawrence went into the holographic room, sat in the chair and had the visidatacom unit project a clear-sparkling pool in a narrow canyon, flanked by red sandstone cliffs, fed by a small waterfall and shaded by trees. When she was satisfied, she had the visidatacom unit place a call to her mother in Amarillo. In less than two minutes a likeness of her mother, wearing a scarlet-red silk caftan with black trim, embroidery, sash and sitting in a chair appeared in front of her. Despite the graying at the temples and a sprinkling of gray through her raven hair, Lawrence's mother at forty-nine years was youthful looking, with the same tall-slender figure as her daughter.

"Hello, Lawrence, it's so good of you to call." Lawrence's mother could see by the look on her daughter's face and her posture that something troubled her. "Lawrence, what's wrong?"

Lawrence tried to lie, but wasn't very good at it with her mother. "Oh, there's nothing wrong, Mom. I was just feeling a little low and decided that a talk with you could cheer me up."

Lawrence's mother could tell that whatever bothered her daughter, she didn't want to talk about it. "Okay, Lawrence, well I see that you're looking well. Last time that you called, you told me that you were going out to check the livestock along the river."

Lawrence started to pull nervously at the fringe of her sash. Her mother picked up on it right away, and thought, something must have happened during that trip along the river. How was the trip anyway?"

Lawrence continued to pull nervously at the fringe of her sash. "Well, Mom, it was a good trip. We found and killed a predator that had been killing our stock. We tracked it down and killed it. It was a large male cougar."

Her mother wondered if something on the trip was troubling Lawrence. "How did it go? Did anything happen that I should know about?"

"No, Mom, Lawrence said, "other than tracking down and killing the cougar, it was a normal check of our northern boundary."

Lawrence's mother kept watching her. She was still pulling nervously at the fringe of her sash. There had to be something bothering her. Her mother decided to try again to find out what it was. "Lawrence, I know that something is bothering you. What is it?"

Lawrence knew that she needed to change the subject. "Oh, Mom, it's nothing to be concerned about; I just can't talk about it now. By the way, how is Rose, Cathy and Cornelius doing?"

"Your sisters are doing well." Her mother said, "They wonder when you'll be coming home to visit."

Lawrence knew that it had been a mistake to call her mother. It had done nothing to resolve her dilemma; and she ran the risk of saying something that would betray the men. "I know that I haven't been in Amarillo much lately. We've been really busy here and I just haven't had the time. I will try to get home soon to visit. Say hello to Rose, Cathy and Cornelius for me. I have to go now, Mom, I love you."

"I love you." Her mother said. They waved at each other as her mother's image faded.

Finally, Lawrence decided that she needed to talk to someone. She called Nancy and asked if she could come over. She then left her bungalow and walked the short distance to Nancy's bungalow.

Nancy waited for Lawrence at the door. Nancy was dressed in a silk lounging pajama of a floral print in pink, rose and pine-green on a yellow background and yellow slippers. Nancy invited Lawrence in and served drinks. They then sat in Nancy's living room to talk. "oh,

Nancy, something has just occurred with Stewart that has changed our relationship, and I needed someone to talk to about it."

Nancy put down her drink on the end table, and gave her full attention to Lawrence. "You know that I'm your best friend. You can tell me anything."

Lawrence looked at Nancy and said in a low-hesitant voice. 'Well, Stewart just kissed me."

Nance's eyebrows came up. "Oh, so he did."

Lawrence continued, "Please, listen. This wasn't like any kiss that I've ever experienced before. It was much more than a friendly kiss."

Suddenly Nancy was very interested and hanging on Lawrence's every word. "Oh, when did this happen?"

Lawrence felt more confidence now. She took a drink from her glass, then put it back down on the table. "It happened this afternoon. It was while we were viewing the computer from the cave. We were watching a military band playing and discussing it; when he just put his arms around me, drew me close to himself and kissed me on the lips."

Nancy was on the edge of her chair now. Kissing on the mouth was the most intimate kiss, usually only between mother and daughter. Everyone else usually just kissed on the cheek. Nancy just had to ask the next question. "How was it to kiss a man?"

Lawrence was glad that Nancy wasn't judgmental, but kept an open mind about it. "It happened so quickly that he was kissing me before I could react to it. When he had me in his embrace and was kissing me, my resistance just melted away. It frightened me, and at the same time it caused a feeling that I've never felt before. I mean strong passions that I'm not sure that I can control. He was in complete control. If I hadn't had run from him right then, I would have done anything he wanted. I think that I would have even copulated with him."

Nancy was momentarily shocked by Lawrence's frankness. She had to ask the next question. "Would you really have copulated with him?"

Lawrence didn't answer right away. She then got up out of her chair, paced in front of her chair a couple of times and sat back down.

"Well, I don't know. I've thought about it; at first the idea of a man entering me was shocking and revolting, but after the shock wore off, the idea begins to intrigue me. I started to imagine how it would be to copulate with a man. Every time that I think of it, a warm flush comes over me and there's a warm feeling deep in my loins. I get a feeling like an itch that you can't scratch, a feeling that just won't go away. As for copulating, I'm not saying no; I just want more time to think about it."

Nancy had a thoughtful look on her face and nodded. " Yes, I know what you mean. I'm having the same thoughts about Ernst. I also have that warm feeling deep in my loins; and that itch that you can't scratch. I have also thought of copulating, or as they prefer to call it 'making love' and it doesn't frighten me. I think at times that I'd like to do it; but how would other people think of me if they knew?"

Lawrence was relieved to know that others were having the same thoughts that she was. If Nancy was having the same thoughts, then Henry, Sean and the others must also be having them. "Nancy, I know that we've always been told that males were subhuman, but I can no longer believe that. After getting to know the men, no one could tell me that they are subhuman. They're as much true humans as we are. I know that a lot of women would see them as subhuman; and to copulate with them would be a base act. If I copulated with Stewart, I'd have to be prepared to deal with it."

Nancy looked at the ceiling for a few seconds thinking, then nodded. "Yes, it's a big step to take."

'Yes, I know," Lawrence said, "but we're infertile anyway. Even if we were to copulate with the men no one need ever know. We can't have children, so what does it matter."

Lawrence felt better now. Nancy and the others were thinking about it and wondering who would be bold enough to be first. They talked more about the men, but the important questions had already been asked.

Knowing what he wanted was not a problem with Stewart. He had never before allowed himself to love a woman. About the closest that he had ever come was with Betty. In his past life there hadn't been any place for love, but now he felt there was, and he loved Lawrence. She could love him; he knew it by the way that she responded to him. He just had to give her a little time. He didn't have a plan for the future yet; he had no idea how they would be received, or how much freedom in their lives that they would be allowed. However, he knew that if he could have his way things would be different than they were before. He knew that whatever happened, he wanted the women at the ranch to be a part of it.

That evening Stewart and Dr. Nichols talked about what Stewart had found out about the worlds declining population from Lawrence. They agreed that they had to learn more about it.

XVII
SLIDE TO EXTINCTION

After talking with Stewart and learning about the startling plunge in the human population worldwide, Dr. Nichols agreed to find out as much as he could about it. The implications of such a dramatic drop in world population was ominous, evening factoring in an expected drop when a population went to a single gender, there was no way that he could account for it. There had to be a reason; he only had to find it.

Nancy had been showing Dr. Nichols how to use the visidatacom unit; and would be willing to let use it to do his research. The operation of the visidatacom unit was simple, most everything could be done with voice commands. Nancy only had to show him how to use it and command it to recognize Dr. Nichols voice as a user. The visidatacom unit was an entertainment center, computer and communicator all in one. It was infinitely more powerful than the computers of his time, and at the same time a lot more user friendly and helpful. The visidatacom units in all of its various models ran modern civilization. They ran the systems of people's homes, buildings, ground and air traffic. They controlled the operation of ships, aircraft and other large land vehicles. The visidatacom units also controlled automated manufacturing processes.

Information on individuals was still confidential, but not population trends and densities. What he found out explained a lot of the questions that had been on his mind. He didn't have all the answers. Some information was closely guarded and could not be accessed. After two days of searching unclassified websites, he had enough to get back with Stewart.

That evening they met in Stewart's room. Stewart had a bottle of brandy that had been a gift from Jerry. He poured glasses for Dr. Nichols and himself, then settled back into their chairs to enjoy the brandy and talk. "Well, Ernst, what have you found out?"

Dr. Nichols took a sip of brandy, put his glass down and shifted forward in his chair. He had a concerned look on his face. "Do I have a story to tell. There are some parts that I don't have, and some parts that I may never have, but here it is as incomplete as it is. To begin with there is no mention in their history of what happened to the men. It's as if men just ceased to exist. Every likeness of men in the world, such as statues, art, pictures, books, even medical reference books, everything was destroyed. I think to get some answers to that question, we'll have to look into secret government or religious records, if any still exist.

"Well, to get back to the story. Their grand experiment of an all-female society seemed to be going just great. Little girls would grow up to become women and have their one girl child. After the expected drop to account for the men, the world population numbers stabilized. Population growth fell to zero and everyone shared in the prosperity. Then about two-hundred thirty years ago a small problem started to develop. Some women had started to have fertility problems. However, as time went by the problem got worse. The number of infertile women rose at an alarming rate. Their experiment in ovum fusion had started to backfire.

"All the governments put a top priority on it and got their scientific communities working on it. They were astounded to learn that the 'Y' chromosome wasn't the only thing that the male contributed to reproduction. There was something else, some essence, that's as good as anything to call it that had remained unknown until it had been removed completely. Ovum fusion worked great for the short term. But over time this essence was lost from the gene pool and women started to build a resistance to this institutional conception method.

"By this time there were no more males. They had completely erased any chance for future men. The population had started to decline. By running the statistics, they found that ovum unions that had the most success was cross-racial unions. By that time, they were getting desperate. Only cross-racial unions were allowed. There was worldwide cooperation. A woman in North America may have her ovum fused with the ovum of a woman in Africa. A woman from South America may have her ovum fused with a woman's ovum in China. The separate gene pools worldwide were being thoroughly mixed. It worked for a while; the declining fertility rate leveled off, then started to show signs of increasing. Everything seemed okay for a couple of generations, then the problem returned. The decline was slow at first, but accelerated. By now the whole human race was one giant homogeneous gene pool. Now human fertility, the birth rate and world populations were all in a nosedive. You said that the world population is now seven-hundred sixty million?"

Stewart nodded. "Yes, that's about it."

Dr. Nichols continued, "Well, as I see it, by the end of the first decade of the next century, the world population will be down to less than three-hundred million. In one-hundred years, or a little more, the human race will be extinct."

This was really bad news for Stewart. It was much worse than he had expected. He just had to ask the question. "Are you sure of this?"

Dr. Nichols looked at Stewart. "I can't put it any more strongly. The percentage of fertile females is between seven and eight percent. Of the women that are fertile, there's still the problem. A small percentage can manage to have five or six children before they start to experience fertility problems. The majority become infertile after two to three children. By the next generation the percentage of fertile females will be down to three percent, or less. As the population falls, they'll reach a point where they can no longer maintain their technology. Then it will be the end."

Stewart sat back and considered what Ernst had just said. "So, that's why all the women look as they do."

Dr. Nichols said, "Yes, actually there's only one human race now; all the human subspecies have been merged into one. Any racial or ethnic group that tried to hold out went into such steep decline that they were no longer viable as a group, and were absorbed by another group. They have played their last card, they're out of options. They're in a slide to extinction that's irreversible. They need a miracle to survive."

Stewart sat back, took a sip of brandy and smiles. "Perhaps we're that miracle."

Dr. Nichols returned the smile and lifted his glass as in a toast. "My words exactly. However, we must be careful. A lot of women will welcome us, but some won't. They now have a very anti-male religious dogma, as you know, in any population you'll have some non-believers, the majority will be lukewarm to religion and some will be true believers. We'll have to be careful."

Stewart now turned retrospective. "I've been giving a lot of thought as to why the women of our century turned against men; and I think that I have the answer."

Dr. Nichols was curious about Stewart's answer. "Okay, what is it?"

Stewart said, "The answer is that love between men and women was lost. It happened when they abolished marriage. We each had to share ourselves with other women. When love was lost between men and women, all that was left was passion and need. The women became frustrated and passion was lost, that left only need. When they no longer needed us, they got rid of us."

Dr. Nichols nodded. "Yes, I see what you mean. What do you suggest that we do about it?"

Stewart took a sip of his brandy before he answered. "I haven't figured that out yet, but one thing I know; I don't want to share myself with several women anymore. I'll help other women as much as I can, but I want a life with only one woman."

Dr. Nichols thought for a moment. "I see your point. Things will have to be different this time around."

Stewart leaned forward in his chair. 'I say that we should have a plan before we make ourselves known to society. Do you agree?"

Dr. Nichols nodded. "Yes, I do. I think that we should talk with the men and see what they have to say. We can also bring the women in on it later on. I'm sure that when the time comes, they'll be with us."

Stewart took another sip of brandy. "Ernst, the women on the ranch say that they are all infertile. Is that just to ovum fusion, or what?"

Dr. Nichols smiled. "Yes, that's true, but only to ovum fusion. As for the natural way, I would say that they're all primed and ready to go. If you get my meaning."

Stewart chuckled. "Yes, I get your meaning, but what about the problem that we had before. Is the environment and food-chain still polluted?"

Dr. Nichols shook his head. "No, they no longer have that problem. They have done an excellent job of cleaning up the environment and food chain. There is no longer the imbalance that we had before. All the other animal species have recovered."

Stewart nodded. "Yes, all but the human race, that's now single gender. What about other areas, how have they progressed in the last two-hundred eighty years?"

Dr. Nichols had been looking into that also, and was ready for Stewart's question. 'In some areas they are rather advanced, like medicine, energy, engineering, metallurgy, composite materials and manufacturing. Their medicine is very advanced. Anyone today can expect to live past one-hundred years, and live in relatively good health. Energy is where they really shine. They now have nuclear fusion. You might say that it's an energy source too cheap to meter. With unlimited energy, they can produce all the hydrogen fuel they need. What petroleum they have is reserved for petrochemicals, medicines and lubricants. All their factories are almost completely automated; and with new building materials and new construction techniques, they can build bigger and better than ever. The minus side, their research, except for new fields and consumer products development, is stagnant. There is still a NASA, but it is just a shadow of its former self. They have given up the manned space flight program. All they do now is launch communication, GPS and weather satellites."

Stewart was impressed by the progress. "It looks like they have done all right on their own."

"True," Dr. Nichols said, "but unless they can solve their declining population problem, all will be lost."

Dr. Nichols stayed with Stewart for a while longer. They talked about what they should do once the secret of their existence was out. They brought up and discussed several ideas, but until they knew societies reaction to them, all they could do was come up with multiple contingency plans.

Dr. Nichols told Stewart about how Nancy was always close by, and always willing to help out any way that she could. He knew that the women were ignorant of and unskilled in the art of courtship. He felt sure that she was just trying to tell him that she was interested in him. He liked having her around, and hoped that they would eventually be a couple.

Lawrence concentrated on her work. She felt that she should stay away from Stewart, but at the same time she wanted to be close to him. She felt pushed one way and pulled the other. She didn't try to avoid him, but she tried not to be alone with him. She wasn't sure yet how this relationship with Stewart would end, but she wanted to maintain control for now.

She was so intrigued by Sherry's computer, that she spent most of her free time on it. She found another subject that had caught her attention. It was called the Holy Bible. She brought it up on the computer. It seemed to be a series of books arranged in two parts, the Old Testament and the New Testament.

She started out at what appeared to be the beginning. A book called Genesis, the same as in their testament. She started to read, but soon found that it was extremely hard to read. Although it had been written in English, it was a very old text. Some of the words had changed meanings and some she had never seen before. After a while, she quit trying to understand it on her own, and went to Stewart for help. He went back to the computer with her to try to help her.

Stewart looked at what she had on the computer, and said, "You're right, this is a very old text. It's the King James version. The text is over eight-hundred years old."

The word king was strange to Lawrence. "Stewart, what is a king?"

The question surprised him. How could they not know what a king was? They must have wiped out all history of men from the history books, or attributed it to women. "A king was a male hereditary leader of a nation who ruled with absolute authority for life and usually passed on his title to his son."

The idea of kings intrigued her. "Did they have kings in your time?"

Stewart shook his head. "No, they didn't. By my time all kings and queens had been replaced by democratic governments."

What is a queen?" Lawrence asked.

Stewart took a moment to determine how he was going to answer it. "Well, a queen is like a king, except for being a woman. Most queens were the wives of a king. However, if a king died without a male heir; his oldest daughter becomes queen. She then rules in her own right, as a king would."

Lawrence would like to know more about kings and queens, but not now. They turned back to the computer and started to review Genesis. They got through the first part of the creation story without trouble. When they got to the part about Adam and Eve, Lawrence had questions. "According to our testament Adam was still was one of the two mothers, and they were created together at the same time. Now, in the Bible, it says that Adam was created first and that he was a man. Then god took a rib from him to make a woman for him, and that was eve."

Stewart looked at her posture, the set of her jaw and the glint in her eyes. He could see where this was going. He decided that it would be the wrong move to get defensive and start to defend the Bible against her. He had to be flexible. 'Yes, that's what it says. Now I know it doesn't agree with your testament, but let's read on a little farther, then we can talk about it."

This ran counter to what Lawrence had been thought, but she was more interested in learning about this than fighting about it. Since Stewart didn't want a confrontation, she reluctantly held her objections for now, to get back to Adam and Eve. They continued to read. After they got past the part where god drove Adam and eve from the garden of Eden, and they started to live as husband and wife and have children; Lawrence wanted to stop and talk about it. Stewart decided to go ahead and discuss it with her.

Lawrence said, "To get back to Adam and Eve, do you believe that they were made as the Bible said? Adam first as a man, then Eve, made from him as a woman?" She waited for his answer. If he agreed with the Bible literally, she was ready to argue with him.

Stewart knew that a lot depended on what answer he gave. He framed his words in his mind before he spoke. "Now, I'll put it this way. I do believe that God made man and Woman. As for the account in the Bible, that's open to interpretation."

Lawrence was puzzled by his reply. "What do you mean by that?"

Stewart was glad to see that he had headed off an argument. He continued, "What I mean is that you don't take it literally, that it's just symbolic. Now I have a question. What does your book say about Adam and Eve being driven out of the Garden of Eden?"

Lawrence was eager to explain it to him. "Okay, when the first mothers were driven out of the garden of Eden, they had fallen from a state of grace and were cursed to share the earth with subhuman males until they could obtain a state of spiritual maturity. God then banished the subhuman males from the earth."

Stewart could see how the story of creation had been rewritten to promote a certain point of view. He wondered just how many generations it took for them to really believe that. He decided to change directions. If he didn't do something they would be at an impasse. "All right, let's talk about it. Now according to what you have been taught God is a woman. Right?"

Lawrence nodded. "Yes, that's right."

Stewart continued, "Now I was taught that God is a man." Lawrence started to speak, but Stewart raised his hand to silence her. "Now I also believe that that is also open to interpretation. As for me, I see God as a spiritual being, a supreme Being. I see God as transcending all things earthly and physical to include gender. God is just God. Can we agree on that?"

Lawrence thought for a while, then nodded. 'Yes, I can see what you're getting at and I'll compromise with you. We'll see God without gender."

Stewart smiled. Now that they had agreed on this, they could view the Bible without gender bias getting in the way. "good, now if you can see that my book was written with a male point of view and your book was written with a female point of view, then you can read the Bible with a more open mind."

Lawrence could see Stewart's wisdom. She continued to read the Bible with Stewart's help. She found it very interesting. The Bible would be seen by most as blasphemous text. Lawrence didn't think the world was ready for it yet.

The next day Lawrence was back at the computer with Nancy, Crystal and Jeff. The computer had become the most popular past time on the ranch. Lawrence didn't want to read anymore of the Bible for now. She decided to let the other women choose what they would view next.

The other women wanted to see what was under the heading of classic cinema. There was a very long list of titles, some highlighted. Classic cinema had been farther divided into categories like drama, historical drama, mystery, comedy and others. When Sherry had made her selections for the time capsule, she had chosen films from the time when society had still been normal. They were all for the flat screen, no holographs among them.

They went to drama and chose one of the highlighted titles, Friendly Persuasion. It was the story of a family living in the nineteenth century. They found it to be a good story, but what interested them the most were the complex relationships between men and women. They were beginning to understand that men and women had different roles within a family unit and their society. It was also true what the men had told them; men and women did dress differently.

The next title that they chose came from the comedy list. The title was, Pillow Talk. It was set in the twentieth century and was a comic view of human courtship. They found it very interesting.

The next day, Lawrence discussed the cinema stories with Stewart. She had enjoyed the stories; and they had gone a long way in explaining the complexity of relationships between men and women. He tried his best to clear up any questions that Lawrence had. He also suggested some titles to look for.

During the next few days, Lawrence and the other women viewed, Gone With The Wind, The Ten Commandments, Titanic, The Story Of Ruth and a title with her name in it, Lawrence Of Arabia. It was true, Lawrence was a name for a man.

By now the women were thinking in terms of gender roles and things that were gender specific. The knowledge and awareness of their own femininity had started to awaken in them. They weren't the same persons that they were a month ago.

Stewart recommended some more titles for Lawrence and the other women to view. They were really moved by On Golden Pond. Lawrence cried when she watched Doctor Zhivago. Lawrence and the other women were beginning to understand what love between a man and a woman was. They now knew that men and women were meant to share their lives. Lawrence found herself anticipating the next time that Stewart would kiss her. This time she wouldn't run away. If he wanted to as he called it, make love to her, then she would let him. Besides, she now looked forward to it herself.

It was early December now and the weather had become really cold. When they didn't have to work out in the weather, they stayed indoors. Lawrence felt comfortable with Stewart in private again. She sometimes went to his room to visit; and sometimes he came to her bungalow.

One evening, after they had watched, A Summer Place, Lawrence invited Stewart to her bungalow to talk about the story. She couldn't understand why the young couple had been having trouble getting married after the girl became pregnant.

Lawrence and Stewart were sitting on the sofa facing each other. She had dressed in a white terry cloth robe and sat next to him with her feet tucked up under her robe. The tie in the waist sash was loose, giving Stewart a glimpse of smooth thigh under the robe. They were very close and he could smell the scent of her hair and hear her breathing. He saw her breast rise and fall with each breath. He looked into her eyes and could see the longing in them. Her closeness became intoxicating. He wanted her more than ever; he had to have her now. He reached out, took her in his arms, and pulled her to himself. She made no objection, but snuggled comfortably into the hollow of his shoulder. Her eyes were locked with his and her breathing had become rapid. He kissed her on the lips. She tilted her head, closed her eyes and parted her lips. She wasn't holding back; and she didn't want to pull away. They kissed again.

Lawrence was really passionate now and Stewart could see that she wanted him. He picked her up and carried her into the bedroom and lay her on the bed. When he laid her on the bed, her robe fell completely open. She was nude under the robe. He quickly removed the robe and his clothing, then got in bed with her.

He started to kiss her again and to massage her breast. She reacted right away to his touch. She had never felt passion like this before. The way Stewart used his hands just drove her wild. Every place that he touched her it made her tingle. He moved about her with his hands, lips and tongue. What he was doing to her was driving her crazy. His fingers traced soft lines and swirls down her ribs and abdomen. It sent shock waves up and down her body. When he touched her inner thighs, it sent shock waves of pleasure through her like electric shocks. She felt for him and took him in her hand, he felt so big. He kissed her breast and she arched her back. Her legs were open. His hand moved up to her volva. His fingers knew just where to go to find that special spot that was the center of her pleasure. She couldn't help herself, she cried out with pleasure. Her skin was flush and slick with perspiration. Her vagina had become warm and moist; she was ready for him.

Stewart rolled atop of her and between her legs, positioned himself and entered her. There could be no holding back. They both had urgent needs that only the other could meet. Their lovemaking became frenzied, fueled by the fires of passion. They built to a climax and then it was over. They lay on the bed in each other's arms. Lawrence never in her wildest dreams ever believed that she could feel passion like this.

Stewart slept with her that night, and they made love again. They made love again when they woke up in the morning.

They got dressed and went to breakfast at the dining hall. They were walking arm in arm. Lawrence's world had been transformed; she now knew a love that she had never known before. As soon as they walked through the door, everyone knew that their relationship had changed in a most profound way.

XVIII

A SECRET REVEALED

After breakfast, **Lawrence and Stewart** went to his room, collected his things and took them back to Lawrence's bungalow. Lawrence instructed the visidatacom unit to recognize Stewart as a resident of the bungalow. They were now a couple and had decided that they were going to live together.

That evening, Lawrence entered the holograph room to call her mother. She wore a silk emerald-green caftan with red-orange trim, embroidery, sash and matching emerald-green velvet slippers. She took her seat in the chair and ordered the visidatacom unit to project a sitting room from the Russian Czar's winter palace in St. Petersburg. The room with its elegance, rich colors and gold leaf matched her mood of being the luckiest person alive. Once she had settled into her chair, she ordered the visidatacom unit to place the holograph call to her mother.

In under two minutes the image of Lawrence's mother sitting in her chair materialized in front of her. Her mother wore a pink silk caftan with purple trim, embroidery, sash and matching pink velvet slippers. "Hello, Lawrence, I'm so happy that you called." Lawrence's mother could see immediately that there had been a change in her daughter. She was all aglow, radiating confidence and happiness. What is it,

A SECRET REVEALED

Lawrence? There's something different about you. What is it?"

Lawrence shifted uneasily in her chair. She should have known that her mother would see the change in her. She wanted to start pulling on the fringe of her sash, but that would be a giveaway to her mother that she was becoming uncomfortable about something. "Oh, Mom, you're imagining things. There's nothing different about me. It's just that everything is going just great and I'm in a really upbeat mood."

Lawrence's mother continued to watch her closely. "I still say that you have changed in some way. I don't know what it is; I've never seen you like this before. Okay, I won't push you, it's your business. You can tell me when you're ready." She wondered why Lawrence had started to keep secrets with her. Lawrence had always been so open to her. "Perhaps I can take the time to come out to the ranch to visit you."

That was the last thing that Lawrence wanted, to have her mother visit. "I don't think that's a good idea, Mom. We're very busy right now. I'll have the time later on to come to Amarillo for a visit."

Lawrence's mother could see that Lawrence wasn't going to give any hint as to the secret that she was keeping. Reluctantly she changed the subject to Lawrence's sisters and family matters. Lawrence and her mother spoke for several more minutes, then signed off.

When the transmission had ended, Lawrence sat in her chair for a couple of minutes before leaving the holograph room. She thought that she would have to be more careful with her mother, so as not to give away what was going on at the ranch.

In seemed as if everyone else had been waiting for someone else to be the first. Now that Lawrence and Stewart had taken the lead, others started pairing up as couples. In three days', time, Dr. Nichols had moved in with Nancy, Benjamin with Sean, Thomas with Henry, Carlos with Jeff and Clifford with Brigitte. By the end of a week, Allen Worley and Crystal Laster were living together. Now every woman on the ranch of childbearing age had taken a man to live with.

A week after Stewart moved in, they were relaxing in the living room after dinner. Jerry had come to visit, and had just left. Stewart and Lawrence were sitting on the sofa talking. Lawrence snuggled up next to Stewart and put her head on his shoulder. Ever since they had started living together, she had wanted to tell him how she felt about their relationship. "Oh, Stewart, I'm so happy. I knew what love for your mother was and what for a sister was. However, love for a man was something new for me. Before now I had no way to understand it. I was like a blind person who was trying to understand the beauty of the sun. people could try to describe it to me, and I could feel the warmth of it on my face, but I didn't have the eyes to see the beauty for myself. Now I have the eyes to see, and I'm starting to understand the love between a man and woman. I love you, Stewart."

Stewart embraced her and kissed her passionately. "I love you too, Lawrence. I've never said that to a woman before. I never had this feeling for a woman before." Stewart paused for a moment, "There is however something that I wish we could do something about."

Lawrence wondered what he had in mind. "What's that?"

Stewart looked into her eyes. "please, don't take it the wrong way, but it's your name. You're a very beautiful and sexy woman, a very feminine person with a masculine name."

Lawrence lay back in Stewart's arms. "You said that there's a feminine variant to Lawrence?"

"Yes," Stewart said, "it's Laurel, or in some cases people prefer Laura."

Lawrence thought for a few seconds, then kissed Stewart. "okay, from now on my name is Laura."

Stewart embraced her and kissed her again. "I love you, Laura."

Laura replied, "I love you, Stewart." Soon they were in bed making love again.

The men and women who had formed couples were starting to take on an identity apart from the others. Stewart and Laura were starting to be looked on as the leaders of the group. When Lawrence started calling herself Laura, the other women with masculine names followed her lead. They all took the feminine variant. Henry was now Henrietta; Carl was now Carlotta and Jeff was now Jennifer. Even Robert Edison started calling herself Roberta.

The women were getting used to and learning more about living in a dual gender community. They were learning that not only did men and women wear different styles of clothing, but that clothing could make one's self more attractive to the opposite sex. They were also learning all the things that must be learned when two people of the opposite sex lived together. The women had finally even started to wear a top to their swimming suit at the pool.

On the fourteenth of February they had the heaviest snowfall in over twenty years. They had to keep the dairy cows at the barn and feed them in the dairy lot. With the heavy snow, all they could do was take care of the dairy cows and the horses. That was just fine for Laura. She had not been feeling well lately.

Laura went to the dispensary and talked to Dr. Nichols. When she described her symptoms to him, he had an idea of what she could be suffering from. He gave her a medical examination and asked her a lot of questions, some of them personal. He then got some urine and a few drops of blood from her for testing.

He ran the tests on his diagnostic machine. The machine was easy to operate. It just took a few drops of urine and a couple of drops of blood from a finger prick. The whole test took no more than a few minutes. When the test had been completed, Dr. Nichols had the results displayed on his desk monitor. Everything seemed to be within normal limits, there was, however, one item that had been flagged that attracted Dr. Nichols attention. He was relieved and pleased to know what had been causing Laura's discomfort.

Laura sat across from the desk from Dr. Nichols, and felt relieved to see him smile. Dr. Nichols still smiling, looked up from the desk monitor and winked at her. "Well, what do you want to hear first, the good news. Or the good news?"

Laura giggled. Dr. Nichols demeanor had put her at ease. "Okay, I'll take the good news."

Dr. Nichols had always been pleased to give good news; and this was especially good news for Laura and Stewart. "Although you're experiencing some discomfort now, that's quite natural for someone in your condition. There's nothing for you to worry about. I don't have much to treat you with, but your illness is normal. However, you're going to have to stop using alcohol for a while and go easy on the coffee. No more than two cups a day." By now Laura had become very confused. Dr. Nichols continued, "Now, do you want the really good news?"

Laura sat nervously on the edge of her chair. "Of course, I do. What is it?"

Dr. Nichols reached out and patted the back of Laura's hand. "From what you've told me and from my examination, I'm certain that you're pregnant. You're going to have a child."

This revelation hit Laura with stunning force. She knew that she hadn't had her period when she should have; but she never considered being pregnant, being that she was infertile. There had to be another reason. She just sat there for a minute looking at Dr. Nichols. She wondered if she had heard him right, or if he really knew what he was talking about. As a youth, she had dreamed of being a mother. She had really been crushed when she had been tested and found to be infertile. This was too good to be true. With a voice barely above a whisper, Laura said, 'Dr. Nichols, this is unbelievable. Are you sure?"

With a big grin, Dr. Nichols nodded. "The symptoms that you have described sound like morning sickness, and other changes taking place in your body. Also, my diagnostic test confirms it; you can believe me, you're pregnant." Dr. Nichols had become as excited for Laura as she was for herself. Laura still had trouble believing Dr. Nichols. As much as she wanted it to be true, how could it be? Laura squirmed in her chair, and her palms started to sweat. "But how can I be pregnant,

I'm infertile?"

Dr. Nichols looked at Laura and gave her a reassuring smile. "Oh, lady, you may be infertile for ovum fusion, but not the old fashion way. When you took Stewart's seed into your womb, that's all it took. For sure you are going to have a child, and Stewart is the father."

Laura finally believed him. She became so excited that she wanted to jump up and down and shout. A strange feeling came over her. She put her hand to her belly, as though she could already feel the new life starting to grow inside of her. Her face lit up with a broad smile and tears started to roll down her cheeks. "Can I tell Stewart?"

Dr. Nichols nodded. "Yes, I'm sure that he would be pleased to get the news. Now, after the snow has melted off and the roads are clear, you need to make an appointment with your doctor and get a prenatal checkup."

Laura jumped up from her chair, gave Dr. Nichols a hug and a kiss on the cheek, then rushed to find Stewart and tell him the news. She burst through the office, almost colliding with Roberta who had just entered the office. Laura hugged Roberta exclaiming. I'm going to be a mother!" Lawrence then rushed out the door; leaving a bewildered Roberta in her wake.

Shaking her head in wonder, Roberta went back to the dispensary to find out from Dr. Nichols what the ruckus was about.

Dr. Nichols felt happy for Laura, but at the same time he knew that their secret would soon be out. He would have to get with Stewart and the others to figure out what was best to do.

That evening Laura sat in her chair in the holograph room to call her mother. Laura wore a pale-blue silk caftan with Prussian-blue trim and sash with floral embroidery in pink, red, yellow and green with pale-blue slippers. She had the visidatacom unit display a sunlit garden surrounded by a tall hedge and filled with rose bushes in bloom, flower beds in full bloom and a water fountain as a centerpiece. The air was filled with the sweet scents of roses and other flowers. The faint sound of falling water in the fountains could be heard. She then had the visidatacom unit place the call.

In less than two minutes her mother's likeness sitting in her chair formed in front of Laura. Her mother wore a dark-green silk caftan with golden-yellow trim, embroidery and sash with dark-green velvet slippers. "Hello, Lawrence, it's good to see you." Laura's mother noticed right away that there was something different about her daughter. "Dear, I don't think that I have seen you like this before. What is it?"

Laura fought hard to control her excitement and present a calm demeanor. "Oh, Mom, I may soon have great news, but I can't say anything about it now."

Her mother's interest was piqued. "Great news you say. Why can't you tell us now? Why have you been so secretive lately? You know that I'm concerned for you."

Just as Lawrence was about to speak, the image of a young girl of almost fifteen years entered and stood beside her mother's chair. Her features were similar to that of Laura and her mother. She was still coming into her womanhood, but showed the promise of being tall and slender like her mother and sister. She wore silk floral print lounging pajamas with large white and yellow flowers with green leaves on a red background and red velvet robe and slippers. "Hi, Cornelius." Laura said.

"Hi, Lawrence," Cornelius said, "I just had to say hello to you." Cornelius was really good at reading her sister's moods. "Are you still keeping secrets from Mom?"

Laura was used to her sister's abruptness. "Yes, I do have a secret and it's wonderful, but I can't say anything about it now. There are a few things that have to be taken care of first, but after that I will tell you."

Cornelius pleaded with her sister. "Oh, please, tell us now."

"I'm sorry,' Laura said, "I can't possibly tell you now, but I promise you that I'll let you know as soon as I can. By the way, how would you like to come to visit me at the ranch this summer when school is out?"

Her mother took a few moments to let some expectation build. "Okay, Cornelius, if Lawrence will have you, you can go. Provided that is, that your final school reports are up to where they should be."

Cornelius kissed her mother on the cheek. "oh, thank you, Mom, they will be."

Her mother patted her on the rear. "Now it's time for you to get to bed. You have school tomorrow."

Cornelius said, "Thanks, Lawrence, good-night."

"Good-night, Cornelius." Laura said. Cornelius turned and left the room with a spring in her step. Laura then turned back to her mother. "Nice try, Mom, but even using Cornelius can't get me to reveal the secret prematurely."

"Does it have something to do with the ranch?" Her mother said.

"Yes, Mom, it does." Laura said, "Now, can we talk about something else."

Laura's mother gave up trying to get the secret out of her; and started talking about what everyone in the family had been doing. Her mother figured that the secret had something to do with Lawrence's job; and decided that she would just have to be patient.

When the call ended, Laura just sat in the chair for a while. She had wanted to share the great news with her mother. It had been hard not to, but the stakes were too high to be careless. This would have to be the last call until they went public.

Eight days passed before the roads became clear. By then Dr. Nichols had also confirmed Henrietta and Nancy as also being pregnant. Stewart called a meeting to decide a course of action. It was known that some scientists, despite the objection of the church, worked to try to reintroduce males back into the human population. Dr. Nichols had been checking and believed that the St. Louis Institute of Genetic Research would be their best bet; but how would it be best to make contact with them?

They had to choose a doctor that they thought would help them. They finally decided on Henrietta and Sandra's doctor. She was a young general practitioner, Dr. Vernon Mays, age twenty-seven. She had established her practice in Amarillo just over a year ago. She seemed to be a liberal opened minded person.

They contacted the office of Dr. Mays and were able to get the last three appointments for the coming Friday afternoon. All they said was that they had been having a queasy stomach lately and had been throwing-up, and that they needed to see the doctor.

On the afternoon of the appointment, all three women left the ranch for Amarillo. They were all nervous and a little fearful of what to expect. They had talked it over at length and knew what they were going to say and do. However, there were so many uncertainties that in the inn they just had to hope for the best.

When they arrived at the doctor's office, they were each shown to an examining room where the nurse took their vitals and took blood and urine samples. The nurse then pulled their medical records through the visidatacom unit from the regional medical data bank. She then used some of the samples to run through the physician's desk top auto lab. All three test results had a flag in one item. The nurse checked the auto lab and ran the test again. The results were the same. She decided that a hard copy of the test should be made for the doctor. She also made hard copies of the pertinent parts of the human's medical records. The nurse checked the printouts and highlighted an item on each of them. She then took them to the doctor's office.

When the nurse entered the office, Dr. Mays was taking a coffee break before seeing her last patients of the day. The nurse stepped up to the desk. 'Doctor, you must see this right away before you see your last three patients." She lay the printouts on the desk.

Doctor Mays picked up the printouts and started going through them as she drank her coffee. She noticed right away the highlighted portions. She went through them again shaking her head. "No, this can't be right. Something must be wrong. You need to run them again."

"This is already the second time I've run them." The nurse said.

Dr. Mays looked at her nurse. "Run them again and bring the

results to me."

The nurse left the office, ran the test again and brought them back to the doctor's office. She placed them on the doctor's desk. Dr. Mays looked at the test results again. "Connie, where do these humans live and work anyway?"

The nurse looked at her charts and said. "They are all drovers from the Farrow Ranch."

Dr. Mays thought for a moment. "Okay, I want to see all of them right now here in my office."

The nurse left the office, got Laura, Nancy and Henrietta and brought them into the doctor's office. They each took chairs and had a seat in front of Dr. Mays desk. They knew that a lot depended on this meeting, and they were nervous. They had elected, that if possible, Laura would be their spokesperson.

Dr. Mays sat behind her desk checking the printouts. Dr. Mays studied the three humans sitting in front of her. They were all wearing floral print shirts, denim trousers, boots, short coats. and were carrying broad brimmed hats. There wasn't anything out of the ordinary about them, but if the printouts were true, these humans had managed to do something incredible; there was a mystery here. Dr. Mays didn't know what it was yet, but she planned to find out. "Nancy Cleveland, Henry Perkins and Lawrence Sherman." The humans nodded as their names were called. Dr. Mays continued, "If these printouts are correct, you're going to make medical history. Here you are three humans living out on a ranch. You're all infertile and you manage to get pregnant without medical intervention."

Laura spoke out, "Yes, the printouts are true; and as for being infertile, that is also true, but only to ovum fusion. E came in today to have it confirmed and try to enlist your aid."

Dr. Mays took a long look at the humans in front of her. Something was very odd here. They admit that they are infertile to ovum fusion, but what other way is there to become pregnant. These humans didn't come in today to find out was wrong with them, they already knew that they were pregnant. Not only that, but there seems to be something odd with the genetic profile of the embryos of Henry Perkins and Lawrence Sherman. She would have to run more tests to determine what it meant. Every medical fact that she knew told her that this was impossible, but the fact was that they were pregnant. She didn't know what it was, but they were keeping some incredible secret from her.

Dr. Mays cleared her throat, and looked at the three humans. "Now I may not be the swiftest person in the world, but I can tell when people are holding out on me. There's something going on out there at the Farrow Ranch and I would like to know what it is."

Laura knew that she couldn't reveal any of the secrets to Dr. Mays here. She would have to convince her to come to the ranch with them. "Well, Dr. Mays, we do have something that we feel that you must know, but we can't tell you about it now. You have to see it for yourself. We can however tell you this, what we have to show you is truly remarkable. You wouldn't think of it in your lifetime. If you have the time, we'd like to invite you to enjoy the hospitality of the Farrow Ranch."

After Laura finished speaking, Dr. Mays sat behind her desk apparently reading the printouts; actually, she was weighing if she should accept the invitation. All the secrecy puzzled her, but she was also puzzled by the fact that three infertile humans could become pregnant. She toyed with the idea that it had to be some kind of a hoax, but rejected it, she couldn't see how they could pull it off. It became clear to her that the only way that she would be able to get to the bottom of this would be to go with them to the ranch. In the end curiosity won. "Okay, I accept your invitation."

Laura and the other women were relieved that Dr. Mays had agreed to go with them to the ranch. They had taken the first step, and it looked like they had gained a supporter. Laura said, "Thank you, Dr. Mays. If you want, you can leave your car here and come with us. We'll bring you back tomorrow."

Now that Dr. Mays had decided to come to the ranch, she had started to think of what she would have to bring with her. "No, thank you. I need to pack an overnight bag. I also want to bring my desk top auto lab and some other equipment to conduct more tests while I'm out there. I'll meet you here in front of the clinic in one hour; then follow you there in my vehicle."

A lot of the tension was gone. Laura and the others shook Dr. Mays hand and thanked her for her decision to come to the ranch. They told Dr. Mays that they would meet her in front of the clinic in one hour, then left the office.

As soon as the humans had left her office, Dr. Mays called her nurse into her office. She told her nurse that she would be leaving for the day; and had her help to load the equipment that she needed to take in her vehicle.

She then drove home to pack an overnight bag. She called a friend to let her know that she would be going out of town, and to have her look after her dog.

She arrived back at the clinic in one hour to meet the humans from the Farrow Ranch. Laura rode with her to keep her company on the drive and to give directions.

Night had fallen when they arrived at the ranch. They had called ahead and dinner had been put on hold till they arrived. When they pulled in, everyone was in the dining hall. They parked in front of the dining hall and went inside. The food had already been put on the tables.

Entering the dining hall, the first thing that Dr. Mays noticed was that there were several strange people here. To say that they were just strange had to be an understatement. To say that they were human was certain, but she had never seen or heard of any humans like these. They were large with mostly pale skin, except for two that had really dark skin and one with tawny skin. Their hair and eyes were of various colors and they had facial hair. The most striking thing had to be their odd body structure. Dr. Mays became intensely curious about them, but since Laura didn't make any comment about them, Dr. Mays figuring that Lawrence would explain them in her own time.

Laura led Dr. Mays to a table where one of the strangers was seated. The person stood up as they approached. This person's height of about two meters took Dr. Mays by surprise. She had never seen someone so tall before. Laura made the introduction. "Dr. Mays, this is Stewart Vaughn."

Stewart shook hands with Dr. Mays. "Hello, Dr. Mays, it's a pleasure to meet you."

Dr. Mays immediately noticed the deep low-pitched voice and the strange accent. Stewart also had Large hands and a strong grip. "It's a pleasure to meet you too, Stewart Vaughn." Dr. Mays looked around. Who are these people? Why are they so unusual/ Where did they come from? And what are they doing here? Dr. Mays in all her experience had never heard of such strange humans. She was eager to ask about these strangers, but she figured that her host would tell her in her own time.

They took their seats and served themselves. After everyone had started to eat, Laura took the lead. "Dr. Mays, you have no doubt noticed that the strangers here with us, to include Stewart are very unusual."

Dr. Mays looked up at Laura. "Yes, I didn't want to mention it, figuring that you would get around to in in your own time"

Laura had a smile on her face, like she was about to play a trick on someone. "well, there's a good reason for it. You see, they're all male human beings."

Dr. Mays was stunned. She just sat looking at Laura and Stewart, not knowing what to do. She opened her mouth to speak, but couldn't say anything. Stewart had a broad smile. He tried hard not to laugh at Dr. Mays discomposure.

Laura continued, "We found them last October in a cave at the edge of the wilderness zone. They were in cryogenic units. They had been there for two-hundred eighty-six years."

Dr. Mays had started to get over the shock. She understood so far what Laura had been telling her. Of all the reasons for their strangeness, the idea that they were males had never occurred to her.

Laura continued, "You see, Stewart is my man. They call themselves men and us females, women." Laura pointed to Dr. Nichols at the next table. "That's Dr. Ernst Nichols, he's Nancy's man." She pointed to the next man at the table with Nancy and Henrietta. "That is Thomas Owens. He is Henrietta's man."

Dr. Mays finally spoke. "I thought her name was Henry?"

Laura said, "Well, Henry is a masculine name, so she now wants to be called Henrietta, the feminine variant of Henry." Laura paused for a moment, then continued, "I believe that you understand the need for secrecy now. I don't think that you would have believed us if we had told you in your office."

Dr. Mays looked around at the men. "Yes, you're right. I couldn't have believed you. I still find it hard to believe even though I can see it."

Laura said, "Now, doctor, to answer your question. The men are our secret. They impregnated us by sexual intercourse."

Dr. Mays was shocked. Stewart couldn't help laughing. He was holding hands with Laura at the table.

Dr. Mays finally exclaimed, "You mean that you copulated with these males like animals! That's blasphemous!"

Laura looked straight into Dr. Mays eyes. "No, Dr. Mays, it isn't blasphemous, it's as natural as nature has intended it. Now we came to you because we thought that you were open minded enough to help us. The world needs to know about these men, but first we need allies. Please, Dr. Mays, will you help us?"

Dr. Mays felt embarrassed now. Her outburst about the humans copulating with the males had been a sudden reaction that reflected her religious upbringing more than her present views. Of course, they were right. It was only natural. After a few seconds she made up her mind. "Okay, I'll help you."

A smile lit Laura's face. She grabbed Dr. Mays hand and shook it vigorously. 'Oh, thank you, Dr. Mays. We were really counting on you."

Dr. Mays pointed to Dr. Nichols. "Lawrence, you said that that male over there is a doctor?"

Laura nodded. "Yes, he's an orthopedic surgeon; and please, my name is no longer Lawrence, it's Laura. Come, I'll introduce you to him. Laura introduced Dr. Mays to Dr. Nichols.

After dinner Dr. Nichols took Dr. Mays up to his dispensary at the ranch office. He also showed her the time capsule. They then examined the three pregnant women again. The additional tests that Dr. Mays was able to run explained the reason for the odd genetic profiles of Laura and Henrietta's embryos. Dr. Nichols was amazed to see Dr. Mays medical equipment. He just couldn't get over how advanced medicine had become.

After the examinations, Dr. Mays had a conference with Dr. Nichols, Stewart and Laura. She then used the visidatacom unit in the ranch office to send an urgent message through her office unit to the Director of the St. Louis Institute of Genetic Research. She instructed her office unit to forward any reply to the ranch unit.

XIX

ALLIES SOUGHT

Dr. Anthony Kirschner, a petite woman of thirty-eight, Director of the St. Louis Institute of Genetic Research, relaxed in the study of her on-campus home. She sat in her favorite chair in peach colored silk lounging pajamas, velvet robe and slippers, while having a brandy before going to bed. This week had been a disappointment to her; and she had been glad to see it come to an end. She had had such hope for the latest research project, but after so much time and effort it had ended in failure like all the others. It angered her that the human race had gotten its self into such a dire predicament that it was in.

What had happened to the human males? She knew, as well as everyone else the fairy tale that the church tells about the males being banished, but as far as she was concerned it was all a lot of hog wash. She had tried to find out what had happened. All she found was a black hole; like the memory of the males had been expunged from human memory. Why had their predecessors taken such extreme measures to destroy all knowledge of human males?

Her thoughts were interrupted when the visidatacom unit chimed to announce an incoming call. She got up from the chair, took a seat at her desk and ordered the unit to connect the call. A young human wearing a white lab coat over dark-blue coveralls sitting behind a desk in an office replaced the scene of wind-swept dunes and surf on her video wall. "Yes, Evelyn, what is it?"

Evelyn cleared her throat nervously before she began. "Sorry to disturb you at home, Dr. Kirschner, but I have an urgent message from a Dr. Vernon Mays in Amarillo, Texas."

Dr. Kirschner didn't like being bothered at home in the evening by work. Especially after such a dismal week. "Can it wait until morning, or is there anyone else who can take care of it?"

Evelyn was very insistent. "Dr. Kirschner, this message is most urgent. I believe that it requires immediate action and should be for your eyes only."

Dr. Kirschner took a few seconds to study Evelyn. She could tell that Evelyn was nervous about something. This wasn't like Evelyn. She didn't usually get so excited about something unless it was really important or unusual. "Okay, Evelyn, send it over."

Dr. Kirschner directed the message to be displayed on her desk top view screen. The message appeared, it read.

February 27, 2375

To
Director, St Louis Institute of Genetic Research
St Louis, Missouri

From
Dr. Vernon Mays
1237 NW 15th Street
Amarillo, Texas

Subject
Unexplained Pregnancies

> This day I examined three patients in my office. All three patients are certified as infertile. My examination shows that all three are pregnant and that their pregnancies were not through medical intervention. For now, I will call them patient 'A' twenty-nine years old, patient 'B' twenty-six years old and patient 'C' seventeen years old. The embryos of patient 'B' and 'C' have the 'Y' chromosome.
>
> Sincerely
> Dr. Vernon Mays MD

When Dr. Kirschner read the final sentence, it couldn't have attracted more attention if it had been a mountain falling on her desk. She read it two more times to make sure she had read it right. She then ordered the visidatacom unit to call Evelyn. As soon as the image of Evelyn came up on her video wall, Dr. Kirschner said, "Evelyn, is this some kind of a hoax?"

Evelyn shook her head. "Not that I know of. It's an authentic message from Dr. Mays."

Dr. Kirschner looked at the message one more time. "This can't be true, It's impossible! There must be some kind of mistake! Are you sure that the message said the 'Y' chromosome?"

Evelyn nodded nervously. "Yes, Dr. Kirschner, that's what it said, no mistake. I forwarded it to you exactly as I received it."

Dr. Kirschner looked at the message again and shook her head. It was a statement of impossible fact. Humans could only get pregnant by ovum fusion, and no human had the 'Y' Chromosome. She didn't know what to think about this message. It was bizarre. She had to get to the bottom of this. She must talk to Dr. Mays personally. "Evelyn, I want to speak to Dr. Mays personally. I don't care how long it takes for you to get in touch with her, or what the time is, you put it right through to me."

Evelyn nodded. "Yes, Dr. Kirschner."

Dr. Kirschner signed off.

Dr. Kirschner got up and poured herself another brandy, then sat back down at her desk. She had a lot on her mind. The human race was sliding towards extinction. The only way to save it would be to breed human males again. The problem was that no human alive in the world possessed the 'Y' chromosome; and all attempts to create it in the lab and breed males had been unsuccessful. Now this, two humans all on their own find out how to conceive a male child. She shook her head in disbelief as she thought. No, there must be something wrong here. It's impossible! It just can't be! She sat at her desk sipping her brandy and trying without success to come up with an explanation for the message. She just couldn't imagine how they were able to do it.

The chime of the visidatacom unit interrupted her thoughts. She answered the call. "What do you have, Evelyn?"

"I have Dr. Mays."

Dr. Kirschner sat up straight behind her desk and assumed a businesslike attitude. "Okay, Evelyn, put her through." The image of Dr. Mays replaced the image of Evelyn. Dr. Kirschner got her first impression of an attractive and well-dressed human in her late twenties, with a serious attitude. "Dr. Mays, thank you for getting back to me. Now, about this message, there must be some mistake."

Dr. Mays stood her ground and replied with conviction. "No, Dr. Kirschner, there's no mistake. It was also unbelievable to me at first. What I have here is a group of isolated humans, all certified as infertile, twelve all total, with seven being of prime child bearing age. I have checked the other four humans of child bearing age and fond a forth patient, call her patient 'D', eighteen years of age. She is also pregnant, and her embryo has the 'Y' chromosome."

Dr. Kirschner looked hard at Dr. Mays. " Look, Dr. Mays, if this is some kind of a joke!"

Dr. Mays looked back at Dr. Kirschner, maintaining eye contact through the video. "It's no joke. Dr. Kirschner, I'll stake my reputation on it,"

Dr. Kirschner slapped the top of her desk. "That you will, Dr. Mays! That you will!"

Dr. Mays gave instructions to her visidatacom unit, then spoke to Dr. Kirschner, "I'm now transmitting the results of the tests that I ran on each of the humans."

After about a fifteen second delay, the tests results started showing up on Dr. Kirschner's desktop viewer. She checked over all the tests results, then checked them again. "Dr. Mays, how could you get such readings? I still can't believe they are true."

"I ran every test at least three times. I checked all my equipment to make sure that it was properly calibrated. Believe me, as incredible as it seems there's no mistake."

Dr. Kirschner looked again at the test results. How could a properly working diagnostic lab give such results, she needed answers. "Okay, tell me how this has happened."

Dr. Mays now started to become secretive. "I'm sorry, Dr. Kirschner, but I dare not risk saying anything over the net. I think that you have to see it to believe it. You must come here to see it without delay."

Dr. Mays evasive behavior perplexed Dr. Kirschner. "Tell me, Dr. Mays, if these humans are infertile, then how can they even conceive a child, much less a male child?"

Dr. Mays smiled as if she were hiding some profound truth. "It's true that they're infertile for the ovum fusion procedure, but there are other ways to become pregnant."

This had become very confusing to Dr. Kirschner. What did Dr. Mays mean by 'There are other ways'? The only way for a human to become pregnant was by ovum fusion. She could see a mystery here and she was determined to get to the bottom of it. "Now, Dr. Mays, you know as well as I that the only way for humans to become pregnant is by ovum fusion. There is no other way. What's happening down there? What are you not telling me?"

Dr. Mays could feel the insistence in Dr. Kirschner's voice, but didn't give in. "I'm sorry, Dr. Kirschner, please accept my apology, but I can't tell you over the net. You must come here and see it for yourself. As for ovum fusion being the only way, that is no longer true. The humans here have found another way."

Dr. Mays urged Dr. Kirschner once again. "Dr. Kirschner, you must come here. The humans here have been keeping a most marvelously incredible secret. This secret will transform all of humanity. I must say that when they revealed their secret to me, I was astounded. I would never have imagined it. You must see it for yourself to believe it."

It only took a moment for Dr. Kirschner to make up her mind. She still wasn't sure if it was a hoax or not; she had to go down there to be sure. "Okay, I'll be there by eight AM tomorrow."

Dr. Mays gave an audible sigh of relief and allowed herself to relax a little. "Thank you, Dr. Kirschner. If you fly into the Trade Winds Airport, I'll have someone there to meet you."

Dr. Kirschner signed off and called Evelyn.

"Yes, Dr. Kirschner?"

"All right, Evelyn, first thing I want you to do is call the pilot for the institute aircraft, wake her up if you have to. Tell her I want the aircraft ready to go at six-thirty in the morning. We'll be flying to Amarillo, Texas. After that you call whoever is on standby and tell her to come in and take over your duty. Then I want you to go home and pack your bag. You're coming with me; and I don't know how long we'll be down there. Now let's get moving, and don't say a word to anyone about this communication from Dr. Mays."

Dr. Kirschner signed off. She then sent a message to Monsignor James Espin canceling their golf date for the next morning, then went to the bedroom to pack.

After signing off, Dr. Mays called her nurse. The chiming of her visidatacom unit awakened Dr. May's nurse, Connie Bosch. Since she was in bed, she ordered her visidatacom unit to transmit only her likeness with the voice transmission. The video wall in her bedroom lit up with the image of Dr. Mays. "Yes, Dr. Mays?"

Sorry to disturb you, Connie. Do you know the way out to the Farrow Ranch?" There's a Dr. Kirschner coming tomorrow to see me. She is the director of the St Louis Institute of Genetic Research. She'll be flying into the Trade Winds Airport at eight AM. I want you to meet her and bring her out here to the Farrow ranch. Oh, one last thing, don't tell anyone about this."

"All right, Dr. Mays, you can count on me."

Dr. Mays smiled. 'Good, then I'll see you tomorrow."

After signing off, Connie ordered her visidatacom unit to give her a wake-up call at 6:30 AM and went back to sleep.

Connie Bosch arrived at the Trade Winds Airport before 8:00 AM the next morning. She took a seat in the visitor's lounge to await the arrival of Dr. Kirschner's aircraft. She had been puzzled by recent events. She thought, Dr. Mays had never been secretive before and now this. Why was Dr. Kirschner, the director of a prestigious institute, rushing down here to see a young general practitioner in a small out of the way town. Perhaps It has something to do with those pregnant drovers from the Farrow Ranch.

Connie's thoughts were interrupted by the announcement of an incoming aircraft. She looked out the window to see the aircraft on its final approach to the landing pad. As it approached the landing pad the aircraft, under control of the onboard visidatacom unit, started to transition from horizontal flight to vertical flight. The blast of the engines kicked up a little dust from the tarmac just before it settled onto the landing pad. The aircraft then taxied from the landing pad to a parking pad.

Just as Connie left the terminal, she could hear the engines of the aircraft shutting down. A cold wind blew from the northwest. Connie pulled her coat closer about herself and turned the collar up. As she approached the aircraft, she saw the rear ramp lower, then two humans in suits and overcoats disembarked from the aircraft. Connie, assuming the older human to be Dr. Kirschner, stepped up to her and held out her hand. "Good-morning, Dr. Kirschner. I'm Connie Bosch, Dr. Mays nurse. I'm here to take you to the Farrow Ranch." They shook hands.

Connie and the pilot took the bags and went to where Connie's vehicle had been parked. After they stored the bags and got in, Connie started the vehicle. The vehicle was red. Connie decided to change the color. She dialed the polarity controls until the vehicle was a light-blue. As soon as the gyros were stabilized, she retracted the parking wheels. There was a slight movement as the gyros stabilized the vehicle, then Connie pressed the accelerator and they were off.

They left the Trade Winds Airport. Connie drove through Amarillo towards Interstate 40. Amarillo was much the same as any other city in the world. It had shrunk to a fraction of its size. Whole sections of the city had been abandoned, with some of the sections demolished and the streets taken up. Prosperity abounded; but that was just the pretty veneer over the ugly truth. With automated factories and a lessening demand on resources, everything had become affordable. They were an opulent society within a dying civilization.

They reached Interstate 40 and turned west. It was a two-lane road that the state kept in good repair. A long time ago, it had been a four-lane highway. However, with so little traffic, the east bound lanes fell into disuse and were abandoned.

The drive took a little less than an hour and a half. Dr. Kirschner questioned Connie to see what she knew. Connie had to admit that Dr. Mays had told her nothing. They arrived at the Farrow Ranch just before 10:00 AM.

Dr. Mays had been watching the road, and saw Connie's vehicle approach. She stood in front of the Ranch Office to greet Dr. Kirschner when she arrived. After the introductions, Dr. Mays took Dr. Kirschner and the other woman into the ranch office. Dr. Mays first showed Sherry's computer to them. "Dr. Kirschner, this was found in a cave at the edge of the wilderness zone last October. It's a time capsule, but it was just a bonus. Also, in the cave were sixteen cryogenic units that were occupied. They had been there for two-hundred eighty-six years.

Three of the units had lost power and the occupants were dead. Two more units lost power during the reanimation process and the occupants died." Dr. Mays paused for a few seconds for effect. "Dr. Kirschner, we have on this ranch the survivors from the cryogenic units. They are eleven male human beings from the twenty-first century

Dr. Kirschner opened her mouth to speak, but could only say. "What!"

Dr. Mays continued, 'We have eleven male human beings right here on this ranch. That is the reason for the unexplained pregnancies. The females, or women, have been copulating with the males, or men and were impregnated by them."

Dr. Kirschner had regained her composure. Connie and Evelyn were disturbed by the idea of humans copulating with the males like animals. Dr. Kirschner, however, was not a religious woman, but a scientist. She didn't give a damn about religious sensibilities, she looked at the benefits. "Male human beings you say! Where are they? I want to see them now!"

Dr. Mays indicated the door. "If you will follow me, they're all in the dining hall."

Dr. Mays led them out of the office to the dining hall. When they entered, Dr. Kirschner saw the strange looking humans. Until she had actually seen them, she still couldn't believe it. All memory of human males had been lost. No one even knew what a human male looked like. She assumed that males would look different from females, but the sight of the men still took her by surprise. She just stood in wonderment regarding the males. This had to be the most memorable event in all her life. She now stood in the same room with the salvation of the human race. All the men were lined up on her left. The seven women who were cohabiting with the men were lined up on the right. Everyone was dressed for the occasion. All the men were wearing dark trousers and jackets, with shirts in bold colors. The women were all wearing dresses of simple but elegant style in bold colors.

Dr. Nichols stood at the head of the line. He stepped up and introduced himself. "Good-morning, Dr. Kirschner, I'm Dr. Ernst Nichols." They shook hands. Dr. Kirschner took a good look at him. He was powerfully built, with dark, almost black skin. He had dark-shining eyes; and a quick smile that split his facial hair to show a perfect set of teeth. Dr. Nichols turned to the next man in line and introduced him. "This is Mr. Stewart Vaughn."

Dr. Kirschner looked at Stewart. She noticed that his skin was very light, his hair a reddish-brown and his eyes blue. She could see that he was the tallest of the males; taller by more than a head than herself. He seemed more reserved than Dr. Nichols, with a more serious appearance.

Stewart shook hands with Dr. Kirschner. "Good-morning, Dr. Kirschner, we're glad to see that you could come."

Dr. Nichols took Dr. Kirschner down the line, introducing her to all of the men. Dr. Kirschner was really impressed by how different and exotic they were. She felt intoxicated to be near them.

After she met all the men, Dr. Mays took her to meet the women. Laura stood at the head of the line. "Dr. Kirschner, this is Laura Sherman. She's patient 'B'."

Dr. Kirschner shook hands with Laura and exchanged a few words with her.

Dr. Mays took Dr. Kirschner on down the line, introducing her to the rest of the women. She pointed out Nancy Cleveland, Henrietta Perkins and Sean Anderson as patient's 'A', 'B', and 'D'.

After the introductions, Dr. Kirschner took Dr, Mays aside. "Dr. Mays, you were right. This is something that shouldn't be mentioned over the net. Secrecy has to be maintained until we can contact the right people and get security in place. Then we can arrange to have the males moved to St Louis. Now I'd like to interview everyone to get to know them."

Dr. Kirschner, Dr. Mays and Dr. Nichols went back to Dr. Nichols dispensary at the ranch office. Dr. Kirschner first interviewed all the men. She then interviewed all the women. At some time during the interviews, someone put down a sandwich and a glass of orange juice in front of her; she ignored it.

After the interviews, she personally retested all the women that were sexually active with the men. Her results were the same as that of Dr. Mays and Dr. Nichols. She then took photographs and holographs of all the men, close up and full body, both clothed and nude. Only then did she notice the sandwich and orange juice.

After she had eaten, she used the visidatacom unit at the ranch office to send a message to the United States Surgeon General. She told the Surgeon General that she had a matter concerning national survival, and must have an immediate appointment with the President. The matter was very urgent. She sent the message through the Institute visidatacom unit and instructed it to forward any reply to the Farrow Ranch.

She then requested that Dr. Mays and her nurse not leave the ranch for now. Dr. Mays asked if she could have her receptionist join her at the ranch. Dr. Kirschner approved it. Dr. Mays called her receptionist and told her to pack a bag and come out to the Farrow Ranch.

After Dinner, Stewart and Laura were relaxing on the sofa in their bungalow. It had been a long and trying day. Stewart and Laura had been apprehensive that morning before Dr. Kirschner had arrived. Dr. Mays had been reassuring that Dr. Kirschner was the best choice to make themselves known to; but until the first meeting, they hadn't known what the outcome would be. As it turned out, Dr. Kirschner had been the best possible choice. She had been very reassuring and had their security and wellbeing as her top priority. In the end, Stewart felt sure that they had,

To relax, they had decided to talk about something else besides the day's activities. Laura talked with him about the latest film that they had viewed, South Pacific. The conversation turned to the women that lived in his time. "Tell me, how were the women in your time? Were they much different than us?"

Stewart reached up behind her and started to run his fingers through her hair. Laura had been letting it grow longer. "They weren't much different then as you are now. If anything, you're more self-reliant."

Laura snuggled into the hollow of Stewart's shoulder. "There's a lot of information about earlier periods, but not much of your period. I would like to know more about it, like how you lived and how the women dressed. What about the clothes they wore? Did they dress differently than we do now?"

Stewart thought for a moment. "The styles were different then, but they wore dresses, skirts, pants, shorts and other things, much the same as you wear today." Stewart stroked his beard. "I wish I had a razor now."

Laura looked at him. "A razor?"

Stewart continued, "You know what a razor is, don't you?"

Laura poked Stewart in the chest with her finger. "Yes, I know what a razor is, silly. They use them in the hospitals to shave the skin before surgery. We also use them in treating our animals when we have to shave an area of skin to be treated."

'Do you have them here?" Stewart said, 'I'd like to shave my beard."

Laura reached up and stroked his beard. "Why do you want to do that?"

"Oh, I used to shave all the time, most men did."

Laura nodded. "Yes, I've seen that in the films."

"Well, as you can see, men used to shave their faces and women shaved their legs."

"You're kidding! Why would they do that?"

"It was thought that smooth skin without hair to be more feminine, and they shaved their armpits too."

Laura grimaced. "Ugh! Why would they want to do that?"

Stewart just had to laugh at her. "Don't worry, if you don't want to, you don't have to."

Laura ran her fingers through Stewart's beard. "Please don't shave your beard, I like it."

Stewart kissed her on the forehead. "Okay, I won't shave it on one condition, that you keep letting your hair grow long."

Laura lay her head on his shoulder. "okay, you have a deal."

He put his arms around her and held her close. "There's something else I want to talk to you about." He paused before he went on. "You know what marriage is all about?"

"Yes, I've been learning a lot about it from the films."

Stewart cleared his throat in a nervous manner. "Well, I've been giving it a lot of thought. I want our relationship to be exclusive and permanent." He paused, then went on again, "Laura, I want us to have a marriage ceremony and be husband and wife."

Laura gave a sharp intake of breath. She could feel her heart beating faster. "I'd love that, but do you think we can do it?"

Stewart said, "Yes, I think so. I don't think that they have a law against it. I don't know what the future will be, but I know I want to spend the rest of my life with you."

Laura's eyes were damp, now that the impact of what Stewart wanted hit her. There was a tear running down her cheek. "Oh, I want very much to spend my life with you. Now that I know what love is, I don't want to live without it."

Stewart smiled at Laura. "I doubt that there's such a thing as a marriage license these days. So, all we have to do is get a minister to perform the ceremony."

Laura thought for a minute. "Roberta has a good friend who's a minister in Amarillo. Maybe she can get her friend to do it. I'll ask her in the morning."

Stewart hugged her again. "Yes, you just do that."

After dinner, Dr. Kirschner received a reply to her message. The President could see her Monday afternoon at three. Dr. Kirschner decided to have a meeting with the men tomorrow.

That evening Stewart called a meeting with all the men and their women. He now had his plan worked out and presented it to them. They talked it over for over three hours. At the end of the meeting they were all in agreement and would follow Stewart and Laura's lead.

PLANS MADE

Sunday morning after breakfast, everyone stayed in the dining hall for a meeting with Dr. Kirschner. Present for the meeting were all the men, the seven women who were cohabiting with them, Dr Mays, Evelyn Watson, Connie Bosch and Joseph Simms, Dr. Mays office manager.

The meeting opened with Dr. Kirschner thanking Dr. Mays for calling her in on the discovery. Dr. Kirschner then told everyone how the human race was in such peril and how the men would bring it back from the brink of extinction. She then told them how they had been trying without success to reintroduce the 'Y' chromosome back into the human race; and how the men were their salvation. She told them how at the institute they were able to separate the spermatozoon with the 'Y' chromosome from the spermatozoon with the 'X' chromosome from the animal sperm in the test and that they should be able to do it with the men. They could then take the most viable and inject a female ovum with a single 'Y' chromosome sperm cell. Then when they had a viable embryo, they could implant it in the mother's womb. With a small amount of sperm, it would be possible to impregnate countless women.

After the lecture, she opened the meeting for questions. There were a few questions about the institute and to clarify the points of what they planned to do. Dr. Kirschner quickly answered all the questions.

After the questions, she continued, "We'll have to move the men to the St Louis Institute of Genetic Research in St Louis."

Stewart stood, he had expected that something like this would be planned, and he had been ready for it. "Dr. Kirschner, pardon the interruption, but we have already talked it over and we're not going to move from here. We're willing to cooperate with you as much as needed to restore the human race, but we don't want to move to St louis."

Stewart's objections took Dr. Kirschner by surprise. She wasn't used to having her plans objected to. She tried to explain her reasons for the move to St Louis. 'Please understand, all our facilities are in St Louis; and we have the amenities that a big city can offer. I'm sure that you'd find it better there."

Stewart wouldn't be put off. "Dr, Kirschner, I'm betting that there's nothing to keep us from doing what we want. Am I right?"

Dr. Kirschner nodded. "Yes, for now you're right."

Stewart didn't fail to notice the implications of Dr. Kirschner's remark. He felt certain that if need be, she could get the authorities to enforce her will. He couldn't just be intractable, he had to win through logic. 'So, there are no legal reasons why we can't go where we want. However, we have no anonymity. We couldn't take more than ten steps on the street of any city or town before we would draw a crowd. So regardless of our rights, we can't go out in public. We are in fact prisoners of circumstance. Now if we went to St Louis, we'd not be able to leave the campus of the institute. We believe that we have the right to choose our place of confinement."

Dr. Kirschner had been listening to Stewart and could understand why they may not want to leave. However, the institute personnel and facilities were in St louis. The institute campus, even though being spacious, would be small and confining if you couldn't leave it. They could acquire more property to give the men some living space. "Okay, I can understand that, but we can provide anything that you would need there. We can expand the campus to provide you with living space and see that every amenity is available to you."

Stewart shook his head in disagreement. "True you could care for us, pamper us and satisfy our every whim, but we would still be like birds in a gilded cage. Now that's not the life we want and that's not all. Our women are part of this now. Once their involvement with us is known, their anonymity will be gone too. Whatever happens, there is one thing that you must understand, our women will be staying with us no matter what; we all want it that way. Now we had a meeting last night and we decided to stay here. We'll cooperate with you fully. You can bring whatever equipment and personnel you need to do the job here. In return we want as normal a life as we can have."

Dr. Kirschner thought for a while before she answered. She realized that the men were right. They were humans, and their rights and desires would have to be respected. They couldn't just be treated like lab animals. There would have to be an outlay of funds anyway to expand the institute campus to provide for their comfort. They could just as easily use the funds to set up here at the ranch. In the end it wasn't such a hard decision to make. "I can see your point; and on reflection I agree with you. I'll make arrangements to have what we need moved here."

Stewart smiled; they had won the right to live where they wanted. Now he would have to enlist Dr. Kirschner's aid to implement the rest of their plan.

Dr. Kirschner ended the meeting. Everyone started to leave the dining hall to go about their own business. As Dr. Kirschner started to leave, Stewart came up to her and asked if he could talk to her in private. They went over to the ranch office where they could be alone. They took the dispensary. Dr. Kirschner took a seat behind the desk. Stewart took a chair in front of the desk. Stewart opened the meeting. "Dr. Kirschner, please forgive me for the interruption during the meeting. I just needed to make my point."

Dr. Kirschner dismissed it with a wave of her hand. "That's all right. I understand why you did it; but this isn't why you wanted to speak to me in private."

Stewart looked at Dr. Kirschner across the desk. "No, it's not. What I want to talk to you about is what's going to happen after we go public; but first I want to tell you a story.' Stewart told Dr. Kirschner about how it had been in his time. Of how marriage had been abolished, and how men and women had started to drift apart. He told her about the ultimate betrayal of the men by the women and the internment camps. "Now, when we go public, everyone is going to want to know everything about us. It's going to be like living in a fish bowl."

Dr. Kirschner had been listening and could understand his concerns. She now understood why there was a black hole in history when it came to the men. What had been done to them was shameful and criminal. It would take women a long time to live it down. "Yes, you're right about that, but you won't be bothered by the public. There will be security around this place to keep them out. You will be well protected here."

"Well. That's not what I have in mind. What you want from us is the seed for a generation of mostly males. What I'm thinking of is our example to the world. There have been no men for over two-hundred years. It's safe to say that no one living today has any idea of what to expect of a man. People will have to understand how men and women interact with the and behave towards each other, and live together. We'll be the role models to the next generation. We need to be a community of families living as normal a life as we can. We need to set examples and precedents. Do you agree?"

Dr. Kirschner nodded. "Yes, I can see what you're getting at, I agree."

"Now, you want a generation of males, but there's more to it than just breeding males. You have to bring them up as males. They have to learn, and we can be the teachers by example."

Dr. Kirschner nodded again. "You have a good point there."

Stewart had come to the most important part of his presentation. He had to sell the idea to Dr. Kirschner. "One other thing, we need to have our own identity as a community. We need to separate ourselves from the Farrow ranch staff. There's the perfect place about three miles up the valley, north of here where we could build a village."

Dr. Kirschner gave it some thought. Stewart's idea of a separate village appealed to her. It would make security easier; and it wouldn't cost any more to build there than anywhere else. "Okay, I like the idea. I'll see what can be done and get back with you. Is there anything else for now?"

Stewart thought for a moment. "Yes, there is. We want to set precedents and the first precedent we want to establish is an old religious rite. It's the bonding together for life of a man and woman to form the core of a family unit. The rite is called marriage. In the ceremony the man and woman exchange vows before God and become husband, the man, and wife, the woman, for life. We believe that the abolishment of marriage in the twenty-first century and the love lost between men and women led to the problem that we have today. I can show you examples of the ceremony in the time capsule."

Dr. Kirschner thought about it for a minute. 'All right, I like it so far. What else do you have?"

"As for the rest of the men who have mates, they'll also be taking their women in marriage. That leaves four men without mates. The other women here at the ranch are past child bearing years. In the past men could just go out and find a mate, but not now. The pairings will have to be arranged. The men are all in agreement on this. The women should be in prime child bearing age. Can you help us out on this?"

Dr. Kirschner took a minute to go over it in her mind. She liked the idea of being matchmaker. "This is great. I see what you're getting at. You and the other men, along with your women will become a social model for study. As for the other request, let me take care of it. I already have the women in mind."

Stewart relaxed and smiled. He had gotten what he wanted from Dr. Kirschner. He changed to another topic. "You know that when we start giving women babies, that's just the beginning. Everything will be turned upside down. There'll have to be new industries to cater to the needs of the children. You'll have to think about new schools right away; and teachers to staff them. You'll need new hospitals. You might say that you will need more of everything. All these additional children will be a burden on your economy."

Dr. Kirschner agreed with Stewart. "True it will be a burden, but a burden she felt sure that everyone would be glad to accept. She liked his ideas and had started to respect him. She could tell why he had become the group's leader.

Before lunch, Dr. Kirschner had a meeting with Dr. Vernon Mays, Nurse Connie Bosch, Evelyn Watson and Joseph Simms. Dr. Kirschner opened the meeting. "I'd like to thank you for the effort that you have given so far. Now I have a proposal for all of you. Evelyn, the proposal will mean that you will stay and work here at the site. There will also be a raise for you."

Evelyn was very excited about the offer. "Oh, thank you, Dr. Kirschner. I want very much to work on this project."

Dr. Kirschner nodded at Evelyn. "Thank you, Evelyn. Now Dr. Mays, can you give up your practice and come to work for me here at the site. I need you very much; and I can promise you more than what your practice is bringing you. Will you come to work for me? I can also use your nurse and office manager."

Dr. Mays thought for a few seconds. "I like the offer, it sounds reasonable. However, I need some time to think about it."

Dr. Kirschner nodded at Dr. Mays. "All right, I can give you until this evening. Now, Connie, same offer. The position will be interesting; and you will have a raise in pay. What do you say?"

Connie gave it some thought. "Okay, I'll come if Dr. Mays does."

Dr. Kirschner looked at Joseph. "Now, Joseph, I'm offering you the same deal as the rest of the women. What do you say about it?"

Joseph looked at Dr. Kirschner. "My answer is the same as Connie's. I'll come if Dr. Mays does."

Dr. Kirschner smiled. They seemed to be willing. "Thank you, Joseph. Now for the rest of the offer. The men and their women are to form a community of family units and be role models for the next generation. They will show how men and women are to behave with each other and live together." Dr. Kirschner paused for a moment before she went on. "Now, here's the rest of the proposal. Four of the men are without women companions. I'd like for each of you to be the companion to one of the men. You will live with him and bear his children."

Everyone just sat there for a couple of minutes. This was a lot to take in all at once. All of them were just getting comfortable with being around the men; now Dr. Kirschner wanted them to cohabit with them. It was an idea that they needed time to consider. They also knew that it would be an offer that they would only get once. Finally, Commie asked a question. "For how long would this be?"

Dr. Kirschner looked at Connie, but the answer was for everyone. "Well, Connie, it will be for a lifetime. Now you can take the rest of the day to think about it. You may talk with the other women if you want. They are ready to answer your questions. I need your decision this evening." Dr. Kirschner excused herself and left them to think about it.

At lunch they observed the women having lunch with their men. It had become obvious to them that the other women were very happy in their relationships with the men. They took a closer look at the unattached men, thinking about their possible companionship. That afternoon they got to talk to the other women about their relationship with their men. The women already in relationships with men were very candid and answered all of their questions, to include how it was copulating with men. They were assured that it was pure pleasure. By dinner they all had made up their minds. They were going to stay and become companions to the unattached men.

Dr. Kirschner spoke with the women and men involved. They decided that they would take a few days to get to know each other, then pair off with whom they felt most comfortable.

Dr. Kirschner then sent Dr. Mays, Commie and Joseph home to

get everything that they needed or wanted to keep. Then be back in the morning. She would take Evelyn with her on the flight back east. She would drop Evelyn off at St Louis on the way to Washington D. C. and pick her up on the way back.

Early Monday morning, Sandra Emory drove Dr. Kirschner and Evelyn to the Trade Winds Airport. Dr. Kirschner and Evelyn flew to St Louis, where Evelyn was dropped off. Dr. Kirschner then flew on to Washington D. C. At 3:00 PM the President's Secretary admitted Dr. Kirschner, accompanied by the Surgeon General to the President's office. The President had cleared her appointments for the rest of the afternoon for this meeting.

Dr. Kirschner wasted no time in getting into the narrative of events since the three women visited Dr. Mays at her office. She told the president about the women finding the cryogenic units and the time capsule in the cave. She told the President about how the women came to cohabit with the men. She went over the interviews with the men, and showed the photographs and holographs of the men. She then reviewed with the President the program to use the men to rescue the human race. Dr. Kirschner told the President that the men would continue to live at the Farrow Ranch.

They agreed to give other Heads of State around the world advanced notice and coordinate news releases. The story would be made public in time for the evening news Friday. The President would arrange with the U S Marshals office, the military and the governor of Texas to provide security. The fact that the ranch was on the edge of the wilderness zone would help with the security.

When Dr. Kirschner left the President's office, she had a sense of urgency. The clock was ticking, and she didn't have much time.

Dr. Kirschner went directly to her aircraft and flew back to St Louis. She told her Pilot to be ready to fly back to Amarillo at 6:00 AM. She then went to her on campus home and called in her Staff. Her cook made her dinner while she waited for her staff to arrive.

When they were all there; she told them, what had happened. They were taken completely by surprise by the news. No one had known what she had been doing in Amarillo. She immediately called a halt to the 'Y' chromosome research, being that it had become moot. She assigned members of her staff tasks to perform to activate the program to use the men to rescue the human race. They were going to have to coordinate with reproductive specialists worldwide. They made up a list of equipment and supplies that they would need at the Farrow Ranch. The equipment and supplies were to be sent to the Farrow Ranch after they went public.

Dr. Kirschner contacted Evelyn and told her when to be at the airport for the flight back to Amarillo. She then got some sleep before flying back.

Connie was at the Trade Winds Airport when Dr. Kirschner and Evelyn arrived. Dr. Kirschner noticed that Connie's vehicle was now dark-green. After the luggage was loaded, Connie drove them back to the ranch.

When they arrived at the ranch, Dr. Kirschner asked to see Dr. Mays and Dr. Nichols. When they were all together. Dr. Kirschner started the meeting. "Dr. Mays, and you Dr. Nichols, as of yesterday you were working for the St Louis Institute of Genetic Research. Dr. Mays, I want you to set up a clinic here at the ranch. You'll be responsible for the health of the men. Dr. Nichols, you'll be Dr. Mays assistant. Your training as a physician may be dated, but you are the only living physician in the world that knows human male anatomy. Dr. Mays, whatever equipment or supplies you need, just give me a list and I'll get it for you. Now the first thing that I want you to do is to give every man a complete physical examination and start a medical history. After the men, you'll do the same for the women. You will also have your nurse with you. Any questions?"

Dr. Mays said, "What about my office manager? I don't think I'll have enough to keep her busy."

Dr. Kirschner said, "I've already thought of that. She'll take all the information from the time capsule and transfer it to our own visidatacom units so that it can be accessed through the net. Any more questions?" Dr. Mays and Dr Nichols said no. Dr Kirschner continued, that's all I have for now. Let's get to work. "

Dr. Kirschner had a meeting with everyone, and told them that they were going public Friday in time for the evening news. She then outlined to everyone what would happen after they went public.

That evening Laura sat in her chair in the holograph room ready to make a call to her mother. She wore a mauve silk caftan with pink trim, embroidery and sash with mauve velvet slippers. She directed the visidatacom unit to display a small sunlit glade surrounded by giant redwood boles. After she had the scene just right, she had the visidatacom unit place the call to her mother. In less than two minutes the image of her mother sitting in her chair, dressed in a teal-green silk caftan with yellow-orange trim, embroidery and sash and teal-green velvet slippers took form in front of her. "Hi, Mon.' Laura said.

Her mother smiled back at her. "Okay, Lawrence, it's good to see you. You look well."

Laura willed herself with all of her self-control to maintain her poise and show no nervousness. "This is just a quick call, Mom. I just called to let you know that something important is about to happen."

"What's that?" Her mother said.

"I can't say, Mom. All I can tell you is to watch the news Friday evening."

Laura's mother was confused by her daughter's strange behavior and had started to worry about her. "Lawrence, why all the secrecy? What is happening out there? I'm worried about you."

"Don't worry about me." Laura said with a smile, "I'm doing just fine. Just watch the news Friday evening."

Laura's mother felt that she had to do something to find out what was going on. "Perhaps I should come out to the ranch for a visit."

Laura was pleased by her mother's suggestion for a visit. "I would love for you to come for a visit here at the ranch. I can arrange for the visit, say next week, or the week after. Will that be all right?"

"Yes, that would be fine, but I would still like to know what the secret is."

"Mom, I can't tell you now, just watch the news Friday evening. I must go for now, Mom. I'll call you again Friday evening. Good-bye, Mom."

"Good-bye, Lawrence, I love you."

"I love you too, Mom."

After her daughter's image faded, Laura's mother sat for a few minutes in her chair thinking. She had observed her daughter during the call. Lawrence had tried hard to remain calm, but she could easily see through her daughter's deception. She didn't know what was going on with Lawrence. All this secrecy had her upset. Yes, she would have to make a trip out to the ranch to see her daughter. She hadn't been out to the ranch in a long time; she enjoyed going out there. She tried hard to figure out what secret Lawrence could be keeping. She didn't even get close.

By Friday the rest of the men and women were paired up. Dr. Vernon (now Verna) Mays had paired with Theodore Conway, Connie Bosch with Douglas Hamilton, Evelyn Watson with Steven Picket and Joseph (now Josephine) Simms with Raymond Moyer.

XXI

GOING PUBLIC

The President had scheduled a press conference for 4:00 PM Friday. Usually the press knew what the press conference would be about, or at least they had a good idea. This time the blackout had been complete. The usual contacts either knew nothing, or weren't talking. That wasn't all, there had been personal messages that had been hand delivered by courier from the President to other world leaders. Nothing had been trusted to electronic communications and no one would talk.

As the people of the news media started to gather for the press conference, there was a lot of speculation. White House watchers had noticed that Dr. Kirschner, Director of the St Louis Institute of Genetic Research, had been to the White House Monday, and had returned for today. There was speculation as to a breakthrough in genetic research. There had also been a lot of looking at national and world events and bets were made.

President Nelson La Vallee wasn't known for her punctuality, but precisely at 4:00 PM she was announced and took the podium. "People of the media, thank you for coming today. I have an announcement to make. It concerns a subject of worldwide importance. As I speak here the same information is being released in major capitals around the world." By now everyone sat on the edge of their seats. They didn't know what was coming, but it must be something out of the ordinary. "This isn't going to be a regular news conference. I will take no questions. I will give a news release, then turn the news conference over to Dr. Kirschner, Director of the St louis Institute of Genetic Research, to answer your questions. Now, this is the news release. There are now at an undisclosed location in the United States eleven male human beings."

There followed a moment of complete silence, as everyone's jaws dropped in stunned disbelief, then the conference room erupted into pandemonium. All decorum was gone; everyone leapt to their feet shouting questions. President La Vallee called for everyone to remain quite, then raised her hands for order. When order had finally been restored, she continued. "The 'Men", as they call themselves, were found last October in a cave in cryogenic suspension. Since they were found, they have been living in a community of twelve infertile humans. Seven of the humans are of child bearing age and have been cohabiting with seven of the males. Of seven of the infertile humans, four are now pregnant; and of the four embryos, three have the 'Y' chromosome. They will be male children."

The conference room erupted into pandemonium again. President La Vallee raised her hands for order. When she had order, she introduced Dr. Anthony Kirschner. Dr. Kirschner talked about the men.

During her talk, holographic projectors were turned on and the images of the men appeared in front of the media, both clothed and nude. No one could take their eyes from the holographic images. Dr. Kirschner explained the program to use the men to reintroduce males to the human population worldwide. At the end of the presentation, Dr. Kirschner handed out photographs and made holographic copies available.

In every newsroom around the world that evening the lead story, in many cases the only story was that of the males. The public reaction had been immediate and profound. Some people understood the dire position of the human race, and the need for the males. Most were unsure of what to think of it. Then there were some that saw the males as a threat. Everyone talked about the males. The world couldn't get enough information about them. Every news service in the world demanded an interview with the males.

Laura's mother made sure to watch the evening news as her daughter had urged her to do. When the newscaster on the video wall started talking about the men who were at an undisclosed location in the United States, everything else was forgotten. She couldn't take her eyes from the video wall as they showed the pictures of the men. This was unbelievable, she had never even seen a picture of a human male; all pictures and other likeness of men had been destroyed before anyone's lifetime. When the newscaster made reference to holograms of the males, she went into her holograph room to view the holograms of the males.

She then recalled that Lawrence had asked her to watch the news this evening. What a coincidence that the story about the male humans should break at the same time. The idea briefly passed through her mind that there might be a connection. She shook her head. That was just too much for her to believe. She decided not to wait for Lawrence to call, but to call her daughter now. She sat up straight in her chair, smoothed out her robe and had the visidatacom unit project a scene of a mountain meadow filled with wild flowers, complete with the scent of flowers and the sounds of nature in the background. She then had the visidatacom unit place the call.

Laura heard the chime of the visidatacom unit with the announcement that she had a call in the holograph room. She went into the holograph room. She had replaced the chair in the holograph room with a short sofa. She took a seat on the left side of the sofa; then directed the visidatacom unit to display the walled garden with the scents of roses and other flowers, then connect the call. The image of her mother sitting in her chair wearing magenta silk lounging pajamas, magenta velvet robe and magenta velvet slippers materialized in front of her.

When Laura's mother saw her daughter's image, she noticed that the sofa had replaced the chair. She also noticed that instead of being casually attired, as was her custom at home, Lawrence had dressed in a frock of a style that she had never seen before. It was made of champagne colored satin. It had short sleeves, a rounded neckline and a snug fitted bodice to the waist, with a full skirt down to mid-calf. She had matching velvet slippers. "Lawrence, have you seen the news this evening about the human males?"

"Yes, Mother, I knew what the news was going to be this evening."

Laura's mother started to speak again, when the realization of what Lawrence had just said hit her. Lawrence did not say that she had seen the news this evening. She said that she knew what the news was going to be. How could that be? She shook her head. How could Lawrence have known? Lawrence had asked her to watch the news this evening. Was the fact that Lawrence had asked her to watch the news have something to do with the males? "Lawrence, why did you ask me to watch the news this evening?"

Laura was very excited now and fought to maintain her poise. "Because, Mother, I wanted you to see the men." Laura paused for a moment, "You see, we already knew about the men. We were the ones that found them. They have been living with us here at the ranch since last October."

Laura then turned and motioned for someone out of the holograph view to join her. Stewart's image entered from the right, took a seat next to Laura and took her hand in his. He was dressed in indigo-blue jacket and trousers and azure-blue shirt. Laura turned back to her mother, and with a smile of real pleasure said, "Mom, I would like for you to meet Mr. Stewart Vaughn."

Stewart smiled at Laura's mother. "Hello, Ms. Sherman, it's a pleasure to finally meet you. Laura is always telling me about you and her sisters."

Laura's mother couldn't take her eyes off of Stewart. That he was one of the males, she had no doubt, having seen his image in the news.

Laura's mother, after a while, managed to nod and say. "Hello, Mr. Stewart Vaughn."

Laura had gained confidence with her mother. "Mom, now that our secret is public, there's something that I can now tell you." Laura took a deep breath and continued, "Stewart has been living with me in my bungalow since November. He shares my bed and we're lovers. "Laura's mother's brow knitted as she took on an expression of puzzlement. Laura didn't give her a chance to say anything, but continued to speak, "Mom, our love making has borne fruit." By now Laura had a broad smile on her face, "Mom, I'm pregnant, I'm going to be a mother."

Laura's mother just sat there for a few seconds in stunned disbelief before she could say a word. Finally, she uttered, "You're what?"

"Mom, that's not all. My child is going to be a very special child, it's a male child. Mom, you are going to have a grandson."

Laura's mother opened her mouth to speak, but couldn't say anything. She had been overwhelmed by what she had heard.

"Mom, Stewart is the father of my child."

Laura's mother finally found her voice. "You said that it is going to be a male child?"

Laura nodded, still smiling. "Yes, Mom, a male child, it's going to be a boy." Laura could see that it would take some time for her mother to come to terms with what she had told her. "Well, Mom, I believe that's enough for now. I'll make arrangements to have you cleared to visit us here at the ranch. Good-bye, Mom, I'll call again tomorrow."

Laura's mother nodded. "Yes, good-bye, Lawrence. I will be waiting for your call tomorrow."

"good-bye, Ms. Sherman."

"Yes, good-bye, Mr. Sherman Vaughn."

After the call had ended, Laura's mother just sat in her chair for a while. She was still in shock from Lawrence's revelations. Her world had just changed. It would take a while to sort out the new order of things. It had been shocking enough to hear of the males. It had been even more unsettling to learn that her daughter now lived with a male. Suddenly a realization struck her and she became embarrassed. Lawrence had told her that she was going to have a child; and she had been in such a state of disorder, that she hadn't even congratulated her daughter on the wonderful news. She would have to call her back to congratulate her.

By Friday, a security cordon had been put in place around the Farrow Ranch. For the most part it couldn't be seen, but it was there. The cordon had been designed to protect without attracting attention. The security force was a mix of state police and federal marshals. Human patrols and remotely controlled security vehicles covered the outer perimeter. They also had a quick reaction force in case the perimeter was breached. The ranch would also be protected from the air by an aircraft exclusion beacon.

The news media and other interested parties tried to get the male's location from the St Louis Institute of Genetic Research and the government without success. It wasn't long however before Dr. Kirschner's movements for the last several days were tracked and noted that she had been spending a lot of time in Amarillo, Texas. All eyes were now on Amarillo. From there it was just a matter of time until they focused on the farrow Ranch.

Suddenly, Interstate 40 west of Amarillo became a very busy highway. The highway became clogged with people trying to get to the Farrow Ranch to see the males, or to protest against them. If people couldn't get there by the road, they tried to get there cross country. The security had their hands full keeping everyone away. Everyone was curious to see the males. In the end the Texas State Police had set up a traffic point to turn back everyone who wanted to try to get to the Farrow Ranch.

Now that they had gone public, there were a few things the men wanted. The St Louis Institute of Genetic Research, in anticipation of the money the men would earn by incorporating themselves, had made arrangements for an advance on their earnings. They first called the Watts Custom Boot Company in Amarillo. The men could now get proper footwear. By late Saturday afternoon the owner of the Watts Custom Boot Company herself came out to the ranch to take measurements for the men's boots. They each ordered two pair of boots in brown and black. The owner of the Watts Custom Boot Company insisted on giving a large discount to be able to advertise that her company was their boot maker. Before leaving, the owner of the Watts Custom Boot Company promised delivery on the boots in two weeks.

Stewart had admired Laura's carbine for a long time. It had a very compact action that fired caseless ammunition. It used preloaded, disposable magazines of twelve, twenty or thirty rounds. Stewart ordered a new carbine like Laura's, with custom silver and gold inlayed engraving and custom French walnut stock made to his measurements. He also ordered new ammunition for his .44 cal. Magnum revolver manufactured to order. The other men also ordered new carbines and side arms for hunting.

At last, even if they couldn't go anywhere, they could at least get the things that they needed to make life tolerable. They would love to have gotten out and seen how the world had changed, but that was impossible; their health and lives were priceless. Perhaps someday they could go out in public, but not now.

Dr. Kirschner guarded the welfare of the men like a she-wolf guards her cubs. Anything that she felt would be a hazard to the men, she tried to eliminate. The men were too precious to risk. Stewart, on the other hand, worked on behalf of the men to keep the restrictions from becoming too oppressive. This led to regular heated debates between Dr. Kirschner and Stewart. The first encounter had been over the issue of the man working around livestock. After a long debate, they came to a compromise. The men could still work with the livestock, but they couldn't come in direct contact with the livestock. That meant that they could still put out feed at the holding pens. They could work the squeeze chute to vaccinate, tag and dehorn. They could also run the dip tank. They could also work the dairy herd, the dairy cows being gentle enough so that they were no threat.

Another confrontation had been over the ammunition and firearms. Dr. Kirschner at first was quite adamant on the subject that firearms were too dangerous. Stewart kept insisting that the men were well trained in the safe handling of firearms. Stewart insisted that all the men wanted was to be able to shoot as a pastime; and have the right to go hunting when they wanted. In the end, Dr. Kirschner gave in to Stewart's demands.

Stewart also complained about the security. If she could do it, Dr. Kirschner would have a police bodyguard with each of the men twenty-four hours a day. This had just been too much for the men to take. Stewart told Dr. Kirschner that they didn't care what kind of security arrangements they had to make, as long as they didn't have to see them. Dr Kirschner made the security arrangements to give the men the space that they desired.

Dr. Kirschner was stymied. She had been used to having her way and expected everyone to abide by her decisions, then to do their part to get the job done. However, with Stewart, she had met her match. For some reason that she couldn't understand, he had been able to get his way with her.

Roberta and Jerry let the institute have use of some of the facilities of the ranch, for which they were compensated by the institute. Temporary housing units and lab units had started to arrive. As soon as they could get the equipment in place, the program would commence.

The news media had been clamoring for interviews. The institute screened all the applications and conferred with the men and their women before awarding the privilege to the North American Broadcasting Company. The Institute cleared Margo Young, the senior news anchor for the North American Broadcasting Company, to interview the men and their women on the next Wednesday. She cleared into the ranch with her news crew Wednesday morning.

She started out by interviewing Dr. Mays and Dr. Nichols at the new clinic on the ranch. There she was given a brief description of how the program to separate the spermatozoon by 'X' and 'Y' chromosome would operate. Dr. Nichols then told her about when the women became pregnant, they had decided to go to Dr. Mays. Dr. Mays told her about when they first came to her office, and the confusion that they had caused before they revealed their secret.

Ms. Young then interviewed the other men and their women around the ranch at work and during the interviews, Margo found the men to be really exotic individuals. The other thing that she had come to notice had been the personal relationships between the man and woman of each couple. Everyone knew of close relationships between humans, but with each couple that she interviewed, she noticed a feeling between them that was more than friendship. They had a love for each other, but different than the love between a mother and child.

She ended up after dinner in Stewart and Laura's bungalow. Stewart and Laura were sitting on the sofa in their living room facing Margo Young, who sat across from them in a large easy chair. The recording crew had set up to record both regular video and holographic. Stewart wore navy-blue coat and trousers, with a light-gray silk shirt. Laura wore a frock of the same style as the one that she had worn Friday evening when she had called her mother, except this one was made of an orchid color silk brocade with matching velvet slippers.

Margo had been satisfied with what she had gotten so far from the other men and women, but she knew that the interview with Stewart and Laura would be the one that her audience would be most interested in. They were the first to cohabit and they were the couple that had emerged as the leaders of their community.

Margo started out with some easy questions to put them at ease before the heart of the interview. "Well, Laura, you call yourself Laura now, but your name is Lawrence. Why is that?"

Laura kept her eyes on Margo as she answered. "Stewart didn't want to call me Lawrence, it being a masculine name, Laura is one of the feminine variants of Lawrence."

Margo nodded. "Yes, I've been hearing about masculine names and feminine names. Some of the other women have also changed their names. This thing about names will require a lot of study. Right now, I'd like to know how different it is living with a man?"

Laura moved closer to Stewart and smiled. "Well, for one thing it's great, I love it. There has been a lot that I had to learn and there's a lot still to learn. One example, in a single gender society there's no sex, so nudity isn't a concern. Now when you live with a man except for changing clothes, bathing or going to bed, you remain clothed in each other's company. For people of the opposite gender, the nude body of the other gender is an object of erotica."

Erotica was a new word for Margo. "What does erotica mean?"

Laura had to stifle a giggle as she answered. "Oh, erotica means an object of sexual arousal."

Margo nodded. "I can see that we have a lot to learn. What else is different about living with a man?"

Laura was ready for this question. "You must keep in mind that there are two different people with sometimes different points of view. Men are different from women, not just physically, but mentally. Men think differently than women do and their learned role as a man is different from that of a woman."

Margo had really been enjoying all this; she had gotten a really great interview so far. "So, you're saying that men are completely different from us women?"

Laura shook her head. "No, that's not what I mean. It means that although we have a lot in common there are basic differences. This is all new to me too. There are also things that need to be kept private from each other. I'm still learning how to live with a man."

Margo now came to the subject that was personal, but what her audience would be most interested in. "Is it true that you and

Stewart were the first couple to copulate and that you were the first to become pregnant?"

Laura got a very pleasant look on her face, and took Stewart's arm. "The answer is yes to both, but we don't use the word copulate. Human relationships are very complex. Sex isn't just for reproduction, it's part of the bonding process between a man and woman. We call it making love."

Margo was really excited now; she had come to the question that everyone wanted to know. "And how is it making love to a man?"

Laura didn't answer. She got a contented look on her face, looked into Stewart's eyes and snuggled up next to him. Laura didn't have to answer the question, her expressions and body language told more than words ever could.

Margo was pleased with the interview so far. She asked her next question. "Laura, you will have the distinction of being one of the first women to have a male child in almost two-hundred ninety years. How do you feel about it?"

Laura, maintaining eye contact with Margo, sat up straighter on the sofa. "Well, Margo, Stewart has been talking to me about this. Our son will be born with a brain that has some basic differences from a female. I will have to raise him different than you do a female."

Stewart had been content to sit back and smile as the questions were directed at Laura. He would be glad to answer any of Margo's questions. However, he also wanted to use the interview for his own purpose. After he had told Jerry that he and Laura wanted to have a wedding ceremony, Jerry had asked some of the priests that she knew if they would perform the ceremony. They had all turned her down; apparently, they were afraid of reprisal from the Bishop of Washington D. C., the head of the Reform Church of North America. After talking it over with the other couples, they had decided to go public with their plans. The interview would be the perfect opportunity.

He cleared his throat to get Margo's attention. "Margo, I have a statement, then an announcement. First the statement, I want to say that Laura is the most wonderful and exciting woman that I have ever known. We love each other and want to spend our lives together. Now I would like to make the announcement. We plan to make out union permanent before God and the state. We're going to revive an old ritual; it's called a marriage. The ceremony is called a wedding. A priest conducts the ceremony. In the ceremony we'll take vows before God to live together for all our lives as husband, that's me, and wife, that's Laura, and to forsake all others. If you want there are some examples of a wedding ceremony that I can show you."

Margo sat on the edge of her chair. This was really great stuff. She had hoped for something really good, but wow, you couldn't get any better than this.

Stewart continued, "Don't misunderstand, I'll do whatever I'm asked to restore the human race, but Laura is the only woman that I'll cohabit with for the rest of our lives. After the ceremony we'll observe one other custom. Laura will take my surname. She will cease to be Laura Sherman and become Laura Vaughn. In the past all women gave up their maiden name and took their husband's surname. We're doing this because we love each other and because this is the way men and women are supposed to live together."

The interview lasted a little while longer. There were a few more questions and answers, but Margo had what she wanted. This interview would make every network and newsroom in the world.

There was plenty of activity at the ranch now. The St Louis Institute of Genetic Research had their equipment and team in place. Dr. Kirschner planned to train some of the men and women to run the operation on this end under the supervision of Evelyn. The sperm, once collected, would have the sperm cells with the 'Y' chromosome separated out by a process developed by the institute. Then all the spermatozoon would be quick frozen and shipped to St Louis; some to be kept in St louis, the rest would be shipped to other fertility centers worldwide.

In the United States and other countries women of child bearing age, who had been infertile to ovum fusion, were being recalled to their local reproductive centers for their ovum to be collected. It would then be quick frozen and stored until they had sperm on hand to fertilize it. Once it was fertilized and they had a viable embryo, it would be implanted in the mother's womb. Strict records must be kept of every step of the operation.

At thirty-seven years of age, Dr. Kirchner would be in the first group to be recalled to her reproductive center. When she realized that she would have a chance to bear a male child, she at first debated with herself if she would have the time for a child. Ever since she had found out that she was infertile, she had given up the of being a mother. She had instead devoted her life to her career. She had put a lot of work into becoming the director of the institute. Now with the men, the role of the institute would be even more vital than ever. She debated if she would have the time to care for a child and oversee the work of the institute. It didn't take long to decide that there was no way that she would miss her opportunity to bear a child. Given her position, she could even choose whom she wanted as the father.

It would be about two months before they started to get ovum and had enough sperm to start fertilizing them. The plan would be to produce all males for the first two years. They would then start to produce an increasing number of females until they had a balance between males and females. It was a grand plan, but there were dangers. There were some people who didn't want the human race to be restored this way.

XXII

BISHOP LANGLEY

Bishop Sonya Langley, Pastor of the National Cathedral in Washington D. C. and leader of the Reform Church in North America, was near the point of exhaustion. She had hardly slept for the last week since the news broke about the male humans being that had been found. This could conceivably be the worst possible blow to the church, and to herself personally. It had taken her completely by surprise. How could this have happened? The Book of God's Truth stated that true humans once shared the earth with subhuman males until God banished them from the earth. Now subhuman males were back to pollute the pure human race. If they allowed this blasphemy to succeed, it may well lead to the collapse of the faith of the church. If all human beings were made in the image of God, then how could these subhuman males be true human beings? How could true human beings stoop to the act of copulating with a subhuman male like an animal?

Bishop Langley had been able to get a list of the names of the humans who were copulating with the subhuman males. She had promptly excommunicated all of them. She felt that they deserved much more than that. They all should be thrown in prison. The absolute final insult had been this blasphemous idea of a religious marriage ceremony. If any pastor of the church performed such a ceremony they would be excommunicated. She would see to it personally.

She had to do something to stop this, but time wasn't on her side. As soon as she had heard about the subhuman males, she had gotten in contact with her supporters in Amarillo. She had first of all told them that no one from the clergy would be allowed to give the subhuman males any assistance. She had also directed those clergy in Amarillo completely loyal to her to do whatever they had to do to get someone on the inside at the Farrow Ranch. There had to be someone completely loyal to the faith that could be counted on to do whatever had to be done to get rid of the subhuman males.

Bishop Langley was desperate; she had perhaps two months to stop it. Once they started to impregnate true humans with that vile subhuman seed, it may be impossible to stop it. She needed allies, but where could she get them. Most human beings were infertile and they now had the hope of having a child. Most wouldn't willingly give up that chance. Also, most people were not as strong in their religious beliefs as they should be. She needed true believers, martyrs to the faith. Too bad they were rare in the police and military, being that only infertile humans could serve in the police and military.

Bishop Langley had no illusions that it would be easy. The only way that they could get rid of the subhuman males would be by violent acts that would take lives. It would have to be a military style operation. As she saw it, they had to strike in two places at the same time. The Institute of Genetic Research and the Farrow Ranch. If they destroyed one, but not the other, the one that survived would be guarded so closely that there would never be another chance. If they didn't destroy both, their mission would be a failure.

Bishop Langley had no compunction about killing the subhuman males. After all they were not true humans. If any true humans got in the way and were hurt or killed, then that would be regrettable, but necessary. Of course, the subhuman male's consorts would also have to die. She saw her duty clearly, she would be doing God's work, but she needed to take action now. She did have some trusted friends in industry and the professions, she could start with them.

Laura's mother and sisters had been cleared to visit the ranch. The next Friday afternoon, after the announcement of the existence of the men, Laura's mother and sisters Cathy and Cornelius were driving west on Interstate 40, heading to the Farrow Ranch. Laura's mother had been able to bring Cathy and Cornelius, they had been eager to come along. Laura's older sister Ruth on the other hand had been torn by religious convictions and for now had hostile feelings towards the men. Perhaps in time she would come to see that the human race needed the men.

They passed through the checkpoint soon after leaving Amarillo. At the check point, stern looking State Police officers turned back anyone whom they thought was trying to gain illegal entry onto the Farrow Ranch. Laura's mother showed her authorization and they waved her on through.

As they got close to the turnoff to the Farrow Ranch, they started to see people alongside the highway. Apparently, the checkpoint hadn't been able to turn everyone back. Some were carrying placards or banners with slogans either for are against the men. There were groups huddled in prayer or singing hymns. There were other individuals ranting about one thing or the other. Laura's mother wondered where all the crazies had come from.

They turned off the interstate onto the road leading to the Farrow Ranch and encountered a roadblock. Laura's mother stopped where directed by one of the police officers that manned the roadblock. Laura's mother had to show her authorization and have her vehicle searched. As they searched the vehicle, Laura's mother looked around. The roadblock was well manned by very serious looking police officers, some with dogs. Off in the distance she could see remote security vehicles patrolling. She felt sure that there were a lot of things she didn't see.

Once their vehicle had been inspected, they were waved through the roadblock and on their way. On the drive from the roadblock to the ranch headquarters they didn't see any more security, but they knew that it had to be there. When they reached the ranch headquarters they drove straight to Laura and Stewart's bungalow.

Laura had been alerted by security that her mother and sisters had been passed through the roadblock. Laura and Stewart were waiting in front of the bungalow when Laura's mother and sisters arrived. The vehicle glided silently into the parking space next to Laura's vehicle and came to a stop. The parking wheels were lowered, the doors were raised and Laura's mother and sisters disembarked from their vehicle.

As soon as her mother emerged from the vehicle, Laura rushed up and embraced her mother and they kissed on the cheeks. "Oh, Mom, I'm really glad to see you." They embraced and kissed each other on the cheek again. Laura then embraced and kissed on the cheeks each of her sisters in turn. Laura then started to introduce Stewart to her family. She wanted very much for her family to accept Stewart and come to love him as she did. Laura's mother and sisters Cathy and Cornelius had seen and spoken to him during holographic calls, but to be face to face with him was a new experience. Laura's mother exchanged formal greetings with Stewart, shaking his hand. She noticed his firm hand shake and direct manner and felt intimidated by his larger-than-life presence.

Cathy followed her mother in exchanging greetings with Stewart. She also was a little awed by his presence and exchanged only a formal greeting and hand shake.

Cornelius also started to shake Stewart's hand. She also felt awed by his presence, but managed to smile at him. Stewart could see the awkwardness between Laura's family and himself. He also knew that if barriers between Laura's family and him were to be broken down, he would have to make the first move. Rather than just shake hands, Stewart hugged Cornelius and kissed her on the forehead. Cornelius had been taken off guard for a moment, she then hugged Stewart and kissed him on the cheek. That was all it took to dissolve the awkwardness of this first meeting. Cathy embraced and kissed Stewart on the cheek, followed by her mother.

Everyone became informal now and everyone started talking with

Stewart and each other. Cornelius had expressed a desire to meet all the men, especially Benjamin. He was about her age and she thought that he looked cute with his smooth beardless face. Cathy also wanted to meet all the men, but she didn't have a favorite. Laura's mother wanted to get to know Stewart first, then she wouldn't mind meeting the other men. It pleased Laura that her family's first meeting with Stewart had gone so well.

Laura then led everyone into the bungalow and got her mother and sisters settled into the guestrooms. Stewart took care of the refreshments. Laura's mother and sisters spent the afternoon getting to know Stewart. Laura explained to her mother that when she and Stewart married, that he would become part of the family. She them explained the relationship of mother-in-law, sister-in-law and son-in-law to her mother and sisters. She also explained other relationships, like aunts, uncles, nephew, niece, and cousins. It was all very strange to them. It would take a little time to sort it out. Finally, Cathy and Cornelius realized that Stewart was to be their brother-in-law; and when Laura's baby was born, they would be aunts and the baby would be their nephew. They found it exciting and couldn't wait to tell their friends.

At dinner that evening, Stewart and Laura introduced her mother and sisters to the other men. When Cornelius started to shake hands with Benjamin, she became giddy and started to giggle. Benjamin smiled at her patiently until she regained her composure. They then had a brief visit.

Saturday, Laura and Stewart wanted to take Cathy and Cornelius horseback riding. When Dr. Kirschner heard that Stewart had gone to the barn to go horseback riding, she rushed to the barn. There she confronted Stewart. She didn't want him to go horseback riding; it could be too hazardous an activity to risk any of the men. A heated debate ensued that was settled only when Stewart agreed to ride a horse of Dr. Kirschner's choosing. Dr. Kirshner made sure that Stewart had the most gentle and harmless animal in the barn.

By Sunday afternoon when Laura's mother and sisters had to leave for the drive back to Amarillo, Laura's mother and sisters believed that the men were just as much human as the women. Her mother had also been convinced that Laura and Stewart's union was a wonderful thing; and that she would accept Stewart as one of the family. Her daughter's Cathy and Cornelius had also accepted Stewart as family.

Jerry and Roberta had a problem. The St Louis Institute of Genetic Research was compensating them for the use of ranch property, but that wasn't the problem. The problem was that they were going to have to hire other drovers to replace the ones that were living with the men; and they would need the bungalows for the new drovers.

They went to Dr. Kirschner to see what could be done about it. Dr. Kirschner also wanted to see them. She had been eager to acquire the land for the men's settlement. To safeguard the health of the men, she needed to isolate them and their women as soon as possible.

Once she had the land, she could have it surveyed, the foundations poured and the family units and landing pad up in two weeks. The clinic, community center and indoor swimming pool would take a little longer to complete. The couples also wanted a stable for their horses. Dr Kirschner felt uneasy about the men riding horses, it being a potential hazard, but she also knew that she couldn't deny them all of life's pleasures.

They negotiated a deal and Dr. Kirschner acquired a section, one square mile, of land for the new settlement, three miles north of the ranch headquarters. She called in surveyors and architects the next day. The women would continue to work for the ranch until they completed the settlement. Jerry and Roberta started interviewing replacement drovers.

Josephine had become curator of the time capsule. She had been able to download everything into the visidatacom unit. She now had the most popular site on the net. This would be a great source of income for the men. Dr. Kirschner had gotten the government to declare the time capsule to be the property of the men; and that they should have all the revenue generated by it.

Another popular item was the tapes of the men and their women as they went about their daily routine. The institute had remote cameras to tape the man and their women in all the public areas. They also had a film crew that recorded certain activities. The tapes were made available through the visidatacom unit to the net. These tapes had already started a new interest in revolvers. One of the tapes showed the men firing their new firearms at the range. Stewart had also been shown firing his magnum revolver. Laura and some of the other women had tried firing it, but found it too much gun for them.

Gun enthusiasts seeing the revolver, wanted one of their own. An instant market for revolvers sprang up. Arms manufacturers were starting to tool up to produce the first revolvers in over two-hundred fifty years. They would be offered in several calibers and styles. People were starting to see that the men were going to be good for business.

The two categories in the time capsule that brought the most interest and the most controversy was history and the Holy Bible. The reform Church long ago had discarded the Bible; they had passed off their own testament as the true word of god. History had also been rewritten to minimize the role of men. Despite the controversy, Josephine didn't try to suppress anything.

The reform church in all its forms had become the major, but not the only church. The Reform Church had only become interested in the Holy Bible in order to discredit it. The other religious groups were also interested in it for the same reason. There were, however, some people, bold clergy and laymen, that were interested in it to see if it could answer some of the questions they had.

The Holy Bible, being the King James version, had been written in an antiquated language that no one understood much anymore. Clifford Johnson had theological training and took over the job of interpreting the Holy Bible text on the net.

Stewart and Laura were going ahead with the planning of their marriage. The institution of Marriage had been abolished even before Stewart's time, so it would be something new to both of them. They looked at the examples of what a wedding ceremony had been like in the old cinemas and in history. The words weren't hard to come up with. Now they only needed a member of the clergy to officiate at the ceremony. No clergy from the Reform Church would do it. There were other churches, but they were not able to get anyone from any of them either.

Dr. Kirschner was aware of the problem of finding someone to officiate at their wedding ceremony. She had offered to get someone to perform the ceremony. She had someone in mind that she felt sure would jump at the chance to do it.

On a Saturday morning, Dr Kirschner finally had her golf date with Monsignor James Espin, two weeks late. It was a cold morning with a gentle breeze coming from the west. The outdoor environmental units that lined the fairways of the golf course easily maintained the air temperature over the golf course at a comfortable twenty degrees centigrade (sixty-eight degrees Fahrenheit). They had a tee time of 8:15 AM.

They teed off on time and both parred the first hole. After driving off the second tee, they started walking down the fairway. Monsignor Espin said, "Well, Anthony, you really stirred up a hornet's nest this time."

Dr. Kirschner smirked. "Oh, how was that?"

"You know, It's the males, or men as everyone is starting to call them. It has had quite an effect on the church. Bishop Langley has been ranting and raving about it since the news broke. She had excommunicated or threatened to excommunicate anyone with an association with the men. The men have a lot of enemies, but I would say that Bishop Langley is at or near the top of the list. Be warned she's someone that needs to be watched."

Dr. Kirschner looked down as they continued on towards the next green. "That was expected. To reveal the existence of males to a society that has never known one is traumatic. As for Bishop Langley, I'll keep her in mind."

Monsignor Espin looked ahead to where her ball lay. "It's not just the men, it's that book, the Holy Bible."

"I havn't had much time to review what's in the time capsule. I believe it has something to do with religion."

Monsignor Espin laughed and slapped Dr. Kirschner on the back. "That's an understatement if I ever heard one. Of course, it's a religious book and it predates ours by several hundred years. That's what has everyone so concerned, that our faith could be based on an untruth."

They got up to where their balls lay and made their approach shots to the green. As they were walking up to the green, Monsignor Espin said, "I know that you don't have much time for religion, so you don't know what has been happening to the church. To make it simple, the church is in trouble. The church has been preaching the truth of a single gender race. Well, as long as it was going great, so were we. When the reproduction rates started to drop, people turned to the church for answers. When we didn't have the answers, the people started to lose faith."

Dr. Kirschner nodded. "Okay, I believe you. I know that most people only play lip service to religion anyway."

Monsignor Espin had to shake her head and laugh a little. "Yes, I know your view on religion and you are still my friend. Now to get back to what I was saying. People have lost faith in the church; and now these men turn up. Is it true that they'll save the human race?"

They were close to the second green. Dr. Kirschner stopped and looked at Monsignor Espin. "James, to be honest with you, it wasn't working. Each generation became more resistant to Ovum fusion. In three more generations we'd no longer be able to reproduce, then extinction. Now the women that the men have impregnated prove that almost everyone can reproduce again, even myself. In short, we couldn't survive as a race without the men."

Monsignor Espin said, "Yes, that's what I figured. As soon as I heard of the males and their time capsule, I got on the net and found the Holy Bible in the section on religion. At first it was shocking, but I got past that and could see it for what it is. I believe it to be the true word of God. What we've believed is a lie. The church must change or perish."

Dr. Kirschner looked at her friend. "James, I know that Bishop Langley has no faith. She believes only in her own power. I also know that she fears you because of your popularity in the priesthood. You must challenge her for control of the church to save it." Dr. Kirschner paused for a few seconds, then continued, "James, I'd like for you to conduct the wedding ceremonies."

Monsignor Espin nodded. "Okay, I'll think about it."

They continued up to the green and made their putts. On the fifth hole, Dr. Kirschner sliced one into the rough and dropped a stroke. At the eighth green she hit a bunker shot too hard and the ball landed off the green on the other side. She missed a putt on the eleventh. Then sliced into the rough again on the thirteenth and sixteenth holes. They both made par on the eighteenth hole and Monsignor Espin won by two strokes.

Monsignor Espin turned to Dr. Kirschner. "Thanks for letting me win. I've given it some thought; and I'll officiate at the weddings."

XXIII

CONSPIRATORS

Bishop Sonya Langley arrived at the office of Casey Toriano, Senior Vice President of the Tidewater Air Cargo Service. Sonya and Casey had been friends ever since elementary school. Sonya knew that she could count on Casey for anything. Sonya felt nervous; she was about to test that friendship to the limit. She planned to draw Casey into the conspiracy.

When Sonya entered Casey's office, Casey came around and stood in front of her desk. Sonya and Casey shook hands. Casey wondered what had brought Sonya to her office all at once without notice. "Good-day, Sonya, you look good."

"Hello, Casey, I'm glad that you could see me."

Casey went to a small bar in her office and removed two glasses and a bottle of wine. "I have something here that I think you will like. It's from the vineyards of North Georgia, it's really good."

They took seats on a sofa in front of a coffee table. Casey poured two glasses, then Sonya tasted the wine. "Yes, it's really good."

Casey brought down her wineglass from her lips. "I'm glad that you like it. I have an extra bottle for you."

Sonya smiled and patted the back of Casey's hand. "Thank you, Casey."

Casey put her wine glass down on the coffee table and looked at Sonya. "Well, what brings you down here to Norfolk?"

Sonya took another sip of wine before she answered. "I had some free time for once in a long time. I just thought it would be nice to come down and pay you a visit."

Casey sat back in the sofa. She had a feeling that it would be more than a friendly visit. Sonya was always busy; and not the person to go out of her way to pay a friendly visit. "Well, that's nice. It's good to see you. I guess that we both work too hard. We need to try to get away more often."

Sonya looked at her friend, knowing that Casey would not believe this to be just a casual visit. She might as well get to the purpose of her visit. "I must confess to you, Casey. I had to make this free time to see you. I'm alarmed at the new developments and needed to talk to someone about it."

Casey took another sip of wine. She had an idea what Sonya meant by new developments. "By new developments, you mean this thing about the subhuman males?"

Sonya continued to look at Casey. Casey's remark had let her know that they shared an opinion of the males. "Yes, I see that you still know me well. I'm sure that we both think the same about this. This is an abomination, a disaster. We just can't allow the purity of the true race to be polluted by these subhuman males."

Casey nodded. "Yes, I'm of the same mind. This is a very unfortunate event. It is contrary to our beliefs. This could seriously affect the doctrine of the church."

Sonya put her wineglass on the coffee table. She was about to make her opening to enlist Casey's aid in her conspiracy against the males. When she spoke, it was with anger in her voice. "It can do more than just affect the doctrine of the church; it can mean the end of the faith! It can destroy the church! It can destroy our pure society! I tell you Casey, this is a catastrophe! Something must be done! These Vile subhuman males and their seed has to be utterly destroyed!"

Casey slowly turned the wine glass in her hand as she pondered the question. It would be a big step to take and she wanted to be sure that she could be equal to it. She also had questions that she needed answers too. She believed strongly in her faith and in the need to keep the race pure. She had also heard the talk about the males being needed. It was a full two minutes before she spoke. "You say that the subhuman males have to be destroyed. I have been hearing that they're the salvation of the human race. What am I to believe?"

Sonya just had to have Casey's support. So, what if they say that the human race is in peril. It's only because of a lack of faith. She felt sure that with God's help, science would somehow find the answer without the subhuman males. "Casey, I respect your concerns, but I firmly believe that God wouldn't let her people perish; she would show us the way. Have you thought that these subhuman males are the final test by God to see if we're really her people, that we have finally earned her favor?"

Casey was a true believer in the pure race. She believed in it so much that she would do anything to safeguard it, even if it meant persecution. She was even prepared to martyr herself for her beliefs. In the end the human race would thank her for it; she would be exonerated by history. "Okay, Sonya, now what can I do about it?"

Sonya smiled; this had been the response that she had been looking for. She now knew that she had Casey's support. 'Casey, are you willing to do whatever it takes to rid us of this problem?"

Casey put her wineglass down on the coffee table, turned to her friend, took her hands into her own and looked into her eyes. 'You can count on me. Whatever you need or whatever I can do for you, all you have to do is ask."

Sonya embraced her friend Casey. "Thank you, Casey. I knew that I could count on you. What we must do is get rid of these males. They can't be allowed to live; they must be killed. Do you have any problem with that?"

Casey shook her head. "No, I don't have any problem with that.

If it's necessary, as distasteful as it might be, it has to be done. What do you have in mind?"

Sonya picked up her wineglass, took a sip, then put it back down on the coffee table. Now was the time to make her case. "Well, Casey, it's easier to say what we don't have. I do have some people that are true believers, that will do anything for me, but I don't have a plan and I don't have time. And where would you get the specialist that you would need to make a plan work? As for most people, they don't care that much about religion. They'll lean in whatever way the wind is blowing. We need people strong enough about their faith to risk everything. I don't think that we can count on anyone high up in the military or law enforcement. As for politicians, publicly they have a strong belief in God; in private they believe only in themselves. As for the military, if they aren't with us, at least they won't be much of a threat. There hasn't been a war in anyone's lifetime. They're now used only for natural disasters and rescue. Law enforcement are the only ones we will have to worry about. There's one thing however that I do have. I have people loyal to me in Amarillo that have been trying to get someone loyal to us hired on as a drover at the Farrow Ranch. If they are successful, we'll at least have someone on the inside."

Casey hoped that they were successful at getting someone hired on at the ranch. She knew that for any plan to work, it was imperative that they have someone on the inside. "Okay, now for the plan. We need to eliminate the males at the ranch, and destroy the lab at the at the St Louis Institute of Genetic Research at the same time. As for the time, we have less than two months."

Casey got up from the sofa and paced in front of the desk for a couple of minutes. Finally, she looked at Sonya. "Let me give it some thought. We can meet this time next week in Richmond at the Redstone Hotel. I think that I can have a plan for you by then."

Sonya, in a show of exuberance, embraced Casey and kissed her on the cheek. "Oh, thank you! Now, if you are ready, I can take you to lunch."

Dr Kirschner had come back to the ranch to check up on the progress of the construction. The contractor had finished pouring the aircraft landing pad. It would be large enough for three medium cargo or executive aircraft. The landing pad would be set hard enough to use in three days. The contractor had started to pour the foundations for the buildings. Once the foundations were ready, they could bring in the prefab buildings and have the living units up in a week. The buildings for the clinic and community center would take another week. The stables, corrals and tack room were almost completed. The indoor swimming pool would be completed soon after the clinic and the community center. The contractor assured Dr. Kirschner that everything would remain on schedule. They would start drilling a new well for the village in two days.

After the meeting with the contractor, Dr. Kirschner had a meeting with Stewart and Laura. Dr. Kirschner had some interesting news for them. Stewart and Laura welcomed Dr. Kirschner into their home and made her comfortable in an easy chair, then served her a drink. Stewart and Laura took their seats on the sofa across from Dr. Kirschner.

Dr. Kirschner put her drink down. "Stewart, I have some news for you. We checked the NASA archives. It seems that when they couldn't find the cryogenic units, they did the next best thing. According to their records those sixteen units never existed. There was never any theft of cryogenic units. No one would ever look for you. It was pure luck that you were even found."

Stewart nodded. He wasn't surprised that they had did something like that "It looks like they didn't want us to turn up ever. By the way, have you found anyone to perform the marriage ceremony?"

"Yes," Dr. Kirschner said, "I have a good friend, Monsignor Espin in St Louis. She has agreed to perform the wedding ceremonies."

Laura and Stewart were really pleased to hear that. "That's great," Laura said, "but I know that Monsignor Espin is in the Reform Church. With Bishop Langley's prohibition on the clergy performing the wedding ceremony, why is she willing to do it?"

This question Dr. Kirschner would be glad to answer. 'It's a long story, but here it goes. There's been a rift developing in the Reform Church lately. Some of the clergy is dissatisfied with the way that Bishop Langley is running the church. They've been looking for a good reason to break away from her, and be able to take part of the followers with them. Monsignor Espin has become very interested in the Holy Bible. It's obvious to her that the Holy Bible is a book of great antiquity. It's much older by many centuries than the book of Gods Truth.

"As soon as she heard of the men, she got on the net and found the time capsule. She found the section on religion and the Holy Bible. She downloaded a copy and it has dominated her waking hours ever since. It didn't take long for Monsignor Espin to recognize the validity of the Holy Bible. On close examination it appears that the Book of gods Truth is a perverted and incomplete copy of the new Testament part of The Holy Bible. Monsignor Espin can see a crisis of faith coming. It was hard at first for her to see the truth, but she got past the period of anger and confusion. Monsignor Espin can now see that the Reform Church has been built on a fraud.

"The people will survive the crisis, but the church won't. She knows that the Reform Church is headed for collapse. She will perform the wedding ceremony for you and Stewart and the others. This is sure to put her at odds with Bishop Langley; and in a position to pick up the pieces after the collapse of the church and the discredit of Bishop Langley."

Stewart and Laura would have liked for their wedding to be just their day, but they realized that they couldn't avoid it also being a political statement. They looked at each other; they didn't have to discuss it; they knew that this would be the best that they were going to get. "Thank you, Dr. Kirschner," Stewart said, 'You can tell Monsignor Espin that we accept her offer. We would be glad to have her perform the wedding ceremony."

That evening Stewart and Laura made a holographic call to Laura's mother. Laura's mother had by now gotten used to calling her daughter

Laura instead of Lawrence. Laura's mother's name was Paul. She had tried the feminine variant of Pauline, but had decided for now not to change it. Laura and Stewart were seated on the sofa. Stewart had dressed in dark-brown trousers, maroon shirt and his new brown boots. Laura was dressed in a jade-green caftan with light-orange trim, embroidery, sash and jade-green velvet slippers.

Laura ordered the visidatacom unit to show a tropical beach in the holograph room. Stewart found himself and Laura sitting on their sofa on a sandy beach being shaded by coconut palms on their left and sparkling-blue ocean on their right. There was even the sound of waves lapping the shore and the scent of tropical flowers and salt air to complete the illusion. Stewart continued to be amazed at how realistic the holographs were; he could swear that they were on a tropical beach. When everything was ready, Laura ordered the visidatacom unit to make the call. Laura's mother's image appeared sitting in her chair facing Stewart and Laura. She was wearing azura-blue lounging pajamas with azure-blue robe and slippers. "Hi, Mom." Laura said. Stewart also said, "Hi, Mom."

Laura's mother smiled. "Hello, Laura, hello, Stewart, it's so good of you to call."

Laura was very excited and grinning with pleasure. "Oh, Mom, I have great news. We're going to be able to get married. Dr. Kirschner has found someone to do it. It's Monsignor Espin of St Louis. We will be husband and wife by the power of the state and before God."

Laura's mother was pleased to hear the good news. "Oh, that's just great, Laura. I'm sure that the wedding will be beautiful. I know that you and Stewart are happy."

"Mom," Laura said, "we'll be sending you an invitation for the wedding. Also, I want Ruth, Cathy and Cornelius to be my bride's maids. We spoke of this when you were out here before. I know that Cathy and Cornelius will be there. What about Ruth?"

With a look of sorrow, Laura's mother shook her head. "I'm sorry, Laura, Ruth's still not willing to make up with you. She said that she wants nothing to do with your wedding, or with any of the men. Maybe someday she'll come around. Let's just hope it'll be soon."

"Mom," Stewart said, "you, Cathy and Cornelius need to come out Friday morning before the wedding. You will be staying with us in our new home. It's going to be a great weekend."

They talked for a few minutes more. Laura spoke of her morning sickness and other changes that were taking place with her. Her mother gave her advice on what to do about it. Stewart and Laura's mother spoke a lot with each other. Laura's mother now regarded Stewart as one of the family.

The young woman entered the vestibule of the cathedral from the bright afternoon sunlight and waited a couple of minutes to let her eyes adjust to the dim light of the interior of the cathedral. The young woman was Francis Tyler, eighteen, petite and slim. She was a student of George Town University in Washington D. C. Francis was in turmoil; all her beliefs were being challenged. Ever since those subhuman males were found everything had been turned upside down. Why didn't those stupid people on that ranch just leave them where they were? She thought. Because of them her religious beliefs were under attack. Something had to be done. It they weren't here, then their damn blasphemous religious book could be discredited.

Francis then went to the altar, where she knelt and prayed. She felt close to God here and maybe God would give her the answers that she had been looking for.

As Francis kneeled at the altar praying, bishop Langley watched her. She wondered what troubled this young human.

XXIV

THE PLAN

Stewart and Laura had been able to speak to Monsignor Espin by visidatacom. Monsignor Espin forthright and gracious manner had put them at ease. After a while, despite the fact that Monsignor Espin was a member of the hierarchy of the Reform Church, Stewart felt sure that they had an ally. Stewart could see that Monsignor Espin, as an independent thinker, would be willing to accept change if it could be shown to be the truth.

They went over the wedding ceremony with her. Stewart and Laura reviewed video clips showing examples of how weddings were conducted in the past with Monsignor Espin. After reviewing wedding ceremonies in the time capsule, Stewart and Laura had written their own wedding vows. They went over the vows with Monsignor Espin, so that she would know them and in what order they would be said. After speaking with Monsignor Espin, they were glad to have her. They could tell right off that She would be just as eager as they were to make the wedding a success, even if for different reasons.

Stewart and Laura knew very well that they were setting a standard for the future, when the children yet to be born came of age and married. Stewart and Laura were aware that theirs and the other wedding ceremonies would be the pattern for the future. They were paying attention to details to make sure that everything would be right. There had been a discussion about having a single ceremony for all the couples, but they had decided not to. They felt that every couple should have their own day.

They knew the costumes and their significance. It hadn't been very difficult to program the sewing machine to produce the black suits that the men and Jerry would wear. They all had decided that instead of tuxedos, they would wear plain black suits with white dress shirts with ruffles and black pearl buttons, but no tie; no one was eager to reintroduce that useless piece of male attire.

As for the bride's gowns, all the women were set on having their wedding gowns with the same fullness of detail and elegance as the examples seen in the time capsule. The machine could be programmed to do most of it. However, there would still be some hand finishing. How much depended on what style of gown the bride wanted. After the machine put the gowns together, they were sent off for finishing. Everything else they needed for the ceremonies would be easy to arrange for.

The entire broadcast networks and independent film companies bid on the rights to produce the documentary on the weddings. The contract went to the highest bidder that had a reputation for quality productions; the Pan American Film Productions of Mexico City. The first wedding would be Stewart and Laura. Dr. Nichols and Nancy would follow them in one week. There would be a wedding every week until all the couples were married.

Two more of the women in the group were now pregnant, they were Jennifer and Crystal. Jennifer's embryo had the 'Y' chromosome. Further proof that the human race was on the road to recovery.

Dr. Kirschner had everything running well. Evelyn ran the project at the ranch, with the help of Dr. Mays, Dr. Nichols and Nurse Connie.

They collected the samples, separated the spermatozoon with the 'Y' chromosome from that of the 'X' chromosome, coded, cataloged and froze them for shipment to St Louis.

At the laboratory of the St Louis Institute of Genetic Research they were logged in and stored in lots. Some would be used in St Louis; most would be shipped to reproduction labs in countries around the world. They were just storing it for now. It would be more than a month before they received the first lots of ovum to be fertilized.

Dr. Kirschner had been busy recruiting more staff for the program. She would like to achieve two million pregnancies in North America the first year of the program. They hoped to have another seventeen to eighteen million worldwide. They would use only the 'Y' chromosome spermatozoon the first two years. They would then start producing an increasing amount of female embryos. Dr. Kirschner planned to run the program for at least fifteen years. By then the new males would be starting to get old enough to make donations. They could then establish sperm banks around the world. Over the next fifteen years the eleven men would be the fathers of over two-hundred million children worldwide. Genealogy would be a big field in the future to keep half-brothers and half-sisters from marrying each other.

Bishop Langley sat at a table in the lounge of the Redstone Hotel in Richmond. She had been waiting for about forty minutes now for Casey to show up. She had been thinking about Monsignor Espin. That bitch would be marrying those subhuman males to their human consorts. Monsignor Espin had become too strong in the church and too popular in her diocese. What she couldn't afford now was a fight for control of the church with Monsignor Espin, or a split in the church. She just had to ignore her for now and wait for the right time to get rid of her. They had to be rid of the subhuman males first. Once the subhuman males were out of the way, things would go back to normal. Then she would be able to deal with Monsignor Espin.

She looked at her watch again. She expected Casey to be here by now. She looked at the door again just as Casey entered the lounge. Sonya smiled at her friend and waved. Seeing Sonya, Casey came over to the table and took her seat across the table from Sonya. "Hi, Sonya. I hope I didn't keep you waiting long?"

Sonya shook her head. "No, Casey, I just got here myself. What are you drinking?"

'I'll take a bourbon on the rocks."

Sonya ordered Casey's drink and a fresh one for herself. They exchanged pleasantries while the waitress got their drinks. After the drinks arrived, Sonya got down to business. "Well, Casey, what do you have?"

Casey looked around to make sure that no one was eavesdropping before she began. "I've come up with a plan. As of yet it's not complete, but I do have it put together enough to give you an outline. Before I get to the plan, I should review the obstacles. First, the Farrow Ranch is in the open far from any population center. It would be far easier if the males were in St Louis." Casey Paused for a moment before she continued. "Well, they have a lot of open space around them to set up security. They have set up an electronic cordon around the ranch with motion sensors, security cameras, robotic police patrol vehicles and troop strong points. There is no way that we can approach it from the ground. Second, the ranch is protected from approach from the air. They have an aircraft exclusion zone with a radius of twenty miles. You can't get within ten miles of the ranch."

Sonya had a worried look on her face. It all looked pretty much hopeless to her. She wondered how they could ever get past all that security. 'If you can't get close by ground or air; then how are we going to get to the subhuman males?"

Casey gave Sonya a reassuring look and continued, "Now, even with the exclusion zone, we must make our assault by air. To try to go in overland would be madness. We can do it by air, but we still need a way to disable the beacon."

THE PLAN

This beacon was new to Sonya, she had never heard of it before. "What is this beacon? I've never heard of it before."

Casey took time to take a sip from her drink before she answered Sonya's question. "That's not unusual that you have not heard of them before, they're not often used. Now, there are certain zones of restricted air space, but if you fly into or through them, you only get a fine, or your ticket is pulled for a period of time. Now the police and military are the only ones that have these beacons. They're used only when for security reasons they must keep all aircraft away from a certain area."

Curious, Sonya said, "How do they work?"

Casey saw that an explanation was in order. 'Well, Sonya, there normal range is twenty miles, although they can be adjusted. When the aircraft hits the outer edge of the exclusion zone, a warning flashes on the pilot's video display, giving a heading to void the exclusion zone. If the aircraft reaches the intermediate zone, the beacon sends a command to the aircraft's visidatacom unit to turn away. If by some way the pilot is able to override the aircrafts visidatacom unit and keep coming, when it reaches the inner boundary, the beacon will fire a powerful electronic beam that will fry the circuits of the visidatacom unit on the aircraft. Without the visidatacom unit the aircraft is uncontrollable and it crashes."

Sonya nodded her head. She realized that it was a system that had been designed not to be defeated, but there had to be some way around it. "I know that there are aircraft that are flying in there. Do they turn off the beacon when the aircraft fly in?"

Casey shook her head. "No, the aircraft are equipped with a beacon disable unit. The disable unit allows the aircraft to fly in and out without being challenged by the beacon."

"Can we get a disable unit to allow us to fly in?"

Casey again shook her head. 'No, the beacon will only recognize its own units. "Casey paused to emphasized what she was about to say. "Look, Sonya, there are only two ways to defeat the system. We could steal one of their units, or disable the beacon. To steal one of their disable units is remote. To even get close to one of their disable units is very unlikely; and even if we were to steal one it would be missed right away and the codes would be changed. To steal one is out of the question. Our only option is to disable the beacon."

Sonya thought for a minute as she turned her drink slowly in her hands, then looked up. "Casey, my people in Amarillo have managed to get someone loyal to our cause hired as a replacement drover at the Farrow Ranch. We now have someone on the inside that should be able to do it."

Casey reached across the table, grabbed Sonya's hand and smiled. "Oh, that's just great! We had to have someone on the inside, or we were defeated before we even started," Casey took a sip from her drink, then continued, "Now, for the plan. We have a cargo flight that flies from Denver to Houston, it's flight 934 departing at 2:15 AM. On days that we have more cargo than one aircraft can carry, we put on a second aircraft. The first aircraft becomes flight 934-A. The second aircraft becomes flight 934-B. It leaves at 2:25 AM, ten minutes behind flight 934-A. The flight time from Denver to the Farrow Ranch is fifty minutes. The attack will begin at 3:15 AM. I would choose a day in the middle of the week, like Wednesday or Thursday."

Sonya showed a lot of interest. Casey took a break to order fresh drinks. When they had their drinks, Casey continued, "Now, we will start the attack with a bomb run, then we will come back around, land and conduct a mop-up operation."

"You say that you will use a bomb. What kind of a bomb?"

Casey took another quick look around to be sure that no one was eavesdropping. 'It will be a hydrogen fuel bomb. It will be a large cylinder filled with over two-thousand gallons of liquid hydrogen fuel. We will come in over the target at two-thousand feet above the ground and drop the bomb by parachutes. A bomb that size will take three parachutes. When we drop the bomb, the parachutes will take about ten seconds to fully deploy. At that time, it will fall between three to four-hundred feet. It will take another sixty-five seconds more or less depending on air density to reach a point two-hundred foot above the ground where it will explode. The bomb will make a huge fireball and shock wave. The shock wave will collapse the buildings and the fireball will burn up all the oxygen in the air. Most, if not all, will be killed by the buildings collapsing on them, or by asphyxiation.

We'll make the run at one-hundred eighty miles-per-hour. As soon as the bomb is released, we'll accelerate at full thrust and be four to four and a half miles away when the bomb goes off. We'll make a one-hundred eighty-degree turn, come back and land. The assault team will make a sweep and take care of any survivors, If any ones still alive. We'll be away before the security force can respond. We'll fly out west into New Mexico, then turn north across the wilderness zone towards Denver, staying below radar. After dropping the assault team off in a remote clearing near the lodge. I'll fly the aircraft to a remote location near Salt Lake City. There I'll disembark and send the aircraft off on a programmed flight to the northwest to run out of fuel and crash in the wilderness zone."

Sonya had been paying close attention to Casey's plan. So far, she liked it. Her one concern was that no investigation leads back to her. "It sounds great Casey, but I'm worried about you and the others getting away after you hit the ranch and kill the subhuman males."

Casey reached across the table and patted the back of Sonya's hand. 'Don't be concerned about it Sonya. I have taken care of it. I have three close friends that will testify that I was on a hunting trip with them in Wyoming near the Yellowstone. As for the assault team, at intervals over the next few days, they will fly back east from Denver. My friends will head back a couple of days after the operation, stopping to refuel at Salt Lake City. There I will join them to fly back east.

"What about the assault team?" Sonya said, "Won't the police trace them to Denver?"

Casey shook her head. 'No, they will make their flights out to Denver and back on Tidewater Aircraft without any record of them making the flights. Besides, with no direct connection, the police won't be looking for them anyway. Anyone involved in the operation can fly on Tidewater aircraft without any record."

So far it sounded okay to Sonya. "Now, what about the laboratory in St Louis?"

Casey had also worked out a plan for the laboratory in St Louis. "We'll have to hit it at the same time that we hit the ranch. It'll be a vehicle bomb. The St Louis Institute of Genetic Research will be easy to penetrate. They have a security fence, but their gates are as not yet high security. They have only two guards on duty at each gate at a time. They believe that with their internal security that's enough. At night only the main gate is open. They have a roving patrol and guards in some of the buildings. All we have to do is crash the gate. Then we can take out the laboratory before they can do anything about it. Now, this is the weakest part of the operation. The person that drives the vehicle bomb will have a difficult time getting away after they deliver the bomb."

Sonya nodded. "The plan sounds good so far. How many people will you need?"

Casey took another sip of her drink. "Well, Sonya, I have someone to fly the aircraft with me. She's our senior pilot from Miami, Troy Quiller. I also have someone to lead the assault team, a former police officer, Lestine Bradshaw. I also have someone to build the bombs. To me she gives the name of Ashley McKibben, but knowing the person she is, I suspect it an alias. Well it doesn't matter what her name is, as long as she serves us well. We can carry as many as fifteen people on the aircraft with the bomb. Lestine will need at least twelve people for the assault team and we still need someone to deliver the bomb to the laboratory."

Sonya had enough people that she could trust to make up the assault team. She also recalled the young human that had been coming to the cathedral. "You can leave that to me, Casey. I can supply the personnel to Lestine for the assault team. As for the person to deliver the St Louis bomb, I already have someone in mind. Oh, Casey, can you have this

THE PLAN

Ashley McKibben give me a call. I need to know where the person that will deliver the St louis bomb needs to go to get in contact with her."

Casey was pleased that Sonya could supply the personnel. "okay, I'll have her get in contact with you."

Sonya and Casey sat in the lounge of the Redstone Hotel for a few more minutes talking, before going to lunch.

Stewart and Laura's wedding would be in less than a week and Laura was really excited. She was aware that hers and Stewart's wedding would be the first worldwide in anyone's lifetime. The ceremony wouldn't be a large one, but they had researched it and every part of the ceremony would be according to custom. Dr. Nichols would be Stewart's best man. The ushers were Thomas Owens and Allan Worley. Laura's maid of honor would be her sister Cathy. Her sister Cornelius would be one of the bridesmaids'. She would've liked to have her sister Ruth as one of the bridesmaids', but her sister Ruth was still under the influence of the Reform Church and wanted nothing to do with the men or their wedding. Laura hoped that over time Ruth's views would change. Nancy would be her other bridesmaid. Jerry Lawton would be walking her down the aisle. The guests would include everyone living on the ranch, to include some of the security personnel; Dr. Kirschner and some of her staff from St louis. The ceremony would be in the new community Center. The media would be broadcasting it live."

Because the men were so crucial to the recovery of the human race, they couldn't be exposed to anything that could be detrimental to their health. With this in mind, everything would be done to give them a fulfilling and interesting life without exposure to the general population. That applied also to their women, because of their closeness to the men. At first the women objected to the idea that restrictions would be placed on their movements, but now that they were known to be the men's partners, they had no anonymity. They were recognized everywhere they went; they soon accepted their isolation with the men.

XXV

MARTYR

Francis Tyler passed from the bright light of the mid-day through the doors of the cathedral into the dim light of the vestibule. She stood there until her eyes became adjusted to the light. She then proceeded down the center aisle. At the alter she knelt and prayed. She didn't know it, but she was being watched.

Bishop Langley stood in the shadows at the back of the cathedral. She had known that this young human would be coming at this time and had been waiting for her. Bishop Langley just hung back in the shadows and waited until she felt that the young human was about to leave. Bishop Langley timed her approach to be face to face with the young human just as she turned to walk back down the aisle.

Francis turned and was surprised to find herself face to face with a middle-aged human dressed in the yellow caftan with emerald-green trim, embroidery and sash of the bishop of Washington D. C. and head of the church in North America. 'Oh, excuse me your Excellency; I didn't hear you come in."

Bishop Langley gave a reassuring smile. 'that's all-right child, I didn't mean to startle you." Bishop Langley reached out and put her hand on Francis' shoulder. "I have seen you come alone before. You pray at the altar, then leave." Bishop Langley paused and looked into

Francis' eyes. "Is something troubling you child?"

Francis became so overcome by the bishop's attention, that it took a few seconds before she could speak. "Oh, your Excellency, my problems are too small for you to concern yourself with."

Bishop Langley could see that this young human was very intimidated and respectful of authority figures. Perhaps she could be turned to her own use. "Nonsense child, despite my title, I'm first of all a priest; and it's my duty as a priest to serve my parishioners. I'm about to have tea. Would you like to join me?" Francis couldn't say no to the Bishop of Washington D. C. The idea of having tea with such an important personage thrilled her. She accepted the invitation to tea.

Bishop Langley took Francis to her office in the rectory, then had her secretary serve tea and shortbread. Francis felt honored by the attention of Bishop Langley. After the tea was served and they were alone, Bishop Langley spoke, "Now, child. Oh, I don't know your name."

"It's Francis Tyler, your Excellency.'

"Good, now, Francis, what's bothering you? How can I help you?"

Francis looked down at her teacup for a few seconds before she spoke. She just couldn't believe that such a dignitary could be interested in her concerns. 'Your Excellency, I don't know how you can help me."

Bishop Langley gave Francis a reassuring smile. 'Come now, it can't be all that bad. Now, what is it?"

Francis became emotional and tears started to run down her cheeks. "Your Excellency, it's about the human males. How can they be? Their an abomination!"

Bishop Langley nodded. This was more than she had hoped for. If Francis could be so traumatized by the subhuman males; she might be willing to do anything to get rid of them. "Yes, Francis, I quite agree with you. They must be the spawn of the devil."

Francis started to feel more at ease with Bishop Langley. She had needed someone to talk to. Now that she had a sympathetic ear, she couldn't hold anything back. "Your Excellency, I'm a true believer in the church and its teaching. That's why these subhuman males can't be allowed to contaminate our pure race. How can a true human ever consider taking the seed of these vile sub humans into their body? My mind rebels at the thought of it."

Bishop Langley chose her words well. She needed to feel Francis out to see just how far she would be willing to go. "I know how you feel, Francis. Like me, your faith is strong, but not all humans share your faith in the true God. They have been beguiled by the devil. All they can feel is an empty womb. They're willing to compromise their faith and their race for the promise of a child."

Francis nodded; she was glad to have someone of such immense stature confirm her beliefs. "Yes, Excellency, I know that the faith of most humans isn't as strong as it should be; that they can be made to do the devil's bidding. I know that nothing can stop them, unless the church can do something."

Bishop Langley smiled, pleased so far with how the conversation had been going. "Well, Francis, I feel as you do, but there isn't much that the church can do. The church can't prevent it. Only the government can; and the government isn't willing to. The real tragedy is that the subhuman males are also false prophets. They have brought with them a blasphemous message from the devil. If they succeed, then their message will be believed. This can be very damaging to the church and the faith, but if they fail, then their message fails." Bishop Langley had reached the critical point in the conversation. She had put it all out there; now it all depended on how Francis reacted to it.

Francis straightened up in her chair; she had come to a decision. She knew the answer to the question before she even asked it. "your Excellency, what has to be done to make them fail?"

Bishop Langley gave the answer without hesitation. "The males and their seed must be destroyed before they can infect the true pure race.' Bishop Langley had made her case. It was up to Francis now. She hoped that she had presented her case well. She felt sure that Francis could be the person for the job of delivering the bomb to the laboratory in St Louis.

Francis sat for over two minutes in thought before she moved. She then stood, smoothed her trousers, straightened her jacket and ran her fingers through her short dark-brown hair. 'Thank you. Your Excellency. I have found out talk very enlightening. I must go now."

Bishop Langley showed Francis to the door. After Francis left, Bishop Langley went back and sat at her desk again. Francis hadn't said yes, but she hadn't said no either.

The next day at noon Francis entered the cathedral again. She waited for a couple of minutes in the vestibule, then walked down the center aisle to kneel before the alter. She prayed a little longer than usual that day. While Francis prayed, Bishop Langley entered and stood off to the side of the alter. When Francis finished praying, instead of leaving, she went over to Bishop Langley. When she got to Bishop Langley, she nodded her head as a show of respect. 'Good-day, your Excellency."

"Good-day, Francis, it's good to see you again. Have you been able to resolve any of your problems yet?"

"Yes, your Excellency, I can see the problem more clearly now."

Bishop Langley put a hand on Francis' shoulder and smiled at her. 'That's good, Francis. I'm glad that I was able to be of help to you yesterday."

Francis didn't respond right away. She just stood in front of Bishop Langley like she had something else to say, but was reluctant to bring it up. Bishop Langley broke the impasse. "Francis, come walk with me. We can have tea."

Francis followed Bishop Langley to her office.

When the tea had been served and they were alone in the office, Bishop Langley said, "Now, Francis, is there anything else that you would like to talk to me about?"

"Yes, your Excellency, there's something that you said yesterday that I can't get out of my mind."

"What's that?"

Francis cleared her throat before she answered. "Your Excellency, you said that the males and their seed must be destroyed. Isn't that murder?"

Bishop Langley had to think for a few seconds. This could be a very tricky question. She had to make Francis see that it would be all right to kill the subhuman males, without actually telling her to do it. It was very important that she have the right answers for Francis. When finally, she had the answer framed in her mind, she said, "If you are killing true humans it would be murder, but we have determined they're in fact subhuman agents of the devil. It would be God's work that's being done."

Francis thought for a moment. "Well, your Excellency, I believe you when you say that it would be doing God's work. However, what if true humans tried to stop it?"

Bishop Langley knew that all depended on the next answer. "Francis, as you know, we all have free will. It's the way God wanted it. We are free to do good or evil. Now any true humans who are assisting these agents of the devil are themselves agents of the devil. Some may be hurt, but you may be saving their soul."

Francis took her time responding. Bishop Langley held her breath in anticipation. "Then, your Excellency, I hope that someone can do something about it. I wish that I were in a position to do something."

Bishop Langley sat back in her chair relieved. She had the person to deliver the St louis bomb. She had her martyr. "Am I hearing you right? You would be willing to take action to preserve the purity of the human race?"

"Yes, your Excellency, If I could do something, I would."

Bishop Langley got Frances' home and web address. She told Francis that there might be a chance for her to do something for her faith and race. When Francis left, Bishop Langley's office, she had a spring in her step. At last she felt reasonably certain that she could do something to defend her faith.

XXVI

WEDDING

Friday morning, Dr Kirschner, along with her staff and Monsignor Espin flew into the village the men had named New Adrian. Monsignor Espin and the wedding party would have a rehearsal that afternoon, followed by a groom's dinner. The film crew that would be covering the wedding were driving in from Amarillo, and would be there in time to cover the rehearsal.

Dr. Kirschner felt good about how everything had gone. Her program was on schedule and everything had been going really well here in New Adrian. She had a feeling that New Adrian would turn out to be a good place to live. In two to three years the program should be doing well enough, and the public would be accustomed enough to the men, that they could start going out in public. It would have to be carefully monitored at first, but they would eventually have a near normal life.

Theresa Matos had been on the move since before sunrise. This was the most important assignment of her career; and she wanted everything to be just right. She had checked the placement of all fourteen remote cameras that she had set up in the community center of New Adrian. She had four technicians to monitor and control the cameras. At the rehearsal yesterday everyone had been very informal in dress and demeanor. Today would be different; the air seemed to have a charge of excitement. Even she wasn't immune to it.

The community center had started to fill up with people. Everyone was in formal dress; most in full-length formal gowns, some in suits. The police officers and military that were attending wore their dress uniforms. The wearing of full-length formal gowns of elegant design as formal wear was new to her. Dark suits of conservative style had always been the norm for formal wear. After it had been explained to her the difference in formal attire for men and women; she had gone to the time capsule on the visidatacom unit to research women's formal attire. She was now wearing a full-length garnet-red silk brocade gown. It was a new experience for her and she liked it.

The Men Really stood out in the crowd. They were all wearing dark suits; and most had the facial hair that they called beards. Theresa was still getting used to being around the men. It was one thing to see the pictures or holographic images of them, but something else to meet them in person. The community center looked beautiful with the candles, fresh flowers, other decorations and everyone in their best formal attire. Theresa felt good about herself. Today she and the pan American Film productions of Mexico City would be a part of history

Laura got dressed in her wedding gown with Nancy's help. Laura had researched the films in the time capsule where she got the idea for the style of her wedding gown. It was an ancient style that hadn't been seen or worn by anyone for over three-hundred years. Nothing like it, or even close, could be found in the visidatacom unit that controlled the sewing machine. There were, however, in the time capsule patterns of seventh, eighteenth and nineteenth century costumes were found. One of these patterns was used to produce a pattern for the wedding dress. Once it had been programed into the visidatacom unit, it took less than an hour to produce it. Even then she had to send it out for a lot of hand finishing. The gown had been made of white satin with fitted bodice, full floor-length skirt, long sleeves and high collar. The gown had plenty of embroidery and seed pearls. It was a heavy gown, with lots of fabric and stiff petticoats. She had spent many evenings wearing it to get used to moving in it. She wasn't far enough in her pregnancy to show yet. To complete her ensemble she had white shoes, white vail and underneath everything a blue garter. With her bouquet of white, pink and red roses she was ready.

Jerry Lawton and the men had arrived wearing their black suits. The suits that the men and Jerry wore had been a lot easier to produce. Even with the formal styling and special details, it hadn't been hard to program the computer to produce them. This would be a special day, not just for Stewart and Laura, but for all the men and women involved. They were reestablishing old customs and traditions; they wanted everything to be just right. Stewart and Laura both had their vows memorized.

Thomas had just escorted Laura's mother to her seat in the front row. Stewart and Dr. Nichols took their places at the altar. Monsignor Espin stood ready in her place. She didn't wear the emerald-green caftan of the Reform Church, knowing how much the men disliked it. She had been doing research of her own and was wearing a black cassock with red trim and waist sash. The statement that she made by discarding the green and wearing black wasn't lost on anyone there. It could only be seen as a direct challenge to Bishop Langley.

The music changed, and everyone stood as the wedding procession started down the aisle. After all the ushers and bridesmaids were in position, the music changed again to the wedding march. Laura started down the aisle escorted by Jerry Lawton. Arriving at the altar, Jerry handed Laura off to Stewart and took her seat. The wedding ceremony went flawlessly, Stewart and Laura exchanged vows and rings. At the conclusion of the ceremony, Monsignor Espin introduced Stewart and Laura to the wedding guest as Mr. And Mrs. Stewart Vaughn. They then walked down the aisle arm in arm.

The reception was going great. Everyone had been able to relax and enjoy themselves. After a while no one seemed to notice the cameras anymore. Theresa Matos was really pleased with herself; the wedding ceremony had really been good, but it had been formal and everyone had been acting stiff and unnatural. Now at the reception everyone had started to relax and be themselves. Her viewers would now be able to see the men as they really were. Theresa by then had gotten used to being around the men. At first their strangeness and casual self-assured manner awed her. She had even at first found their strong-deep voices and large size intimidating, but it wasn't long before she was at ease and on friendly terms with them. She found them to be not much different than anyone else.

After the cake had been cut and the toasts made, Monsignor Espin, Stewart and Laura found a quiet place where they could talk in private. When they were comfortably seated, Stewart said, "Monsignor Espin, Laura and I would like to thank you again for coming here to perform the ceremony."

Monsignor Espin smiled at him. "It was my pleasure; this was something that I really wanted to do."

Laura still had some concern for Monsignor Espin; she, like everyone else, knew of Bishop Langley's threats. "We didn't know if we were going to be able to get anyone to marry us. Bishop Langley has threatened to excommunicate anyone who performed a wedding ceremony. Are you afraid that she may try to excommunicate you?"

Monsignor Espin laughed. "Fat chance! She would like to, but she wouldn't dare. She doesn't want to risk a rift in the church."

Now Stewart became curious and asked, "I thought as head of the church, she could do as she wished?"

Monsignor Espin could see that an explanation of what went on behind the scene in the church would be needed. She said," Of course, you don't understand what is happening in the church now. There has been a long running division of loyalties in the church. Bishop Langley is more a politician than a priest. She was just enough of a priest to get by. Most of her time and energy was spent involved in church politics. Her rise in the church hierarchy was meteoric. She has her supporters in the church that wield the power. On the other end is a group of priests who see the church as becoming corrupt under Bishop Langley's leadership. Most of the priesthood and sisters are in the middle waiting to see who wins out. I've always wanted to be just a priest that serves the church, but I've become by acclamation the leader of the opposition."

Stewart had been listening intently to Monsignor Espin. "So, that's why she won't excommunicate you."

Monsignor Espin nodded. 'That's part of it, but the main reason is you and the other men. Finding you has upset everything. She's afraid that if she excommunicates me, I'll take most of the church with me. You and Laura wanted to get married in part to set a precedent for the institution of marriage. I wanted to perform the ceremony to set the precedent that it's a religious ceremony performed, recognized and defended by the church. I can see now that the church has been taken down the wrong path. The church must change and I want to change with it."

"Yes, it's a whole new world," Laura said, "it'll never be the same again, and that's good. The old way wasn't working."

Stewart nodded in agreement. Monsignor Espin said, "Everything's on the table. Bishop Langley's betting on the status quo. I'm betting on a future of change in the church. At stake is the control of the church. Today when I put on this black cassock, I made a break with the past, or perhaps I should say the present; the black represents the old-true church. I'll continue to wear the black. Bishop Langley can't ignore me now; and the priesthood will have to choose sides.

Tuesday afternoon Bishop Langley sat in her office at the rectory. Since Monsignor Espin performed that wedding Saturday, the church and priesthood had been in rebellion. By Sunday some priest was wearing black cassocks. By yesterday there were more and now today black cassocks were being seen in every parish in the country. Times might be difficult now, but in the end Bishop Langley felt sure that she would prevail. When the males were taken care of and this was all over with, she would remember who her friends were. There would be a purge of the priesthood, she would crush this rebellion.

Her secretary announced Ashley McKibben and admitted her to Bishop Langley's office. Bishop Langley stood up behind her desk as Ashley entered and they shook hands. Ashley took a seat in the chair across the desk from Bishop Langley, as the secretary brought tea. After the secretary left them, Bishop Langley said, 'Thank you for coming, Ashley."

Ashley took a sip of her tea and put the cup back down. "I'm glad to come, your Excellency; after all you're the one that I'm really working for."

Bishop Langley kept studying Ashley. She had a good idea that Ashley was a human that knew whom she had to please; and that she could be relied on to be discreet. 'I'm glad that you see it that way. What I have asked you here for today, is to find out how long it'll take to get the job done."

Ashley had begun to feel that this wasn't the only reason that Bishop Langley wanted to see her. She would have to play along to see what the real reason was. She gave a look of wonderment with raised eyebrows and wrinkled brow. "Hasn't Casey told you yet?"

Bishop Langley nodded. "Yes, she tells me everything, but I need to hear it from you. After all, you're the expert and nothing can happen until the bombs are ready.'

"Okay, your Excellency, three weeks to get everything ready."

Bishop Langley nodded again. 'Yes, that's what Casey told me. I just needed to hear it from you. I would also like to know if there's anything I can do for you?"

"What about the bomb that will be dropped on New Adrian?"

"Everything I need is easily obtainable from legitimate sources, your Excellency."

"That's good. By the way, are you sure that it'll be powerful enough to do the job?"

"Yes, your Excellency, if they get it on the target, it's powerful enough to do the job."

Bishop Langley paused for a moment and gave a satisfactory nod. "Fine, now what about the St Louis bomb?"

"On that one, your Excellency, I'll have to steal a delivery van and make modifications, but it'll also be ready."

Bishop Langley took her time before asking the next question. 'do you have someone to deliver it yet?"

"No, your Excellency, this is the most hazardous task in the whole operation. I still need someone to deliver it."

Bishop Langley drummed her fingers on her desk for a few seconds before she continued. "I've someone in mind. Is there any special skill required to do this job?"

Ashley shook her head. "No, your Excellency, all they have to do is drive the delivery vehicle and follow instructions to the letter."

Bishop Langley smiled. "good, then I have that person for you. She's perfect for the job. She's a true believer and will carry out her assignment without fail." She handed Ashley a card. "This is her home and web address. You can get in touch with her."

Ashley took the card from bishop Langley, and checked the name and address on the card. "I'm leaving for St louis tomorrow, your Excellency. I'll get in touch with her and take her with me. Casey already has a house rented for us to do the work."

"Good, now there's one thing you can do for me."

Ashley could feel that the true purpose for this meeting was about to be revealed. 'yes, your Excellency, what's that?"

Bishop Langley looked hard at her. "I must not be linked to this. Will this person, Francis, be able to avoid capture by the police?"

Ashley thought for a moment before she answered. "She'll have a good chance to evade capture after the bomb goes off, your Excellency.'

Bishop Langley shook her head. "That's not good enough. I need an absolute guarantee that the police will never get her, if you know what I mean."

Ashley nodded. "Yes, your Excellency, I know all too well what you mean." Knowing that Bishop Langley didn't want Francis to survive the attack.

"You don't have any qualms about it? Can you do it?"

It didn't make any difference to Ashley either way. Bishop Langley would owe her for it. "It will be done, your excellency."

Bishop Langley felt pleased by the response. "Good, now to the other group. Casey tells me they'll be able to get away, but I also need a guarantee on them. Do you have any problems with that?"

Ashley could do it; and it meant that Bishop Langley would be in her debt for the rest of her life. She could imagine the doors of opportunity that could be opened for her. "No, your Excellency. After all, you're the one I'm working for."

Bishop Langley felt so relieved that she was almost giddy. "thank you, Ashley, I'm glad that we understand each other."

Ashley got up to go and shook hands with Bishop Langley. "You can count on me, your Excellency. Now, I must go and see this Francis Tyler."

XXVII

PLANS COUNTER PLANS

Casey had been busy lining up the aircraft for the mission. She had to make sure that they had one of the companies' medium size cargo carriers equipped to make air cargo drops by parachutes ready at the Denver air terminal when they needed it. She would send the aircraft out four days ahead of time, then show it down for maintenance so that it would remain available for the mission.

As for the bomb, she had acquired a compressed gas tank ten feet long and six feet in diameter. She was having skids attached so that it could be loaded into the aircraft and dropped by parachutes. The parachutes and other equipment were easy to obtain. When the tank was ready, they would fly it out to Denver on the same aircraft that would drop it and just leave it on the aircraft.

Two to three days before the operation, Ashley would come from St. louis and complete the bomb, except for the liquid hydrogen fuel. The afternoon before the operation, Casey would have the tank filled with liquid hydrogen fuel. Casey had also rented the house in St Louis for Ashley, and a lodge west of Denver for Lestine Bradshaw to train her assault team of twelve humans.

Wednesday morning, Ashley and Francis departed from the tidewater

Air Cargo terminal at Richmond on a flight to St Louis. Upon arrival, Ashley had Francis rent a car. They then drove out to the house that Casey had rented for them. Casey had rented a house with a barn on the outskirts of St louis. The house was located away from major roads with no close neighbors. They needed the isolated location and the barn to build the bomb.

After dropping off their bags, they took the car and went out to make a reconnaissance of the area around the St Louis Institute of Genetic Research. They then purchased the supplies and equipment that they would need during their stay in St louis.

The next day Ashley stole a light delivery van. After disabling the tracking system, she brought it back to the barn. The vehicle belonged to the Simon's Florists Company. She reprogrammed the signs on the sides of the van to that of the East Central Missouri Industrial Machine Repair Service LTD. She then changed the polarity of the vehicles surface finish to change it from light-green to dark-blue. After the outside changes were made, the vehicle had to be modified on the inside to carry the bomb. The vehicles electronics also had to be shielded against being disabled. On Friday, Ashley had received an airfreight delivery by Tidewater Air Cargo from Baltimore. This was everything that she would need to make the fuses and triggers for the bombs. After they had the delivery van ready, Ashley started to work on the fuses and triggers. She did this work alone.

Francis had work of her own to do. She would be the one to deliver the bomb. The target would be the reproduction laboratory where the male sperm was being kept in a frozen state. Ashley had a map of the St louis Institute of Genetic Research to study and memorize. The institute was planned around a twenty-seven-acre lake. The main entrance came in from a main thoroughfare and ran three-quarters of a mile where it forked left and right to circle the lake. In the fork in the road at the head of the lake stood the administration building. A three-story building of red sandstone and copper colored glass and metal. The administration building sat inside the road next to the lake. The other buildings were arranged around the lake. The laboratories and other buildings were located on the outside of the road around the lake. Located inside the road, on the lake, were on campus residences for some of the senior staff of the institute. The grounds were well kept, with open space, trees, ornamental shrubs and flowers. Dr. Kirschner's residence was inside the road on the lake, across the lake from the administration building. One other road came into the institution campus from the rear of the lake.

The target for the bombing would be the forth building to the right of the administration building, as viewed coming in from the main gate. It was a compact five-story building made of stainless steel and reflective glass. There were driveways on both sides of the building, leading to a large parking lot in the rear of the building. The bomb vehicle would have to be parked in the driveway, on the far side of the administration building, as close to the building as she could get it. That way they would be sure to destroy the freezer units where the male sperm and female ovum were being stored.

Francis had even been able to get a look at the campus when she went out to the administration building to get an application for employment. She now knew where she had to go to deliver the bomb.

Three days after they completed the modifications on the delivery van, the explosives arrived. The explosives had been shipped from Chicago on Tidewater Air Cargo aircraft. The cartons were listed as crockery and marked handle with care. Ashley and Francis picked up the cartons from the airfreight terminal and brought them back to the barn. To make sure that the bomb would do the maximum damage, it would be made of over one-thousand five-hundred pounds of the most powerful plastic explosive.

They started by packing all the explosive blocks tightly in the cargo compartment of the van. The bomb would be set off by a timed fuse and blasting cap in a one and one-quarter pound block of plastic explosive. A military type waterproof fuse lighter, with a pull ring, would light the fuse.

After all he explosives had been arranged in the van, Ashley took a roll of waterproof timed fuse. She first cut off one foot of the fuse and discarded it. She then measured, then cut off another foot of fuse and showed Francis how to attach the fuse lighter. Ashley then had Francis pull the ring on the fuse lighter. They heard a pop and the fuse started to burn. Eighteen seconds later, a small tongue of flame spit out the end of the fuse. Ashley calculated that they would need thirteen foot of time fuse to give them four minutes of delay. Ashley had Francis cut off thirteen foot of time fuse. Then holding it away from her body, with the dikes between the front end of the blasting cap and her face, with her eyes turned away, to crimp the back end of the blasting cap to the time fuse. Ashley then showed Francis how to use the pointed end of the dikes to poke a hole in the end of a one and one-quarter pound block of plastic explosive, then insert the blasting cap. They then attached the fuse lighter to the time fuse, then taped it to the steering column of the van. The bomb was ready.

Casey Troiano sat in Bishop Langley's office having tea and scones. Casey had come to brief her friend on the operation. "Well, Sonya, everything is coming together. We have the twelve humans that you provided to be the assault team. They're short on experience in this sort of thing, but they're true believers, and can be trusted not to say anything about this ever. Lestine Bradshaw will start training them as a team next week at the lodge west of Denver.

"We have managed to get a plan of New Adrian. It's laid out on a north/south grid. The landing pad and its supporting structures are in the southeast quadrant. The community center, swimming pool, dispensary and other community buildings are in the northeast quadrant. The southwest quadrant is a park with stables for their horses. The northwest quadrant is where the private residences are.

'we are going to hit the place at 3;15 AM. At that time everyone should be in their homes asleep. We just need to concentrate on the homes in the northwest quadrant."

Bishop Langley gazed out the window as she let her imagination paint a picture of the destruction that would befall the males and their consorts. She was brought back to reality by Casey's silence.

"That sounds good. How long will it take you to kill all the males?"

Casey put down her tea and scone, then brushed the crumbs from her suit. "We won't have long to do it, ten minutes, fifteen if we get really lucky. The bomb will do most, if not all of it for us. We just have to land to check for and take care of any survivors. We should be away from there long before the police can respond."

Casey paused before she continued, to emphasize what she was about to say. "Sonya, we have a good plan; and I'm sure that it will work, but unless we have someone on the inside we're defeated before we even try.'

Bishop Langley smiled, she felt really pleased with herself. "I have some good news; we have someone on the inside.'

Casey was overjoyed with the news. 'That's great, who is she?"

"She's one of the new drovers hired by the Farrow Ranch to replace the drovers that they have lost. Her name is Darian Jansen. The pastor of her church is loyal to me. She knew that I was looking for someone close to the males. When Darian Jansen approached her expressing misgivings about the males being used to introduce males into the human population; the pastor questioned her and found that she was willing to take action to prevent the males from being used to pollute the true human race."

Casey was really enthusiastic about this development, now they could carry out the plan. "I can have Ashley go down to Amarillo. Can you arrange a meeting with Darian Jansen?"

Bishop Langley nodded. "Yes, I can arrange for them to meet through the pastor of Darian Jansen's church. Can you have Ashley in Amarillo by Sunday when Darian comes to church?"

"Yes, I can have her there. I just need to know who she needs to contact."

Bishop Langley wrote the name of the pastor and the church on a card and handed it to Casey. "Okay, Casey, now how are you doing on the St Louis operation?"

"Everything's ready. The bomb's completed and the person that's going to drive it is being trained. She'll be ready in plenty of time. They will time their attack to take place at the same time as the attack on the males at the ranch.'

Bishop Langley opened a drawer in her desk and took out a bottle of light blended whiskey and two shot glasses. She poured a drink for Casey and herself. "God is on our side. I'm certain that we will prevail. Let's drink to it." They raised their glasses.

West of Denver, at a lodge in the Rocky Mountains , Lestine Bradshaw worked to get her team ready. They were all true believers, but that didn't make them expert killers. She did her best with the people and time that she had and hoped that it would be enough. Good organization was one of the keys to success. There was no way that she could control twelve people in an attack. In a fight one person could control at the most three other people. She had organized the team into three groups of four, with one human in each group designated as the leader. She would control the leaders and they would control their own people. That way no one had to control more than three people.

With the plans to the community of New Adrian, Lestine had set up a sand table. It would be better to visualize things with a sand table, than with a simple plan on paper. She was giving them training with their weapons. She was also teaching them how to move and fight in the open and inside buildings. She didn't have to tell them what the targets looked like; the whole world knew what the males looked like by now. Besides, some of the male's consorts were pregnant with male children. All the people on the ground were targets.

Each day her team got better; they would be ready. As for the equipment, she wished that they were better prepared. They had no problem with communications; the whole team would have two-way communications with each other. As for weapons, they had only semiautomatic carbines and pistols, but that would have to do. They had no way to get any automatic weapons, or heavy weapons. At least they had plenty of ammunition packed in disposable magazines. They had some pyrotechnics and flares, but nothing lethal. No matter the limitations of the equipment, she was confident that they could get the job done. She just hoped that the team in St Louis would be able to hit their target on schedule; timing was important for success.

Dr. Kirschner was at the reproduction lab. They were having good results with the separation process. All the chemicals that had caused the reproduction problems in the twenty-first century had long since been eradicated from the environment; and were no longer in the food chain. The men were now producing spermatozoon of 'X' and 'Y' chromosomes in more or less equal amounts. They already had enough on hand to start their impregnating program. Dr. Kirschner planned to include herself in the first group of women to be impregnated. She had chosen Stewart to be her male child's father.

In one month, they would start shipping to other reproduction centers around the world. Dr. Kirschner was well aware that despite the peril to the human race, there were some people that would like to see it fail. The sooner they had a large number of women worldwide pregnant with a male child the better. Only when there were too many males for anyone to do anything against them would the human race be safe.

The person that she most distrusted was Bishop Langley, the head of the Reform Church . She would be desperate to hold onto what authority over the people that the church had left. In the early days the church enjoyed a position of immense popularity and respectability with the people. As long as the fantasy of an all-female utopia held up, the people bought into the dream. They bought the dogma of the church;

they believed everything that the church told them. When it all started to go wrong; and fewer humans were reproducing, everyone looked to the church for divine intervention. When the birth rate continued to fall, so did the popularity of the church. If Bishop Langley maintained control of the church, she would take it down with her, unless she could destroy the males. If she got her way, not only would the church be finished, so would the human race. Dr. Kirschner supported Monsignor Espin. Bishop Langley would try something, she had to; and when she failed, Monsignor Espin could take control of the church. If she could safeguard the males and the program here in North America, the programs throughout the world would be safe. No one would want North America to have a monopoly on males.

Everyone had gotten settled into the new community. It had been Stewart's idea to name the community New Adrian. He felt that the name had been necessary to give them an identity separate from the Farrow Ranch. Old friendships were maintained with some of the women at the ranch, but the new drovers were discouraged from coming around. Dr. Kirschner wanted all unnecessary contact to be kept to a minimum.

Dr. Nichols had started to give lectures on male anatomy, male human disorders, diseases and their treatment. Other members were also giving lectures on history, male culture and other subjects of interest. Dr. Nichols and Nancy were now married; and so were Thomas and Henrietta. Everything was going according to plan.

XXVIII

ATTACK

Friday, the aircraft to be used for the attack was flown from Richmond to Denver. The aircraft had on board some air cargo, along with the unarmed bomb. Upon arrival, they unloaded the air cargo, then parked the aircraft in the company maintenance hangar. Ashley McKibben had been waiting for it. After the aircraft was parked, she went aboard as a maintenance worker. She installed the bomb fuse and trigger. When she completed her work, she covered the bomb with a tarpaulin. Before leaving the aircraft, she took care of one other thing for Bishop Langley.

Sunday morning Ashley met Darian Jansen in Amarillo. The meeting took place in the garden of the church rectory. The pastor of the church had been willing to assist Bishop Langley to get someone that they could trust hired on at the Farrow Ranch; and set up the meeting between Ashley and Darian. Now, with all that had happened in the church, she had been having second thoughts about having helped Bishop Langley. She now had an uneasy feeling about the meeting and kept her distance, not wanting to know what the meeting was about.

At the meeting Ashley gave Darian a platter charge, about the size of a large dinner plate with tripod to use against the aircraft exclusion beacon; and instructed her on how to use it. She then hid it in Darian's vehicle in a place where it wouldn't be found by a police check. Before Darian departed, they each wished the other good fortune in the coming venture.

Tuesday afternoon Lestine Bradshaw started to send her teams out to Denver. She had them depart from the lodge in groups of two, at intervals of twenty minutes. After two hours the last group departed to Denver. Lestine then made her departure. The plan would be for the groups to enter the cargo terminal at different times during the evening; and assemble at the Tidewater maintenance hangar by 11:00 PM.

When Lestine got into Denver, she checked the weather again. There was a cold front moving out of the central plains, with a line of rain and thunder storms running from southwest Texas. Through Louisiana, Arkansas and up through the Mississippi River Valley. The weather from Denver to the target would be clear, everything would come off on schedule. She had a lot of time before she had to be at the cargo terminal, so she went sightseeing in Denver. That evening she had dinner at the Rocky Mountain Gateway Hotel.

Tuesday morning, Dr Kirschner worked at the reproduction lab of the St Louis Institute of Genetic Research. They had received their first shipment of frozen ovum from the Los Angeles Reproduction Lab that served California, Arizona and Nevada last Friday. Yesterday, they had received a shipment from the Boston Reproduction Lab serving Massachusetts, Rhode Island, Connecticut, Vermont, New Hampshire and Maine. To give every woman a chance to reproduce, they were concentrating first on older women of childbearing age from thirty-five to forty-five years of age and in good health. The younger women could afford to wait a little longer. They already had ovum from the St Louis region. Dr. Kirschner's ovum had already been harvested. It had already been fertilized with one of Stewart's spermatozoon. In a few days her embryo would be safely in her womb. A shipment would be coming in this afternoon from the Chicago Midwest lab. A shipment had arrived from the Atlanta Southeast Region the last weekend. As soon as the shipments arrived, they started to fertilize the ovum. When the fertilized ovum had grown into a viable embryo, they were frozen, then shipped back to be implanted in the mother's womb

Dr. Kirschner hardly spent time in her office at the administration building these days. Most of the time she now spent in the reproduction lab. Their overseas distribution would start in two weeks. The first shipments would be to Paris, Moscow, Cairo, San Palo, Peking and Sidney. That was where Dr. Kirschner wanted to be. This was her life's work now and she wanted to make sure that everything went right.

Francis Tyler had a long day ahead of her, so she slept late that morning. Ashley had her breakfast ready when Francis came out of her bedroom. Francis liked Ashley. Ashley had gone out of her way to make things comfortable and pleasant for her. At breakfast, they talked and watched the news on the video wall. A lot of the news was still devoted to the males. Francis hated to even think of them, or see or hear of them even less. They were talking about the weddings on the news. She thought, as she watched the video. Well, let them have their fun. It will all be over with tomorrow. They needed to kill the evil consorts of the males too. Nothing of them must be left.

After breakfast, Francis and Ashley drove out to check the area around the target. They then checked again the place where Francis would wait for the right time to deliver the bomb. Ashley went over the sequence of events that would take place when Francis delivered the bomb. After Francis had broken through the main gate and parked the bomb vehicle beside the target building; she would stop the motor, break the key off in the ignition, light the fuse, then lock the door when leaving the vehicle. She would then move quickly without running to the rear of the parking lot, then on through the woods to the road where Ashley would pick her up.

After the final reconnaissance, they drove back to the house and checked the bomb vehicle, to make sure that everything was ready. Ashley showed Francis that she had put additional tape around the fuse lighter and fuse, to make sure that it stayed in place. Everything was ready.

That evening, Ashley took Francis to dinner. Francis talked about how she looked forward to hearing on the news tomorrow about how the males were all dead and their seed was no more. Ashley listened to her talk and told her how they would have a big laugh together when they heard the news at breakfast the next morning.

Bishop Langley sat in her office in the rectory having a late lunch. She felt really good today, better than she had felt in a long time. Tomorrow her problems would be behind her. Casey had called her before leaving on her mission expressing confidence in their success. She looked forward to good weather and a perfect flight. She knew that Casey would do her job well and not fail her. It was too bad that she would have to be sacrificed. She would miss her.

The problem in St Louis had also been taken care of; there could be no link of this plot to her. She had been assured that there would be no connection with St Louis. Ashley McKibben had assured her that the plan was flawless. They wouldn't catch Francis; Ashley had assured her of that. She could get someone later on to take care of Ashley. Her greatest victory would be after it was over with. Then she would take her revenge on Monsignor Espin.

Lestine Bradshaw had done wonders with her assault team. They were amateurs, but they were true believers and willing participants. With her leadership they would succeed.

At 9:00 PM, the members of the assault team started to show up at the air cargo terminal. Casey had been busy preflighting the aircraft with Troy Quiller. The bomb had been filled that afternoon with two-thousand one-hundred gallons of liquid hydrogen fuel. They then attached the parachutes and prepared the bomb for the drop. Casey had been instructed on how to arm the bomb.

By 10:00 PM the preflight was completed. All the assault team was in the hangar. At 10:40 PM, using the onboard visidatacom unit, Casey filed a flight plan as flight 934-B to Houston, Texas, departure time 2:25 AM. They had nothing to do now but wait.

At 11:00 PM, Francis woke up from her nap. She went to the kitchen and had some soup and coffee. At midnight she got ready to go. Ashley went out to the barn with her. Francis got into the driver's seat and checked to make sure that everything was still in place. She then received her final briefing from Ashley. "Okay, Francis, when you leave here, you'll drive to the start point. Now, from the start point it takes twenty minutes, driving at the speed limit to get to the main gate. You'll leave the start point at 2:55 AM and drive the speed limit, arriving at the main gate at 3:15 AM. As soon as you crash the main gate, drive as quickly as you can to the target building. Now, when you have the bomb next to the building follow this sequence, turn the motor off, break off the key in the ignition, pull the ring to light the fuse, then exit the vehicle and lock the doors. From there you have four minutes to get clear. Walk as fast as you can, but don't run, to the rear of the parking lot, then keep going into the woods. Once in the woods, pick a large tree and stand behind it. After the bomb goes off, just keep the light from the fire to your back and I'll see you at the rendezvous. Any Questions?"

Francis shook her head. "No questions." They had gone over all this before, but Ashley figured that it didn't hurt to go over it again.

"Okay, then good luck, Francis. May God be with you." Ashley put out her hand and they shook hands.

"Thank you, Ashley, you've been really good to me.' Francis embraced Ashley. Ashley patted her on the shoulder. Francis said, "I love you Ashley."

Francis started the van, as Ashley went to open the doors to the barn. As Francis started to drive out of the barn, she waved at Ashley. Ashley waved back at her. Ashley watched the vehicle as it rolled down the drive, turned onto the road and drove out of sight. She then closed the barn doors, then went to the house to pack and clean up.

After leaving the barn and pulling onto the road, Francis started to drive to her start point. She looked again at how Ashley had put more tape around the fuse lighter and fuse. It was sure to stay in place and function as required without fail. It was good of Ashley to think of all the little things like that. She felt honored that Bishop Langley and Ashley had the trust in her to carry out such an important mission. She was determined not to let them down.

That late at night there wasn't much traffic on the roads. When she arrived at the East Central Missouri Industrial Machine Repair Service LTD. She backed the van into the drive and parked next to the building. It was 1:20 AM; she had arrived at her start position with plenty of time to spare.

At 1:30 AM Lestine Bradshaw gave her team one last check; and they boarded the aircraft. Casey watched them board and take their seats for takeoff. Once everyone had strapped in, Casey went forward to the flight deck and took her seat. Everything was ready for now. Troy Quiller would be doing most of the flying. Casey would be dividing her time between the flight deck and the cargo bay. Now came the hardest part, waiting for the time to pass. Casey ordered the onboard visidatacom unit to display engine diagnostics and fuel load status on the pilot's video display. Everything was ready for engine start.

At 2:00 AM, Casey ordered the visidatacom unit to signal for the hangar doors to open. As the hangar doors started to slide open, Casey ordered engine start. The engines came to life with a low hum, that built to a high-pitched whine. When everything was ready, Casey ordered the navigation lights to be turned on and the aircraft to taxi to the takeoff standby position behind Flight 934-A. The engines increased thrust and the aircraft taxied to the standby position behind flight 934-A.

At 2:15 AM flight 934-A took off and climbed to cruising altitude in the direction of Houston. Casey ordered her aircraft to the launch point.

At 2:24 AM Casey started to give the launch orders. "Aircraft, hover at two meters, maintain station," The engines increased from a whine to a roar and the aircraft picked up to a hover two meters off the ground and held position over the white painted cross on the launch pad. "Aircraft, rotate to heading of 165 degrees true, maintain station." The aircraft while still at a hover, rotated to a heading of 165 degrees true, while maintaining station over the white painted cross.

At exactly 2:25 AM, Casey called terminal air control. "Terminal control, Flight 934-B departing 165 degrees true for Houston."

Terminal control responded. "Roger 934-B cleared for departure."

Casey commanded the aircraft. "Depart 165 degrees true, climb to 12,000 feet at an eight-degree angle of assent, then proceed at economy cruse."

The aircraft started forward in a nose down attitude at first, then as the aircraft started to gain speed, the nose came up and it transitioned to horizontal flight. When the aircraft reached 12,000 feet, it automatically leveled off and throttled back to an economic cruse speed of three-hundred fifty miles-per-hour.

Casey ordered a course change for Houston. She then left Troy to monitor the flight and went back to the cargo bay. She removed the tie downs; leaving only the magnetic anchor that would automatically be released when they reached the drop point. She then set the release mechanism for the drogue parachute and attached the static lines for the main cargo parachutes. She then activated the ground proximity trigger and removed the safety from the bomb fuse; the bomb was now ready to drop.

The police cruiser turned the corner and started down the street. Officer Levi Adams drove the cruiser. She had been on patrol for over four hours now and she was bored. It had been a slow night, with not much going on. It was 2:35 AM now. She had over three more hours to go before the end of her shift. She passed by the East Central Missouri Industrial Machine Repair Service LTD and gave it a casual glance.

Francis watched the police cruiser pass by, being careful not to be seen sitting in the vehicle. Just twenty more minutes and she could go.

Officer Levi Adams had gone almost three-hundred yards past the East Central Missouri Industrial Machine Repair Service LTD before she realized that she had seen one of their vans parked outside of the gate. She had never seen one of their vans parked outside of the gate at night before. At least it would be a break in the monotonous routine. She decided to go back and have another look.

Francis watched as the police cruiser made a U-turn and started back. She started to feel that knot in the pit of her stomach, as fear started to build in her mind. Why were the police coming back? She started the vehicle motor.

Officer Levi Adams decided to check the vehicles registration. She beamed the electronic signal for the subject vehicle to disclose its registration number and other registration information; she got no response from the vehicle. Something had to be wrong, every vehicle was supposed to be programed to respond to her inquiry. She turned on the blue lights and started to pull around to block the drive with her cruiser.

Francis panicked, pulled out of the drive and started racing toward the institute. Officer Levi Adams turned on the siren and gave pursuit. She got to within two-hundred foot of the fleeing vehicle and fired a high-power electronic beam to fry the electronics and disable the fleeing vehicle. The vehicle kept on going, unaffected by the beam. The vehicles electronics had to be shielded. She called for back-up.

Francis had been forced to move prematurely. She wasn't sure if this would upset the operation or not. Even after she crashed the gate, she would still have the police in pursuit.

As the pursuit continued, a second, then a third police cruiser joined the chase. The pursuit had been going on for over ten minutes when

Francis started to get close to the main gate of the institute. The police realized where she was going, but had no one to block her.

Francis crashed the gate and headed for the laboratory, with the police in close pursuit. She needed to light the fuse before she got to the laboratory. The police may not give her the chance to light it when she got there. As she got near the fork in the road, in front of the administration building, she pulled the ring of the fuse lighter. There wasn't a pop of the fuse lighter, but the blast of a detonator. It didn't light a time fuse that burned at a rate of eighteen seconds per foot, but detonating cord with a burn rate of over a half a mile per second. The explosion was virtually instantaneous.

A tremendous explosion jolted Dr. Kirschner awake. She jumped out of bed, put her feet in her slippers, then rushed to the game room at the rear of the house, that over looked the lake. Some of the windows had been blown out. Shards of glass and dust were everywhere. She looked out the window to see a glow of a fire the other side of the administration building across the lake from her house.

She rushed to the visidatacom unit in her office. The explosion hadn't damaged it. She first called the administration building, but got no response. She then called the main gate. The security guard that answered looked to have been tossed about and she had a deep cut on her cheek that bled. "Yes, Dr. Kirschner."

Dr. Kirschner asked, 'What happened?"

The security guard brought up a handkerchief to her face, to try to stem the flow of blood. 'We had a delivery van crash the gate, with the police in pursuit. It exploded in front of the administration building."

Dr. Kirschner had a sudden-frightening realization. The men! She ended her transmission to the main gate, then gave an order to the visidatacom unit. "Emergency! Immediate conference call, all units in New Adrian!"

Darian Jansen looked at her watch again; it was almost 3:00 AM.

She had already set up the platter charge provided to her by Ashley McKibben. Her target would be the aircraft exclusion beacon. The beacon sat on a hill top one and one quarter miles southeast of New Adrian. The beacon sat on a concrete pad. It had a seven-foot square base five foot high. From the base rose a thirty-foot high telescoping tower. On top of the tower sat a four-foot diameter dome. The base was surrounded at a distance of fifty-foot on all sides by a ten-foot-high chain link fence, topped by razor wire. Around the fence were security devices to prevent anyone from cutting through or climbing over.

The platter charge consisted of a nine-inch diameter steel plate one-quarter inch thick backed by plastic explosives. It was supported by a tripod with a crude aiming device. Darian had set it up just five-foot from the fence; and had aimed it at the access panel at the base, as Ashley had told her. A hit anywhere in the panel would disable the beacon. She looked through the aiming device one last time, to make sure that it was properly aimed. She checked the wires one last time, to make sure that they were properly hooked up to the platter charge and the triggering device. The triggering device was a hinged hand-held device that when you squeezed it closed, sent a small electric charge down the wire to set off the blasting cap.

She looked around; it was almost time to set off the platter charge. She moved a safe distance from the platter charge and took cover. She kept looking at her watch. At exactly 3:05 AM, she squeezed the triggering device. There followed a deafening explosion and a blinding flash. The steel platter was propelled forward at over two-thousand foot per second. It tore through the chain-link fence like it was a spider web. It continued on to crash through the access panel, carrying away wiring and other hardware; the beacon went dead.

Casey had fed the parachute drop coordinates, drop weight, wind speed and direction into the aircrafts visidatacom unit. At 3:00 AM she ordered the aircraft to change course, start its run into the drop point at one-hundred eighty miles-per-hour and descend to fly the terrain at two-hundred foot. The aircraft changed heading to 235 degrees true, slowed to one-hundred eighty miles-per-hour and descended to fly the terrain at two-hundred foot

At two minutes out from the drop point, the aircraft climbed rapidly to two-thousand foot over the terrain. At the same time a digital count-down began on Casey's video display. She gave a standby to the people in the cargo bay. The count-down reached zero. The magnetic anchor released and the drogue parachute deployed into the aircraft's slipstream. The parachute filled with air and the drogue line snapped taut. For a moment there seemed to be no effect on the bomb, then there was movement and the bomb rapidly accelerated and exited the rear of the aircraft.

Casey ordered the aircraft. "Accelerate full thrust." The aircraft surged forward, rapidly picking up speed. Casey and the others were pressed back into their seats.

Stewart, Laura and the other couples were just over a half-mile west of New Adrian. As soon as the call had come in from Dr. Kirschner, Stewart and Laura had led everyone west to get a hill between themselves and New Adrian as soon as possible. They took time only to put on coats over pajamas or nightgowns, put on their boots and grab their weapons and some ammunition.

After the bomb exploded, Casey ordered a one-hundred eighty degree turn and took manual control of the aircraft for landing. In the cargo bay Lestine got her team ready to disembark. At one mile from touchdown, Casey decelerated and transitioned from horizontal to vertical flight. Some of the buildings were starting to burn ferociously. She picked a level area just south of the residential buildings and sat the aircraft down.

As soon as the aircraft touched down, Lestine led her team down the ramp. With one look at the devastation, Lestine felt sure that it would be a walkover. As she deployed her team, she spotted someone approaching at a run from the right of the aircraft; it was a true human.

The person was Darian Jansen. As she got close, she pointed to the hill to the west and shouted, "They went that way!"

With a look of surprise, Lestine said, "What! What did you say?"

Darian had come up beside Lestine now. "They went over the hill to the west!"

Lestine had become really concerned now, the plan had started to unravel. 'Damn! How did they manage to escape?"

Darian was now bent over with her hands on her knees, trying to catch her breath. " They must have been warned. Just before I disabled the beacon, I saw them fleeing their homes, and I believe that they're armed."

Lestine had some decisions to make and almost no time to make them. It wasn't going to be the easy walkover that they had expected. They were now facing a force almost twice their size, that had been alerted and was armed. She only had minutes to salvage something from this. Success was doubtful now, but they had to try. She directed her team to give chase. The team broke into a run and started to race up the hill.

When they saw the aircraft return, land and disembark a force of armed women, Stewart directed everyone to get into a reverse slope defense. That way they would have their targets silhouetted against the light of the fires, while they would be in darkness.

Lestine's team reached the crest of the hill in three minutes. They were moving from the light of the fires, into the darkness of the reverse slope of the hill. Gunfire erupted and two of Lestine's people went down immediately with bullets in their chests. A third turned and ran back down the hill holding her arm. They started to fire blindly into the darkness. They needed to get close to their adversary, but her people were faltering. She started to urge her people forward.

Stewart saw someone in front of him. He took aim with his .44 cal. Magnum and fired.

There was a flash and a loud report from a powerful large-caliber weapon in front of her. Lestine's heart exploded and she was knocked to the ground. She didn't retain consciousness long enough to realize that she was dying.

When Lestine fell, her team lost the determination to press the attack. They turned and made a hasty retreat back to the aircraft. Casey had been waiting in the cargo bay when the survivors of the assault team returned. She knew that the mission had failed; and that they were out of time. She reluctantly gave Troy the order to takeoff.

Stewart and Laura were still in the prone position when they saw the aircraft takeoff. Their defense plan had worked as expected, resulting in a short one-way fight. Stewart called around and found that there were no casualties on their side. They were really lucky that Dr. Kirschner's call came just in time.

They got to their feet and walked back up the hill, to check the bodies of the attackers that had fallen. The one that Stewart had shot must have been the leader. As soon as she fell, the others fled. A quick check assured them that the attackers still on the hill were all dead.

As they topped the hill, they could see the security force coming up the road from the direction of the ranch headquarters. They got a look at their homes and were sickened by the sight. They rushed down to see if they could salvage anything from the fire.

Casey monitored the flight as they made their way back to Colorado. As soon as they got back to the lodge, everyone would exit the aircraft, to include Troy Quiller. Casey would then fly the aircraft on to Salt Lake City, then program the aircraft for a flight into the wilderness zone northwest of Salt Lake City. She would then send it off on an unmanned flight until it ran out of fuel and crashed. She felt very depressed; all the planning and resources for nothing. The operation had been a failure. She had a desperate hope that perhaps they could try again, but she knew that there would be no second chance. The police would be after them now. If they had succeeded, the males and their consorts would have been no more. Then the people backing the cause of a pure race would again be in charge. However, with the failure everyone would be against them.

The aircraft was flying through the Cimarron Canyon. Casey would turn north at Eagle Nest Lake. She ordered a review of fuel consumption and remaining load. That was her last conscious act; a bomb hidden under the flight deck exploded and sent the aircraft plunging to the canyon floor in flames.

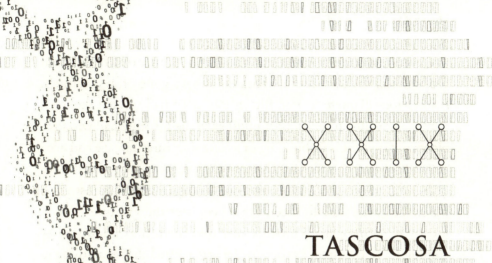

XXIX

TASCOSA

They reached their burning homes at about the same time as the police rescue force. As soon as the force commander had been assured that the attacking force had gone and the emergency passed; her force gave the residents of New Adrian a hand at putting out the fires. Dr. Kirschner's warning had come just in time. A few more minutes and they would have been caught in their homes. It was certain that if that had happened, no one would have survived.

After they got the fires out, they went over to the community center. A lot of the windows had been blown out, but the building wasn't seriously damaged. Everyone had mixed emotions of anger, relief and sorrow over their losses. The police commander was livid, how could it be possible that her security had been breached.

They made coffee or hot chocolate for everyone. The police commander had some self-heating ready to eat meals sent to the community center for breakfast. After breakfast, when it was light enough. They would go back to their homes to see what they could salvage of their personal property.

As soon as they had arrived at the community center, Stewart and Laura had checked the center visidatacom unit and found that it hadn't been damaged. They contacted Dr. Kirschner to let her know that everyone was uninjured and safe. Dr. Kirschner told them about the bomb at the institute. It appeared to have gone off prematurely. A forty-foot diameter crater, fifteen-foot deep had severed the main road into the institute. All the buildings in the institute had windows blown out, but the only building to receive structural damage had been the administration building. Three police officers in close pursuit were killed, along with the bomber and two persons in the administration building. There were fourteen other people at the institute injured, mostly by flying glass. Dr. Kirschner told them that she would be coming to New Adrian as soon as she was assured that everything in St Louis was okay.

Bishop Langley ordered the visidatacom unit in her office off. She was feeling rage and despair. All the planning and resources for nothing. What went wrong? They had had a good plan. Casey and the others had put a lot into it. Casey had assured her that it would work. It was just as well that Casey had to die; she had let her down. What would she do now? She had run out of time. She couldn't stop Dr. Kirschner from carrying out her plans. It had become painfully clear to her now, that she would have to accept the inevitable, that those males would always be with them. She must now look to her own survival. She had to do whatever she had to do to keep control of the church. Even if she had to embrace this new religious belief, she would.

Ever since word of the attack got out, it seemed like every news media person in the world had been trying to get in touch with the institute. Dr. Kirschner didn't want to be bothered with it now. She had detailed as many people as needed to keep the media happy, while she got everything under control; and made assessments of the damage that had been done.

As soon as she had sent the warning to New Adrian, she had gotten into her vehicle and rushed to the reproductive lab to see what impact the explosion had on the lab and the project. An inspection reassured her that apart from some broken windows, everything was fine. She had been relieved when she got the call that all the men were safe.

Dr. Kirschner contacted the pilot for the institute aircraft and had her make the aircraft ready for a flight to New Adrian. She made sure that all the dead and injured were taken care of. She then gave orders to her staff to get the institute cleaned up and running again.

At 5:20 AM Dr. Kirschner was able to leave for the airport. As soon as she arrived at the airport, she had her aircraft depart for New Adrian.

Dr. Kirschner's aircraft sat down on the New Adrian landing pad at 7:45 AM. She was glad to see that all the men and their women were safe and well. As for New Adrian, the sight of the damage sickened her. There had been some damage to the community center, mostly blown out windows; the dispensary, being on the other side of the community center from the residential area, had received less damage. All the homes would have to be rebuilt.

Stewart asked Dr. Kirschner if they could talk in private. Dr. Kirschner agreed and they went into a conference room in the community center, Laura went with them. When they were alone, Stewart said, "Dr. Kirschner, you said that there had been an explosion at the institute. How bad was it there?"

"We incurred some damage," Dr. Kirschner said, "mostly to the administration building. There were a lot of injuries , mostly from flying glass and some deaths. Some police, some of our people and the bomber. We're almost certain that the intended target was the reproduction lab. For some reason the bomb exploded prematurely."

Stewart said, "You say that some police died. I thought that you had your own security. What were they doing there?"

Dr. Kirschner replied, "They were in close pursuit. The bomb vehicle ran when it was scanned by one of the police officers. We believe that this forced the bomber to make her move early. That was very lucky for us."

Laura had been listening. "Dr. Kirschner, what are the chances of this happening again?"

Dr. Kirschner reflected on Laura's question for a few seconds before she gave an answer. "I'll not go as far as to say that there's no more danger, but I believe that they took their one chance and failed. It would take them a month or more to try again, if they could. By that time there will be over a million pregnancies worldwide. By then it would do them no good to try to kill the men."

"That's good to hear." Stewart said, "I'm sure that everyone will be reassured to hear that. Do you have any idea who was behind it?"

Dr. Kirschner said, "We know that the aircraft came from the Tidewater Air Cargo Company. It was scheduled as flight 934-B from Denver to Houston. The persons listed as being the aircraft crew were false. They were in New York at the time. I've been in touch with the President. One of our surveillance satellites picked up an explosion and fire in the Cimarron Canyon, east of Eagle Nest Lake at about 4:00 AM this morning. I think that when we find out who did this, we'll find that most of them are dead. I have no proof yet, but I believe that Bishop Langley could be behind all this."

"What about the person that knocked out the beacon?" Laura asked.

Dr. Kirschner answered, "The police are working on that now. We'll soon have her."

Stewart had a subject that he wanted to bring up with Dr. Kirschner. He felt that this would be as good a time as any. "Dr. Kirschner, what we wanted to see you about is the rebuilding. We would like for you to hold off for a few days before you do anything. There's something we want to do first before we rebuild."

Dr. Kirschner looked at Stewart. She could tell that he had something unusual in mind. "Why do you want to hold off on the rebuilding?"

"We've been talking it over, " Stewart said, "We think that we're too easy to get to here. We also want something more permanent. New Adrian was all right for now, but it was more of a transient camp than a real town. We need a place where we can build a real town. All eleven couples could eventually have sixty to seventy children or more.

In twenty years or more, there will be grandchildren. We need to plan for a proper town with a civic center, commercial district, hospital, school and residential area. It needs to be a regular town with streets and sidewalks. We would like to move across the Canadian River into the wilderness zone. I have a place in mind that's a lot better for us than here in New Adrian. We're going to go and check it out."

Dr. Kirschner knew by now that it did no good to disagree with Stewart; he would end up getting his own way in the end. "Okay, I won't do anything until you tell me to."

Dr. Kirschner, Stewart and Laura spoke for a while longer. Dr. Kirschner then left to have a meeting with the police commander.

The next morning four ATV's, each with two riders and a trailer, left New Adrian heading northwest. On the ATV's were Stewart, Laura, Thomas, Henrietta, Benjamin, Sean, Allen and Crystal. They traveled most of the morning, reaching the Canadian River by 11:00 AM. They crossed down river from the bluffs into the wilderness zone and turned east.

At 11:40 AM they crossed the Tascosa Creek and came in sight of the Tascosa Court House ruins. When they got close, they could see the state that the old building had fallen into. All the old cottonwood trees were gone, long dead. The roof was gone, along with windows, doors, floors and anything else that had been made of wood; having long ago rotted away. Everything was overgrown with weeds and brush. They all dismounted to have a good look at it.

After looking it over, they met in front of the ruins. Thomas asked Stewart, "What do you think, can it be rebuilt?"

Stewart took one last look before he answered the question. "Well, it may look in a sad state now, but those walls are well over a foot thick and made of dressed limestone blocks. The walls and the four large-square columns in front are sound, it can be rebuilt."

Everyone looked at the ruins of the old building. "It must have been an impressive building at one time." Crystal said.

Stewart nodded, as he looked over the ruins. "Yes, it was and it can be again. It can be rebuilt to be modern on the inside, while keeping its traditional appearance on the outside. We can even replant the trees, cottonwood if you want, or something else." In his mind Stewart could already see the old Tascosa Court House restored to its former glory. It would be a great centerpiece for their town.

After checking out the ruins of the old court house, they explored the rest of the area. Benjamin served as a guide for the party. He used to come here with his mother and knew more about the area than anyone else.

The area under consideration for their new home had been the former township of Tascosa and lands to the east. The area had a lot of resources. It was mostly rich bottom land, with lots of grass and trees. There were two lakes, each about twenty acres in size. One was about three-quarter mile north of the court house. The other was about two miles east of the court house. The lakes were mostly spring fed and there were other natural springs in the area.

They spent the remainder of the day exploring the area, drawing maps and taking pictures. Everyone was really impressed with the beauty of the area. It was like an oasis amidst this semi-arid land. They camped out that night next to the ruins of the old court house. The next morning, they returned to New Adrian.

As soon as they returned, they called a meeting with the rest of the couples. At the meeting, the couples that had went on the reconnaissance to Tascosa briefed the others on what they had found. They also shared the images of the old court house and the area with the others. The buildings that had been there, except for the old court house, were mere heaps of rubble. Despite its appearance the foundation and walls were sound, it could be rebuilt. The old court house would make the ideal centerpiece for their new town.

After seeing the area, Stewart could understand why the old town of Tascosa had first been founded there. It was a beautiful place, with lots of trees and plenty of water. Once everyone had seen the pictures there was no need for discussions, everyone wanted to relocate there. Stewart and Laura were elected to speak to Dr. Kirschner.

Stewart and Laura found Dr. Kirschner at the ranch headquarters office. Dr. Kirschner had just come from a meeting with the police commander on scene. Dr. Kirschner took Stewart and Laura into the ranch office to speak in private.

As soon as the door was closed, Dr. Kirschner turned to Stewart and Laura. "I have good news, we have one of the conspirators in custody. She's Darian Jensen. She's one of the new drovers."

"That's good," Laura said, "now we can find out who was behind all this."

Dr. Kirschner took a seat in the chair behind the desk. Stewart and Laura took seats in chairs that were before the desk. Dr. Kirschner looked at Stewart and Laura. "Eventually we will, but we'll have to overcome her defiance first. Right now, she sees herself as a martyr on a holy crusade. We also found the wreckage of the Tidewater aircraft in the Cimarron Canyon; there were no survivors. The police are in the process of making identifications."

Stewart said, "What about this interrogation cap that I've been hearing about. Can they get the information they want from it?"

Dr. Kirschner replied, "Well, Stewart, the interrogation cap can do a lot of things, but it can't just read a person's mind. Whatever knowledge a person has about something, you can find out by asking the right questions. However, we first need to know the right questions to ask. The way the cap works is by reading the brain waves to see if a person has knowledge of the facts of the questions being asked. As an example, say that you want to know if the person being interrogated knows certain people. You make up a list of names of people that you are sure she doesn't know. Interspersed within this list are names that you want to know if she knows them. Now the person being questioned doesn't even have to be cooperative, or give a response. All you have to do is make sure that she hears the names as they are being read. The brain will react different to the name that is unknown that to the one that is known. We need to know more facts before we can ask the right questions."

Stewart nodded. "Yes, I have a better understanding about how it works now."

"What about the three that were killed on the hill during the fight; and the bomber in St louis?" Laura asked.

Dr. Kirschner said, "They've been identified, even the one that drove the bomb vehicle in St Louis. In St Louis there wasn't much body left, but they did find enough pieces for DNA testing. Now, you said that you wanted to see me about something?"

Laura took a deep breath to calm herself before she spoke. "Yes, we have talked it over, and we have decided not to rebuild in New Adrian. We're going to move to a new location in the wilderness zone."

Dr. Kirschner nodded, knowing that had been what they wanted to do.

Laura continued, "We'll be moving to the old township of Tascosa, northeast of here on the other side of the Canadian River."

Dr. Kirschner looked at Stewart and Laura. It would be a lot easier to rebuild in New Adrian; and it would be a lot closer to everything. However, they now had the funds to do anything they wanted. "You know that you have access to a road here. If you move into the wilderness zone, the only access you'll have is by air."

'Yes, we know that." Stewart said, "That's what we want. We'll be forty miles from Amarillo and over twenty miles from the nearest road. We can easily secure it. It's what we have been needing all along; and it's much better than we have here."

Dr. Kirschner thought for a while. It would be a lot more work to relocate than to remain here. She also thought about the men and their wives and what they wanted. She was also sure that they could make the move without falling behind schedule. As long as they remained on schedule, what did matter where they lived? "Are you sure that's what you want?"

Stewart and Laura nodded, Stewart said, "Yes, we're sure; and we need to do it now. We have two more women. Brigitte and Crystal pregnant. We need to be resettled before the women are too far along in their pregnancies."

Dr. Kirschner was also in favor of Stewart's idea of a permanent township. She made her decision. "Okay, you and the other men are an enterprise now. You have the financial resources to do what you want. We'll start the relocation as soon as we can. Where you live makes no difference to the operation of the program."

Stewart and Laura stood to leave, Stewart said, "Good, then we need to get the architects and builders going. We would like to have temporary housing at the new site until the new homes are completed."

Dr. Kirschner took care of everything; they were able to start moving to the site of the township of Tascosa the following week.

XXX

INVESTIGATION

Darian Jansen knew that she was in trouble; she had been charged with destruction of government property and conspiracy to commit murder. The police had started their interrogations within two hours after the attack. They had questioned everyone on the ranch, using the interrogation cap. It only took the police a few minutes to determine that Darian's answers to their questions were deceptive.

Darian wasn't worried, she had prepared herself for the harassment that she expected from the police. She had done god's work and was prepared to martyr herself for her beliefs. The police could ask all the questions they wanted, she would give them nothing. She only regretted that the effort had failed. Even without Darian Jansen's cooperation, the police were not completely stymied. They had an investigator that was very skilled with the interrogation cap. They were able to determine that she hadn't built the platter charge that she had used, but had gotten it from another person. As for the names of the person that had recruited her and the person that had given her the platter charge; they had no suspect names to quiz her with. If later they had suspect names, they could quiz her with them and her brain patterns would confirm who her accomplices were.

INVESTIGATION

Since the crime crossed state lines, the FBI took charge of the investigation. Special agent Carmen Fry of the St Louis field office had been named the lead investigator. She had the sites in St Louis, New Adrian and Cimarron Canyon to investigate.

Within five days, they had received the results of the DNA test on the remains from St louis and New Adrian. The bomber at St Louis had been identified as Francis Tyler, a student of George Town University in Washington D. C. The three dead women at New Adrian had also been identified. Two were from the Washington D. C. area, the other one from Richmond. One of the women had been a former Richmond, Virginia police officer. The bodies at the Cimarron Canyon crash site were badly burned, identification would take two to three days more. One other thing they had to think about; Casey Troiano, Vice President of Tidewater Air Cargo and Troy Quiller, one of their senior pilots were on vacation, but couldn't be located. Perhaps when they got the DNA back, they would know where they were.

Special Agent Fry had a lot of questions. She had begun to think that the answers were to be found not in St louis or Texas, but back east around Washington D. C. She needed to look into the lives of all these people to see what they had in common. She had all their personal effects and personal Visidatacom unit data sent to her in St Louis.

Dr. Kirschner was very busy now. The Lab had started to fertilize ovum. Dr. Kirschner had recently had the time to have her fertilized embryo implanted in her womb and was now pregnant. It had become a thrill to put her hand on her belly, knowing that a new life grew within. She was determined that no harm would ever come to her child.

The reproduction lab now worked a twenty-four-hour schedule, seven days a week. In the first month they planned to fertilize 240,000 ova. The other reproduction centers around the world, were shipments were sent, would start their own fertilization programs in about one week. In the first month of their programs, there would be an additional 1,560,000 ovum fertilized worldwide. After that no one would be able to stop the project. In one year, there would be over twenty million males conceived, with five million of those already born. After that, they could start to relax the vigilance on the adult males slightly.

At first when Stewart came to her with the idea to move the community, she hadn't liked the idea very much. However, since she had seen what they had in mind and had become enthusiastic about it. New Adrian, for all its amenities and services, still looked like a transient labor camp. Their new home, that they had named Tascosa, would be permanent. They were isolated now, accessible only by air or cross-country trek. Later, when they were ready, they could build a road to connect with Interstate 40 to the south. Dr. Kirschner could envision someday a real town with church, school, hospital and businesses.

Dr. Kirschner had taken a break from her busy schedule to have lunch with her good friend, monsignor Espin at their country club. She wanted to bring Monsignor Espin up to date on the investigation; and find out what was happening in the church. They were seated at a table in the dining room, with a view of the putting green and the tee for the first hole.

Dr. Kirschner put her menu down and signaled the waitress to come and take their orders. She then turned back to Monsignor Espin. "I talked with Special Agent Carmen Fry. They have identified the bodies at the crash site in Cimarron Canyon. Casey Troiano and Troy Quiller are no longer missing, they're two of the bodies at the crash site."

The waitress arrived at the table. The conversation was interrupted while she took their orders. After the waitress departed for the kitchen, Monsignor Espin continued, "What about the remainder?"

Dr. Kirschner took a drink from her glass of tea, wishing that it were something stronger, but with the embryo developing in her womb, alcohol was out. "They were all young women. The FBI found no connection between them and either Casey Troiano or Troy Quiller. However, they have found a link between them and Lestine Bradshaw. She was one of the women killed during the assault on New Adrian. She's a former police officer and did security consulting work for Tidewater Air Cargo. There's your connection to Casey Troiano."

Monsignor Espin nodded. "What about the bomber here in St Louis?"

Dr. Kirschner started to take another drink from her tea; she grimaced at the lack of a strong taste and put it back down. "That was Francis Tyler. All of her friends agree that she knew nothing about explosives. She was only the driver; someone else built the bomb. They found a diary on her visidatacom unit. It was filled with a lot of tripe about preserving the purity of the race; and wanting to do something about it. There was also something about talks with Bishop Langley and being told that she could serve. Later she had been contacted by Ashley Mckibben

Monsignor Espin swirled the ice in her bourbon and water, while looking at Dr. Kirschner. "So, you're saying that there's a connection with Bishop Langley on this."

Dr. Kirschner had been watching Monsignor Espin's drink with envy. She shook her head. "No, it's close, but the connection hasn't been made yet. However, she knows two of the conspirators and I would say that was more than just a coincidence. The FBI thinks that she's involved, but they have no proof yet. Okay, by the way, how is your campaign to take over the church from Bishop Langley progressing?"

Monsignor Espin was about to answer, when the waitress came with their orders. Once the waitress had served the meals and departed, Monsignor Espin said, "She's trying to hang on. She's no longer trying to defend the old faith. She had announced the appointment of a counsel to study and authenticate the Holy Bible. She's trying to align herself with the majority of the clergy, but her days are numbered. Both you and I know that Bishop Langley's involved in this conspiracy, she may have even put it all together. What are the chances of her being linked to it by the police?"

Dr. Kirschner stopped cutting her steak and put her knife and fork down. "So far Darian Jansen's saying nothing. She's a true believer with illusions of grandeur. She sees herself as a soldier of God. Perhaps a dose of reality from being incarcerated will make her talk."

With a smile and a chuckle, Monsignor Espin said, "I wouldn't count on it; that kind doesn't break easy. What about this Ashley McKibben; do you have a lead on her yet?"

Dr. Kirschner had just taken another bite of steak. She put her fork down, shaking her head. "No, not yet. It seems that the name Ashley McKibben is an alias. The police are trying to find out who she really is."

They continued to talk during lunch. Monsignor Espin told Dr. Kirschner about the plan of her supporters to question Bishop Langley's fitness to continue to lead the church; and call for a referendum by the clergy on her fitness. With over eighty percent of the clergy openly supporting Monsignor Espin by wearing black cassocks, the outcome wasn't in doubt.

The construction crews were on the site at Tascosa; and the work was progressing on schedule. Everyone had been housed in temporary housing, with temporary buildings for the medical complex. They already had a roof on the old court house and were starting to rebuild the interior. The work on the court house would be complete in a little over three weeks. The foundations for the rest of the buildings and homes were being built. Everything should be completed in less than four months.

This time they had laid out a real town, with the court house centered on the south side of a one-hundred-yard square lot. The front of the court house looked south, across a rectangular common that ran one-hundred yards east to west and two-hundred-twenty yards north to south. On a one-hundred-yard square block to the south of the common, a three-story building, facing north, was being built. It would be a guest house to accommodate people who would be visiting Tascosa on business, or other reasons. The property on the east and west sides of the common would be zoned commercial. Two blocks of land west of the court house was for the medical complex. Two blocks east of the court house was for the new church and church yard. Two blocks north of the court house would be reserved for a school, that would be built later. The town had been laid out with wide streets, sidewalks and street lights. The court house grounds would be planted with cottonwood trees. All the streets in the town, except for the streets that ran around the common, would be lined with cottonwood and sycamore trees. It was going to be a beautiful place to live. The airfield had been constructed one-mile west, across Tascosa creek from the town. A dairy barn and stable was being constructed by the lake north of the courthouse. There was land being fenced for pasture. They also planned to put some of the land to the plow. They were going to be self-sufficient.

The state police had built a police barracks on the block south of the guest house. There would be a permanent force of eighteen officers to look to the safety of the community. There they had located a new aircraft exclusion beacon. Monsignor Espin had sent a priest, the Reverend Carrie Morales down from St Louis to be the pastor of their church. She would officiate at the weddings of the remaining couples to be married. Everyone soon came to respect their new pastor.

Stewart had taken a direct interest in the construction of Tascosa. He and the other men were still amazed by the modern construction techniques. Buildings were no longer stick built on site. They were engineered in factories, manufactured in sections, then trucked, or air lifted, to the site for assembly and finishing. It had really helped that there were more than adequate deposits of sand and gravel close to Tascosa for concrete. A mobile concrete plant was air lifted into the site to provide the concrete for the foundations, streets and sidewalks. Through the whole construction process Laura was at Stewart's side. The other couples brought their request for special features for their homes to Stewart, who passed them on to the architects and builders.

XXXI

TASCOSA REBORN

There had been a financial trail that Casey Troiano had tried her best to hide with fictious companies' and dummy accounts, but in a society where most transactions were electronic, with currency used only for trivial transactions, it hadn't been possible to completely hide financial transactions. The FBI had uncovered the purchase of the components for the bomb and the rental of the lodge west of Denver and a house in St Louis.

At the lodge the crime scene unit found a multitude of finger prints. They also found genetic evidence and best of all, clothing and personal items of the deceased persons at New Adrian and the crash site in Cimarron Canyon. They already knew the identity of the dead members of the conspiracy. They hoped to uncover additional clues from the scene that would lead them to members of the conspiracy still at large.

The House in St Louis had been where the vehicle bomb had been built. The place had been cleaned up, but there was still enough evidence to confirm that someone had made a real effort to sanitize the place. The crime scene unit dusted for fingerprints, but came up empty. Every surface in the house had been wiped clean. They vacuumed for bits of DNA, like skin flakes or hairs; again, they came up empty handed.

Whoever had been here really knew their business. They seldom found a crime scene that was so devoid of clues. However, as good as their adversary had been, they were the best at what they did. Their diligence finally paid off. The sheets and bedspreads on the beds were clean, but under powerful magnification they found a barely perceptible stain on the edge of one of the mattresses, it was most likely menstrual blood. It wasn't much, but it could be the break in the investigation that they were looking for. They could get a DNA profile and compare it with the FBI database and see if they could come up with a match. The evidence sample had been carefully packaged and sent off to the FBI laboratory in Washington D. C.

From the first day Special Agent Carman Fry had the FBI and police under her control looking into every aspect of the case. The bomb experts picked up everything at each of the bomb sites and examined everything collected. On the steering column of the van used in St Louis Bombing they found something that had been attached with tape. Removing the tape an object was revealed, that despite the damage, that because of the general shape and color, was believed to be a waterproof fuse lighter. After close examination, they realized that it had been a lighter modified to be a detonator. So, if the driver had been on a suicide mission and knew that pulling the ring would cause an immediate explosion; then why did she pull it when she did?

A few days later, after the investigation of the crash site in the Cimarron Canyon; and finding out that a small bomb under the flight deck had brought down the aircraft. Special Agent Carmen fry had her answer. The bomber in St Louis didn't know that she had been on a suicide mission. She thought that she was just lighting a fuse. It wasn't suicide, but murder. The twelve people in the Cimarron Canyon crash were also murdered.

Two names started to come up in Special Agent Carmen Fry's

investigation with ominous regularity, Ashley McKibben and bishop Sonya Langley. Ashley McKibben had been known to have been in St louis, Denver and Amarillo. Special Agent Carmen Fry was sure that Ashley McKibben was the bomb builder. Bishop Sonya Langley and Casey Troiano were long-term friends and saw each other often. This by its self could just be a coincidence, but Bishop Langley also knew Francis Tyler. Now what's the likelihood that Bishop Langley knew both women and now both women are dead?

Special agent Carmen Fry would like to question Bishop Sonya Langley about her knowledge of this, but Bishop Sonya Langley was too powerful a person and had too many influential friends. Special Agent Carmen Fry knew that she would have to connect all the dots before confronting her.

Ten days after it had been sent in, the bloodstain from the house in St Louis had come back. A search was made of the data bank and a match made. The DNA sample belonged to Amos Tomasello, age twenty-nine years, salvage diver and demolition specialist living in Baltimore. FBI agents were sent to her home. Her neighbors told the agents that she hadn't been at home for over a month. They checked with her employer and found that she hadn't been at work for over a month. No one knew where she was at the time. They put an all-points bulletin out on her. She was wanted for questioning about the bombing in St louis, New Adrian and the Cimarron Canyon.

Pastor Corey Upshaw was having a crisis of faith. Up to now she had been an unwavering supporter of Bishop Langley. She believed that as head of the church, Bishop Langley would be an unwavering champion of the true faith. She now saw Bishop Langley as a person without honor or integrity. When the faith had been challenged from within the clergy and her position as leader of the church was in jeopardy, she abandoned her supporters and the true faith, to do whatever she had to do to maintain control of the church. Pastor Corey Upshaw had been rethinking her loyalty to Bishop Langley. She could see the other priests giving their support to Monsignor Espin. If nothing else, Pastor Corey Upshaw was a realist. She could see that the human race would once again be male and female. God must want males, or they wouldn't be succeeding. Pastor Corey Upshaw decided to support Monsignor Espin. She also had to protect herself; and the best way to do that would be to tell of the meeting that she had arranged between Darian Jansen and Ashley McKibben, at Bishop Langley's request. She made the decision to go to the police.

The rebirth of Tascosa was coming along on schedule. The court house had been finished; and the construction of the rest of the buildings was well along. The completion of the court house had been a milestone in the rebirth of Tascosa., so they had a ceremony to mark the beginning of their community. Persons from the institute in St Louis and the State Government were invited. Dr. Kirschner had also been invited as a guest speaker. She had been pleased to be invited as guest speaker. She now felt that she was one with the group, being that the embryo that would become her male child now grew in her womb. She rejoiced in every aspect of it. She even found a perverse delight in morning sickness. When she had made her decision to become pregnant, she had thought for a while of making Dr. Nichols the father of her son, but in the end, she had chosen Stewart.

When as a young woman finding out that she was infertile, she never expected to be a mother. That's when she dedicated her life to her career. When she found that the procedure had been successful and that the seed of a man now grew in her womb, she became very emotional and cried. Suddenly her priorities were different. She now lived for her son; he had become the most important thing in her life. She had already planned the addition to her quarters for the nursery.

As she spoke to the residents and guest at the court house in Tascosa, she felt pride in what they had accomplished. The human race was being pulled back from the brink of extinction and was now on the road to recovery. They still had a way to go, but she felt sure that they would get there.

During the speech she also outlined how they would choose the other inhabitants that would staff the guest house, run the general store to be built in the commercial zone, next to the commons; and fill other jobs in the town. They would all be women who had already been impregnated with male embryos, or had newborn or infant girls. They would also be given lots to build their homes.

After the ceremony, Stewart and Laura took Dr. Kirschner on a tour of Tascosa, to show her what had been done so far. The barn and stables would be finished within two weeks. They were fencing in one-hundred acres of pastured east and north of the barn. Stewart and Thomas were plowing the bottom land next to the river for vegetables, corn and alfalfa. All the streets and sidewalks had been paved; and the street lights were now being installed. Also, another bit of good news, all the women were now pregnant. It looked like there would be a lot of growth in their community.

Amos Tomasello, alias Ashley McKibben was on the run. She had used the alias of Ashley McKibben in St Louis, Denver and Amarillo. She had had had Francis Tyler use her hand or eye scan to make all rentals, purchases and other arrangements where identification had been required. Casey Troiano had provided the explosives and the other bomb building material. The fuse lighters, time fuse, detonation cord and blasting caps were items that she had pilfered from other jobs and couldn't be traced to her. Almost everyone directly involved in the operation was dead. She had been so careful to sanitize the house. She wondered how the police had got on to her. Some of her friends had told her that the FBI and police had been around asking questions. Amos had been hiding with a good friend of hers, but she could no longer hide out with her friend. It was a small apartment and only a matter of time before she was found out. As much as she wanted, there was no way that she could create a new identity. She lived in a world without personal documents. There were no identity cards, driver's licenses, credit cards, check books, passports or any other personal documents. Everything was in the central data bank and your hand or eye scan accessed everything. Amos had several thousand credits in her personal account, but she couldn't get to it. When she went on the FBI wanted list, her accounts had been frozen. She had cash, but cash was not much used. Most people carried just enough cast to make small purchases. Any cash purchase of over twenty credits attracted a lot of attention.

Amos couldn't even use her private vehicle to go anywhere; especially to try to leave the city. The first time her vehicle was scanned by a police cruiser, or she passed through a check point, the central data base would flag her vehicle as belonging to a fugitive wanted by the FBI. She had a chance to get away from North America. There was a ship leaving for Rio de Janeiro and the captain was willing to take her. She only had to get to Wilmington, Delaware from Baltimore. She was lucky to have a friend that was going to drive her to the ship.

The ship was due to get underway at 2:00 AM. They would leave at 8:00 PM. That would give them plenty of time to make the drive. The ship was the Amapa Zephyr: a large ocean-going surface-effect flyer. The Captain was sympathetic to her cause. If Amos could get out of North America, she felt that she would be safe. She feared that Bishop Langley might try to have her killed to keep her involvement in the conspiracy secret.

At 8:00 PM, Amos and her friend left for Wilmington, Delaware. It wasn't a long drive; they should be there in a little over an hour. There wasn't much traffic at this time in the evening.

They arrived in Wilmington a little before 9:30 PM. Like most cities and towns, Wilmington had abandoned neighborhoods. Some still had abandoned buildings. Some still had the streets, but the buildings had been razed; and some had even had the streets taken up. Most buildings that survived were along major arteries, or in the center of the city. Wilmington now had a population of about twenty-thousand. About two thirds of the dock space was no longer in use. Ocean shipping had become just a fraction of what it used to be. There were a lot of old ship hulks beached and abandoned along the Delaware River.

They arrived at the berth where the Amapa Zephyr was tied up. Everything looked clear, but Amos decided to have her friend park close to the head of the pier; and watch for a while to make sure that it was clear before she boarded the Amapa Zephyr. They were there for about five minutes; and Amos had decided that she should go aboard now, when a vehicle pulled up behind their vehicle and the blue lights begin to flash. Another police cruiser pulled up in front of them.

The police ordered them out of their vehicle. Amos and her friend got out and stood at the rear of their vehicle. One of the police officers that approached them had a hand print identity pad in her hand. She spoke first to the driver. Are you the operator of this vehicle?"

With a hint of nervousness in her voice, the driver said, "Yes, I am the operator."

The police officer could see that the women were nervous and started to get suspicious. "What are you doing parked here?"

The driver replied, "I drove a friend of mine to the ship; and we were saying good-bye to each other when you showed up."

The driver tried to be casual, but the police officer could see through it. The police officer held out the identity pad to the driver. "Please place your right hand on the pad."

The driver placed her hand on the pad. In less than ten seconds the display revealed, 618 332 9103, Marie W. Hudson, no warrants.

The police officer with the pad now turned to Amos. "Are you a crew member of the Amapa Zephyr?"

Amos shook her head and tried to act casual without much success. "No, I'm a passenger."

The police officer held out the pad to Amos. "Please put your right hand on the pad."

Amos considered running, but where would she run to; and she knew that she wouldn't get more than a few steps anyway. Reluctantly she placed her right hand on the pad.

In less than ten seconds the police officer had the readout, 618 328 5732, Amos K. Tomasello, capital murder warrant, FBI. The police officer making the identity check gave a quick signal to the other officers. The reaction was immediate. The police officers grabbed them, threw them up against the car, searched them and handcuffed them. They were both placed under arrest.

XXXI

BISHOP LANGLEY'S END

The rebellion in the church had started. There was however, nothing violent about it. It started with the Archbishop of San Francisco, Gary Mercer, calling a council of Bishops, Monsignors and church pastors. Archbishop Mercer already had the supporters for Monsignor Espin lined up. Monsignor Espin had already left for San Francisco.

Bishop Langley, on the other hand, wouldn't be there. Her supporters would be there to make her case. They tried to portray her as a person that had seen the fallacy of church doctrine; and had now become a tireless reformer, but it was too little too late. Most of her supporters had deserted her. The only supporters she had left were the ones that were so closely tied to her, that they shared the same fate. Bishop Langley was finished.

Everything had already been scripted. The calling of the council by Archbishop Mercer would be the first step. When the council convened, there were supporters of Monsignor Espin ready to be called to speak about Bishop Langley's corruption and lack of leadership. Then other supporters would call for a change in the church leadership and nominate Monsignor Espin to be the new Bishop of Washington D. C. and head of the church in North America. When she was elected, she would accept with humility. She would be the head of a new church. Her first act would be to abolish the present testament recognized by the church in favor of the Holy Bible. Her second act would be to appoint a council to study the Holy Bible and recommend change in church doctrine.

Special Agent Carmen fry watched Amos Tomasello through the one-way mirror. Federal prosecutor Melvin Sanders stood next to her. Melvin Sanders turned to Agent Fry. "How long has she been in the room?"

Turning to look at Melvin Sanders, Agent Fry said, "A little more than two hours. I think that she's just about ready to talk. Let's go in and introduce ourselves."

Special Agent Carmen Fry opened the door and entered the interrogation room, followed by Marvin Sanders. Amos Tomasello sat at the single table in the interrogation room. She faced the door and mirror in the wall, with her ankle shackled to the floor. Special Agent Fry could see that the leg shackled to the floor shook nervously, A technician followed them in and fitted the interrogation cap on Amos. She then hooked it up to the monitor that Carmen and Melvin could see from their side of the table. As Carmen and Melvin looked at Amos across the table, they could see the fear in her eyes. The technician took her seat at the far end of the table, in front of her own console; everything was ready for the interrogation to begin.

Agent Fry, with a stern face, looked directly into Amos Tomasello's eyes. "Amos Tomasello, is that your name?"

Amos nodded. "Yes, you know damn well that's my name!" The monitor of Amos Tomasello's brain waves showed that to be true.

Agent Fry could see that despite her disadvantage, Amos still had some hostility left in her. Agent Fry looked up from the monitor. "You are also known as Ashley McKibben?"

Amos managed to keep a straight face as she replied. "Who's Ashley McKibben?" Her brain waves showed intimate familiarity with the name.

Agent Fry said, "You were in St Louis with Francis Tyler."

Amos didn't have to answer; her brain waves showed the statement to be true.

Agent Fry continued, "You were also in Denver for Casey Troiano."

Again, Amos was betrayed by her own mind.

Agent Fry then said, "You were also in Amarillo for a meeting with Darian Jansen, arranged by Pastor Corey Upshaw,"

Amos was shocked that they knew about that too; her brain waves showed Agent Fry that the statement was true.

Finally, Agent Fry said, "You were the one who built the bombs used in St Louis and New Adrian."

Amos just had to respond. 'No, I had nothing to do with that!" Her brain waves told another story.

Agent Fry confronted Amos. "Amos Tomasello, you can't lie, or even try to conceal the truth. We know that you built the bombs. We know of your involvement with Francis Tyler and Casey Troiano." Agent Fry pointed to Mervin Sanders. "Amos, this is Federal Prosecutor Melvin Sanders. She will be the one to decide what to charge you with, where you serve your time; and to the extent that she can influence the judge, for how long you serve. Now, I'm going to ask you some questions, then Melvin Sanders will have something to offer you. Now, first question, the premature detonation of the bomb in St Louis, was that accidental?"

Amos answered, "Yes, that's what it must have been, a premature detonation."

Agent Fry watched the readout from the interrogation cap monitor. Amos' answer was partly true; there was, however, deception in her answer. She was hiding something. "Okay, question two, was the bomb meant to be detonated at the reproductive lab?"

Amos answered, "Yes. I imagine so."

Agent Fry checked the readout, this was true. It confirmed what they had always determined from their investigation. It had become clear that Francis detonated the bomb prematurely, thinking that she was just lighting the fuse. Agent Fry was also sure that Amos had set the bomb that had destroyed the Tidewater aircraft. It was certain that she hadn't done it for her own reasons. She must have done it for someone else; and that someone else, Agent Fry suspected, was Bishop Langley. "Now, Amos, the third question, did Francis Tyler know that she was on a suicide mission?"

Amos' response was immediate. "Yes, she knew what she was doing; she wanted it that way. She even installed the detonator herself."

Agent Fry watched the readout from the interrogation cap. Amos was lying. Agent Fry took Melvin Sanders aside and discussed the results of the interrogation out of the hearing of Amos.

After the conference, Melvin Sanders spoke to Amos, "Amos Tomasello, we know that you were in St louis with Francis Tyler. We know that you were in Amarillo for a meeting with Darian Jansen. We have the statement from Pastor Corey Upshaw. We know that you built the bomb that was used in St Louis, the bomb to take out the beacon at New Adrien and the one used to bomb the family units there. We know that it was a bomb that brought down the Tidewater aircraft; and that it was your handy work. We also found bomb-making material like that used to build the bombs in your home. We also know that Francis Tyler had not been aware that she was on a suicide mission. If she had known, she wouldn't have tried to arm the bomb before she reached the target.

Now, here's the offer. You were working for Casey Troiano, yet you killed her and everyone else on the aircraft. You also killed Francis Tyler. There's someone else that you were taking orders from. That's the person we want. Now, if you ever want to have a life again someday and not spend the rest of your life in prison. You can give us the person that gave the orders and we will allow you to plea to a lesser charge."

Amos sat there for a while unresponsive. She knew that she couldn't get out of it. She needed some time to think about it.

Melvin Sanders didn't want to give her any time to think about it; she wanted her answer now. "Amos, we know that that person was Bishop Sonya Langley. We have other sources, but you were the one that she gave the order to. Tell us about it and we will reduce the charges and you can plea to just one count of first-degree murder. Then with my recommendation, you will be able to get parole someday."

Amos knew that she had been beaten and started to tell her story. She told of how she had been recruited by Casey Troiano and the meeting in Bishop Langley's office; and Bishop Langley wanting a guarantee that Francis Tyler would never be caught. The implication of the request had been clear to her. The only way to guarantee that Francis Tyler wouldn't be caught, was to have her die in the attack. Amos then told them how Bishop Langley then asked for the same guarantee on Casey and her group. She told Bishop Langley that it would be done. They questioned Amos farther, but they already had what they wanted.

Bishop Langley sat in her office having tea. She thought about what she could do next to try to maintain her control of the church. Everyone around here at the national cathedral had remained loyal to her. No one here had started wearing black. However, this had not shielded her from the fact that most of the priesthood now supported Monsignor Espin. This council that Archbishop Mercer had called would choose Monsignor Espin to replace her. Bishop Langley still had some supporters; perhaps she could take her supporters and start her own church. The Idea of starting her own church wasn't all that appealing to her, but it might be her only option.

The voice of her secretary over the intercom interrupted her. "Bishop Langley, there's a Special Agent Carmen Fry of the FBI to see you."

Bishop Langley knew what Special Agent Carmen Fry was here for and didn't want to see her. "Not now, tell her that I'm busy."

The secretary came back on a few seconds later. "Bishop Langley, I'm sorry, but they insist on seeing you now."

Bishop Langley couldn't put them off. She had to see them now. "Okay, send them in."

Special Agent Carmen Fry entered Bishop Langley's office with two other agents. She stopped in front of Bishop Langley's desk and showed her identification. "Bishop Langley, I'm Special Agent Carmen Fry of the FBI. We would like for you to come with us."

Bishop Langley said, "I can't right now, I'm busy. If you need to talk to me, I can make time to see you later."

Special Agent Carmen Fry said, "Bishop Sonya Langley, you don't understand. We are not asking you to come with us. We have a warrant for your arrest. You will come with us now."

Bishop Langley didn't even bother to ask why she was under arrest, she already knew. "Agent Fry, can you do one thing for me?"

Special Agent Fry responded, "What is that?"

Bishop Langley said, "Will you not handcuff me until we're off cathedral grounds."

Special Agent Fry nodded agreement. "Okay, we won't handcuff you until we're off cathedral grounds. Now, please come with us."

There was nothing more that she could do. Bishop Langley got up from behind her desk and left her office for the last time in the company of FBI agents.

XXXII

RECOVERY

When the church council convened in San Francisco, Monsignor Espin's supporters had no opposition. Those that were still willing to support Bishop Langley were so shamed by the arrest of Bishop Langley, that they didn't even bother to show up. The council declared the office that Bishop Langley had held vacant. The council elected Monsignor Espin to the office of Bishop of Washington D. C. and head of the church in North America.

Bishop Espin's first act had been to declare that the Holy Bible to be the only true testament of the church. She then appointed a theological council of ten to interpret the Holy Bible and set church doctrine.

There had also been a copy of the Koran and other religious text in the time capsule. There were other religious reforms going on around the world.

Dr. Kirschner had everything running according to plan. Her plan had been to have twenty-million conceptions the first year worldwide. Dr. Kirschner's prediction that once the program got started, it would be impossible to stop was true. Now that countries on every continent had women carrying male children, no one wanted anyone else to have more than their share. Every country would now take steps to safeguard their males. There was still a small minority to guard against, but most people were glad to have the men.

After the FBI had arrested Bishop Langley, the charges were made by the states where the crimes had occurred. Texas wanted her for twenty-two counts of conspiracy to commit murder. New Mexico had charged her with twelve counts of first-degree murder. Missouri had charged her with one count of first-degree murder, and five counts of second-degree murder. After all the trials, she would serve life without parole. It was agreed that she would serve her time in Missouri. Two months later Sonya Langley hung herself in her cell.

All the homes and other buildings in Tascosa were now completed. Tascosa was now a town with beautiful homes and tree-lined streets. They even had a sign over the road coming in from the airfield that read
WELCOME TO TASCOSA GATEWAY TO THE FUTURE

As soon as the churchyard had been consecrated, the bodies of their five dead comrades were exhumed and reburied in the churchyard.

In late summer, the citizens of Tascosa erected a monument on the common of the town, across from the front of the court house. It was an obelisk of red granite eighteen-foot-tall, set on a three-foot-high base. They dedicated it to their lost comrades and the women of the twenty-first century who had helped them survive into this century. The names of each were carved on the obelisk.

Dr. Kirschner had also been there. She now felt that Tascosa was as much her home as St Louis; and wouldn't have missed the ceremony. She could see that some of the women were now quite heavy with child. Her own belly had now started to swell with child; and she could now feel her son moving within her womb. She remembered the first time that he had moved. What a glorious feeling it had been. She had spent some time researching male names. She had decided to name her son, David, meaning beloved.

After the dedication ceremony was completed, Stewart and Laura invited Dr. Kirschner to walk back to their home and have dinner with them. As they walked along the sidewalk, they passed the new homes, with beautifully landscaped yards. Dr. Kirschner remarked, "I must say, you have really made a wonderful place for yourselves here."

Looking around at their new town, Stewart said, "Yes, we're really proud of what we have built here; and we will always be grateful for the help that you gave us in realizing our goals."

They were now almost to the walkway leading to their front door. Dr. Kirschner looked at Laura. "Laura, I know that this is your first child. How many do you plan to have?"

Laura smiled. "I don't know. I would say that I'll have as many as God will let me have. We both want many children.'

Dr. Kirschner took Laura's arm. "I'm sure that you and Stewart will have many children, and many more grandchildren. Oh, Stewart, how long do you think that you will remain isolated here?"

Stewart said, "I would say about two to three years. After that we can ask the state to build a road to connect us to the interstate. By then, we would want people to settle here to help our town grow. By the way, I know that you are a person with many responsibilities. Is this going to be your only child?"

Dr. Kirschner thought for a moment. She hadn't given it much thought, but it would be nice for David to have a brother. "For now, I'm happy to have this one child. As for later on, let's just say that I'm keeping my options open."

They all laughed. They were almost to the front door, Laura said, "Door open!" The door slid aside and they all entered the house.

On the twenty-third of October, Laura became the first of the women of Tascosa to give birth. Stewart had been able to go with her to the hospital in Amarillo. At the hospital, Stewart had been an instant celebrity with all the staff and patients. He and Laura were attracting considerable attention, not only from the hospital staff, but also from the news media. The birth of the first male child in almost two-hundred ninety years was an historical event; and they had been anticipating Laura's labor.

Laura's mother and sisters were also at the hospital when she arrived. Even Ruth had come. After the disgrace of Bishop Langley, and the change in church doctrine. Ruth saw the fallacy of the old church teachings. She finally swallowed her pride and apologized to Laura, begging for forgiveness. Laura was glad to have her sister back again. Laura's family would enjoy some notoriety; Her mother being the grandmother to the first male child born in anyone's lifetime. Her sisters would also be aunts to a nephew that they could dote on.

Dr. Kirschner had also anticipated Laura's labor; and had come to Amarillo for the birth. She met Stewart and Laura at the hospital. The birth of Laura's child was going to be an historic event and she wasn't going to miss it.

After the birth of Stewart and Laura's son, whom they named Adam meaning man. Laura rested in her bed in her room with Adam at her side. There came a knock at the door and in walked Stewart, followed by Dr. Kirschner. Laura gave a big smile for her husband, that he returned. Dr. Kirschner also gave her a big smile. Stewart stepped up to the bed and kissed Laura on the lips. 'How do you feel, my love?"

Laura let out a sigh. "Very tired."

Stewart looked at Adam. "I'm very proud of you. You have made us a beautiful son."

Laura smiled at Stewart's compliment.

Dr. Kirschner stood beside the bed and looked at Adam. "Laura, may I hold him?"

Laura nodded approval. "Yes, just be careful with him."

Dr. Kirschner reached out and took Adam in her arms. Adam opened his eyes for a moment, yawned, then went back to sleep. He had the black hair and dark complexion of Laura and the blue eyes of Stewart. Dr Kirschner unfolded the blanket from around him, so that she could view him fully. This was what she had worked for all of her working life to see, a male child. She viewed him for a couple of minutes, then wrapped him in his blanket and handed him to Stewart.

Stewart took Adam and cradled him in his arms. Without opening his eyes, Adam yawned, moved his arms a little, then went back to sleep. Stewart looked at his son and remarked, "Looks like all he wants to do is sleep."

Laura said with a smile. "Of course, he wants to sleep. Being born is hard work." Everyone laughed.

Stewart looked again at his son. He had had children in his former lifetime, but he hadn't been able to be a proper father to them. In that time the mother had sole responsibility for her children. The fathers were not expected to take any roll in their upbringing. This time it would be different.

Dr. Kirschner could see that Stewart and Laura wanted to be alone. She excused herself and left the room. As she walked down the hospital corridor, she thought of how fortunate that Laura and Adam were to have a husband and father. The men were providing the seed, but the women now becoming pregnant would have to raise their children without fathers; thanks to the short sightedness of their foremothers. However, they wouldn't have to raise them alone. Other women, who were close to or in retirement, wanted to be a part of the rebirth of the human race and were eager to help. Dr. Kirschner already had a nanny who would live with her and care for her son, David. Dr. Kirschner was now confident that the human race was no longer sliding towards extinction, but on the road to recovery.

CPSIA information can be obtained
at www.ICGtesting.com
Printed in the USA
BVHW071936170223
658737BV00002B/193